The
Secret
Life of
Teachers

DAVID ADAMSON

DAVID ADAMSON

DEDICATION

This book is dedicated to my wife, Rachel, who has
supported me throughout my long teaching career
and to my sons, Peter, Ben and Mark,
who have made it all worthwhile.

"If you're going through hell, keep going."
Winston Churchill.

A NOTE FROM THE AUTHOR :

The inspirational quotes at the start of each chapter are genuine inspirational words of wisdom from the walls of Wildside Academy.

I hope they inspire you as much as they did me as they probably cost somebody a lot of money.....

WILDSIDE ACADEMY TERM DATES :

Autumn Term : September 3rd – December 21st.
Spring Term : January 2nd – April 12th.
Summer Term : April 29th – July 19th.

DAVID ADAMSON

TERM 1

SEPTEMBER

CHAPTER 1

"Be careful what you wish for."

They never used to have adverts encouraging people to become teachers. Bright young teachers at the start of their career, surrounded by a small class of happy, smiling pupils, all quiet and eager to learn, watching their Science teacher do something fascinating with a Van de Graaff generator. They didn't have adverts like that because they didn't need to. You just wanted to be a teacher, share your knowledge, shape the future. You saw it as a vocation but now you'd be thinking more about the vacations.

They say all good things must come to an end. So as the calendar is turned from August to September, the Sunday night feeling returns with a vengeance and another school year at Wildside Academy begins. What can you say about Wildside Academy that hasn't already appeared in the local press? Well, let's start with the basics. Wildside Academy can be found in the northern town of Lower Steem in the Metropolitan Borough of Wildside. It is a group of modern, glassy buildings, hiding from anybody choosing to walk down Cemetery Road the magnificent stone building at the centre of the site, a building that was once the original Wildside School, founded in 1965.

If you were to visit Wildside Academy - and to be fair the majority of visitors tend to be delivery men, Ofsted inspectors or irate parents - the first person you'd probably run into would be

Darren Froggett. And yes, we do mean *run into*! A former pupil of the school, Darren left with nothing more than a GCSE in Drama eight years ago and subsequently decided to re-train as a lollipop man after an unfortunate incident on the production line at Grimshaw's Glue Factory. Having never managed to pass a driving test, the Highway Code is more like the Da Vinci Code to Darren. His dramatic, almost suicidal, way of stopping the traffic by lunging out into the road without any warning has led to the pupils giving him the nickname 'Frogger' after the old computer game. Drivers, on the other hand, use a few other choice names for him that can't be printed here.

Over the years Darren has found the most convenient place to cross the road. The brow of the hill gives him a good view of the oncoming traffic whilst at the same time making sure that he is not obscuring the motorists' view as he waits behind the bushes. The *"No Stopping at any time"* sign also acts as a convenient place to prop his lollipop up between battles.

Darren prides himself on the fact that he's never been late to his job and believes he should qualify as employee of the month. If asked what he does for a living he always gives his job title as *'Advanced Road Safety Operations Lead Executive.'* Hurrying past Reaper's Funeral Directors and The Golden Dragon Chinese takeaway this cold September morning he spots two boys coming out of Booze 'n' Fags on the other side of Coronation Street. Within seconds he has dived into the road amid a squeal of brakes and a storm of expletives.

"They could 'ave told us it don't start till tomorrow, eh?" said the first boy to his mate as he crossed over.

Darren had never bothered getting to know the names of the boys and girls he helped across the road. There were too many of them. These two he simply thought of as Ginger and Curly after their wild hairstyles.

"I 'ate this place," he said, looking across at Wildside Academy and five long years of his life. "They didn't bother telling me it were shut neither."

Ginger took a swig from his can of Red Mist as if noticing the lollipop man and the traffic for the first time. "You smell of fish, Frogger."

"I could've stayed at home on Zombie Kombat 6," Darren continued, opening his luminous raincoat to reveal the ZK skull logo on his tattered black t-shirt. "I've reached Level 4 y'know, lads!"

Safely on the pavement Ginger chucked the empty can towards the wheelie bin and the two boys headed slowly off.

"Level 4 on ZK?" the first boy mumbled. "Loser, eh?"

"Too right," said his mate.

Uninterrupted by any words of thanks, Darren carried on with his monologue. The banners on the high perimeter fences around the school caught his eye. *"This school is outstanding -* OFSTED 2008."

"Outstanding!" he exclaimed, startling a little old lady who was patiently waiting for a bus to Upper Steem. "Pah! You know what the full quote is?"

The old lady shook her head nervously and pulled her wheeled tartan shopping basket a little closer.

"It actually says *"Nobody in their right mind would say this school is outstanding."* Same when I went 'ere. If it's outstanding, why do they need to train teachers the day before it opens, eh? I 'ate this place!"

And with that his job for today was done. Heading back past Reaper's Funeral Directors he smiled. Level 4 on Zombie Kombat 6 awaited him...

CHAPTER 2

"The scenery only changes for the lead dog."

Mr Ivor Haddenough stared up at the banner on the perimeter fence of the school and smiled. Maybe he should tell somebody but it was more than his life was worth to criticize and anyway it amused him. *"Our GCSE results are beter than last year,"* the banner proudly announced. It had probably cost as much as a new Teaching Assistant but nobody had bothered checking it first.

The toot of a car horn made him turn around.

"Do you know the entry code for the gate?" the man behind the wheel called out, wanting to turn in to the school grounds. Mr Haddenough didn't recognise the driver. He was probably one of the teachers in this week's Science Department.

In spite of a large panel announcing that *"gates open automatically"* the gun-metal gates remained as firmly closed as the minds of senior management. The entry control panel at the side was still out of order and barbed wire topped the perimeter of the grounds. The school itself sat proudly in the shadow of the busy chimneys of Grimshaw's Glue Factory and the gasworks which almost obscured the enemy, Upper Steem Academy or USA as it was affectionately known.

"We've been here twenty minutes," said Mike Stringer, a balding PE teacher who was busy doing star jumps to occupy himself. "I'm giving it two more minutes then I'm off home." Watching Sky Sports could surely count as training, couldn't it?

Then for no discernible reason the heavy outer gates swung slowly open.

"Abandon hope...." muttered Mr Haddenough.

The gates *had* opened for a reason, of course, not simply to spoil the fun. Three cars back in the queue of traffic waiting to turn into the school, Ms Mina Malik, Second-in-Department for Geography, was, as always, prepared for every eventuality. She had the entry code stored on her mobile phone to bypass the entry panel in case of emergency. Now everybody could get into work. Good old Mina!

Once through the outer gates most teachers get out of their vehicle to clock in before driving off to the staff car park some distance away. Another member of the PE Department, the appropriately named Jim Fitt, had abandoned his red Citroën by reception in the space reserved for police, wrongly believing it would only take seconds to sign in.

"*You're listening to Wildside FM,*" the radio blasted out of his open window to nobody in particular, "*and that was Chris Rea and* 'The Road to Hell'..."

Mr Haddenough smiled to himself, noticing that only Ms Malik was following the correct procedure of finding a designated parking space before walking back to sign in. It'd probably make her late.

A noisy crowd of teachers was gathered outside the main reception, trying to solve the second stage of the puzzle.

"Does nobody know t'entry code?" asked Mr Capstick, gripping his pipe firmly between clenched teeth.

Ms Grimley peered through the frosted glass of the double doors where she could see a lady on reception. Tapping on the glass had no effect, other than causing the receptionist to turn her back on them.

"Why doesn't she press the button and let us in? She must know we're teachers. The look of eager anticipation after six weeks away from here!"

Mr Jones tried to get a better view.

"Is that Julie or Julia?"

"That one's Juliette, isn't it?" said Mrs Rigby. "Julie's a bit taller. Unless you mean the other Julie in Finance?"

"I mean Julie Thompson in the Data Office not Julie Tomson that does photocopying. You know, sits with Julia Thomas?"

"It always reminds me of '*Escape from Colditz*' this," said Mr Haddenough, almost to himself. "Only in reverse and with poorer lighting."

"Ay up!" exclaimed Jim Fitt. "'Ere's Bob. 'E's important. 'E'll know t'code t' get us indoors. By 'eck, 'e'll do us champion!"

And indeed the figure lurching down the drive towards them was important. As Head Caretaker Bob had the key to every room in the school, including the special washrooms that were only meant for the Senior Leadership Team or Governors. It looked like Bob had decided to change his appearance after all these years. The faithful black donkey jacket was still there, of course, a scruffy, spotted red hanky trailing from one pocket, but he was now wearing a bright white baseball cap with "I♥NY" emblazoned across it.

"'ow do, Bob? New 'at?"

"I got it in New York over the summer." He blipped the entry panel and the doors opened on to the reception area with a weary sigh.

"I'd never have guessed!" said Ms Grimley sarcastically, forgetting she'd soon be needing Bob to unlock a computer room for her.

"New York!" spluttered Jim. "On your wages? You must 'ave more brass than us. Me 'n' t'missus managed a week in Blackpool. Chucked it down all week."

"I, erm, went with a friend," said Bob, suddenly more interested in the broom he was carrying.

As the teachers reluctantly poured through the open doors, the lady on reception continued to take calls.

"Good morning, Wildside Academy. You're speaking to Julie. How may I help you?"

"I said it was Julie!" exclaimed Mr Jones.

"Ah, but which one?" replied Ms Grimley, not wanting to be wrong.

"I'm sorry, sir," continued the Julie on the phone, "we don't actually serve sweet 'n' sour chicken..."

Having managed to clock in at reception, the next stage of the team-building exercise would be to get through into the main school building. This Julie was busy on the phone so obviously couldn't press the release button under her desk at the same time.

"Does anybody know the entry code?" asked Mr Eccleston, randomly pressing buttons on the keypad.

At that point Ms Malik arrived at reception, her laptop safely in its bag on her shoulder. She clocked in and looked round at the other teachers.

"Am I the only one who remembered my lanyard today?"

"It's an INSET day, Mina," said Mr Jones.

"People still need to know who's who," said Ms Malik.

"Oh we all know who you are, Mina," chuckled Mr Jones.

"No, sir, we don't do prawn crackers either," said one of the Julies calmly.

It was unfortunate that the school phone number and that of The Golden Dragon were so similar but at least it was keeping somebody in a job.

Jim Fitt walked back to his car. Bob was sweeping up nearby, having removed his baseball cap.

"So what y'up to t'day, Bob?" he asked.

"She wants me to paint a new STOP sign at the gates," said Bob, pointing towards the gates for extra clarity.

"To stop t'kids getting in or us gettin' out?" Jim chuckled rhetorically before racing off in search of an elusive parking space near the Sports Hall.

Bob leant on his broom for a minute and gave it some thought.

CHAPTER 3

"If you fail to plan, you're planning to fail."

As well as jetting off to New York Bob had obviously found time over the summer to replace all the lightbulbs in the Main Hall. Only later did he find out she'd just meant the lightbulb in the hall at her house. Without thinking he'd also set the Assembly Hall up with rows of rickety exam desks and hard plastic chairs as he'd done each day before the school had closed in July. As a result it looked as if the teaching staff, all seated the regulation distance apart from each other to avoid cheating, were about to take an exam about their recent holidays.

"Oi! Stop copying off me, yer swot!" called out Miss Armitage, pretending to cover up her exam paper.

"They've done this on purpose," muttered Ms Grimley, always ready to spot a conspiracy. "Divide and conquer. Sit us apart so we can't talk about what SLT are up to. This is exactly how Nazi Germany started."

Unnoticed by most of the staff, the 'Headteacher' (as she liked to be known) had appeared on stage. Half-hidden behind the coffin-shaped mahogany plinth that bore the school crest and the slogan *"Tempus fugit"*, Ms Janine Stonehart was hardly an imposing figure. If people said anything about her - glancing round first to check it was safe to do so - it would be that she looked rather like a smaller version of a former Prime Minister. Sadly the person they named was never a great leader like Winston Churchill. Ms Stonehart was more the kind of lady who was not for turning once she'd written a policy.

Ms Stonehart glanced up at the computer screen behind her

and was surprised to see it simply said "NO SIGNAL" rather than displaying the PowerPoint she had spent the evening putting together with a little help from a friend. She straightened the prepared speech she had printed off as back-up and coughed, hoping to inspire her staff.

"Welcome back to a new year at Wildside Academy!" she began enthusiastically. "*Tempus fugit*! I hope you all had the kind of holiday you deserved. I spent four weeks in the Seychelles myself followed by a fortnight in New York..."

"Everybody's off to New York these days," said Jim as he watched Bob the Caretaker start to paint a large S on the tarmac by the gates.

"The agenda for today will be emailed out to you later this afternoon," continued Ms Stonehart, checking her schedule, "along with an email showing you how to log on to our new email system. At this point I'd like to thank Trevor Rojan in IT Support who's worked tirelessly over the whole summer while the school's been empty, installing the new computer system. He'll be back in next week if you have any problems..."

"What?" whispered Mr Lazenby to a nearby colleague. "I spent two weeks in Madeira with my wife and Trev was staying in the same hotel. We even had a few piña coladas together one night!"

"I bet you couldn't get a word in edgeways," smiled Jim.

"I heard she's given him an extra week's holiday now that hotel bookings are cheaper," added Ms Grimley, looking round to check she wasn't being overheard.

"...now in Trevor's absence I'll pass you over to Adil," continued Ms Stonehart.

Adil Bhatti made his way up on to the stage and glanced nervously out at the sea of faces. He was more used to re-attaching loose cables on whiteboards or quietly trying to beat his personal best on Zombie Kombat 12. Unused to public speaking, he wished he'd thought to bring along a prepared speech like Ms Stonehart had.

"Well, as far as I can make out," he began, "Trev's updated all the computers to Windows 7 and installed a program called the Schools Computer-Assisted Management System that will control everything you do. When you open SCAMS you'll get a homepage like this..." He looked up at the screen which now displayed an egg timer patiently trickling everybody's life away. "Well, it'll work better on your laptops, of course. Now to log on, we've streamlined the start-up system..."

There was a triumphant *ping!* Adil looked surprised as the screen above him displayed photos of two members of staff, clearly recognizable as Bob Ellinson and Ben O'Carrob who were both members of the Maths Department.

"Nice beard, Ben!" somebody called out, but Ms Malik wasn't fast enough to spot who it was.

"For the new log in you'll all have a three-letter code that's unique to you. It's made up of the first letter of your first name, followed by the first and last letter of your surname..."

On the screen the code BEN appeared below Bob Ellinson's photo and BOB below Ben O'Carrob's picture.

"There you go. That should make things a lot easier," concluded Adil, "but if you do have any problems just log them on the help desk once you've logged on."

"That seems really complicated," said Ms Amy Mountjoy taking notes. "I'll never remember my code if I don't write it down."

Ms Murkett was already muttering that the new system was sexist whilst Nelson Gwanzura complained that it was an insult to his Jamaican heritage.

The large screen resumed the message "NO SIGNAL" as Adil hurried off to his den and Ms Stonehart began again.

"Thanks, Asad. On the subject of laptops can I remind you all that you must carry them round in their protective bags. Laptops are the most valuable resource in a school - along with teachers, of course - and we can't afford to replace any more..."

"Laptops or teachers?" whispered Jim to the rest of the PE Department near the back of the hall. Luckily for him Ms Stonehart didn't hear him.

"...now it's not all about Ofsted," she continued, "but those of you who came in for results day tell me we did even better than last year..."

"True," mused Mr Haddenough, thinking of the banner outside the school. "19% pass is better than 17%. Or do we mean beter?"

"...in addition all our Year 11 pupils got to where they wanted to be..."

"Out of here and down t'pub," grumbled Mr Capstick. "They took my place at t'bar. I could hardly get a round in."

"Malibu 'n' lime followed by a double vodka for me," added Ms Shakespeare from the English Department out of force of habit.

As Ms Stonehart continued her speech Mr Haddenough looked around the room to see how many faces he recognized. Going by the number of yellow lanyards it looked like some of the supply teachers from last year had been replaced by new supply teachers.

Mr Hayes, one of the longest-serving members of staff was sitting in the next row. Whatever his teaching abilities might be, Roger was famous for one particular skill : knowing *exactly* how long he had left till retirement.

"How long now then, Roger?" asked Ivor.

"1169 days, 5 hours and 42 minutes," Roger replied glumly without hesitation.

"You could commit manslaughter and get out quicker!"

"...and under my leadership Wildside Academy goes from strength to strength. Now it's not all about Ofsted," Ms Stonehart emphasized again, "but with exam results improving at this rate we'll soon be graded "*Approaching adequate*". As I said the day before Ofsted last came in, 470 days ago, I value you all and wouldn't want to have anybody else under me at this moment in time. So if you all give it 110% we shouldn't have to let anyone else go. Before half term anyway."

There was a quiet splutter from the display screen and the SCAMS logo appeared, rotated for a moment and then froze.

"Well, next on the agenda : Heads of Department will need to get their Curriculum Review Action Plans to me by close of business tonight..."

On the front row the Head of History, Mr Harry Ford, leaned a little closer to Mr Hamish Buonanulla, Acting Head of MFL.

"I'm going to pass the History CRAP on to the Department to do," whispered Mr Ford. "I think it's important to hear their views, make sure everybody feels they're part of the team. Career development really."

"Yeah, yeah, yeah!" said Mr Buonanulla, only half listening as he thumbed through his phone. "So, I've got mine on an email somewhere.... Somewhere here.... So anyway, I'll send it out to the Department tomorrow. They'll be too busy today. You've got to be considerate. C'est la vie, mon ami."

"When is 'close of business'?" wondered Mrs Mower, the Head of Girls' PE.

"Business? It's meant to be a school for crying out loud!" gasped somebody at the back. Ms Malik thought the comment came from one of the Art Department.

"I'd like to welcome all the new members of staff joining us today," continued Ms Stonehart. "This is our school and you're welcome to it. I won't introduce you all as it'd take too long but their photos are all on the shared area of SCAMS. Next Sally's going to tell you about the INSET she's organised for today..."

"Sorry, Janine, can I just ask when we're going to get our new timetables and class lists, please?"

It was Tim Cocker who had dared to ask what most of the other teachers were wondering. Nobody was ever quite sure which Department Tim worked in : sometimes he said Geography, other times IT and he did seem to spend a lot of time over in the Sports Hall. With nobody quite sure as to where Tim should be it was a very effective way of avoiding any Departmental meetings.

Ms Stonehart gave Tim one of her coldest stares, a stare that would have immediately warned anybody else to stop talking but Tim, being Tim, carried on regardless.

"Just so that we can get everything ready for tomorrow..."

Tim glanced round at his colleagues but few of them made eye contact.

"That isn't on my agenda for today," Ms Stonehart cut him off. "I'll see you in my office straight after this, Mr Cocker. Now, over to you, Sally..."

Ms Stonehart actually smiled at this point.

Tim rubbed his chin and looked round as if he'd missed something.

Ms Sally Lovall had made her way up onto the stage by now. She had started her teaching career at Wildside Academy the year before as a trainee RE teacher before soon being promoted to the post of Lessons For Life Co-ordinator following the sudden disappearance of the previous Co-ordinator. It was a rôle which now clearly included teaching experienced teachers how to do their jobs. Not knowing whether it was informal dress on an INSET day

Ms Lovall had chosen to play it safe by wearing her normal working clothes : a spiral tie-dye skirt with green and purple Doc Martens, a red tartan scarf and a pink t-shirt with the words "LOOK AT ME!" printed across it in bold. The flower in her hairband was only there to add an element of individuality to her appearance.

"Hiya," she began. "Well first up it's only 100 days to Christmas so I've put a sheet up in the staffroom for you all to sign up for the end-of-term do..."

"108 days, 4 hours and 28 minutes actually," Roger corrected her quietly.

"So if you can all get your deposits in asap that'd make my job easier as these places get booked up well fast. You'll all remember Shazza on karaoke at The Cock 'n' Bull last year! Fab! Yeah, so for today as Chairperson of the Staff Well-being Committee I've organised a series of workshops on stress management for us all. Details are on SCAMS and if you could all just fill in the feedback form at the end that'd be groovy as it's one of my Bright Sky targets. Cheers!"

Mrs Felicity Lambert found herself sitting in a circle of chairs with around twenty other colleagues from different Departments in one of the Lessons For Life classrooms on the ground floor. She could only name two of the other teachers, Lesley and Michelle, who were, like Felicity herself, members of the English Department. Although they had never met before joining Wildside, they all held degrees from Oxford and Cambridge and had taught for many years in other schools producing outstanding results. The other thing that they had in common was that they had all been turned down for the post of Literacy Co-ordinator in favour of Ms Lynne Winter. Whilst Ms Winter's understanding of English grammar was far from outstanding, she knew exactly what to say in interviews, a skill that had led to her also securing the post of Assistant Head. The door opened and Ms Winter herself appeared followed by a lady.

"Hiya guys!" said Ms Winter, squeezing herself onto the edge of a desk before taking a slurp of her coffee. "Now you should of looked on SCAMS and be in the right room but you need to tick your name off of the list." She passed a sheet of paper to the nearest teacher. "Just to make sure you're all sat in the right

27

group, yeah? Brill. And can you let Sally or I know if there's a problem of any sort no matter what."

"And if Sally's busy we should probably see *I* then?" wondered Lesley quietly.

"You should *have* thought of that yourself, Lesley, since you're *seated* with other English teachers," smiled Michelle.

"Right," said Ms Winter, glad that people were getting involved in the workshop. "This is Barbara and I'll be back when I've just checked up on the other groups, yeah? Brill." And with that she left, depriving the group of any further senior leadership.

"Well, good morning everybody," began the lady nervously, "or should I say *Hi?* Oh dear. Never quite sure there with greetings in a social context. Erm, I'm Brigitte - not Barbara, sorry, my fault - and I'm here from Sunshine Training & Development and my colleagues Brian and Cynthia are around somewhere too. Give them a wave later. We've got other workshops and some online tests for you to do too. You'll each get a certificate at the end. Well, erm, stress. It affects us all. Please help yourself to the *Love Hearts* on the table by the way and please do grab a Sunshine stress ball and squeeze it if you feel the need. It's got our email on it too. Erm, right."

Jim Fitt picked one up, launched it into the air and headed it straight into the bin by the door.

"Oh dear. Erm, but good shot," smiled Brigitte nervously, a little unsure what to say. "Yes, jolly good."

She seemed to glance down at some notes for guidance.

"So, how are we all feeling? Generally. Stress-wise. Alright? Lovely! A bit of background first then. Now I was a teacher for ten or maybe twelve days and there was an awful lot of stress. So that led to us setting up Sunshine Training & Development away from the classroom. But stress is always with us. Today I've had a very stressful day myself. Oh dear! First, I had to decide what I was going to wear today, choice of breakfast cereal, hoping my Satnav would get me here, wondering if the computer system would work..."

There was the scrape of a chair being pushed backwards as Mr Doug Digby stood up.

"I'm sorry," he said pleasantly. "I don't want to be rude, but I've got a lot of planning to do for tomorrow. I've not even got my class lists yet. I'm really sorry but I'm going to have to leave you to this. Sorry."

There was an awkward silence as Mr Digby made his way to the door.

"Oh dear," said Brigitte, a little shocked. Nobody had ever walked out of one of her workshops before and if truth be known she was finding it a little bit stressful today. "Well," she continued bravely, "I think he just didn't know how to cope with stress. Oh dear. You need to be able to verbalise your stress before shutting those nasty anxieties away in a box. I've got some leaflets he can read when he's found his own inner tranquillity. Bless. Well, let's move on to our first activity if everybody's OK with that, shall we? We don't need to rush. We've been given the full morning, so we can take it at your pace. Jolly good. So, our first activity is called "Good stress, bad stress" and we're going to begin by getting into groups to share our experiences of potentially stressful situations and activities that raise our blood pressure. We'll start with a rôle play..."

Tim Cocker started the ignition and attached his seat belt. The first day was done and whilst he still had no timetable or class lists for the next day, he had completed the stress management workshop and a certificate from Sunshine Training lay proudly on the passenger seat. Perhaps he could have done with the stress management training before his summons to see Ms Stonehart but at least he had survived the meeting. His survival was probably down to Janine not really knowing which Department he worked in. She'd got a bit confused. In fairness she probably realised that without him coming in dressed as a giant banana once a year the school website would probably struggle to justify Wildside Academy being labelled as a Fairtrade school.

Bob had just finished painting those four large letters across the tarmac as Tim drove up to the school gates.

"Mind you don't smudge it, Tim," said Bob, wiping the sweat from his brow with his hanky. "It's taken me all day. I hope she likes it."

Tim was going to ask why Bob had painted the word SPOT across the tarmac but it'd been a long first day and he just wanted to get home. If the traffic wasn't against him, he'd be just in time to catch *Midsomer Murders*.

CHAPTER 4

"If you can't say nothing nice, don't say nothing at all."

Cemetery Road was a dead end. Quite literally. At the far end of it were the imposing black wrought iron gates of Lower Steem Cemetery and just before you reached that was Wildside Academy. After six weeks of almost endless rain the sun had finally put in an appearance as the new Year 7 pupils made their way towards "big school." In many ways Darren Froggett enjoyed his rôle on the first day. Whilst there were very few pupils needing him to help them across the road, there were around two hundred additional cars trying to manoeuvre their way in and out of the little cul-de-sac to get their kids as close to school as possible. Some parents seemed like they would not be happy unless they could deliver their son or daughter right up to the very desk they would be sitting at.

Darren had never been abroad - in fact he'd never gone further than a pub in Upper Steem - but the scene always reminded him of a travel programme he'd seen once. The traffic fighting its way around the Arc de Triomphe was nothing compared to the things he saw on Cemetery Road. But just then he was distracted from his daydreams by the appearance of the one car he always looked out for every morning. Just coming over the horizon was the red sports car that belonged to Calvin Armani. Calvin had been in the same class as Darren but had followed a different route : teachers' pet, Head Boy, more GCSEs and prizes than you could shake a lollipop stick at, a place at University before returning to join the school as a Science teacher. What he didn't have though was a GCSE in Drama! Darren was just getting ready to stop Armani from turning onto Cemetery Road when he heard a familiar phrase.

"I 'ate this place!" It was the ginger kid again. "They could 'ave told us Year 9 ain't in till ten, eh?"

"Too right," said his mate. "I ain't comin' back in again. Fancy a Red Mist, Kev?"

And with that they headed off to Booze 'n' Fags. Mr Patel was busy putting out newspapers, still optimistic that one day he'd sell his old stock with the latest photos of the Falklands War. But when Darren turned back, Armani's sports car had turned the corner and was already pulling into the school grounds.

"I 'ate this job," scowled Darren, kicking an apple core into the road.

There had to be some logic in putting two hundred new Year 7 pupils into the forms of teachers who were themselves new to the school, along with a Head of Year who had only just started in the rôle too. Perhaps between them they would all manage to work out what was going on? It was nearly breaktime and already Mr Ball had lost about half of 7X by giving them a guided tour of the school. It was hardly surprising really. It had probably been a mistake for all the form teachers to attempt a school tour at the same time and not expect some losses. Everywhere you looked pupils were climbing up and down flights of stairs, marching along corridors, almost, it seemed, making their way along the ceiling upside-down like an impossible Escher print. He thought his particular missing pupils were somewhere in the Science block but with most of the Science Department being new as well, it was unlikely he'd see them again before dinnertime. He'd found one of his form in tears after a teacher in the Science Department had shouted at her that she was feckless for asking for directions. It hadn't helped that she'd asked what 'feck' was. Mr Ball had been told Year 7 were going early for dinner all this week, to give them more time to choose which particular flavour of pizza they wanted. Perhaps he'd find them in the canteen?

Mrs Eleanor Sellers had come in early to set up her classroom ready for 7Y's arrival and had felt quietly confident before the day began. Once her laptop had updated she'd managed to log into SCAMS just long enough to write down the names of her new form. A seating plan was now displayed clearly on the interactive whiteboard with the tables similarly labelled with small stickers. After some initial disorientation the pupils had managed to work out where they should be sitting and were now listening to their new form tutor as she went through her expectations with them. It was a system that had always worked in her previous school and she could see no reason why things would be different at Wildside Academy.

"So it's rather like going on an aeroplane," Mrs Sellers continued. "You've all been on holiday on an aeroplane, haven't you?"

"Miss, my nan got lost at an airport once. She said she'd gone to buy some jam."

"Thanks for sharing that, Nicola," said Mrs Sellers, looking at her seating plan. "Well, when you go to an airport you plan in advance. You might need to get a passport, foreign money, book your tickets and a hotel. Then you turn up at the airport in good time with everything you need, you queue up quietly in the right place and check-in. You're given a particular seat, get out what you need for the journey and put your bag safely in the storage area. And you follow all the instructions you're given, sensibly, without disturbing other people, don't you?"

There was a certain amount of nodding around the room.

"So why do you think I'm telling you this, 7Y?"

"Miss," ventured a boy near the front of the class, "are you going to take us on holiday?"

"No, Colin. No," said Mrs Sellers calmly. She hadn't gone into teaching to be a travel agent. The Geography field trips she'd had to go on were more than enough. "No, it's a metaphor. Can anybody tell me what a metaphor is? Yes?"

"We saw one in Spain, Miss," said a boy sitting near the back. "He were fighting a bull. My sister said it were cruel."

"Will you be taking us to Spain, Miss?" asked Colin hopefully.

"No, Colin. Mr Buonanotte, your Spanish teacher, might though. No, a metaphor is a bit like..." Mrs Sellers paused. If she mentioned similes, would they end up discussing emoticons? She decided it was best to move on and leave grammar to Ms Winter and the English Department. "No, I'm telling you about going on an aeroplane because it's a lot like being in my classroom. You arrive here in good time, with your books, equipment and homework ready, sit where I tell you and follow my instructions, sensibly, without disturbing other people. So that everybody learns something. Our destination is your GCSEs, isn't it?"

There was some nodding but a few puzzled faces too.

"Miss, when I went to Majorca, I spent the whole time looking out of the window at the clouds..."

"Well, you won't be doing that, erm, Joe. This is a classroom not an aeroplane."

That only seemed to confuse some of them still further. Very soon Mrs Sellers regretted asking 7Y if they had any questions. It took her about twenty minutes to explain that there wouldn't be an in-flight movie or a snacks trolley and that there wasn't a toilet. When a girl called Katy burst into tears because she couldn't find a life jacket under her seat Mrs Sellers decided it was time to move on. If only the pupils' timetables were ready they'd have something to keep them busy, copying the details out into their planners. Then she remembered : the Head of Year had said she'd been told the planners would be arriving in the afternoon. Tomorrow at the latest.

"So, did your nan manage to find some jam, Nicola?" she asked, hoping to fill the remaining time before dinner.

CHAPTER 5

"Working hard or hardly working?"

At some point in the last two years the wall separating the HR offices from the rest of the school had become known as the Berlin Wall. There was a large set of double doors in the wall and to be fair the sign on the wall only strengthened the image.

> ➤ *Pupils must not come through to the Student Welcome desk without a pass signed by both their Head of Year and Form Tutor.*
> ➤ *First Aid is only available between 12 and 2.*
> ➤ *Teachers (especially the Art Department) are not permitted to use the Office photocopiers at any time.*
> ➤ *In case of fire, please find an alternative exit.*

Getting through the school's main gates was nothing compared to the challenge of trying to get to the front office. With the entry code changing daily, you really needed to be summoned if you ever wanted to see how the other half lived. Those who worked in HR were clearly far too busy to be interrupted by either teachers or pupils.

Mrs Norma Spratt had only been Head of HR for six months following the sudden disappearance of her predecessor. She'd heard that nobody ever stayed in the rôle very long with the record going to a woman called Kirsty who had held on to the post for nearly nine months if you included time off work ill. Mrs Spratt was sure she would beat this record. It was just a matter of following each policy to the letter and making sure Ms Stonehart was happy.

So it was that this morning, as ever, she delivered a fresh pot of lapsang souchong to the Headteacher's office at eight o'clock sharp, together with the local and national newspapers. As this was Friday, the end of a very busy week for the non-teaching staff, she'd also brought along some tasty croissants for Ms Stonehart and everybody working in administration. She carefully closed the door and went back to her own office having set aside the morning for reviewing school policies. As she'd said at the interview, she was very experienced in HR, although in truth the policies she'd inherited here were nothing like the ones she'd had to deal with at the dog food factory. At the last count there were more than three hundred and sixty school policies to review even before new ones were written. Just finding them on the shared area of the computer system was like searching for a hidden Easter egg on a DVD. Perhaps when that nice Mr Rojan was back in he'd show her an easy way to use SCAMS. It would be good to see old Trev again. He was such a calm, reassuring person to work with and such a good listener. Now, where had that Leave of Absence policy got to?

Across the corridor from Mrs Spratt's room the Main Office was a hive of activity. With less than a hundred days to go, Julia Thomlinson was busy on the phone trying to arrange the best venue for the office Christmas party. Julie Tomlinson was printing off amusing quotations for the office wall which Julie Thompson was trying her best to laminate. In the well-stocked kitchenette Julie Tomson was on tea and coffee duty, checking her texts while the kettle began to boil.

"Just wait here," said Judy Timson, the Office Manager, Attendance Officer and First Aider, "I'll just need to get an ice pack."

The boy with a bruised knee sat down outside the office and prepared to wait. He'd tripped over a *'Caution! Slippery floor!'* sign that had been left at the top of the stairs. As he waited he looked up at the framed portrait on the wall opposite, wondering why there was a photo of that Prime Minister his Dad didn't like.

"Ladies," said Judy to her team in the office, "if I can just break you off from your work for a minute, we have a new colleague joining us today."

A young man stepped forward. The ladies in the office were a little taken aback. Nobody had ever heard of a man working in the office.

"Hello, everybody, I'm Julian Humphreys but my friends call me Jules. Ooh, well I never! Is that a quote from *Mamma Mia?*"

"It's Julie's favourite film," said one of the other Julies.

"No!" exclaimed Jules incredulously. "Me too! My partner and I have seen it twelve times! Would you like me to help with the laminating machine? I know just the knack for making it turn out straight. Give it here. *Here I go again!*"

As the mid-morning cakes were passed round, all the ladies agreed that Jules would fit into the team nicely.

"Delicious tarts," said Jules as he helped himself to another. It was mid-afternoon and the office team were taking a well-earned break now that the pupils were all heading home for the weekend.

"Julie made them," said Julia. "Should we put you down on the rota for next week, Jules?"

"My baking's to die for!" exclaimed Jules enthusiastically. "My partner can't get enough of my fairy cakes."

"So how was your first day then?" asked Judy.

"You've all been absolute darlings," said Jules. "It all seems like so busy in here though."

"Oh don't worry about that," said Julie. "We get sent a lot of emails with things to do but you can ignore most of them as they're usually meant for somebody else. I get a lot that should have gone to Julie."

"I'm the same," agreed Julie.

"That'll probably change with the new staff codes," said Julia.

"We thought we'd put you in charge of exams," said Judy. "Julie's off on maternity at the moment, so that desk's yours. Next to Juliette. You'll like her. She's off ill today. You can also be the Fire Safety Officer if you like. You'll get a luminous tabard and a clipboard."

"Ooh, that sounds very exciting," said Jules, clapping his hands.

"Well, that's all you need really. Just make sure you look busy when Ms Stonehart comes in. Putting documents through the shredder or stapling things together always seems to impress her."

"I heard somebody say something about her not actually being a teacher?" continued Jules.

"Keep your voice down," said Julie Thompson. She quickly slid the glass partition shut between the Main Office and the corridor. "She's one of us but she certainly wouldn't want to be reminded of it."

"Go on," smiled Jules, eager for all the gossip.

"Well, what I heard from Juliette," said Judy, "and you mustn't ever repeat this..."

Jules nodded earnestly and crossed his heart. "I'm the soul of discretion," he said. "You ask anybody."

"What I heard was that Janine Stonehart never trained as a teacher. She's never taught a single lesson in her life. The nearest she's ever been to teaching was working as a secretary at some primary school up near the motorway before she started here. Somewhere up near Berryfield, I think."

"No!" exclaimed Jules, cupping his face in his hands in shock. "Go on."

"Well, about six years ago I'd say she applied for a secretarial job here but there was some sort of a mix-up with the paperwork in HR, nobody really knows quite what happened, and she was offered the top job. Headteacher! One of the candidates who'd been interviewed for the post of Headteacher on the same day was offered the job of secretary."

Jules looked round at his colleagues in the office.

"He turned it down," explained Judy. "Running USA was obviously more appealing."

"The President?"

"The Deputy Headteacher of Upper Steem Academy," said Julia.

"Nobody knew who'd screwed up," added Judy, "so it was agreed that Janine would just continue as 'Headteacher'. It's working out quite well really...just as long as Toby doesn't find out."

"Toby?"

"Toby Chambers. Chair of Governors," added Julie. "Horrible man. Hands like an octopus. Thinks he owns this school.

It was his idea to run it as a business."

"Probably because they keep us busy!" joked Julia. "I mean you couldn't call it an organization, could you? This place is about as organised as…"

"Anyway if you think about it," Judy continued, "we've got a lot of job security here. We know Janine's little secret and she thinks the paperwork from her interview has all been shredded. It's a very well-equipped office here I think you'll find, Jules. Lots of photocopiers and it's so easy to send emails with attachments if you know what I mean…"

Jules looked round at the photocopiers before he realised what she really meant.

"If you want job security you're best on this side of the wall," Judy said.

"As long as you don't do what Mrs Speke did," said one of the Julies quietly without looking up from her mobile phone.

"We don't mention her," said Judy. "Let's just say you don't normally find office staff disappearing like the teachers do."

"Don't worry, said Jules. "I'm not one of them."

OCTOBER

CHAPTER 6

"Worry about today before tomorrow."

Not for the first time Ms Stonehart looked around her vast office, then out at the sunshine shimmering across the roof of her top-of-the-range Mercedes and patted herself on the back. She'd come a long way since Berryfield. If only her ex-husbands could see her now! Suddenly though reality returned with a bump as she realized that she'd have to get Bob to re-paint the STOP sign at the gates correctly. It was just one thing after another. She even had to remind him to take the bins out each week, making sure he didn't leave them too close to her car, of course.

The first month of the new school year had gone well but she was still rushed off her feet with the number of things she had to do as Headteacher. It could be lonely at the top, carrying the burden of leadership on her shoulders alone. Nobody really appreciated how much she did. She had two meetings pencilled into her diary this morning. She needed to meet with two of her Assistant Heads to discuss the Curriculum Review Action Plans to improve teaching and learning throughout the school as well as the Finance Department to discuss money. She'd do the more important of the meetings first. It was always nice to spend time talking about money and it would do her Assistant Heads no harm to be kept waiting outside, reminding them that nobody is indispensable. A quick phone call to Norma resulted in Alex Goldbloom and Julie Thomas being shown through to her office along with a fresh pot of her favourite tea.

Ms Stonehart came straight to the point.

"Do you have the figures for last month, Alex?"

Alex often couldn't help picturing Ms Stonehart stroking a large white cat as she sat in her black leather chair behind an acre of polished mahogany. He passed over a stapled sheaf of papers inside a beige folder.

Ms Stonehart took another sip of her lapsang souchong before looking up.

"I like the colour of this folder, Alex," she commented. "Do you want to go through everything and explain all the numbers? Just in case Julie's not seen it, of course."

Julie had seen it but smiled politely. If it hadn't been for her Alex might have forgotten how much Ms Stonehart was impressed by papers that were stapled nicely together. Or shredded, depending on the content. Even though she had not been employed at Wildside when Ms Stonehart had been appointed as 'Headteacher' Julie still had a copy of the paperwork from that interview hidden away at home between the pages of her diary. Nobody was indispensable unless they knew where the bodies were buried.

"September was a very good month for the business financially," said Alex. "The devil's in the detail. So, for example, here we saved nearly £6000 on planners. Instead of putting in an order for teachers' planners we kept them all waiting for nearly three weeks saying there'd been a delay at the warehouse. By then most staff had gone out and bought themselves a planner from a pound shop. Except the PE Department, of course."

"That's even better than last year," smiled Ms Stonehart.

On that occasion teachers had been asked whether they'd prefer an A4 or an A5 planner but then regardless of their choice they had all been given the smaller, cheaper option. She'd had to let one Science teacher go because she'd kept insisting that she wanted one of the more expensive planners.

"We've also made a saving this year by not providing the pupils with a student diary. There's a new website called 'S'Cool Homework!' that pupils can log on to for homework tasks. The first year is free and then I thought next year parents themselves could maybe subscribe to it?"

"That sounds like an outstanding idea, Alex. Just the kind of thing Ofsted are looking for. Pupils taking ownership of their own learning and developing their IT skills at the same time. Parental involvement too. And what do you have for me, Julie?"

"Well, since we introduced the online payment system in the canteen last September we've made a profit of over £800 per term. What happens is a lot of parents put money on to their child's account, then they forget the password and the child then ends up bringing in sandwiches. In fact some of the parents of last year's Year 11 are still putting money into their account by standing order even though they've left."

Involuntarily Ms Stonehart glanced over at the shredder in the corner.

"Just make sure all the accounts are in order before Ofsted come back, won't you? I've heard they take a keen interest in Free School Meals data."

"We'll look into it straight away," Alex assured her. "I think there's an edit option on SCAMS. We've also come up with another little tweak to the system that I think you'll like. If we increase the price of every item sold in the canteen by just 10p the amount we take each term will increase considerably."

"Won't anybody notice?"

"We chose 10p in line with the cost of buying a plastic bag in a supermarket. I think Ms Lovall could probably do some L4L lessons about the harm plastic is doing to the planet? I picture Year 7 designing posters for the canteen saying that everything bought there is helping to protect the planet?"

Ms Stonehart was already making a mental note to make sure that Ofsted saw the canteen during their next visit. Ideally earlier on in the morning, before the pupils had been let loose in there. Under her leadership Wildside Academy really was going from strength to strength.

Being members of the Senior Leadership Team Ms Lynne Winter and Ms Sharon Payne were more than capable of keeping themselves occupied whilst waiting for their meeting with Ms Stonehart.

"This'll be brill," said Sharon trying to hold her mobile phone far enough away to get them both in shot. She couldn't quite fit all of Lynne into the picture but it still looked hilarious with them both sticking two fingers up in front of the Head's office. It had all started because they hadn't wanted to hang around looking like two naughty schoolgirls waiting to be expelled. They'd been looking at the framed photos of the Senior Leadership Team that ran the entire length of the corridor when they decided they could do better themselves.

"When I started there was loads of photos of the different Heads going back to the 1960s up here," said Lynne. One of the first things Ms Stonehart had done as 'Headteacher' had been to get Bob to take them all down. Nobody knew what had happened to them. There'd been an awkward moment when the widow of old Mr Buckingham had come in wanting to retrieve a photo of her late husband for the funeral but somebody on the SLT had sorted it somehow.

Lynne looked up at one portrait where she'd taken her glasses off and was squinting at the camera.

"You don't think this one makes me look fat?"

"It's well brill. You've lost loads of weight since you joined that gym," said Sharon. "I reckon all them photos should be updated anyway. Janine's hair isn't those colours now anyway."

"I hope she don't go on too long this time," said Lynne. "I'm hungry."

Their last meeting with Ms Stonehart had gone on for nearly two hours and she'd never even said what it was about.

Around twenty minutes into their meeting with Ms Stonehart Lynne was starting to feel that they were making some progress.

"So, just to clarify what you're saying," Ms Stonehart continued, "in case I ever meet one, they're called Year 7 because they're in their seventh year of education?"

"Yes. Well, technically it's their eighth year if you include Reception," explained Lynne.

"That's their first year at school," added Sharon to avoid any ambiguity.

"And Year 11 is their last year, their twelfth year then? The one with the GCSE exams?"

"Unless they go on to a Sixth Form…" added Lynne.

Sharon was wishing her friend hadn't overcomplicated things for the Headteacher.

"And that'll be the Lower Sixth, their thirteenth year?"

"Year 12, yes," said Lynne. "But we don't need to bother about that. Just up to GCSE." Ms Stonehart had closed the Sixth Form two years earlier in order to make more office space and save money on staffing. Few people understood the reasoning behind why the teachers who lost their jobs weren't actually ones who worked in the doomed Sixth Form.

"And there's a new grading system for GCSE, isn't there?" Ms Stonehart had read it in a Sunday supplement but it all sounded so different to when she'd got her three 'O' Level results.

Sharon glanced across at Lynne, wondering which of them would take on the task of explaining the new system to Ms Stonehart. As it turned out they were saved by a rough tap on the door followed by the clatter of Bob coming in with his toolbox.

"Alright if I get it up now, is it?" he asked.

There was a slight pause before Ms Stonehart realized what he meant.

"Of course, Bob. That wall there I think."

As Bob hammered a nail into the wall it gave Lynne and Sharon twenty minutes' grace to consider how to tackle their explanation. Bob looked pleased with himself as he straightened the picture frame, put his tools away and left. It was hard to tell from this distance but Sharon thought it looked like it was a framed cycling proficiency certificate.

"Now you were about to tell me about the new GCSE grades," Ms Stonehart resumed. "I assume first-class students are looking for grade 1s in their GCSEs?"

Never before had Lynne and Sharon been more delighted to hear the shrill sound of the fire alarm blaring out through the building.

CHAPTER 7

"If a person has a match they will find a place to strike it."

"There's absolutely no way in the world I can wear that," said Jules, holding up the tabard. "Not with this tie."

"I hear what you say," said Mrs Spratt, "but you're the designated Fire Safety Officer. It's a very important rôle."

"The most important rôle in the school right now," added Judy Timson, pleased that it was one less thing she'd be responsible for.

"Well, I suppose just this once then," said Jules. "If I button it up. But hi-vis yellow really clashes with mustard. Perhaps if I'm told in advance when the school's going to be on fire I could wear something that goes with this? My colour therapist would probably advise pink or slate grey."

And so with the fire alarm still ringing in their ears the office staff made their way out of the building, pausing only to collect their coats and one of the chocolate muffins that Julie had brought in.

The evacuation seemed to be progressing well. Ms Malik had taken it upon herself to re-direct those pupils who were trying to leave via the main reception back into the building to exit by the correct route.

"I really don't know why you think we have these procedures to keep you safe if you're not going to follow them!" she called out as the pupils went back in through the double doors.

As it was only his first ever fire drill Jules wasn't quite sure what to expect. As far as he could tell the whole school was out on the front field. They all seemed to be looking at him and it was at that point he wished he'd remembered to bring a list of all their names so that registers could be taken. To his left the Year 7s looked like they'd been getting changed for PE, standing there in variations of the school sports kit. Over to his right Year 11 were keeping themselves entertained by seeing which form could do the best Mexican wave. Last to appear were Adam and Sonya from Year 10, arm-in-arm again, with Adam proclaiming that he would always save Sonya from a burning building.

"It's always when I'm on a free," grumbled Ms Grimley. "I bet they look at my timetable before they hit that alarm."

As the fire bell continued to echo around the area, causing nearby residents to open their bedroom windows and curse the school, Jules felt the weight of hundreds of pairs of eyes staring at him with expectation or annoyance. Just as he was starting to wish that the ground would swallow him up the piercing sound of the alarm was drowned out by the siren from an approaching fire engine. Everybody, especially Ms Lovall, became much more interested in the sight of the firemen who had been stopped by Darren Froggett at the zebra crossing. Perhaps he genuinely thought the school was ablaze and that he was doing everything he could to help by keeping people back? At the school's main gates Bob and Stan the Assistant Caretaker were struggling to remember the entry code.

"I think it'd be fab if we could get some of these firemen in to give a talk about fire safety," sighed Ms Lovall. "I'm gonna see if we can do that instead of the online Fire Safety training this term."

Mr O'Reilly, the new Maths teacher, was always looking for opportunities to make his subject relevant to the pupils. Having counted that his class were all safe and lined up roughly parallel to the other Year 10 forms, he decided to set them a puzzle.

"So if a thousand pupils exit the building in five minutes, what's the average time taken by each pupil?"

At the front of the line Kevin had reluctantly agreed to join in, taking out his calculator to work it out.

"It's about three seconds each," he concluded.

"That can't be right," pondered Mr O'Reilly. "Can I borrow your calculator, Kevin?"

He tried two plus two and got the result 42.

"Where did you buy this calculator, Kevin?"

"From the Maths Department. We was told we needed a scientific calculator for the exams. Mr Mason sold me it last year."

Mr O'Reilly had replaced Mr Mason towards the end of the summer term when Mr Mason had suddenly disappeared.

"Hmm, three seconds. You may need to replace the batteries, Kevin."

"It says it's solar…Uses like nuclear bombs do."

"That'll be why then. It's not that sunny today."

"Sir," said Josette. "Is this another of those things where we have to find x? 'Cos if it is, I think it's over there. On that number plate on the fire engine."

Not for the first time Mr O'Reilly was glad that they'd decided to get rid of slide rules.

In many ways there was a lot more furious activity going on waiting for the fire alarm practice to end than ever went on inside most classrooms at Wildside Academy. Mr Armani had hauled Ryan Spivey out of his line to give himself more room to shout at him at the front of the field. Ryan, it turned out, had been up to his old trick of taking the opportunity to sell sweets and drinks to the other pupils at exorbitant prices. Nobody ever argued back with Mr Armani - it would have been like trying to reason with the Exterminator from Zombie Kombat 3000 – but as far as Ryan was concerned he was just like that wrinkly old bloke he'd seen on TV who fired people all the time. One day Ryan would be a millionaire and he'd get him fired!

"I can tell when you're lying, Spivey!" continued Mr Armani. "I can see your lips moving. Now get back in line and just repeat the bit where you weren't talking!"

As for the other staff some were about as happy as Ms Grimley on a Sunday evening whilst others were just glad to be out of the classroom.

"You know why we have so many fire alarms here, don't you?" joked Tim Cocker with Miss Fullilove, the Assistant Teaching Assistant. "It's the school uniform. Too many blazers!"

Miss Fullilove smiled politely as though a diagram would help her understand the joke.

Brigadier Vernon-Smythe, the Head of DT, was busy making a few calls on his mobile phone. Having a second job wasn't technically in breach of contract as long as there wasn't a conflict of interest. In Vernon-Smythe's case selling top-of-the-range second-hand cars, like the one he'd sold Ms Stonehart for a very reasonable price, pretty much guaranteed him job security. He noticed that cones had been put down around her Mercedes to keep pupils away from it. To be fair if her car did get scraped he could get it repaired for her at a very reasonable rate.

Just as breaktime was due to come to an end the all clear signal was given for everybody to return to the building. Ms Grimley wasn't sure whether to grumble that she'd lost her break or be grateful that she'd not had to do her break duty in the canteen. In the end her natural instinct took over but she compromised by complaining about the amount of mud now covering her shoes.

Having checked that her car was safe Ms Stonehart returned to her office where a fresh pot of tea and biscuits awaited her after her busy morning. As instructed Jules was sitting outside as though on naughty step, ready to report back on the fire alarm. Julie had told him that he'd have to do a back-to-work meeting with everybody before they could go back to their duties but he hoped she was joking.

"You wanted to see me, Ms Stonehart?" he began nervously when the door opened and he was summoned inside.

"Mrs Spratt has given me the information," said the Headteacher. She drew Jules' attention to a figure on her computer screen.

"Time to evacuate the building during a fire alarm practice : 3 minutes and 27 seconds."

Jules breathed a sigh of relief. Under five minutes from the alarm being first sounded to the total evacuation of over a thousand pupils, sixty teachers, all the office and admin staff along with any random visitors or delivery people who may be in the building seemed pretty good to him. It had seemed longer but he found things often seemed longer than they really were.

"That," said Ms Stonehart sternly, "is from the Upper Steem Academy website under Health and Safety. The time for Wildside Academy this morning was 23 minutes and 19 seconds! We can't put that on our website! What would Ofsted say?"

Jules was already trying to find a solution to the problem.

"Perhaps if we were to start the timer from when the firemen actually arrive," he suggested. "I mean, they're the professionals. It seems a bit rude starting without them."

"We'd still be waiting for them if Ms Lovall hadn't known the codes to the school gate and let them in."

"Sorry," said Jules, wondering whether bringing in some of his fairy cakes tomorrow would help her forget this failure. Still, he was also the Exams Officer. He could impress her with how well he got the GCSE exams organized.

Looking out of the window at Upper Steem Academy Ms Stonehart was muttering quietly to herself. It sounded to Jules like she was repeating the same words as though in a trance : twenty-three-nineteen-twenty-three-nineteen-n-n-n-nnineteen…"

"You may go," she eventually said.

Just as she was reflecting that nobody understood the pressure she was under, Bob clattered on the door and came in.

"It's all sorted, that sign by the gate," he said, glancing over to check the certificate was still hanging on the wall.

"We'll have a Chinese tonight," said Janine. "But don't get it from The Golden Dragon this time!"

CHAPTER 8

"Food tastes better when the table is well set."

They say you only get one chance to make a first impression and so standing out prominently in any school's calendar is the night of the Open Evening. It's a chance for the world to see what your school is really like, to lift up any rock and see what's crawling underneath, to see where you've papered over the cracks. Perhaps that's why Ms Stonehart always found Open Evenings so scary. Oddly enough it's the only time when staff are provided with free cakes and hot drinks, in the hope that this will keep them smiling and making the right noises to parents for the next five hours.

With just over an hour to go before the Open Evening, Ms Mina Malik, Second-in-Department for Geography, looked at the plates of treats laid out on the worktop in the staffroom.

"It's so nice that they've put these out for us all," she said. "We're so lucky to work here."

"What are you going for?" asked Mr Jones in the queue behind her.

"Mmm, these chocolate brownies look incredible," said Mina. "One of those and a black coffee, I think."

"Chocolate brownies and a black coffee!" repeated Mr Jones in mock indignation. "A little bit racist, if you don't mind me saying, Ms Malik. I didn't expect that kind of language from you of all people."

Mina looked round quickly to check that nobody important had heard her *faux pas*. "But…What are *you* having then?" she asked anxiously.

"I'm having a cocoa sponge square," said Mr Jones,

reaching for a chocolate brownie, "although I've heard the gingerbread people are very good too. This'll go well with a coffee without milk."

As Mr Jones made his way to the seating area to enjoy his chocolate brownie and black coffee Ms Malik chose an iced finger and a seat in the quiet corner. She realised that if anybody on the SLT had heard her she wouldn't have scored any brownie points in her plans for promotion. Even then the thought crossed her mind that she shouldn't really be calling them brownie points either...

Once the free cakes had run out in the staffroom Ms Winter and Ms Payne had decided the most useful thing they could do as members of the SLT would be to go round each Department to check that everybody was ready for the Open Evening. It'd be a good way of offering support to colleagues at this busy time and where better to start than over at the Food Tech classroom.

As they got there, Bob was busy fixing a photocopied sheet on the door of the Food Tech room and Sharon cursed when she read what it said. There were no tempting smells drifting out from the classroom, no freshly baked cookies or fruit scones. Instead the room was in total darkness, the cooker lights dimmed. Mrs Carter was absent and there'd be no cookery demonstrations tonight.

"I was looking forward to one of her cheese toasties," said Lynne, swigging the last of her diet cola.

Bob blew his nose before starting to sweep up in the corridor. "I've heard she went home this afternoon with suspected food poisoning."

"Is the canteen still open?" asked Lynne hopefully.

As it turned out there was other food somewhere in the building but the dynamic duo had not yet realised. Up on the second floor Mr Hamish Buonanulla, Acting Head of the MFL Department, was trying to create the atmosphere of a *café français* in his classroom with help from his best friend and colleague Madame Céline Loups-Garoux. Red checkered tablecloths covered three of the tables by the bin whilst accordion music streamed quietly out of his laptop. The other members of the Department had been banished to set up displays of textbooks in another classroom down the corridor.

Simply for purposes of quality control Mr Buonanulla had

decided it would be worth tasting a little of the cheese before any of the parents arrived. Neither he nor Madame Loups-Garoux could actually be certain when they'd opened the second bottle of wine but it had helped put them in a reminiscent mood *à la recherche du temps perdu*. It was as if they were back in a café on the Champs Élysées in the days before the school became an Academy with the pupils displaying independence by exploring Montmartre on their own.

"So," he said, topping up his friend's glass again, "what I don't get is why I'm still only *Acting* Head of MFL after nearly three years doing it."

Madame Loups-Garoux helped herself to another piece of edam, realising that her friend had bought the wrong thing again but not wanting to hurt his feelings. They still hadn't found a use for the sixteen boxes of exercise books with squared blue paper he'd ordered in September. Luckily they'd found a way to blame it on Ivor.

"You should 'ave been made 'ead of Département as soon as Chris retired," she said. "Why we 'ad to 'ave all that brouhaha is beyond me."

Shortly after Ms Stonehart had taken over the school it had been decided that the MFL Department was in need of reorganisation. Mr Thicke had been the member of SLT in charge of curriculum planning that year and not being a great fan of the Germans after an unpleasant incident with a flat tyre outside Düsseldorf whilst on holiday, he had decided to remove German from the curriculum and replace it with Spanish. The fact that the school didn't employ any Spanish teachers wasn't really a concern as one foreign language is pretty much like another. Mr Thicke had said that the plans looked good on paper and the Governors had agreed without hesitation. Chris Carpenter, the Head of MFL, had then mysteriously disappeared around this time, although the official version had said he'd left to spend more time with his family. Fraulein Eva Schadenfreude, the Head of German, had always believed that she would be promoted to Head of MFL when the post became vacant, largely because she had worked in the MFL Department longer than anybody else. As it turned out her refusal to teach Spanish meant that she was just one of the four MFL teachers that the school had had to let go. By a strange coincidence it was around the time that these redundancies were made that Hamish and Céline started giving up their evenings to learn Spanish at Wildside Community College together. Within a few weeks a desire to play a more active rôle in the life of Wildside Academy had blossomed in them along with a sudden interest in the positions of Head of MFL and Head of Year 9. One outcome of this perceived new job security was that Mr Buonanulla had a progress meeting with Ms Stonehart scheduled for every Monday morning.

"I absolutely dread these meetings with Janine," he confided to his friend, not for the first time. "So, I get a wee migraine on a Sunday night just thinking about it. I nearly rode my bike into a lamp-post this morning! And I hate having to explain myself all the time. Don't ask me why."

"You know when I was a little girl in Cafard-sur-Mer my grand-mère always used to sing '*Non, je ne regrette rien!*' to me," said Madame Loups-Garoux, gazing out at the rain and feeling nostalgic. "You 'ave nothing to worry about with Janine. We did the right thing getting these jobs and we will just 'ave to look after each other like *les trois mousquetaires!*"

"Yeah, yeah, yeah, but the GCSE results in MFL are getting worse each year," said Mr Buonanulla, opening a jar of olives. "I think even Janine is beginning to notice."

"It is not your fault, mon ami. There are four of us in the Département, not just you. Ivor teaches far more pupils than the rest of us put together, so if results are bad it's 'is fault. You're just 'ead of Département."

"*Acting* Head of Department. And I can't even get on the Upper Pay Scale till Janine says so."

In the classroom down the corridor Mr Haddenough and Miss Brown had just about finished getting the room ready for the Open Evening on their own. They'd managed to find a few copies of the textbook "*Bof! On est français!*" that weren't covered in graffiti, two Spanish dictionaries and a German flag from Fraulein Schadenfreude's old room. Games from the *Joie de Vivre* website were already bleeping on the interactive whiteboard in anticipation of hordes of enthusiastic Year 6 pupils bursting through the door.

"So," said Mr Buonanulla, checking his phone again, "the parents will be here in about half an hour. So, I think there's some red wine in the storeroom too if you fancy a drop."

"I don't mind if I do, 'amish," grinned Madame Loups-

Garoux. Whatever they said, he was a good 'ead of Département.

With little else to do Mr Jamie Humble, Co-ordinator of Behaviour and Attitudes, was making his way across to the staff toilets when he noticed two pupils over by the bike shed. As he got closer he saw that it was the twins Freya and Maddie from his Year 7 Drama class, two of the canniest bairns in the year group.

"What's up, pet?" he asked Freya. He wiped some of the rainwater off the bench and sat down next to them. He'd noticed that most pupils took him more seriously when they didn't realise they were actually taller than him. Tim Cocker had once described him as *smaller than life!* He was thinking of growing a beard.

"We don't want to get anybody into trouble," said Freya, glancing nervously at her sister.

"Something to do with t'bikes?" prompted Mr Humble. After a tough childhood growing up in Sunderland, he prided himself on being able to get straight to the heart of a problem.

"No, sir," said Freya uncomfortably. "It's just we offered to help with setting up the Open Evening."

"And you forgot to tell your parents you'd be away late getting home. I see." A safeguarding issue. "We can fettle it. Just give 'em a bell from the Student Welcome desk…"

"It's not that, sir," said Freya. "It's just that there's some boys who've been picking on us. Calling us swots and horrible names for helping tonight." Maddie looked like she was about to burst into tears.

Bullying! Even though he was only in his second year of teaching Jamie knew how to deal with bullies as he'd been on a course and had helped Ms Payne write Wildside Academy's anti-bullying policy. It was one of the things that had impressed Ms Stonehart enough for her to create the post of CBA just for him. If he spent enough time with the right people down at The Cock 'n' Bull he was sure he'd be promoted to the SLT within a year. In the meantime he had his sights set on Mr North's job as he was retiring at Christmas.

"Away man," he said to the twins, leading them back into the main building and down the corridor to the office of the School-Home Intervention Team.

As the lights flickered on Freya and Maddie sat down on the beanbags and looked round at the colourful posters on display.

"Now then, now then," said Mr Humble, logging onto SCAMS at the nearest computer. "The first thing I'm going to do is give you both some achievement points to say thank you for helping tonight. Looks like you're already top in your class for achievement like. Y'Mam'll be proper proud."

He then gave them both a large piece of paper. "And I need you both to fill in one of these forms. Do you know who the lads were that were bullying you?"

Freya and Maddie shook their heads silently.

"Well, just leave that part of the form blank," continued Mr Humble. "You just need to fill in all the other details so that I can follow it up – where it happened, exactly what they said, if anybody witnessed it, how it made you feel, what you think the next steps should be, you know, yeah?"

Freya and Maddie slowly started filling in their names at the top of the sheets.

"What's the date today, sir?" asked Freya, looking round for help.

"My pen's not working," pondered Maddie.

"Listen," said Mr Humble, "I'm just going to pop over to the staffroom while you're doing that, but I've also got these for you. Something those bullies won't have though but!"

He handed them each a massive sticker to put on the lapel of their blazers. *'I'm a Wildside superstar! I helped at the Open Evening!'*

Yes, that would really help stop the bullying.

"And I'll get Miss White to give you a special shout out in the next Year Assembly. Champion!" He held his palm out to give them a high-five before he left. "Tara f'now, bonny lasses! Won't be long."

On his way back from the toilets twenty-five minutes later Mr Humble was distracted by odd noises coming from the Music block. It sounded like a cat or something had made its way into the building and got hopelessly stuck. He knew exactly what to do. Standing on tip-toes he cursed as he realised that he still couldn't see in through the window. The rain had started lashing down again so he made his way round to the side door and tapped in the three-digit code as he had forgotten his security lanyard. On his sixth attempt the door clicked open and he hurried in out of the rain. Failing to find a light switch, he cursed again, stumbling about in the darkness as he tried to operate the torch on his mobile phone, and tripped over some sort of metal contraption.

"Everything alright out there?" asked Mr Jones innocently as light flooded out of the Music room to spotlight Mr Humble lying face down under a twisted music stand, his hair wet and one trouser leg ripped. Sheets of music still fluttered in the air like autumn leaves.

Five or six small faces peered out from behind Mr Jones, their rendition of *"London's burning"* having abruptly stopped as soon as they heard the commotion in the corridor.

"Ah, you've come for a sneak preview of Recorder Club," smiled Mr Jones. The pupils behind him giggled.

Mr Humble stood up and dusted himself down.

Have you given them all *Wildside superstar!* stickers?" was all he managed to say as he left.

They say that there's no fool like an old fool but some of the young fools were starting to show real promise.

It was as if Miss Linda Armitage, Head of Geography, had developed a knack for hearing SLT approaching long before they ever appeared on her corridor. To be fair, the arrival of Ms Winter was hardly a patter of tiny feet. The tins of sweets Miss Armitage had bought for Open Evening had been secured in her top drawer under a pile of Ordnance Survey maps even before the classroom door crashed open.

"Hiya," said Ms Winter, almost knocking an illuminated globe to the floor as she squeezed in, followed as always by Ms Payne.

Before Miss Armitage could return any greeting, formal or otherwise, Ms Mina Malik, Second-in-Department, steered the two members of SLT over to the activity she had been setting up before she'd gone for a cocoa sponge square.

"Let me show you what I've prepared," said Ms Malik.

The table by the window was covered in a giant map of the world with a colourful border displaying the flags of every different country. Gold stars on the flags indicated which countries Ms Malik herself had visited. Beside this display were spotless atlases and examples of the pupils' work in their best handwriting with encouraging comments from Ms Malik. The wall behind was covered with photographs from various field trips with Ms Malik herself in nearly every shot. It really was an outstanding exhibition of Ms Malik's contribution to the school but it seemed to have left little in the way of display resources for the rest of the Department. Even the term's quota of Blu-Tack had been used up with no chance of borrowing any from another Department.

"I've also made this quiz for the new pupils to complete as they look at my display," said Ms Malik, handing full-colour photocopies to her senior colleagues.

Ms Winter glanced at the quiz sheet.

"*Spot each country's flag,*" she read out slowly, pondering each word. "You should of come to Sharon or I to check the grammar. We're English teachers us."

"This is well bad," agreed Ms Payne, throwing the sheet back on the desk.

"Yeah. Need to sort out them apostrophes," continued Ms Winter. "You'll have to photocopy them again."

She looked round the room as though she'd lost something.

"Have you got any sweets for the winners?" she asked.

On the basis that he couldn't really add anything to the preparations in the Geography Department Tim Cocker had spent the last hour alone in the Sports Hall. He was just about to beat his own personal best on the rowing machine when he heard somebody going into the sports equipment store. Although he'd told Harry Greenfield, Head of Boys' PE, that he was in there, he still had flashbacks to that night last year. Keen to get home early and watch Wimbledon that afternoon, Harry had locked everything up without really checking, leaving Tim to spend the whole night locked in the gym with nothing but a dead mobile phone and a packet of prawn crisps for company.

"That you, Harry?" called out Tim, forfeiting his score on the rowing machine as he looked out into the Sports Hall entrance. It was unusual for the Head of Boys' PE to come out of the PE office during working hours but these were unusual times. As it happened it was Stan Lawrence, the Assistant Caretaker, who appeared in the doorway of the storeroom.

"Tim," he said, looking guilty. "You nearly gave me a heart attack. I thought you were bloomin' Greenfield. I just need to borrow these."

He revealed the two red table tennis bats he'd been hiding

behind his back.

"You and Bob having a ping-pong tournament?" smiled Tim as the two of them walked to the exit doors.

"Directing traffic!" moaned Stan. "Not directed time but Bob's putting chairs out in the Main Hall so I've drawn the short straw."

"I'll come with you," said Tim, as Stan locked up after them. "I'm going to move my car to the main road anyway. It's always a nightmare getting away at the end with all the extra traffic."

"All in hand this year, Tim" said Stan, demonstrating his semaphoring actions with the table tennis bats. Tim noticed a four-digit number written in black marker pen on the back of Stan's hand.

"Are you sure that's today's gate code?" he asked helpfully.

As Tim drove past the school reception and out on to Cemetery Road to look for a space he noticed that Bob had found time to lay a roll of red carpet up the steps to the main entrance. Ms Stonehart herself was standing there, no doubt waiting for Toby Chambers, the Chair of Governors, who would be arriving any minute now. She checked her watch and made a mental note to summon Mr Cocker to her office first thing in the morning. Not being a Maths teacher, or indeed any sort of teacher, Ms Stonehart had once again put two and two together and got five. All staff should be involved in the Open Evening and certainly not be leaving early.

Nobody really appreciated how much time and effort she'd put into the preparations for this Open Evening. She'd probably put more effort into this one event than all her weddings put together, especially the third one which had had to be a very hurried affair down at Berryfield Registry Office. Being Headteacher it could be lonely at the top, carrying the burden of leadership on her shoulders alone. Then she remembered she needed to see Mr O'Brien and inform him that it was his job as Assistant Head to do the welcome speech to parents, not hers. He'd still got about ten minutes to write something. She needed to wait here and see if the local press arrived and wanted some photos of her in front of the school.

It was never easy to find a parking space on Cemetery Road.

If local residents popped out to the shops they'd usually put their wheelie bin out in the road to reserve their spot. So when Tim Cocker got back to the school gates twenty minutes later, having left his car on the waste ground behind KwikShop, Toby Chambers' chauffeur had dropped him off and the school entrance was virtually empty again. Luckily Stan had had the good sense to leave the main gates open tonight. Tim sneaked in through the main entrance, hoping that parents would think he was a PE teacher, rather than somebody who'd accidently left their work clothes locked in the Sports Hall changing room. A few parents were arriving and Stan was directing them to the few remaining spaces in the staff car park. He lowered his table tennis bats as a mark of respect when a hearse pulled in slowly through the school gates.

"Looks like Graham's got a younger brother or sister," said Tim to Julie on reception, realising that the Reaper family had come straight from work in the company car.

A group of parents had arrived in reception just as Tim was starting to go through to the corridor.

"Welcome to Wildside Academy," smiled Julie. "Please help yourself to a full-colour prospectus, a form and a Wildside Academy limited edition pen. One of our prefects..."

"*Wildside* Academy?" repeated a bearded man at the front of the group. "I said this wasn't Upper Steem Academy. Come on, our Chelsea-Lou."

And with that most of the group turned and left.

"We've ordered takeaway," said another man stepping forward. "Two lemon chicken, one beef in black bean sauce, prawn toast..."

"I'm afraid you want The Golden Dragon across the road," said Julie as patiently as she could.

The entrance was deathly quiet by the time the Reaper family entered.

"I do love this entrance parlour," said Mr Reaper with an air of quiet dignity, solemnly removing his black hat. "Such a tranquil atmosphere. We'd like to look round the RE Department if you'd be so kind."

"...and so finally, Ladies and Gentleman," said Mr O'Brien, smiling as he eventually came to the end of his impromptu speech, "it only remains for me to wish you all the best and let you look round our school. I've kept you for too long. I think if you ask the teachers here they'll tell you how under Ms Stonehart's leadership the Wildside Academy you see today has come about."

There'd never been such a small audience at an Open Evening in the whole history of the school but being a Maths teacher Mr O'Brien was used to working with very small groups.

"Does anybody have any questions?" he asked generously.

A pale man in a morning suit and half-moon glasses raised his hand slowly.

"Good evening," Mr Reaper said quietly. "I was just admiring your lovely plinth. Finest quality mahogany if I'm not mistaken. *Tempus fugit!* So true! Pray tell me, how much did you purchase it for?"

"I'm afraid I really don't know," replied Mr O'Brien having never been asked that one before. "I could find out from Mr Goldbloom in Finance if you like?"

"Speaking of finance," said another parent, "is there a free school bus? Our Harry can't be walking all this way twice a day you know."

"There are some free school buses for pupils with Free School Meals. Whereabouts do you live?"

"Cemetery Road. Number 3, by Booze 'n' Fags."

It didn't take Mr O'Brien long to work out that the walk up to the bus stop was actually twenty times longer than the actual walk down Cemetery Road to the school gates.

"I'll get you a bus timetable from reception," he said diplomatically.

With no further questions the six parents and their offspring made their way out of the Main Hall to tour the buildings.

"Do I hand this in 'ere?" asked a lady with curlers in her hair, following Mr O'Brien through to reception. She handed Mr O'Brien the parent feedback form she'd been given when she'd first arrived. He smiled as if nothing in the world could make him happier and glanced down at her answers. She'd ticked that Wildside Academy was their third choice of school, having put Upper Steem Academy in both first and second place. Next to the gap to explain their "reason for attending the Open Evening" she'd simply written "*nowt on telly.*"

That's probably a fair comment, thought Mr O'Brien,

recalling the time a Parents' Evening had been scheduled on the same night as the one football match nobody had wanted to miss. What a long night that had been, only to hear the score from a parent as he'd left!

"Thank you," said the lady in curlers as she left to make her way home. Watching her go Mr O'Brien reflected on the fact that she'd witnessed nothing of Wildside Academy except the Main Hall and his welcome speech. He hoped he hadn't put her off!

As they toured the school together Toby Chambers and Janine Stonehart made an odd couple. Where Ms Stonehart was an unremarkable little figure - apart from her unusual hair colouring - Mr Chambers was totally bald. With his all-year tan he resembled a scrubbed potato that had been squeezed into a tweed three-piece suit. A pungent trail of cigar smoke followed him down the corridor. Yes, there were rules about not smoking in the workplace but surely statutory regulations didn't apply to him if it was *his* school? Mopping up a spillage further down the corridor Bob watched them suspiciously as they headed up to the first floor.

"He does a good speech that Mr O'Brien," the Chair of Governors was saying. "Mind you, love, it should be good. He's had since September to prepare it."

"I'm pleased with how he's coming along," agreed Ms Stonehart. "I suppose I'm like a rôle model to him. He's learned a lot from seeing me up there talking to staff. I'm sure he'll go a long way." Under her leadership Wildside Academy was going from strength to strength.

"Now then, love," said Mr Chambers, his voice echoing down the empty corridor, "let's see what you've done with my school. I hope you haven't broken it while I've been off in the Bahamas." He winked at her.

Ms Stonehart was unsure whether she was meant to laugh or not. As a compromise she let out a nervous high-pitched sound that was open to interpretation. It turned into a cough as she breathed in too much cigar smoke.

"We're at 508 days without an Ofsted visit," she managed to say, thinking back to the display on her office wall that she updated each day, "but we're ready for them."

"You know, love, the other Governors all thought I was mad putting a little woman in charge," he said. "But you're doing a cracking job and a lot cheaper I told them. More pleasing on the eye than Mr Taylor too. I'll tell you what I've noticed though. There seem to be a lot more teachers than parents. Do we need all these teachers here?"

"Well, Open Evenings are directed time. When I saw Mr Cocker..."

"I don't just mean tonight, love," said Mr Chambers slowly. "In general. We can't be carrying passengers. It's not a charity, it's a business. To make the most profit you need to get the most out of your resources. I mean, do we need two Music teachers, mmm?"

Ms Stonehart immediately regretted taking him to see the Recorder Club. They'd all been in a giggly mood for some reason.

"An excellent suggestion, Mr Chambers. I'll look into it. I think Mr Gordon can always play the piano in assembly so we can probably let Mrs Jones go."

"I knew I could rely on you," said Mr Chambers as they headed towards the Art Department. "Bad news is best coming from the gentle sex, love."

In point of fact Ms Stonehart generally found it best to leave it to Mr Wingett to deal with the actual conversations with staff when they had to let people go. As Headteacher she was there to make the big decisions. Mind you, her door was always open if they needed her support.

In spite of the absence of parents Ms Stonehart felt her guided tour with the Chair of Governors was going well. There'd been an awkward moment when Miss Skellen, the Acting Head of Science, had come over to report that a parent had got an electric shock from the Van de Graaff generator. She'd left Mr Campbell, her Second-in-Department, to sort the situation out while she told Ms Stonehart. Luckily Mr Chambers had been too busy looking at a display of colour-by-numbers David Hockney pictures in Mrs Thorne's room. She'd heard him mutter something about a load of Jackson Pollocks. The ambulance had arrived in no time at all and people rarely sued once they'd had time to calm down.

"Well, it's all looking good, love," mumbled Mr Chambers, glancing at his watch, "but I've told James to pick me up at nine. I'm off to the South of France tomorrow. A man needs a chance to relax from business once in a while. A change from 'er indoors' cooking too!"

In fairness if the *Marseillaise* hadn't been blaring out quite so loudly Mr Chambers might not have decided to get in the holiday mood by looking in on the MFL Department before he left. Perhaps Mr Buonanulla might have heard his bosses approaching down the corridor if he hadn't been so engrossed in conducting the music with a fake cucumber from his bag of plastic fruit and veg. And if Madame Loups-Garoux hadn't been quite so enthusiastic in her rendition of the can-can, twirling a string of plastic onions in the air as she danced on the table, things might have gone so much better for the two amigos.

"Eight o'clock tomorrow morning, my office," was all Ms Stonehart could bring herself to say as she witnessed the cabaret. And then he wonders why he's still *Acting* Head of Department!

"Two meetings in one week," said Mr Buonanulla to his best friend once they were alone again.

"Blame Ivor," said Madame Loups-Garoux, struggling to focus. "Where is 'e when you need him? In the room down the corridor, that's where! Anyway, mon petit chou, it is the 'alf term tomorrow and this will all soon be forgotten."

The Town Hall clock in Lower Steem was just chiming half past ten as the teaching staff made their weary way out to the car park, the last parent having left shortly after eight. Ms Grimley was muttering about the amount of planning she still had to do, having convinced herself that her lessons would be watched the next day. Finding that his car had been clamped Mr Cocker had arranged a taxi and had kindly agreed to help get Mr Buonanulla and Madame Loups-Garoux safely home.

As he was waiting for a lift home with a friend Bob found himself chatting to Mr Humble beside Ms Stonehart's car.

"Long days these," said Bob, trying not to sneeze in the dust from the red carpet he'd rolled up. "Still, the overtime's good."

"Shame the pub's closed though but," said Mr Humble.

"I'll be locking up then," pondered Bob as he walked back inside the main building. "You get yourself home, Jamie."

As Mr Humble got to the open school gates a couple of parents were hurrying in.

"Are you one of the teachers?" asked the woman, unsure because of his size and youthful appearance. "We didn't know what to do. I've been worried sick."

"Is it about the Open Evening? Don't worry you've missed it 'cos I can get you a prospectus and there's probably still some of the limited-edition…"

"It's the twins," said the woman's husband. "They said they were stopping to help with the do but it finished hours ago and they're not home yet."

"We should call the police!"

"Don't worry, Cathy. This young lad will know what to do. I'm right aren't I, son?"

Suddenly the penny dropped faster than a school's rating after an Ofsted inspection. Twins! Freya and Maddie! *Wildside superstars!* Oh dear!

"S.H.I.T!" exclaimed Mr Humble aloud.

"Well really!" said the woman as if she'd never heard the brown word before.

"The School-Home Intervention Team," clarified Mr Humble. "If you'd like to come with me, I think I can help…"

NOVEMBER

CHAPTER 9

*"We are sometimes taken into troubled waters not to drown,
but to be cleansed."*

After a week off for good behaviour it only took five minutes for
the half term to become a distant memory for the teaching staff
arriving back at Wildside Academy. Opposite the school a couple
of boys were dragging a Guy Fawkes effigy onto the bonfire that
was mounting up on the waste ground. For Ms Stonehart the fiasco
that had been the Open Evening was still very much in her mind,
like a smouldering firework that you really shouldn't go back to. As
Headteacher she was determined to find out who was at fault for
the poor running of the school.

She'd seen Mr Buonanulla the next morning, taking some
comfort from the fact that his bike had been stolen from the
school premises, probably whilst he'd been enjoying his second
bottle of Beaujolais. In the end she had decided to let him stay on
as Acting Head of Department with just a verbal warning. It was
cheaper than employing somebody better and there weren't actually
that many people willing to teach foreign languages these days.
Providing Mr Buonanulla kept taking advice from Mr
Haddenough, an experienced teacher too expensive to put in
charge of MFL, the Department would do alright. Toby Chambers
seemed to have something of a soft spot for Madame Loups-
Garoux and Ms Stonehart wanted to keep in his good books. That
was why she'd let her have time off to be on *'The Weakest Link'*

when other teachers didn't even get to attend family funerals. It was only fair that each request was judged on its own merits. It was just a shame she hadn't won as that would have looked good on the school website.

Ms Stonehart had gathered all the Senior Leadership Team together for an emergency meeting in her office this morning. There had been a little bit of confusion about when the meeting was due to start as Bob had had some trouble altering all the clocks. Sipping her cup of tea whilst she made everybody wait, Ms Stonehart looked at the motley crew of individuals gathered around her conference desk. Some of them she had inherited from her predecessor, Mr Taylor, and some, the better ones, she had employed herself. No matter how long they had been there however they could all remember the sudden disappearance the year before of Mr Ellery, Deputy Head in charge of timetable and curriculum planning. They were wise enough not to say anything that would upset Ms Stonehart, the top misdemeanor being to imply that they knew more about teaching than she did as Headteacher.

The seats either side of her were occupied by her two Deputy Heads, Mr Thicke and Mr Wingett. Mr Richard Thicke had been at the school the longest and as far as she was aware this had been the reason he had been promoted, along with a desire to move him as far away as possible from actual pupils in a classroom. His main responsibilities included Bright Sky target setting, litter and delivering a Key Stage 3 assembly every other week. The other Deputy Head, Mr Gary Wingett, came across as somebody whose rôle model was Eeyore. A tall, gaunt man, desperately in need of a haircut and a new suit, it was said that nobody had ever seen him smile during the working day. In charge of assessment data analysis and communication with parents, it seemed his guiding principle was "every silver lining has a cloud."

Next around the table, sitting beside each other as always, twins in every sense except size, were Ms Lynne Winter and Ms Sharon Payne. Lynne had been the first to get promoted to the SLT before convincing Ms Stonehart that her friend needed to be on the team too. Both were members of the English Department, although in truth they only taught three hours a week between them as they had far more important things to do. Together they saw themselves as being in charge of the day-to-day running of the school with the onerous tasks of observing lessons, scrutinizing marking and generally criticizing any teacher on a full timetable. Ms Stonehart valued their comments about teaching as they rarely contradicted anything she read on the internet. If ever there was an acronym Ms Stonehart was not sure of, these two members of the Senior Leadership Team would be able to remind her. That was how she'd discovered that Ofsted didn't stand for OFficial STuff about EDucation. Lynne unwrapped another chocolate bar and nudged Sharon to put her mobile phone away. Nobody knew why Ms Stonehart did not allow phones at the table and she certainly didn't feel a need to justify her decisions. Better concentration, not wanting any conversations to be recorded, reminding them who was boss? It was probably all of the above.

The final member of the SLT, directly opposite to Ms Stonehart, was Mr Samuel O'Brien. He'd been at Wildside Academy just over a year before Ms Stonehart had taken over but she saw the two of them as very similar in many ways. They were both "people people", able to communicate very well and get the best out of everybody. They were both well-liked by staff, pupils and parents. Mind you, even though he'd worked in schools a long time Sam did still have a lot to learn. It was lucky for him that whenever he needed to know how to run a school effectively he could just watch what Ms Stonehart did.

Thoughts about the Open Evening had spoiled her week in Madrid and she was determined that was never going to happen again. She put down her empty cup and coughed to bring the meeting to order.

"Open Evening : our one big chance to show off. I did everything I could to make it a success," she began as she passed some photos round, "but what did you do? What did the staff do? Where were the parents? It's them we do it for! Not just Ofsted."

The members of the SLT welcomed the photos as a chance to avoid making eye contact with her.

In the absence of any photographers from the national or local press Ms Stonehart had instructed Trevor Rojan from IT Support to go round and capture the evening with a digital camera. It wasn't immediately obvious that he'd used photo editing software to increase the number of parents present until you got to the pictures of the RE Department where the duplicated Reaper family made Reverend James' classroom look like a funeral directors' convention. Interestingly there were no photographs of the *café français* nor the performance of '*Romeo and Juliet*' that Adam and Sonya from Year 10 had helped stage in the Drama Department. There were a lot of well-lit shots of Ms Stonehart shaking hands with parents and smiling at a small child which would probably already be on the school's website. Ms Malik featured heavily in the pictures taken in the Geography Department, of course.

"These things usually don't go well," muttered Mr Wingett with a sigh. "What did Chambers think of it? I bet he won't have liked it after that incident with the Van de Graaff. What are they playing at in Science?" He looked meaningfully across at Mr Thicke who was the SLT-link with the Science Department this year.

"By the way I phoned the hospital again this morning," said Mr O'Brien diplomatically. "She's off the critical list. Should we send the family some flowers?"

Ms Stonehart seemed not to have heard the suggestion.

"To be honest Toby seemed quite pleased with it all," she continued. "He said he loved the motivational message from the moment he arrived and saw what's painted across the entrance."

She'd thanked Bob on the way home for having changed the white letters on the tarmac to "TOPS", although she wasn't quite sure why he'd done it. Bob himself had seemed puzzled too and seemed more interested in what Mr Chambers had said to her. She liked it when Bob took an interest in her work.

"Toby said it won't be long before Wildside Academy TOPS the league tables again."

Instinctively the members of the SLT found themselves looking up at the digital display on the wall. The 510th day without an Ofsted visit and counting...

"He did think we're overstaffed and I want you to look into what we can do about that," she continued, pointing at Ms Winter who smiled at the prospect.

"I can help with that," volunteered Ms Payne instantly. And so it was agreed.

"And do you know why we had so few parents after all I'd done?" Ms Stonehart continued. The reason was probably common knowledge to everyone but nobody has ever listened themselves out of a job.

Ms Stonehart held up an old copy of *The Wildside Gazette*

folded back to the page that advertised the forthcoming Wildside Academy Open Evening. It must have cost as much as a Teaching Assistant for a whole term, the colour photograph of Ms Stonehart alone taking up a third of the page. The printers hadn't quite got the colours of her hair right. Then she silently turned back a page to display the advert for Upper Steem Academy.

"And what do you notice?" she asked.

Mr Thicke leaned forward for a closer inspection. A large banner announced USA's 97% GCSE success rate and their Outstanding Ofsted grading.

"It's not the same font size in the two adverts," he commented as though it were a Spot The Difference competition.

"But it's the same date!" shouted Ms Stonehart as Richard once again lived up to his name.

It was true. Both establishments' Open Evenings had been scheduled for the same night. In addition the Upper Steem Academy event was to be opened by none other than the winners of this year's *Celebrity Love Rock Star Academy*. It turned out one of the band had gone to USA as a pupil and they were naming the new Music block after him. No wonder there'd been so few parents yet so much traffic trying to get home that night.

"I've given it a lot of thought," continued Ms Stonehart, "and in a situation like this the person to blame can only be the Headteacher."

Ms Winter nearly spat her diet cola across the mahogany but other than that everybody else was wise enough to remain silent.

"Hoskins knew we were having our Open Evening on that night. We'd had adverts in *The Gazette* for three weeks before. Typical USA dirty tricks!"

There was almost an audible sigh of relief from the rest of the Senior Leadership Team.

Next Ms Stonehart passed round a pile of beige folders with the word "CONFIDENTIAL" typed in red across the top of each one. For extra security each folder had the name of the SLT member on it, as well as their name stamped on each sheet of paper inside. She had labelled it "*Operation Stargazer.*"

"Upper Steem Academy is our enemy," she announced in no uncertain terms. "This is my plan to beat them." She'd run it past the Governors who had agreed without hesitation. Money would not be an issue in a case like this. Anyway it would probably cost less than the helipad they'd had painted on the playground last year only to find it wasn't this Academy in Wildside that a member of the Royal Family had been planning to visit. That was the first time she'd had an argument with Bob. He'd initially painted the helipad himself but it'd been too small. His excuse was that she'd said size wasn't important.

What Ms Stonehart was proposing was to buy the most powerful telescope they could find, ostensibly for the new Science Department but in reality with a view to focusing it on Upper Steem Academy. Forewarned is forearmed.

"Brill!" said Ms Winter. "It'll be like we're astrologers. That's wicked!"

"Yes, it'll be great to have a telescope," agreed Mr O'Brien. "Can I also make a suggestion?" Once Ms Stonehart had nodded her approval he continued. "Well, I'm no astronomer but let's say USA make it difficult for us to see what's going on there somehow, well maybe we could look on their website?"

"I was waiting to see if you'd deduce the second part of my plan," said Ms Stonehart. "That's why I didn't put it in the folder. Keeping you all on your toes." She turned to Mr Thicke. "I'm putting you in charge of updating the Wildside Academy website, Richard. It's not right. There are more photos of Ms Malik than there are of me!" She knew because she'd counted them whilst trying to relax in Madrid.

"There was nothing like this when I was at school," grumbled Mr Wingett. "Didn't even have a colour TV when I was growing up we were that poor. Didn't even get Ceefax! It'll be that unsocial media stuff next."

"Another excellent suggestion," said Ms Stonehart. "It's probably fair that you take charge of that, Gary, seeing as you came up with it. You can work with Richard."

Neither of the Deputy Heads looked too happy at the prospect of working together.

"What about the Local Headteachers' meetings that they have at the Town Hall each term?" ventured Mr O'Brien. "I've heard they're great for sharing best practice and new ideas."

"They're for…" Ms Stonehart paused as the phrase 'proper teachers' didn't sound quite right. "They're for schools that need help and we don't. Just look at all the ideas my SLT have come up with today…" She paused again. "I'm too busy to go to them anyway. Perhaps you should go along, Sam, to help those schools less fortunate than us. And you can let me know what daft ideas Hoskins and the others come up with."

Now that everybody had been given their allotted tasks Ms Stonehart was beginning to tire of it all and it would soon be time for Mrs Spratt to bring in her mid-morning tea and biscuits. After that she would need to call in Mr Goldbloom to see how much they could claim back on the insurance for a faulty Van de Graaff generator.

CHAPTER 10

"The wisest mind has something yet to learn."

For a school the size of Wildside Academy it was perhaps surprising how few IT rooms it had, given that computers are the future. Mr Dave Benson, Second-in-Department for IT, was already on his second mug of coffee when his computer finally spluttered into life. *"I'm an IT Teacher! What's your superpower?"* read the amusing slogan on the mug. He glanced through the glass pane in the door across to the smallest of the computer rooms, ICT-3. Miss Gilbert was clearly still waiting for her computer to load, making the most of the time to browse through a glossy catalogue of wedding dresses.

Once the familiar SCAMS page had loaded on Mr Benson's screen it only took him a few moments to take the register. There were, allowing for absences, only five pupils in his GCSE Computing class today.

"Right," he began. "We're still on Module 1, so you just need to open your files and crack on with it."

"Sir," said a small blond boy with glasses at the computer nearest the teacher's desk. "There's a message popped up. It says I need to change my password? What's my password?"

"We did about this in the first sub-unit of this Module, Wayne. *'Keeping your details safe.'* I asked you all to write your passwords down somewhere." It was a shame they no longer had planners.

"Oh yeah," said Wayne, looking in his bag for the post-it note he'd used in September. His books, muddy P.E. kit and an apple core tumbled out at his feet. "I can't find it but it don't matter 'cos I've remembered. It's *Password123* 'cos you said *123* weren't long enough."

"Well you'll definitely have to change it now," said Mr Benson as the pupil sitting beside Wayne wrote the password on the back of his hand. "You don't want your password to be insecure."

"You'd be insecure if somebody kept changing you every six weeks," said a girl near the teacher's desk.

"I mean it'll need to be seven characters or more."

Wayne struggled along on his own, deep in concentration, as Mr Benson loaded his email page.

"It's not working, sir!" called Wayne in frustration.

"Have you got Caps Lock on?" asked Mr Benson helpfully.

"Sir," interrupted the girl to his left. "Why isn't the Caps Lock key written in capitals if it's Caps Lock?"

"I'll explain later, Brooke," replied Mr Benson.

"Has your password got at least seven characters, Wayne?"

"Yes. I typed *Spongebob, Patrick, Squidward, Plankton*…Maybe I didn't spell them right, sir?"

"Let's just try something a bit shorter shall we?" said Mr Benson calmly. "Here, this should work but keep it safe. Don't forget the capital P." He passed Wayne a post-it note on which was written *123Password*.

Wayne's cry of "Wicked!" was enough to tell Mr Benson that his superpower was still working. It was like the first time he'd shown him how to copy-and-paste a picture into a document and Wayne had thought he was witnessing magic!

He turned back to his emails. Even though he'd checked his messages before leaving work the previous day, there were already 42 new unread emails awaiting his urgent attention. He did wonder how teachers who weren't sitting at a computer all day managed to keep up. Opening the first email he discovered that Miss Gilbert had mislaid her mug again and she just wondered if anybody had seen it as her fiancé had got her it.

"Sir," interrupted Wayne again. "How do you get it off all being in capitals?"

Before he could answer Brooke wanted to help.

"I know, Wayne," she said, running round to his seat and stabbing at the keyboard with her sparkly nails. "Press Caps Lock!"

Wayne looked up at her like she was winding him up. "Don't

be daft. That'll lock it on capitals!" A look of utter surprise crossed his face as he peered back at the monitor and discovered that one key could do two opposite things.

"Wicked!"

"Don't call me daft!" smiled Brooke as she went back to her place. "You can have brains or beauty but you can't have all three."

Mr Benson opened up the next email that had been sent to all staff. It was from Mel.

From : MWE - MWhite@WildsideAcademy
To : AllStaff@WildsideAcademy
Sent : Tues 13 Nov 09:23
Subject : Harry Warren

Hello,

If you teach Harry Warren in 7Y please be aware he's having a bit of a tough time outside school. He's not feeling himself at the moment and it's making him quite unhappy.

Thanks,
Melody W
Head of Year 7.

"Sir," called out another boy in the group. "It says we need to use a search engine to research this bit. Where do we find that 'cos Wayne says the internet will explode if you type *"search engine"* into a search engine?"

Mr Benson could understand why they might think that and to be fair Charlie had come a long way since Year 7 when his computer monitor used to be covered in correcting fluid whenever he'd made a mistake.

"I'll tell you what," said Mr Benson. "I'll show you."

All the pupils paused what they were doing and looked up. Still got that old superpower, thought Mr Benson to himself, the ability to get pupils' attention in a second. In truth the pupils were just waiting to see if he would actually leave his chair to come over and help them. Very few of them had ever witnessed that before. As Mr Benson loaded up SpyOnKids, the whole-class monitoring software, they realised that they would not have a story to tell their grandchildren after all.

"Woah, sir!" exclaimed Charlie, pushing his chair away from the monitor and standing up quickly. "My computer's working by itself!"

"Don't worry, Charlie," said Mr Benson. "I'm just loading up the search engine for you. I can see everything that you're all doing from here."

At the computer beside Charlie, Nathan minimized the muted game of Zombie Kombat he'd been playing.

"You know what, sir," smirked Nathan, hoping to distract Mr Benson. "My Dad once read online maps backwards and he just got spam!"

"I don't get it," muttered Charlie, looking up from his keyboard.

"He tried to buy a toaster online," the class joker continued, "but he said there were too many pop-ups."

Nathan made the most of the moment to plug in a USB stick and load up a program that he believed would block SpyOnKids from interrupting him as he switched back to ZK Level 18.

You got a different class of question from the pupils in this group compared to those in Set 1. They were Mr Lazenby's concern because being Head of Department he had all the top sets. As Mr Benson had gone past ICT-1 earlier, the largest and best-equipped of the computer rooms, he'd heard one pupil ask his line manager, "*Sir, if Microsoft's as big a company as you say, why isn't it called Macrosoft?*" He was a very pleasant man was Alec Lazenby, but answering smart-alec questions was not *his* superpower!

Checking that the pupils were all on task, Mr Benson minimized the SOK screen and returned to his emails. He opened the first one from Ms Stonehart, fearing the worst, only to find that it was a montage of the photos from the Open Evening. He'd been about to download the pictures, thinking they would be useful for the Year 9 Module on Photoshop, when he decided that might not be the most sensible thing to do.

"Sir," called out a voice from behind a monitor. "I was just thinking. Is there a copyright on the copyright symbol or can anybody use it?"

Looking at the photos from the Open Evening reminded him that Vicky Shakespeare had shared some pictures with him on social media. He'd not seen Shazza for a while as she'd gone home ill on the morning of the Open Evening so now would be a good chance to catch up with her, if only online. There were some nice pictures of her at a concert by this year's winners of *Celebrity Love Rock Star Academy*. What a coincidence : it looked like the Headteacher of Upper Steem Academy had gone to the same event.

"Sir," interrupted Brooke. "Wouldn't it be easier if all the keys were in alphabetical order?"

Glancing at his watch Mr Benson realised it was nearly time for break. Just time to work on his daily steps total by popping down to the staffroom for another coffee. Mr Jones had sent another of his funny emails but he could decipher it after break.

"Nathan! You're banned from Computer Club today. I think you've played enough Zombie Kombat for one day."

Nathan looked up. It was like Mr Benson had X-ray vision or something.

"Right, log off everybody and leave it tidy. You can carry on with Module 1 next time."

As he eased himself out of his chair, picked up the empty mug and headed for the door Mr Benson realised that unlike the other pupils Wayne had not yet left.

"How do I turn it off?" he asked.

"When you want to finish, you click '*Start*'," explained Mr Benson, exiting swiftly before Wayne could ask him why.

CHAPTER 11

"If you do nothing, nothing will happen."

Whilst Ms Stonehart might *think* she was the most important person in the school, Mrs Irene Ramsbottom knew that actually she herself was. How could meetings run without her? How could teachers deliver their lessons without her? How could pupils pass their GCSEs without her? Without her in charge of the Reprographics Room, operating her magnificent photocopiers with such skill, the whole of Wildside Academy would come crashing to a halt in minutes. Not only that but she was also in charge of maintaining the Science Department stock room. Luckily that did not include her being responsible for the Van de Graaff generator.

Although she was actually shorter than the average Year 8 pupil Irene made up for it by hurtling down the corridors with all the determination of a bowling ball. She was a woman on a mission and her grim face said *"Don't even think of interrupting me from what I'm doing! You're not important enough!"* She carried a clipboard everywhere and although nobody had ever seen what was on it, it had to be really important because she'd pause every so often, tick something off and frown.

That wasn't to say she didn't find time to talk to people, or perhaps we should say talk *at* people. It's good to talk but she needed somebody other than just Julie and the photocopy repair men who called in regularly. She needed to tell people how busy she was, how rushed off her feet she was, how lucky they all were to have her working here. How could meetings run without her? How could teachers deliver their lessons without her? How could pupils pass their GCSEs without her?

Mr Ash, one of the new Science teachers, gave her a nervous wave as she steamed down the corridor and back towards the Reprographics Room. He'd been trying to unjam the one photocopier than staff were allowed to use, the noisy old machine in the staffroom, and an older teacher had suggested he ask Irene for help. Mr Ash didn't know the name of the teacher but he'd been very helpful, just what you need when you're a Newly Qualified Teacher in your first week in a new school. From the description given he'd been able to recognise Mrs Ramsbottom by her white coat and air of importance.

"Can't stop now!" Irene called out, tapping her clipboard as if this would explain everything. "Too busy. See Julie."

Julie Tomson was Irene's unofficial assistant, but there was no way Mr Ash would know that. He decided to go see if there was anybody called Julie working in the Main Office.

A large group of pupils scattered like ten pins as Irene ploughed her way across the canteen, turned the corner and disappeared beyond the Berlin Wall where she hoped not to be disturbed.

She added another tick to the list on her clipboard and went through to what she saw as the very beating heart of Wildside Academy, the Reprographics Room. The largest of the three machines was methodically converting a large part of a small rainforest into thick stapled booklets which Julie Tomson was stacking on a nearby table. A second machine stood idle with a laminated "DO NOT USE" sign stuck over the keypad. A pair of legs protruded from behind the final machine, indicating that a repairman from Speedy Copier Repairs And Parts was back again.

"Och, it's nae use," said Alan, easing himself out from behind the faulty photocopier. "Hello there, Mrs Ramsbottom. I dinna hear ye come in."

"What seems to be wrong this week?" she asked, helping herself to a chocolate biscuit.

Alan stroked his beard, leaving a trail of black ink across it. A distinct smell of toner fluid drifted from his clothes.

"It's them wee pangolin wires again," he said. "They're just nae managing to coat the photoreceptive drum and the copy paper with a layer of positively charged ions. Aye, getting a build-up of static electricity. You've nae been keepin' something like a Van de Graaff generator near it have ye? Nae matter, I've reversed the polarity of the neutron flow. That should sort it." He paused to look at a code flickering on the display screen. "It's nae made a wee bit o'difference though. I'm gonna have to take it all t'bits again. New toner unit'll cost a pretty penny I'm afraid, Mrs Ramsbottom. It's nae easy to get one that has the wee sprockets what with this being an old ZX-63."

Alan pulled his toolbox closer, prised open the front panel of the machine and set to work again. The photocopier made an unearthly wheezing, groaning sound.

As the print run on the largest photocopier came to an end, silence descended across the Reprographics Room, broken only by Alan's occasional swearing. Julie had been busy at the machine all morning without even a break for a drink of water or a quick trip to the loo. When she looked all the biscuits she'd brought in had been eaten.

A small girl appeared at the open door and smiled.

"Excuse me, miss," she said quietly, "Ms Grimley says would she be able to have two more copies of this as she hasn't got enough." The girl held out an information sheet about Adolf Hitler.

"Tell Ms Grimley I'm too busy here, as well she knows," replied Irene. "Tell her to try downstairs. They've got their own photocopier in the staffroom."

"OK," said the girl as she left. It didn't really matter to her anyway.

Ms Grimley was always doing that. Not getting the right number of copies and then expecting Irene to drop everything to sort out everybody else's problems for them. She'd been far too busy at the start of term to go to the stress management training and she could see this job making her ill if she wasn't careful. And then how would they all cope? How could meetings run without her? How could teachers deliver their lessons without her? How could pupils pass their GCSEs without her?

"What should I do next?" asked Julie, resigned to her fate.

Irene looked at the thick stapled booklets that were now piled so high by the window that they blocked out any natural light. It would make her ill, she thought, not getting any fresh air in here. Maybe she should go over to the Science Department till dinnertime?

"What was that last job?" asked Irene as she picked up a

sheaf of papers from those in the in-tray.

"Mr Thicke," said Julie.

"Ah, yes." Irene ticked it off the list. Two hundred copies of a forty-page document, enlarged, colour photocopied, double sided, stapled with a card cover. It had taken most of the morning to photocopy Mr Thicke's guidance to staff on how to reduce paper wastage in the school. It would have been done quicker but fifty minutes into the job Mr Thicke had turned up to cancel his request in favour of a second version. Apparently he'd found a fault with the font size on page 26. Now the copies of the original document about saving paper were piled against the bin ready to be shredded. Another job for Julie when she was free.

Alan was heading towards the door.

"I should be able to get one by the end of the week," he said. "The week after at the latest."

"You're going to have to speed up a bit if you've only got one job done this morning," said Irene to Julie when they were alone again. Young people these days just didn't have her work ethic!

Julie unwrapped another ream of paper and started loading it into the large photocopier.

"Hello," called a voice from the doorway behind them. "I'm really sorry to bother you. I've started back this week. Mrs Brydon? Just back from maternity leave?"

The thought crossed Irene's mind that it must be nice to have such an unimportant job that you could be off for a year and the school not come to an immediate halt. How would Wildside Academy manage in the unlikely event of Irene being off with a baby? How could meetings run without her? How could teachers deliver their lessons without her? How could pupils pass their GCSEs without her?

Suddenly she realised that this Mrs Brydon was still talking to her.

"I know I'm being a bit silly asking really," she smiled, "but I put something in for photocopying before I went off on my mat leave. I don't suppose it's up here still is it, after all this time?"

"I have a system here," replied Irene, frowning again. "Works like clockwork. Julie, pass me the file for completed jobs. Last year."

She ran her finger down the list of entries and then after

some searching pulled out a slip of yellow paper from the tray beside her.

"Here we are," she said proudly. "Mrs Brydon. September 23rd last year. Thirty copies of "The causes of the Franco-Prussian War : worksheet 2." From *"Exploring History Through Pictures and Worksheets."* Black-and-white copies, single page. Couldn't be easier!"

"I'm so grateful," said Mrs Brydon. "That's marvellous. Thank you so much. I'm doing the same topic with Year 10 tomorrow and I thought I'd have to find the sheet in the storeroom and put it in for photocopying again. After all this time! You're a lifesaver!"

Irene looked at the sheet that she'd been given to photocopy the year before. How would Wildside Academy ever manage if she weren't there?

"It'll be ready Tuesday," she said.

CHAPTER 12

"Nothing is permanent except change."

With cover arranged for their lessons, this being the one time of the week when both of them were teaching, Ms Winter and Ms Payne settled themselves into the Assistant Heads' office to begin their work. They'd both set silent reading from *'Lord of the Flies'* as cover work as this would be easy for colleagues to supervise for an hour. It would help improve the pupils' literacy skills and there wouldn't be any marking at the end of it either.

"We'd best let the noise die down on the corridor," said Lynne. "We'll have to give this our full attention, you and I. I'm gonna make a hot chocolate. D'you want one?"

"I'm alright," said Sharon, pulling a can of Red Mist out of her bag and flicking her phone on.

Twenty minutes later it sounded like everybody had made it to their lessons and there was a relatively quiet working atmosphere about the place. A muffled warble of *'Frère Jacques'* drifted across from the Music rooms as Year 7 worked on their recorder skills but it was not enough to disturb the concentration of two members of Wildside Academy's SLT.

"Right, this is what I think, yeah?" began Lynne. "Janine wants us to look at the school being overstaffed with too many teachers. I think the best way to sort it is by making two lists, those teachers we want to work with and those we want to get shut of. I mean, it wouldn't be fair on us, you and I, if we had to waste our time going round observing lessons of teachers we don't actually need to lose, yeah?"

Sharon nodded enthusiastically, in total agreement as ever

with her friend.

"Then we can see what they all have in common in each list," added Sharon, "to see what we're looking for." She was busy searching something on her phone. "It's called criterion-referenced selection!"

"Yeah," said Lynne, a little unsure of the term. "Then it won't just be up to you and I to make a decision. We'll be able to tell Janine who's the most unique and who's the baddest."

Logging onto SCAMS she brought up the staff list whilst Sharon put two pieces of file paper on the desk in front of them and took the top off a felt-tip.

"Right, let's start at the top of the list to begin with first," said Lynne.

The first names on the screen were the English Department, led by Mr Kaye who'd joined the school the previous year. Well, they couldn't get rid of Billy, could they? He was doing a fantastic job as Head of Department. He made everybody laugh with his funny stories about teaching and the nicknames he gave the kids.

"Hey," said Lynne, smirking at her friend. "D'you remember Nick the Thick?"

Nick Johnson had been in Billy Kaye's Year 11 English group the year before and Billy had been making the gang all laugh in The Cock 'n' Bull with his account of the lesson he'd taught that day.

"*So there I was and I says to Nick, 'Nick, what does the word* indescribable *mean?' And he says, 'I dunno, sir, I can't really put it into words!' What a thicko! Nick the Thick!*"

Hilarious! He was so good with words was Billy. It'd also helped Nick fit in with the other kids in Year 11 as he'd always been a bit of a loner lower down the school. They seemed to be talking to him a lot more after Billy had given him a nickname. Things wouldn't be the same in the pub after work if Billy wasn't there.

Next on the list was Victoria Shakespeare, Second-in-Department. Shazza was a team player, always straight in there, buying a round of drinks for the other members of the English Department. It was never quite the same on those occasions that she had had to go home from work early because she was ill. Poor Shazza! The school had a duty of care to look after her a bit better. In fact the more Lynne looked at the list the more she realised it would be difficult to get rid of anybody in the English Department. English was such an important part of the curriculum and they needed every single English teacher they'd got in the classroom, helping to raise results.

The task didn't get much easier as they moved on to the Maths Department. Sharon had always had a bit of a thing for the Assistant Head of Department, Mr Devlin, and her flirting with Sean would come to nothing if he went off to work in another school. It had been hard enough when his wife was working part-time in the Science Department. Luckily they'd separated six months ago and the school had had to let Mrs Devlin go shortly afterwards.

"I think we should take a break," said Sharon. "Janine didn't say she wanted this by close of business or anything."

"Yeah, there's no rush. And we need to do it proper," agreed Lynne. "I'm gonna go get a bacon butty before the canteen gets busy." There was nothing worse than being in there when it was full of kids. "D'you want anything?"

"I'm alright," said Sharon, "but I'll come with you."

"Brill. I'll get two bacon butties. In case you change your mind."

It was an indication of why Ms Winter and Ms Payne were on the Senior Leadership Team that they'd managed to complete the task by the end of the school day. As the bell rang two minutes after three o'clock, soon drowned out by the stampede of pupils determined to get the best seats on the buses, Lynne and Sharon had completed their wish list. Their moment of inspiration had really come once they'd finished their dinner and had been making their way back past the Finance Office. Bob had put up another oil painting of Toby Chambers and was just checking that there were no fingerprints on the gold frame. Lynne called into the Finance Office and got Mr Goldbloom to print off a copy of the staff list that showed everybody's monthly salary. If they cross-referenced this list with their own two lists of teachers, they should soon be able to save the business money.

They could pass their hitlist on to Janine before heading off to the pub unless she'd already left. They both deserved a drink after such a busy day, especially as they still had to work out what the next steps in their plan would be tomorrow. One thing was clear though. It would involve a lot of extra work for the two of them. There would be even more lesson observations, additional work scrutinies and further meetings. Cover for their lessons would be needed next week but on the plus side the pupils probably hadn't finished '*Lord of the Flies*' yet.

"I've just had a brill idea!" said Lynne. "We get everyone to write out lesson plans for all their lessons so that we can just drop in for a few minutes rather than having to watch whole lessons."

"Yeah, it gets dead boring," agreed Sharon, "and it won't be any extra work for them as they'll be planning their lessons anyway."

"Actually, we probably only really need to see the lesson plans from them on this list," Lynne reflected, "'cos we've got bags of stuff to do in English already." She slammed her laptop shut.

"Same with Sean and Maths," agreed Sharon.

It was, as Ms Winter herself said, the most fairest way that you and me can do things proper, yeah? Brill!

CHAPTER 13

"Learn from the mistakes of others as well as your own."

Mr Thicke had been busy all morning. After much thought he'd planned his Lower School assembly on the theme of the dangers of procrastination. Now with his desk tidy, all the pencils in his pot nicely sharpened and all the files on his computer meticulously labelled, it was time to think of something else to do. He didn't really want to go across to Mr Wingett's office and work with him if he could help it.

He idly clicked on his computer to see whether there were any important emails for him. There were five new messages! It *was* a busy morning! Miss Gilbert had bought herself a new mug so people could call off the search for the other one. Ms Grimley had had some food taken out of the fridge in the staffroom and wasn't happy about it. There was an email from the retired Headteacher of Brewery Road Primary School, a Mr Hedley Cox, asking whether the school wanted him to do his usual talk in Year 7 assembly about the history of Steem. Mr Thicke didn't reply but found himself searching out that Lower Steem's twin town was a place called Pokójiszczęście in Poland. A company called Whamspam24/7 had sent him an unsolicited email about some software they sold that would reduce the amount of junk mail you received.

Finally, highlighted as priority, was an email from Ms Stonehart herself. She wanted to know how he was progressing with updating the school website and demanded a progress report by the close of business. Mr Thicke wondered why she didn't just look at the site but then in fairness he himself hadn't gone on it since the summer. With Ms Stonehart herself in New York at that point he'd been ordered to find a way of burying the GCSE results. He'd done it by emphasizing the news that the school was getting a new statue of Toby Chambers, designed by somebody who'd lived next door to somebody who'd gone to school with Henry Moore's uncle. In the end nothing had come of the statue and the school had lost a lot of money but at least the GCSE results had been largely overlooked.

Before typing in the address of Wildside Academy's website, Mr Thicke decided it would be more beneficial to look at that of the enemy first. As the Upper Steem Academy website bathed his tidy desk in sunshine he looked up guiltily to check his office door was still closed.

It was an odd website, he thought. You'd expect the first thing you saw to be photos of the Headteacher and the SLT but instead you were welcomed by actual pupils, smiling as though they were at a theme park rather than a school. Wait! As the photo slideshow continued to the rousing tune of '*Simply the best!*' as played by the school's orchestra, there were pictures of pupils at an actual theme park as part of something called a "rewards trip." There were shots of happy pupils holding giant "9" and "8" shapes on results day, the sunshine bouncing off their GCSE certificates, pupils taking part in sporting and musical events, Geography field trips and residential visits abroad. The new Music block had just been opened by somebody he'd never heard of and Year 9 had been packing bags for people in KwikShop which was surely something they could do for themselves, wasn't it? There were shots showcasing the school's facilities, including the computer rooms, library, MFL language laboratories, tennis courts and Olympic-sized swimming pool. There were even pictures of a member of the Royal family planting the first of twenty-five trees to commemorate the school's involvement in the Duke of Edinburgh Award scheme over the last twenty-five years. Eventually he clicked on a tab that led to a page that opened with a photograph of Mr Hoskins, the Headteacher, smiling proudly in front of the school. Even without measuring Mr Thicke could tell that throughout the welcome message to parents the font size was consistent. Enough! Unaware that he'd been holding his breath, Mr Thicke let out a sigh, clicked off the website and hurriedly deleted his search history.

As the website for Wildside Academy was taking some time to

load Mr Thicke decided that he could do with another cup of tea. Other teachers might have needed something a little stronger after seeing such startling images on the internet but he disapproved of alcohol. He was pleased that he'd managed to stop the school's tradition of offering staff a small glass of sherry when they broke up for Christmas. The Governing Body had thanked him for the annual savings they'd made as a result of his proposal.

He looked into the Main Office to see if anybody could make him a cup of tea like they did for Ms Stonehart but everybody said they were too busy. Even Jules didn't have time because he said he thought there might be another fire alarm at any minute. Mr Thicke plodded on down the corridor until he came to a door opposite Mr North's office. The blue door was identified only by a bright yellow radiation symbol and a sign telling everybody to keep out. Mr Thicke went in without even knocking.

It wasn't so much that the room was tiny but it appeared to be smaller on the inside because of the amount of junk that was stored in there. Partially dismantled computers fought for space with old computer monitors, masses of different coloured cables and circuit boards whilst the floor was hidden beneath cardboard boxes filled with who knew what. On the wall opposite there might possibly be a small window looking out onto the school car park whilst the other walls displayed film posters from obscure science-fiction films. A dusty scale model of the Millennium Falcon hung from the ceiling by a wire whilst the light on a small Police Box flashed erratically in the corner by the printer.

"Hello there," Mr Thicke called out into the seemingly deserted room. "Any chance of a cup of tea?"

As if by magic the Head of IT Support appeared from behind twin monitors. A chubby, middle-aged man with a thick, drooping moustache, Trevor Rojan always wore the same outfit, a stripy brown tank top over a checked shirt with a pair of corduroy trousers. It was as if his clothes were actually part of him like on the plastic action figures he collected.

"Erm, yeah, I think so," he said, nodding towards a kettle and supplies resting on a laptop balanced on a filing cabinet in the corner.

Knowing this was the best offer he was going to get all day, Mr Thicke clicked the button and dropped a teabag into a chipped mug. *"You don't have to be mad to work here,"* read the amusing slogan on the mug, "*we'll train you!*"

"I'm busy trying to update the school website," said Mr Thicke, hoping to get a conversation started with Trevor. "Might be just up your street if you're not busy?"

"Erm, yeah, I think so," replied Trevor without looking up from the screens. Mr Thicke couldn't see what he was doing there but it couldn't be as important as what he himself had to do. Probably just more Photoshop.

The kettle boiled, filling the room with steam and as it wouldn't switch off he had to resort to turning it off at the wall socket. There was a blue flash and the lights went out, causing the TARDIS to make its usual wheezing, groaning sound in the darkness.

"Was that me?" asked Mr Thicke.

"Erm, yeah, I think so," came the usual reply from somewhere to his left.

Then blinding light spilled into the room as first the door opened and then somebody pulled a lever in a fuse box somewhere.

"Anybody made me a cuppa too?" asked Adil as he squeezed into the room.

"Erm, yeah, I think so," said Trevor, looking towards Mr Thicke for confirmation.

"Milk and sugar?" asked Mr Thicke. He wasn't used to helping people like this but maybe Adil could sort out the school website for him in return. As it happened Zombie Kombat had crashed on the school server so he'd caught Adil at just the right time. He was looking for something more challenging to keep himself occupied till home time rather than just reattaching monitor cables in the History Department.

"You could do loads on the website," he said with some enthusiasm. "Tell you what, if I had a few biscuits to inspire me I could have it all done in an hour. I could email you a load of suggestions. You'd be up for that, wouldn't you, Trev? Bouncing ideas about for the website?"

"Erm, yeah, I think so."

Mr Thicke was just considering whether there might be biscuits in the Reprographics Room when the door slammed into his back and his mug of tea went flying.

Mr Wingett pushed his way into the room, looking down at

the other Deputy Head but then ignoring him. He too had had an email from Ms Stonehart and close of business was approaching fast. He looked even more gloomy than usual.

"Do you know anything about social media?" he asked the two IT technicians hopefully.

CHAPTER 14

"Each person must live their life as a model for others."

As one of her Bright Sky targets Ms Sally Lovall, the Lessons For Life Co-ordinator, was partly in charge of organizing staff training at Wildside Academy. She'd been set this target because she was one of the most experienced teachers in this area, having only recently been trained herself.

As November was drawing to a close it was her job to sort out the after-school INSET again. To be honest, it hadn't been easy, even with her lessons being covered throughout the day to give her time to make phone calls. It turned out that Sunshine Training & Development, the company that had run the stress management course on the first day, weren't even in business anymore. Apparently Brigitte in particular had found the whole thing too stressful and was now running a small pottery painting tearoom near Oxford. Sally idly peeled the Sunshine Training sticker off her laptop cover as she pondered the situation, replacing it with a bright rainbow.

Sally had already planned four two-hour after school twilight sessions on 'Managing Work-Life Balance' for January but the school calendar said this month's training had to be on fire safety. She'd contacted the Fire Service but apparently November was a busy time for them. Still it had not been a total loss. At least she now had somebody to take to the staff Christmas do.

As the bell would be ringing to signal the end of the school day in twenty minutes Sally decided to go back to her original plan and book the online fire safety training for staff.

She'd had to hurry as Fireman Sam, as she'd affectionately

nicknamed him, said he'd be able to get to The Cock 'n' Bull for half past three.

There were mixed feelings amongst the staff about staying behind for two hours the following Friday afternoon. Having forgotten that she'd been granted leave of absence that day to go to the wedding of a friend of a neighbour, Sally had arranged for Ms Winter to get the INSET started. It was beneficial really because you got two members of the SLT for the price of one. Where you found Ms Winter, there you'd find Ms Payne also. The two of them were busy checking the staff lists and herding colleagues to the right computer room.

"By 'eck," said Jim Fitt who had had to cancel the under-16 rugby match, meaning that the team had lost by default, "how comes we've been relegated t'ICT-3?" He looked at the state of the room which made the boys' changing rooms look a lot better somehow. "Bloody 'ell!"

"This is exactly how apartheid started," grumbled Ms Grimley. She wasn't keeping her voice down this time as she felt she should be free to express her own views at the weekend. "They've done this on purpose. Divide and conquer."

In fairness it did seem as though those colleagues who got on with Ms Winter were going into the well-equipped inner sanctum that was ICT-1 whilst the rest were ending up in a room that didn't even have enough chairs, let alone keyboards.

Ms Mina Malik, Second-in-Department for Geography, had looked somewhat crestfallen to find herself being directed towards ICT-3 with the likes of the PE Department. She'd stood quietly at the side like the last team player waiting to be picked until Ms Winter was free.

"Thank you so much for organizing this training for us. It's so important," she began. As Ms Winter seemed happy with her opening comment Mina continued, trying to make sure her suggestion didn't sound like a criticism. "So anyway, is it alright if I go work over in ICT-1 please? I don't need a computer." She indicated the laptop that was securely in its case in accordance with school policy.

"Sharon and me have spent ages on this to get the right mixture of staff in both of the three rooms," said Ms Winter.

Mina couldn't see any PE staff in the other rooms but knew

better than to say anything.

"Is there a problem?" asked Mr Wingett glumly in a tone that said he expected there would be. He could be described as an optimistic pessimist, always looking forward to thinking the worst.

"Mina was a little confused where to go," said Ms Payne, looking out from behind her friend and nearly causing her to spill the diet cola she was balancing on the laptop keyboard.

"Sharon and me have sorted it though," said Ms Winter.

"Thanks," said Mina, going through to ICT-3 where she realised she would now have to stand for the next two hours. Surely Deirdre who cleaned her classroom didn't need a computer?

Whilst everybody in economy class waited for their computers to consider the possibility of joining in, colleagues found themselves talking to people they wouldn't normally have the time or the inclination to talk to.

"It's the same every time," continued Ms Grimley's monologue to anybody who would listen. "*All animals are equal but some animals are more equal than others!*"

As none of Ms Winter's colleagues in the English Department had ended up in ICT-3 there was nobody to tell the PE Department where this quotation came from.

Deirdre the cleaner started to tell Ms Grimley about her sister's operation but she ignored her and carried on with her latest grievance.

"So how come I've got to learn about fire extinguishers when my Head of Department doesn't?" she asked to anybody who would listen. Ms Winter had agreed that Harry Ford did not need to do the fire safety training, having spent the term covering the Great Fire of London with Year 7. Ms Grimley's request to be exempt from any First Aid training as she taught the Jack the Ripper topic to Year 9 had fallen on deaf ears.

Deirdre turned to Mr Cocker and started to tell him about her sister's operation.

Then for no apparent reason all the computer monitors in ICT-3 went blue before displaying a warning that they would be installing important updates for an unspecified amount of time.

"Dave's not had to stay either," said Marcus Deeside as they waited.

Dave Benson had been the first person to complete the fire

safety training, having managed to get most of the modules done whilst teaching his Year 11 Computer Science group earlier in the day. Once he'd handed his training certificate in to Mrs Spratt, the ink still wet from the printer in his room, his weekend had begun. He was meeting Shazza at the pub to see if she was feeling better after three days off ill.

The computer screens in ICT-3 all announced that they were unable to install updates due to an unspecified network restriction and that they just needed to restart again.

"There won't be much of the weekend left," commented Mr Haddenough as he stared at the blank screen.

"Just 63 hours, 11 minutes and 23 seconds," said Roger without hesitation from the other side of the room.

Downstairs in her office Ms Stonehart was tidying up any loose ends before heading off for the weekend. She'd looked over the proposals that her Deputy Heads had sent her after the Open Evening postmortem. Both Mr Thicke and Mr Wingett had surprised her by coming up with some good suggestions for the school website and social media. As a result the whole of the SLT were going to go on a two-day brainstorming session at the Premier Inn to come up with a new slogan for the school, undisturbed by the daily pressures of work.

She hadn't been quite as impressed by Mr O'Brien's suggestions that staff could maybe be trained in something called metacognitive ability differentiation, whatever that was! Fire safety was surely the most important training for any teacher. How could you teach anything if the school had burned down? And what would Toby Chambers say if that ever happened?

She looked at her watch as Bob still hadn't managed to set her clock to the right time. Four o'clock. The school should be empty of pupils by now. Upstairs in the IT suite staff would be about halfway through their training. It would be a good way of showing her support as Headteacher if she went along and checked everybody was there before she left.

Ms Stonehart experienced a brief flashback to the events of the Open Evening as she passed the empty MFL rooms but she hurried along the first floor without looking in. It was then that she heard voices. Not the voices that she usually heard telling her what to do, but voices of actual people who clearly thought that directed time meant having a laugh on the corridor! She quickened her pace and turned the corner onto the History corridor.

"Thick Mick! Thick Mick! Thick as 'is brother Nick!"

Ms Stonehart had no idea who the two boys were who were pushing a third boy about. They were not like any of the pupils she'd met before as they didn't have 'Prefect' badges on. There was no way that she would know that Mr Kaye's affectionate nickname had been passed on to the next generation. What she did know though, was that this was bullying and bullying was something she knew a lot about. The Wildside Academy anti-bullying policy said that serious bullying needed to be reported to the Anti School Bullying Officer straight away. So, without any hesitation, she hurried off to find Mr Humble.

"I'm not impressed with this," said Harry Greenfield watching the screen die for the third time. He'd only agreed to come across from the PE office when Jim Fitt had convinced him that Sue Barker might be presenting fire safety videos as part of the training.

"So where's that young lad?" said Harry. "Jules! What kind of a name is that for a man?! This stuff's for fire safety officers and he's one of them."

Harry had only seen Mr Humphreys twice but he had taken an instant dislike to him to save time. The first time he'd come round with a clipboard looking for smoke detectors and the second time had been that fire alarm when they'd ended up with muddy boot prints all over the gym.

"I heard he's gone down to the fire station to get some posters," said Mr Ansari as he checked his watch. Three o'clock was a distant memory.

Ms Malik was feeling more and more uncomfortable with the situation and she really didn't want to hear about Deirdre's sister's leg. Luckily as she'd come prepared she'd managed to log on to the training resources on her laptop and was now busy making notes on a pad on the floor beside her. *A red fire extinguisher is water for use on wood, paper and fabric, not safe on electrical fires or flammable liquids ; a cream fire extinguisher…*

"Ay up, Tim!" Jim Fitt called across to Mr Cocker. "Can't you get these beggars workin'? You're an IT teacher!"

Today was a day when Tim saw himself more as a Geography teacher. He'd even brought along a copy of *"Exploring Geography*

Through Pictures and Worksheets."

"You know why we have so many fire alarms here, don't you?" replied Tim who worked on the basis that if a joke is worth telling it's worth repeating several times. "It's the school uniform. Too many blazers!"

Two seats further on Miss Fullilove laughed.

"Hey, I've a good one for you," said Jim. "If firefighters fight fire and crime fighters fight crime, what do freedom fighters do?"

"Fight for freedom?" suggested Miss Fullilove, somewhat puzzled.

"Did I tell you my sister's gone in for an operation?" Deirdre asked her, even though she'd never met Miss Fullilove before.

"That's interesting," said Ms Malik, so engrossed in the training that she perhaps didn't realise she was talking aloud. "The first fire sprinkler system was patented by H.W.Pratt in 1872..."

"Well, I never," said Mr Jones, drumming his fingers rhythmically beside the mouse as he waited. "Pratt."

"I bet they've all left in t'other rooms," reflected Jim Fitt as his screen finally illuminated.

"What do you put where it says 'password'?" asked Harry Greenfield hopefully.

"Welcome to the Twilight Zone..." a voice said quietly from behind a monitor in the corner.

It was going to be a long night.

DECEMBER

CHAPTER 15

"He who follows another is always behind."

One of the keys to a successful organization, whether it be a business, a charity or a school, must surely be good communication. To be fair to Wildside Academy, what it lacked in quality of communication it more than made up for in quantity. As well as the private conversations that SLT had on the other side of the Berlin Wall and the hushed conversations some colleagues dared to have in a corner of the staffroom, there were pigeonholes, noticeboards, emails, SCAMSconnect+, Bright Sky messaging and an endless variety of meetings. Sometimes teachers even spoke to each other in person.

The most regular of the meetings were the weekly staff briefings before school which were held every Monday morning without fail, apart from those Mondays when they weren't. It was unclear quite why they were called briefings as they neither briefed staff effectively for the week ahead nor were they brief. Perhaps they were called briefings because nobody was ever longing to go to them? Some teachers might have said they were just there to check that staff had arrived at work on time but teachers who said things like that never usually came to briefings or indeed work ever again.

"Morning. Nothing from me," said Ms Stonehart, her traditional way of beginning briefings if she was there. Under her leadership Wildside Academy was going from strength to strength. "Gary?"

Mr Wingett was standing beside Ms Stonehart with Mr Thicke on her other side. It was as though they were the props in a rugby scrum with Ms Stonehart as the hooker.

Behind this triumvirate stood Mrs Spratt so that she could hear what people said, surrounded by some of the Julies. None of the office staff were ever sure whose turn it was to take the minutes so what was said would probably go undocumented again.

The staffroom wasn't really designed to hold so many people and the piles of abandoned paperwork on various seats didn't help. Nobody ever took Ms Grimley's place. Those teachers who could get a seat had done so, with the latecomers standing by the noticeboard as though in naughty corner. It was really about the only time Mr Greenfield could be found outside of the PE office.

"Well, I'm afraid it's bad news from me," Mr Wingett began gloomily. "HR have only had a few certificates in from people who completed the Fire Safety training last month. Sally's going to set up another training session next Friday after school for anybody who hasn't handed their certificate in by close of business today."

"Sorry, Gary," came a solitary voice from the corner. "I think there was an issue with downloading the certificates at the end of the training?"

It was Tim Cocker, just putting his colleagues' thoughts into words again. Standing beside him Jim Fitt put a hand on his arm to try and bring him back to reality. It didn't matter if they had to do the training again. It didn't matter if Mr Goldbloom took the cost of the extra training straight out of their salaries.

"The printers were being a bit temperamental too..." Tim continued.

"I hear what you say," piped up Mrs Spratt as though a button had been pressed.

"Tim," cut in Mr Wingett, ignoring the Head of HR. "You're an IT teacher. You should have been able to get a simple printer working."

"I did," said Tim, not even bothering to point out that he

taught Geography. "I was just thinking of other people." It was a bad habit of his.

"There's too many people poking their noses into other people's business," said Ms Stonehart, more than doubling the amount she usually said at briefings. "I'll see you in my office straight after briefing, Mr Cocker."

"Sorry, mate," Jim Fitt said quietly.

Over by the fridge Mr Buonanulla looked relieved that he wouldn't be the only teacher waiting outside Ms Stonehart's office this Monday morning. He'd already had one migraine today when he'd discovered that his replacement bike had also been stolen during the night. Madame Loups-Garoux had come to his assistance but they'd nearly both been late for briefing.

With Mr Wingett not being able to think of any other bad news to share, it was the turn of the other Deputy Head. "Richard?"

Mr Thicke had already told Julie to distribute the ten-page supplement to his document on paper wastage to staff as they'd arrived. There really wasn't much for him to say at the briefing but as the longest-serving member of the SLT he felt obliged to say something.

"Just to let you know that I've been busy and come up with a lot of ideas for the website," said Mr Thicke. "So if you see me at your door this week I'll just be taking some photos of what's going on that I can use for it."

Ms Malik made a note of this in her planner.

As Mr O'Brien was on duty at the school gates Ms Stonehart turned to Ms Winter next.

"Lynne?"

"Yeah," Ms Winter put her mug of hot chocolate down on her laptop. It was important to appear professional in front of staff. "The Curriculum Review Action Plans have been collated by Heads of Department putting them together and they have all been totally reviewed by Sharon and I in their entirety. As a result of that the consequence is that we're going to increase the lesson observations so there'll be more as a way of supporting colleagues and sharing best practice and things. Now the lesson observations can't all be done by Sharon and I, so there'll also be additional drop-in observations as well, like Heads of Department, Jamie as CBA and whatever. So we've come up with a very unique system,

Sharon and I, that should make it all well fair, yeah? Every lesson taught needs a lesson plan like this one." She held up a blank four-page document that was held together with a paperclip. "One for each lesson with a seating plan and a SCAMS data sheet for each and every pupil and then just scan a copy into the shared area, log it on the database for the right Key Stage and pop the originals in this folder." She held up a large black ring binder which had been specially printed with the school crest and the slogan *Tempus fugit."* Looking at the size of the box containing the ring binders it didn't look like there'd be enough for everybody. "The lesson plan template is on the shared area and you'll just need to pass your Planning Folders to your Head of Department to check every Monday morning. It'll be brill, I'm really excited about it, but if you've got any questions just see Sharon or I. Cheers!"

"Thanks, Lynne," said Ms Stonehart. "Sharon?"

Ms Payne looked up from her phone. "Just what Lynne said really. Make sure you fill in every box on the lesson plan. Copies on the shared area, database etc. Yeah. Not long till Christmas. Utterly brill." She gave everybody a thumbs up in a supportive way.

Ms Stonehart coughed as she usually did when she wanted to get the attention of her staff. She'd remembered something else she'd meant to say. Colleagues had already started shuffling as the bell for period one had rung ten minutes ago. They were probably about to get told off by Ms Winter for being late to lessons.

"One other thing," said Ms Stonehart. It was unusual for her to say this much but it turned out that she was going to read a prepared statement like she used to do in the early days of morning briefings.

"It's not all about Ofsted," she read, "but we need to be conscious of the impression we make from the very moment inspectors arrive here. Just because Ofsted haven't been in for 530 days doesn't mean I couldn't just get a phone call today and they arrive tomorrow…"

She was interrupted by two pupils banging on the window. Mr Armani glared back at them and they ran off with Mr O'Brien in pursuit.

"With this in mind," Ms Stonehart continued, a little shaken but remaining professional, "the whole of the front drive is going to be resurfaced next week. So the staff car park will be out of action. Just for a couple of days. Obviously for Health and Safety reasons you'll all need to enter on foot by the pupil gates at the bottom of Cemetery Road, instead of the main gates near my office."

Mr Cocker was silently reflecting on the parking fine he'd got after the Open Evening when Ms Stonehart came up with the solution to the forthcoming lack of parking space.

"I've spoken to the landlord at The Cock 'n' Bull and he's agreed that staff can use the pub car park as long as they buy a round."

Ms Shakespeare looked up eagerly at this point while Mr Thicke was silently shaking his head disapprovingly. Mr Capstick was no Maths teacher but he was not the only teacher to realise that the pub's five parking spaces would not be enough. As an experienced teacher he had the good sense to say nothing.

"Also," continued Ms Stonehart, "as you're teachers the Council have offered us a special flat rate of £12 per day at the municipal car park up on Cromwell Way. And it's free after 6pm anyway if we have parents' evenings for example. The work on the drive should only last a couple of days anyway, so it shouldn't be too much of an inconvenience."

Ms Stonehart wouldn't have her staff suffer anything she herself wouldn't do first. So her parking space at the front of school would be resurfaced first. At the weekend. That would give it a couple of days to settle before she was then away with the SLT at the Premier Inn for those brainstorming sessions.

Ms Stonehart folded her speech and put it safely away in case it was needed when the history of Wildside Academy came to be written. Staff were busy digesting the implications of her words.

As always Mr Billy Kaye, Head of English, was propping himself up against the worktop beside Ms Winter, already an honorary member of the SLT. He broke the silence as though he were appearing on *Live at the Apollo*.

"This'll be what Ofsted mean when they talk about teachers going the extra mile!" he joked.

If Tim Cocker had made a comment like that he'd have been collecting his P45 faster than you could say 'Fairtrade School' but Billy was so funny, so clever with words, such a fantastic Head of Department.

Once Ms Stonehart herself had smiled, the majority of the SLT burst into laughter and other staff joined in on cue. It would be hard to tell who started applauding first, Ms Winter or Ms Payne. It was a lovely way to start the week. As Mr Wingett had once quoted at a morning briefing, "*A day without laughter is a day wasted!*" Fortunately for Mr Hayes the laughter and applause drowned out his comment that actually it wasn't a mile to the pub car park. It was 3.7 miles. Each way.

CHAPTER 16

"Something is lost whenever something is gained."

"I think I found it this time, didn't I, sir?" Josette beamed up at Mr O'Reilly as he gave her back her Maths homework.

This time she had indeed managed to find x. In response to question one she had drawn a wavy pink line pointing to the small x in one corner of the triangle and had written *"It's there, sir!!!"* Having managed to find it on the very first go she clearly hadn't seen any point answering any of the subsequent questions, signing off with a smiley face.

As Mr O'Reilly handed back her book he tried to make his comments as encouraging as possible whilst still giving her advice that could lead to her passing her exams.

"Yes, you found it, Josette," Mr O'Reilly agreed. "Well done. But you won't get a mark in the real exam I'm afraid. You haven't put how big x is."

Josette read the question again.

"It doesn't say you have to say how big it is," she replied, having read the question a second time just to make sure.

"But that's what the examiner means," continued Mr O'Reilly patiently.

"Well, he should say that then," mumbled Josette. "It's not my fault!"

"Why do we have to do this?" asked Lewis. "I don't mean to be rude, sir. I mean you're a good teacher an' all but Mason used to just set us it on that website. You could do it on your phone."

"I had Devlin last year," said another boy turning round, "and he just used to read the answers out for us to fill in."

Even though he was only in his second year of teaching Mr

O'Reilly knew better than to pass comment on his colleagues. Anyway he was quite happy to spend his time marking half a dozen books. He didn't really understand why other teachers always complained about having so much marking to do.

"That was lovely too, Luke," he said, returning a book to another boy in the group. "Did you have History homework to do as well?"

Luke nodded. He wondered how sir knew but was too quiet to ask. It was actually the question on percentages that had given the game away. He'd written that 12.5% as a fraction was Henry the One-Eighth.

Brian seemed a little distracted as Mr O'Reilly went to him to return his book.

"Which set are we, sir?" he asked.

"Well, you're Set 6," he replied, wondering if this would knock their confidence.

"'Cos there's six of us in the class," said Brian, seemingly content with this explanation. "So, is that right up there, 'cos that means we're better than Set 1?"

He pointed to above the whiteboard where another of Mr O'Reilly's many colourful displays ran the full breadth of the room. The number line went from minus fifty by the door, through zero, right up to one hundred over by the far window. It had taken him ages to make and put up the display and now somebody had swapped all the numbers around. He'd just have to stay back tonight to rearrange it all. Sarah would understand as she was a teacher too. He really hoped they hadn't taken any of the Blu-Tack though as he didn't have any more.

"I thought we were Set 3?" commented another boy, holding up four fingers to make his point. Mr O'Reilly decided to move on.

"So, let's look at today's puzzle, shall we?" he began. "Three men go out for a meal…"

"Why does it have to be men?" asked Libby sitting near the back.

"Well, it doesn't really," reflected Mr O'Reilly. "Three people go out for a meal…"

"Nando's?" asked Lewis.

"Well, it could be," agreed Mr O'Reilly. "The restaurant's not really the important thing it's just that these three men…"

"People," corrected Libby again. "Or it could be three women."

"I love their peri-peri chicken," said Lewis. "What about you, sir?"

"Yes, it's very tasty…" agreed Mr O'Reilly, hoping to steer the conversation back to the point of the Maths puzzle.

"Does Mrs O'Reilly like Nando's, sir?" Lewis continued as though he was a researcher on *This Is Your Life* rather than a pupil studying Maths.

"You can't just assume there's a Mrs O'Reilly," Libby interrupted, glaring at Lewis.

"It's alright, Libby," said Mr O'Reilly good-naturedly. "There *is* a Mrs O'Reilly and *yes*, she does like Nando's." As a matter of fact he'd got thirty pounds out of the money machine this morning to take her out for a bite to eat later.

"So the three of them go out for a meal," he continued carefully, "and the meal comes to twenty-five pounds…"

"You won't get much for that!"

"Except at The Golden Dragon," added Josette. Dave had taken her there a lot but he was now her ex.

Feeling the mathematical point he was trying to get across was drifting away again, Mr O'Reilly thought of a different way of making it more relevant for his class. He took out his wallet, removed the thirty pounds and five pound coins that he had in change. The six pupils immediately seemed more interested.

"Right," he said, holding the notes out for all to see, "who'd like to play the three customers? Male or female, it doesn't really matter."

A few moments later Brian, Libby and Josette were sitting around the desk at the front of the room whilst Lewis hovered nearby, playing the waiter.

"Do you want me to go up to Buonanulla's room and get some menus and some plastic onions or summat to make it more realistic, sir?" asked Lewis.

"No, it'll be fine, thanks," said Mr O'Reilly.

From what he'd heard in the staffroom the Acting Head of MFL had got rid of his bag of plastic fruit and veg shortly after the Open Evening.

Mr O'Reilly handed a crisp ten pound note to each of the pupils at the table before continuing to set up the Maths puzzle for today.

"Right. Good. Three people go into a restaurant, two women and a man on this occasion, and the bill comes to twenty-five pounds."

"My restaurant is very good value," commented Lewis, smoothing out the ends of his imaginary moustache.

"A bill of twenty-five pounds," continued Mr O'Reilly. "So each of them puts in ten pounds, giving the waiter a total of…?"

"Thirty pounds!" exclaimed Brian.

"Thirty pounds," agreed Mr O'Reilly. "So how much change does the waiter bring them back?"

"Five pounds!" exclaimed Brian again.

"Exactly!"

To demonstrate the point Mr O'Reilly indicated that the three customers should give their three ten pound notes to Lewis. Next he gave Lewis the five pound coins to put on the table in front of the three imaginary diners.

"I hope everything was alright for you?" adlibbed Lewis, starting to get into the part. He always loved rôle plays when they did them with Mr Haddenough.

"And so," said Mr O'Reilly, not wanting any of the class to lose the thread of it all, "each customer decides to keep one pound. The rest they leave as a tip. How much of a tip do they leave?"

Even before Luke had had a chance to turn his calculator on the rest of the class could tell by the two coins left on the table that the answer was two pounds.

"Two pounds!" they said and after a moment Luke nodded also.

"Perfect!" exclaimed Mr O'Reilly before asking all the pupils to return to their places.

"Now we've only got five minutes to the bell, so here's my question. Each person came into the restaurant with a ten pound note and left with a pound coin. So how much did each person spend?"

"Well, nine pounds, sir," said Lewis.

"Perfect again! And if three people each spent nine pounds how much was spent there altogether?"

"Twenty-seven pounds, isn't it?" said Lewis. Luke checked the figure on his calculator and nodded silently.

"Perfect yet again!" This was working out nicely. "So what's the total with the twenty-seven pounds between them and the two pound tip they've left for the waiter?"

"Twenty-nine pounds!" most of Set 6 called out in unison.

"But they came in with thirty pounds," said Mr O'Reilly in a hushed tone. He left a dramatic pause. "So where's the other pound gone?"

The puzzled look on the faces of his pupils as they left for break was nothing compared to the look on Mr O'Reilly's face when he realised that actually there wasn't just one pound missing. He was now thirty-three pounds short!

Helpfully, one of Set 6 had left the takeaway menu from The Golden Dragon next to his laptop.

CHAPTER 17

"The journey of a thousand miles begins with a single step."

As often happened, Bob had got a lift in with a friend that morning. He yawned, wishing that he too could spend a few days away from work. He really wasn't getting much sleep at the moment and you can always rely on a Premier Inn.

"You know yawning means 20% battery remaining," joked Stan, the Assistant Caretaker, but Bob had more pressing matters on his mind.

"You know what worries me?" he said, pausing to lean on his broom.

"What's that?" asked Stan.

"Well, I don't think the gates have really moved since last Friday. That's..." he counted up, "...five days. I just can't remember the entry code now. Can you?"

He looked to Stan for some reassurance.

His colleague gave it some thought before answering.

"Ms Malik'll probably have it on her phone," said Stan. "I think it's got a 6 in it. Maybe a 3?"

Last summer to avoid this very problem they'd written the code on a post-it note but then forgotten where they'd posted it.

There had been no sign of the contractors' vans since they'd dropped their equipment off before the weekend, blocking the drive and preventing the catering lorry from delivering a week's supply of frozen pizzas.

"Ah well," said Stan. "At least the new tarmac will sort everything out."

He looked down at the large white TOPS sign beneath his feet.

"How d'you mean?" asked Bob.

Ms Stonehart was still parked on the double yellow lines outside the school gates. As she started the engine to head off to the Premier Inn she was thinking that it was time to see Vernon-Smythe about upgrading the Mercedes to something better. The windows were always steaming up and she couldn't make hands-free calls since her friend had broken the speaker as he was climbing into the back.

Setting off up Cemetery Road, she looked across at Wildside Academy. It concerned her that the resurfacing looked like it was going to take longer than expected. They needed to start on her parking space because it was important for the school to look as normal as possible should Ofsted arrive. Keeping one hand safely on the wheel she dialled the School Office, hoping to find out if there was any news about Ofsted, but she got a message saying that The Golden Dragon was closed.

Bob and Stan watched her leave. It would be good to have the STOP sign finally painted correctly, of course. She was just pondering how difficult it could be to get the right four-letter word when she was forced to swerve and use other four-letter words. The group of boys doing wheelies down the middle of the road disappeared in her rear-view mirror with Darren Froggett in pursuit. Somebody should have a word with those unruly kids, she thought, pausing at the top of the road. The lollipop man probably didn't realise she was the Headteacher. Few people did. As she forced her way into the rush hour traffic she wondered if the Premier Inn had a jacuzzi with its swimming pool.

As a result of the work on the drive, some teachers actually found themselves in school earlier than they would normally be. Mr Lee Chang had stayed overnight with his cousin and then it was only a short walk to work from the restaurant. He liked his room in the Art Department. High up on the top floor, it was one of the larger rooms with a good view of the front drive and the staff car park at the rear of the building. Once he'd checked that his supplies were ready for the classes that day he boiled the kettle, made a cup of herbal tea and went to look at the sunrise over Grimshaw's Glue Factory. Calming music tinkled soothingly from a small speaker on his desk. The wind chimes he'd hung by the classroom door were really only there to announce the arrival of anybody coming to observe his lessons.

Mr Chang had eclectic tastes in art, although he drew the line at Mrs Thorne's adoration of David Hockney. Unlike his days at the call centre, the good thing about this job was that it gave him time to paint his canvases during working hours. The portrait that was partially completed in the corner was not only a demonstration of the proportions of the human figure for Year 10, it was actually a commission for one of his cousin's regulars. *'Crimson Orb'*, however, the large red circle of paint filling another canvas, had not proven to be quite as popular as he'd hoped. Ms Murkett had complained it was sexist. Never mind. Each to their own. She'd said the same thing about Da Vinci's *'The Last Supper.'* He slowly dipped a pink wafer biscuit into his tea and hummed quietly to himself.

The thing that kept Mr Chang sane in this job, the art he felt most proud of, was not even in the building. Every day when he got out of his car in the staff car park he added a little bit more to his masterpiece before going up to his studio. Sadly as he'd had to walk to work today he'd not been able to be creative. If and when the resurfacing of the staff car park was complete, his *pièce de résistance* would be gone, buried beneath the tarmac, lost to the art world forever. I bet Banksy never has this problem, he thought.

Lowering his gaze to the empty car park he could see how close he had been to completing the biggest canvas he'd ever attempted. Spitting his daily chewing gum out with precision over the years his message to the SLT was so large that it could really only be read from up here. It was just a shame he'd never get a chance to finish the word *"OFF!!!"*

If Mr Chang had looked out of the other window and past the water-logged rugby pitch he would have been able to see many of his colleagues struggling in from the car park of The Cock 'n' Bull and beyond. The blast of several car horns broke the eerie morning silence as their headlights picked out figures crossing the busy road. Several teachers had either refused or been refused Frogger's help in getting across. It was difficult to tell at this distance but it looked like Mr Armani was arguing with the lollipop man in front of Lee's cousin's restaurant. Mr Chang turned back to his canvas and began squeezing fresh oil paint out onto his palette.

Down at ground zero, Darren Froggett let out another

stream of abuse at the man who seemed to have plagued him all his life since Brewery Road Primary School.

"I could agree with you," replied Mr Armani, "but then we'd both be wrong."

Instead he turned, knocked a speck of dust off his sleeve and continued calmly down Cemetery Road.

"Well, at least I've got a GCSE in Drama!" shouted Darren at the former Milk Monitor, Form Captain, Head Boy, then Teacher of Science and Head of Year. "And you haven't!!!"

The man waiting for a bus to Upper Steem looked up from his phone and glanced round nervously. He hoped the madman in the white coat wasn't shouting at him as actually he *did* have a GCSE in Drama.

"I 'ate this job!" moaned Darren, not for the first time.

If Mrs Sellers liked to compare her classroom to an aeroplane then it was now time to take her image further. Cemetery Road echoed to the sound of teachers trundling wheeled cases along behind them each morning, infuriating the neighbours who didn't want to wake up till midday. The cases were not full of holiday clothes and sun cream though. Since the possibility of further redundancies had reared its ugly head again many teachers at Wildside Academy had found this the easiest way to demonstrate how much marking they were doing at home each night. As with an airport the teachers found themselves trundling back at the end of it all, tired, delayed, with some items lost on the way, having spent their time with people they couldn't understand and not being able to find where they'd parked their car.

"It'll look so nice when it's all been spruced up," said Ms Malik, Second-in-Department for Geography, as she marched with determination towards the school. "It's a shame nothing came of that statue of Mr Chambers."

As she only worked part-time Mrs Sellers didn't get quite as many opportunities to talk to Mina as other people but from what she'd seen she always seemed so optimistic about everything. Maybe going away on residential trips with the Geography Department would be more enjoyable at Wildside Academy than it had been at her last school. She'd asked Tim Cocker what the school was like but he'd simply commented that of all the schools he'd taught in Wildside Academy was the most recent.

Mr Dean Gordon, one of the DT teachers and part-time pianist, had managed to park in the pub car park this morning because he'd arrived just as Ms Shakespeare was vacating her regular spot. Shazza had decided she was still ill. She had a splitting headache and really needed to go home right away. There was an amusing sticker in the rear window of the car he parked next to. *Warning! No unmarked books are left in this vehicle overnight!"*

Describing himself as a recovering workaholic, Mr Gordon would talk to almost anybody and today he found himself accompanied by one of the new Science teachers, Dr Whittaker. As they passed by the launderette next to Tangelo's tanning studio a figure huddled under a blanket in the doorway called out to them.

"Spare some change?"

Mr Gordon immediately searched his pockets and threw a handful of pound coins into the man's empty cap on the pavement in front of him.

"How are you keeping, mate?" he asked the man.

The two of them exchanged a few words before reluctantly Mr Gordon said he'd have to head off to work for fear of being late.

Being new to the school Dr Whittaker hardly knew Mr Gordon well enough to ask who the stranger was. Passing the Cemetery View Care Home the two colleagues caught up with Mr Hayes, checking his watch as he waited to cross over.

"Morning. It's sad, isn't it?" he greeted them, looking back at the lonely figure by the launderette.

"Really sad," Mr Gordon agreed. "Dave was one of the best teachers we had," he explained to Dr Whittaker. "All the kids loved him, great to work with, got outstanding results. He used to do these amazing caricatures, spoke three foreign languages but was really modest about all his talents. Ofsted called him "a renaissance man" when they came in."

"A really decent bloke," added Mr Hayes. "I miss him."

"What happened?" asked Dr Whittaker.

"He got called for jury service last year," said Mr Gordon. "Inhuman Resources said he wouldn't get paid."

"You don't get a choice, do you?" asked Dr Whittaker. "They've got to pay you, haven't they?"

"It depends who you are," said Mr Hayes as he stepped

back to avoid a cyclist heading towards them on the pavement. The cyclist swore at them and sped on. "Like most things here."

"He ended up on a massive murder case. It went on for ages! Roger could probably tell you exactly how long. He lost his job, his house, his wife. I don't think he sees his kids much now."

"The case was eventually thrown out of court on a technicality, wasn't it?" added Mr Hayes.

Dr Whittaker didn't know what to say. She'd never been called for jury service herself but surely there must be statutory regulations that Wildside Academy would be obliged to follow?

"So how long has Ms Stonehart been Headteacher here?" asked Dr Whittaker after a moment.

"Just before the school went down from Outstanding to Inadequate," said Mr Gordon. "Do you remember, Roger, it was an April Fools Day wasn't it? Appropriately!"

"It was the same day the President of Mexico died," replied Mr Hayes. "2,444 days ago to be precise. Seen by most people as a distant leader, inexperienced, with little concern for other people, making bad decisions and some very dodgy financial dealings."

"And what was the Mexican President like, Roger?" smiled Mr Gordon.

"Hiya, sir," a boy said to Mr Gordon as they continued down Cemetery Road. The boy had a small dog on a lead and had obviously taken him out for a walk round the block before school.

"You know I thought your dog would be bigger than that, Craig, given the amount of homework he eats!"

"We've not got any meetings tonight, have we?" asked Mr Hayes as they approached the school gates. "I want to try and get away at three."

"Just the Staff Well-being meeting," said Mr Gordon. "Although it'll probably be cancelled again."

Mr Buonanulla had got into the habit of walking from Steem Junction tram station even before the situation with the car park had arisen. This morning he found himself heading towards work with Ms Grimley who was, after Madame Loups-Garoux of course, one of his best friends amongst all the staff. They'd both started at the school on the same day, long before it had converted to Academy status, and had found that politically they had a lot in common.

"So, Thora," said Mr Buonanulla, carrying little more than a tartan manbag, "you must do loads of marking going by the amount of books you bring in each day."

As Acting Head of Department he left most of the MFL marking to Ivor. It was only fair as he taught the most pupils in the Department.

Ms Grimley herself was actually only carrying her handbag, her lunchbox and a well-thumbed copy of *"Exploring History Through Pictures and Worksheets."* Following on behind her however, like a team of Sherpas on this frosty morning, were three Prefects, pulling along two suitcases each and carrying her laptop bag. The boys were three of the most pleasant pupils in the school and the fact that they liked Ms Grimley proved the old saying that opposites attract.

"I'll let you in on a secret," said Ms Grimley quietly, looking round to check that nobody could hear her, not even her servants. She could trust Hamish. They'd both voted the same on Brexit. "I don't do any marking at home!"

"Yeah, yeah, yeah," said Mr Buonanulla looking at all her luggage as if he didn't believe her. "So, what's all that?"

"I do take every book home every night," Ms Grimley agreed. "I'm not stupid! I'm not leaving them in my room for the Thought Police to come poking about. Speaking of which I bet the Gestapo started out doing work scrutinies."

A group of boys came cycling past, practising their circus skills in case their GCSEs came to nothing.

"Anyway," continued Ms Grimley, "what am I meant to mark when they never bother to do their homework?"

As far as Darren was concerned this was only a minor skirmish in the Froggett-Armani War. It wasn't even worth calling today's encounter a battle. Mind you it didn't help that he now taught Science to his little sister who came home every night and said what a wicked teacher Mr Armani was! Darren was so busy trying to work out how he could get Armani's sports car wheel clamped at The Cock 'n' Bull that he failed to notice the increasing warble of a siren.

"You goin' across or what?" grunted a ginger kid beside him.

As Darren woke up from his planning and stepped into the

road the fire engine turned right onto Cemetery Road, narrowly missing him.

Once on the other pavement Darren propped his lollipop up against the bus shelter and watched as the fire engine raced down Cemetery Road towards Wildside Academy. It might not be such a bad day after all, he thought, visualizing Armani's Science lab burning down. That'd teach him a lesson! As he made his way to the school gates this had to be the first time in his life he'd ever gone there with a feeling of eager anticipation. The fire engine would not be able to get in. It felt like his birthday.

The siren and flashing lights stopped abruptly with a slight echo as the fire engine pulled into the kerb in front of the large gun-metal gates. Never had the sign announcing that *"gates open automatically"* seemed more mocking than today.

"This is dreadful!" announced Ms Malik who had hurried out to help as soon as she'd heard the fire engine approaching. "They can't get in! SLT aren't here!" Nothing had ever prepared her for such a crisis and she looked round desperately for help.

"'Ow do?" an old man greeted her as his dog relieved itself against the school sign.

With a slight hiss, a door opened on the fire engine and a pair of purple and yellow Doc Martens appeared on the steps leading down from the driver's cabin. The crowd of pupils gathering by the gates had never seen a firefighter like this before. The figure who climbed down to the pavement was dressed in what looked like a pair of red tartan pyjamas, a yellow woolly bobble hat, a long lime green scarf and pink sunglasses. She nearly dropped her open laptop in the process.

"Cheers, Sam! See ya, lads!" Ms Lovall called out to the firemen as she slammed the door. "That was groovy! Keep it warm for me now, Fireman Sam!"

As always somebody had their phone out. This video was going to be even better than all the other clips of Ms Lovall's driving that had been posted on social media.

CHAPTER 18

"In total darkness a little light goes a long way."

Staff surveys weren't popular at Wildside Academy as too much paper tended to block the shredder. However if you'd been able to ask the teachers if they approved of the SLT going off to the Premier Inn and leaving them to cope on their own, the unanimous answer would have been yes! If pushed, provided they weren't pushed out of a job, many teachers would even have said the place ran better without the SLT. It was calmer. Everyone looked happier. There even seemed to be less litter about the place as if the kids only dropped it to annoy Mr Thicke.

For their part the SLT felt they had got a lot out of the brainstorming exercise, so much so that they had extended it to the full week. They had even agreed that as it had been so successful it was something that should be repeated on an annual basis. Maybe even termly?

Just for the record, there *was* a jacuzzi with the swimming pool.

As a result of all the SLT's hard work there were various initiatives to implement that would have a massive impact on the progress of the school. The increased number of emails awaiting the attention of staff the following week when they switched on their laptops indicated that it was business as usual again.

From : JST (Headteacher) - JStonehart@WildsideAcademy
To : AllStaff@WildsideAcademy
Sent : Mon 17 Dec 07:50
Subject : School Values

Good Morning

The first SLT brainstorming session was a tremendous success. Thanks to Mrs Spratt and the HR Team for organizing it. As so many good things came from our discussions I will not inundate you with all the details. My Senior Leadership Team will cascade the information to you gradually as appropriate.

One exciting innovation I do want to share with you is that as well as our traditional school motto "Tempus fugit!" we now have a new way of expressing the values we stand for here at Wildside Academy. When you go on the school website you will see our unique new look.

In order to cement our values firmly in our pupils' minds staff will now read them aloud at the start and end of each lesson. Wisdom, Inspiration, Leadership, Determination, Success, Integrity, Dedication, Excelence. Under my leadership we are going from strength to strength.

Ms J. Stonehart, Headteacher, *Wildside Academy,*
Diploma in Human Resources, TGCSEC, CPT, BPB.

From : LWR - LWinter@WildsideAcademy
To : AllStaff@WildsideAcademy
Sent : Mon 17 Dec 08:21
Subject : Teaching and Leaning

Hiya!

Just to let you now that as a result of SLT planing the school logo will change from a dark gray background to a black background. This will be rolled out across all of the whole brand in it's entirety.

Make sure that the lesson plans in your folder are on the one's with the black logo and school values by tomorrow. This will also need to be done on all the old lesson plans that are in your folder for the lessons from the previous week's before this too.

Ofsted needs to see consistency and we need to raise standards, yeah? More folders are on order. Any questions just see Sharon or I.

Cheers!
Lynne
Assistant Head i/c Teaching & Leaning,
Literacy Co-ordinator, Advanced Skills Teacher for English.

From : IRM - IRamsbottom@WildsideAcademy
To : AllStaff@WildsideAcademy
CC : Office@WildsideAcademy
Sent : Mon 17 Dec 09:08
Subject : URGENT! Photocopying policy

Please read. This is important!

Just a quick note – staff must hand any photocopying in at least three weeks before it is needed, especially lesson plans which are back-to-back and need to be stapled so take longer. I have a lot to do as this is the busy season for me.

Also if you don't use the new photocopying sheets with the updated logo I won't be able to process your request.

On the plus side, the repair man for the staffroom photocopier should be in next week.

Must dash!
Mrs I. Ramsbottom DipP&R (Hons.)

From : RGT - RGilbert@WildsideAcademy
To : AllStaff@WildsideAcademy
Sent : Mon 17 Dec 10:37
Subject : Lost mug

Hi,
Has anybody seen my new mug? It's white with a shamrock on it. My fiancé got me it.
Think I left it in ICT-3 before the INSET maybe?
Thanks, Rowena.

From : NST - NSpratt@WildsideAcademy
To : AllStaff@WildsideAcademy
CC:SLT@WildsideAcademy
Sent : Mon 17 Dec 11:42
Subject : Fire Safety Training

Good morning staff,

For those of you who didn't hand in your Fire Safety Certificate by close of business on Monday, there will be a further online training session in ICT-3 at 3:30 this Friday. I hear what you say about the printers but the downloaded certificates could also be sent to the staffroom photocopier or printed elsewhere.

Under the Health and Safety at Work Act 1974 it is a legal requirement that you attend this training. A list of staff is attached and a register will be taken.

Mrs N. Spratt,
Head of HR, Wildside Academy.

From : JTN - JTimson@WildsideAcademy
To : FormTutors@WildsideAcademy
CC : AGM - AGoldbloom@WildsideAcademy
Sent : Mon 17 Dec 12:48
Subject : New school blazers

<u>Notice to Form Tutors Years 7-11</u>

Hello,

Please let your forms know that the school blazer with the new black background logo will be available from our uniform supplier by next week. Details and prices are available on the school website and from Alex Goldbloom in the Finance Office.

Also please can staff be aware that the photocopiers in the Main Office are not to be used by teachers. Even for photocopying lesson plans.

Judy Timson, Office Manager, Attendance and First Aid Officer.

From : RTE - RThicke@WildsideAcademy
To : AllStaff@WildsideAcademy
Sent : Mon 17 Dec 13:13
Subject : Updated school website

Morning,

The new website is up and running after initial teething problems with the consistency of the font size across each page. If you have any photos or success stories send them to me so that Trevor can upload them.

Mr Richard Thicke,
Deputy Head, Wildside Academy

From : JST - JStonehart@WildsideAcademy
To : AllStaff@WildsideAcademy
CC : RTE - RThicke@WildsideAcademy
Sent : Mon 17 Dec 13:14
Subject : Updated school website

Re : Wildside Academy website

Important.

If staff have any photos or stories for the school website they **MUST** be forwarded to me as Headteacher before being published.

Ms J. Stonehart, Headteacher, Wildside Academy,
Diploma in Human Resources, TGCSEC, CPT, BPB.

Wisdom, **I**nspiration, **L**eadership, **D**etermination, **S**uccess, **I**ntegrity, **D**edication, **E**xcelence.

From : JHE – JHumble@WildsideAcademy
To : FormTutors@WildsideAcademy
CC : HoY@WildsideAcademy
Sent : Mon 17 Dec 13:14
Subject : Uniform check

Notice to all Form Tutors

Hello there!

Just a heads up that there will be a drop-in uniform check in lessons next week to make sure pupils are wearing the correct uniform. No trainers, piercings, tattoos, jewellery, old-style school logo etc.

Ta,
Jamie, CBA.

From : RTE - RThicke@WildsideAcademy
To : AllStaff@WildsideAcademy
Sent : Mon 17 Dec 13:15
Subject : URGENT!

URGENT!
Re : Wildside Academy website

Please remember to forward any photos or success stories directly to Ms Stonehart if you want them to be considered for inclusion on the school website.

Mr Richard Thicke,
Deputy Head, Wildside Academy

From : LAE - LArmitage@WildsideAcademy
To : AllStaff@WildsideAcademy
CC: ITHelp@WildsideAcademy
Sent : Mon 17 Dec 14:48
Subject : Has 'S'Cool!' crashed again?

Help!

I'm still having trouble getting on 'S'Cool Homework!' to set homework. Does anybody know if the site's crashed again? Also has anybody seen a class set of "Exploring Geography Through Pictures and Worksheets"?

Thanks,
Linda, Head of Geography.

From : SLL - SLovall@WildsideAcademy
To : AllStaff@WildsideAcademy
Sent : Mon 17 Dec 14:49
Subject : Christmas do! Yeeaaaahhhh!!!

Re : The Agaar do's due

Hiya!

Quick reminder – don't forget the final payment for the Christmas bash at Agaar's due! Do pay up! No excuses 'cos we got paid on Friday! Wooooo!!! Get your groovy dancing gear on folks! Shazza – you owe me a double!

Cheers! Sally L4L xxx

From : HJS - HJones@WildsideAcademy
To : AllStaff@WildsideAcademy
CC : AGM - AGoldbloom@WildsideAcademy
Sent : Mon 17 Dec 15:06
Subject : A message to everybody

Harmonious Greetings!

I'm thinking of setting up a school band but we don't have many instruments (just recorders and the piano.) Do you have any old musical instruments lying around at home that you don't use? Please let me know. Any unused drums (either new / second-hand) are welcome. I'd start trying out xylophones in class too if we get any. Does anybody want to start the staff choir going again?

Thanks in advance,
Huw, Head of Music.

CHAPTER 19

"Do not look too far ahead or you lose sight of the road."

"You're listening to Wildside FM and with the time just coming up to half past seven that was Michael Bublé and 'Winter Wonderland'," continued the voice on the radio as Mr Haddenough switched his engine off. *"First the latest from the Met Office. With Storm Jeanette continuing to batter the country and many roads still impassable, police are warning motorists not to venture out unless they really have to. In other news the Minister for Education, Mr Jeremiah Grimes, CBE, said today that teachers just needed to stop moaning and work harder if standards..."*

Ivor switched the radio off and looked out at the Cromwell Road car park where he'd ended up after a hazardous two-hour journey. The only tyre tracks across the endless snowy wasteland had been created by his car and the only prints looked like those of a cat. When he reached the ticket machine the remains of a small bird added a splash of colour to the blank surroundings. The machine spat some of Ivor's coins back out again before flashing up an "OUT OF ORDER" message on the display and refusing to issue a ticket. Hoping that he'd parked fully within the hidden markings of a single parking space, Ivor left a note on his windscreen about the faulty ticket machine and set off on his mission to the unknown. There was no way of knowing if Wildside Academy was open today. Nobody had answered when he'd phoned the school and his *Acting* Head of Department did not reply to texts.

Ivor wasn't into computer games but he did wonder whether this Zombie Kombat thing had a scenario as bleak as this one. There were no vehicles and very few pedestrians. Nobody had thought to grit the roads or pavements and he'd never seen icicles as long as these in the thirty years he'd been a teacher. In one sense it was all quite beautiful. Taking it slowly he'd only slipped twice by the time The Cock 'n' Bull came into sight. There was no chance of replacing the sandwiches he'd dropped in the snow as even the 24-hour filling station opposite the pub was closed.

A muffled thump drew Mr Haddenough's attention back from the empty garage forecourt. By the time he'd slid his way across snowman's land to the pub car park Mr Cocker had already got out of his vehicle and was inspecting the damage.

"Morning," Ivor called out as he approached. "That looks bad. Odd place to put a bollard."

Tim, being Tim, still managed to remain cheerful.

"Could be worse," he said. There'd been that time he'd scraped the car of one of the Julies when he was reversing but as nobody knew which Julie nothing had really come of it. Brigadier Vernon-Smythe had managed to sort it all out for the cost of a couple of pints. Good old Monty!

"Not long now," said Tim, as the two of them headed up Coronation Street together.

"Eight more get-ups."

It didn't take Roger's special gift to work out that in less than ten days the longest school term would be drawing to a much-welcomed close.

The house at the top of Cemetery Road had been hidden beneath Christmas lights as soon as Bonfire Night had been ticked off and it now stood like a beacon, guiding them through the frosty, quiet morning air.

Two doors down from the lighthouse Darren Froggett had scraped the ice off his window and looked out. What he saw was enough to convince him that it wasn't worth getting up for so few pedestrians. He had better things to do. Delores had decided that she was going in, she said, because she had Science first lesson. She could make her own way across the road if she was so smart! As it turned out the complete absence of traffic meant that the few pupils who had been sent off to school on what was probably the coldest day in living memory could cross safely on their own. Provided they avoided the barrage of snowballs from Kyle who had based himself strategically behind the bins outside Booze 'n' Fags.

As the snowy expedition continued Ivor and Tim caught up

with other colleagues heading towards Wildside Academy. It was probably just a coincidence but these were all teachers who'd had to re-do the Fire Safety training the previous Friday afternoon. What a difficult journey home that had been as Storm Jeanette had first arrived!

"Maybe, but if the school's closed we'd have been told," Mr Digby was saying reasonably, struggling to pull his suitcase along behind him. "And look! There are pupils arriving too."

He pointed through the mist. It looked like Nathan and Jack from his Year 9 class. The ginger hair was unmistakable, as was the endless commentary on how much he 'ated everything in existence.

"We never get snow days now we're an Academy," said Mr Jones sadly.

"I bet they just haven't bothered telling us," replied Ms Grimley as her breath formed in the air. She had enough worries today. In the absence of her porters she'd had to leave all the exercise books in the boot of her car, abandoned behind the sewage farm. She was convinced her lessons were going to be observed today and they'd do a work scrutiny. Maybe there was a computer room free? She paused to light another cigarette with shaky hands.

Mike Stringer jogged on the spot for a moment while he checked his mobile phone.

"Well I've not had a text message or anything," he said.

"And there's nothing on the website," said Mr Curry.

"The local radio didn't say it's closed," added Mrs Walker. "USA's closed and WCC. My Paul's off today."

Wildside Community College seemed to close at the slightest opportunity but it was unusual for Upper Steem Academy to do so.

Eventually their resilience paid off and the titanic form of Wildside Academy appeared through the icy mist. The school gates were frozen open with an unearthly clicking sound emanating from the entry control panel being the only thing that broke the silence. They had not only arrived in time for morning briefing, if it was on, but there might even be time to get a hot drink and knock the snow off their shoes first.

The group of teachers crunched their way through the thick snow towards the main entrance. Other footprints across the untreated surface showed that they were not the first to arrive. As the main drive was fenced off beyond Ms Stonehart's personal parking space it seemed that stage one of the resurfacing had been completed. But her Mercedes was not in its usual place and the contractors and their vans were nowhere to be seen. At least the teachers wouldn't have to carry on to the pupils' entrance but could go in through the main entrance again even if the car park was still out of action. It would just be a matter of remembering the entry code to the main building or getting one of the Julies to help them. Business as usual.

But today was different. Before any of them got a chance to attempt the icy steps that led up to the entrance the doors slid open and Deirdre the cleaner appeared, followed by the other members of the Maintenance & Facilities Early Morning Shift.

Deirdre looked surprised as if a school was the last place she expected to encounter teachers.

"You know it's closed, don't you?" she said looking up at the cloudy sky as snow started to fall again. Even on snow days it seemed the cleaners had to be in to keep it all tidy. You never knew when Ofsted might arrive.

If a text message had gone out warning of the school closure then it had not been sent to the people who'd done their Fire Safety training in ICT-3.

"I'm just off up the hospital," she continued. "Did I tell you my sister's got worse?"

Mr Haddenough wasn't sure what he'd done to upset Ms Stonehart but when school opened again the following day he found himself puzzling over the email he'd received from her. It was best not to reply to it.

From : JST (Headteacher) - JStonehart@WildsideAcademy
To : IHH - IHaddenough@WildsideAcademy
CC : HBA - HBuonanulla@WildsideAcademy
    LWR - LWinter@WildsideAcademy
    NST - NSpratt@WildsideAcademy
FILE : (HR) IHH Personal File
Sent : Wed 19 Dec 08:20
Subject : Following school policies

Mr Haddenough,

Mrs Spratt has informed me that you did not phone in yesterday to explain why you were absent when the school was closed due to snow. She was not satisfied with this and neither was I.

Can I remind you that Section 13.9(ii) of the Staff Handbook clearly states that any staff absence must be reported before 7am on the school absence line and the appropriate Head of Department must also be contacted via email.

Whilst I appreciate that you were driving (and presumably don't have hands-free) nevertheless you did not phone the school to advise that you were going to be absent. In future, can I request that you pull over somewhere and contact the school as per procedure in order that we can make provision for your absence which did not happen yesterday.

Your failure to follow the correct school procedures will again be recorded on your confidential personal file in HR.

Ms J. Stonehart, Headteacher, Wildside Academy,
Diploma in Human Resources, TGCSEC, CPT, BPB.

Wisdom, Inspiration, Leadership, Determination, **S**uccess, Integrity, **D**edication, Excelence.

It was two days later before Mr Thicke updated the school website, informing staff, parents and pupils that Wildside Academy had been closed due to snow.

CHAPTER 20

"A fire is not out until the last spark is extinguished."

It wasn't just the end of a term it was the end of an era. Thirty-eight years ago Mr North had arrived at Wildside School as it had been called in the days when Mr Cruikshank had been the Headmaster, when pupils listened and when the idea of Ofsted would have seemed like something from a science-fiction novel. He'd seen a lot of changes in that time and had hopefully made a difference to the people he'd encountered but now he was ready for some rest and relaxation.

He wasn't really sure what retirement would be like. He'd been sent an email informing him that Wildside Academy didn't have enough funds for him to go on the half-day course to prepare him for such a major change to his lifestyle. When he'd offered to pay for the course himself he'd been told it was an issue of covering lessons. His email pointing out that he didn't need cover that morning had not yet had a reply. He paused at the main entrance to admire how the resurfacing of the main drive was coming along. There'd been a lot of work done on the front of the school over the last five or six years. It all looked very expensive.

With the drive to the staff car park still fenced off Bob had cleared the last of the snow away from Ms Stonehart's parking space which was now occupied by a new silver Jaguar. It was her early Christmas present to herself because she'd worked so hard. The red postal van was parked at an angle inside the gates which was hardly surprising as the word POST was clearly marked across the tarmac in large white lettering.

"Not long now, Andy. Just five hours, forty-two minutes and nineteen seconds," said Mr Hayes enviously as he arrived for yet another day as a teacher. "And then you're history."

"No, Roger, you're History," smiled Mr North.

As they walked in together Mr North told his colleague about his dreams for the future. Mrs North would be retiring in six months, their house was already on the market and they had their eye on a small tea rooms that they'd seen in the Lake District. There'd be plenty of fresh air, walking and cycling and space for the family to visit.

"You don't need anybody to help serve tea, do you?" asked Roger hopefully.

Dressed like a Christmas fairy the Julie on the main reception desk was just finishing a call as they entered the building. The evocative smell of pine needles and a gentle wave of festive melodies filled the sparkling air.

"Yes, the school is open today," she was saying. "No. I know. Yes. I did too. I'm afraid the website hasn't been updated yet. Thank you. And a Merry Christmas to you too. "

"Morning, Julia. Anything for me?" asked Andy, looking at the pile of envelopes the postman had left. Andy was one of the few people who'd taken the time to work out which Julie was which. Having started as a Maths teacher he had now reached the dizzy heights of Co-ordinator of the School-Home Intervention Team (Exams) and there were occasionally letters from The Dyslexia Trust for him when they got the address right.

"Nothing today," said Julia without checking. The two teachers blipped their lanyard passes to document their arrival at Wildside Academy. As it was the season of goodwill Julia pressed the buzzer to unlock the inner door for them.

"How was the office party?" asked Andy before he went through.

"Amazing," said Julia. "Even better than last year. I'm so glad I booked us somewhere local what with the weather. Sounds like the place you lot had booked was a bit of a disaster."

Mr North hadn't gone to the Christmas party Ms Lovall had arranged. It wasn't really his thing. In fact, he hoped there wouldn't be a great fuss about him retiring after thirty-eight years here without a single day's absence. Having said that, he'd prepared a speech just in case he needed to thank everybody before he left.

It was very clear on this side of the Berlin Wall that Christmas wasn't very far off. As well as the large Christmas tree taking pride of place in the reception area, Jules had put fairy lights all over the HR corridor and around the Main Office. Cheeky laminated signs asked Santa to stop here and announced that nobody had been naughty. There was even a little plastic Santa on top of the counter that kept mooning at people when they walked past. The office staff, in colourful paper hats, were as busy as ever, pulling crackers, exchanging secret Santa gifts and setting out their mince pies and sherry glasses. A party popper showered Mr North with colourful streamers as he walked past the Student Welcome desk where a pupil on crutches sat quietly waiting.

It was somewhat different when Mr North and Mr Hayes went through to the workhouse where the heating was clearly still broken. The first thing they saw was Ms Winter and Ms Payne, both wearing flashing reindeer antlers and festive jumpers, telling Mr Gordon off for having a snowman design on his tie.

Mr North brushed the colourful strands of paper into the bin as he entered the staffroom. There was always a briefing on the last morning, even though it rarely fell on a Monday. He took a seat in the corner and waited for his final briefing or as he liked to call them "fun-sized staff meetings." There was a general atmosphere of relaxed anticipation about the room with some of the teachers, largely the Maths Department, having all decided to come in Christmas jumpers. The English Department had set up camp in their usual seats in the centre of the staffroom. They were all busy exchanging presents in bright wrapping paper, hugging each other and laughing raucously. Ms Shakespeare unwrapped a present from Billy, adding it to the other nine bottles in a box beside her as she blew her Head of Department a kiss. There was no sign of Felicity Lambert and as Mr North looked round the staffroom he realised there were a few other familiar faces missing too, quietly replaced by people he didn't recognise. He was under no illusion about being indispensable.

In the quiet corner Ms Malik was checking her Christmas card list, wondering if she'd sent them to all the right people. She obviously had not looked at the noticeboard behind her. A message from Ms Stonehart decreed that staff were not to send Christmas cards to each other as it wasted valuable teaching time. Instead there was a large card to all staff pinned to the board which teachers could sign if they paid two pounds.

Over near the fridge Ms Grimley was busy picking up her

lesson plans from the floor. Fearing one last lesson observation she'd just been looking through her folder when it had given way under the weight of all the paperwork and had popped open.

"Are you new as well?" the young man sitting beside Mr North asked him. "I've just joined the Science Department this week. Bryan Collins. It's dead exciting." A copy of *'Exploring Science Through Pictures and Worksheets"* lay on the cluttered table in front of him.

Mr North was just about to introduce himself and explain that he'd been here a while, when Mr Wingett and Mr Thicke entered the staffroom.

"Briefing's cancelled," Mr Wingett announced bluntly in a tone that sounded like he hoped Christmas would be cancelled too. "Janine's tied up in her office."

Unfortunately it turned out he'd been speaking metaphorically.

"Can I remind you all," added Mr Thicke before staff had a chance to move, "it's business as usual. This is Wildside Academy. Not some Cinerama multi-screen."

"We're watching a movie, right?" demanded a boy when Mr Milton turned up to cover Ms Lovall's L4L lesson with Year 10. Further back in the line Ryan Spivey was quietly dealing in popcorn.

"'Fraid not," said Mr Milton. "It's not the Cinerama multi-screen."

"Aw, go on, sir," continued the boy. "Every other teacher's let us today."

The boy seemed oblivious to the fact that this was only the first lesson of the day but then they all tried that argument at this time of the year. It was as if saying something over and over again would make it somehow believable. It was the same tactic the SLT used when they kept repeating that the school was improving under their leadership.

"Where is Ms Lovall anyway?" muttered another boy. "She always lets us watch movies."

She probably did, which would perhaps explain why she hadn't left any cover work for them.

"I don't know where she is," Mr Milton found himself saying as he considered what they could do for the next hour without breaking any of the school's commandments. Watching movies was right up there with *Thou shalt not do wordsearches.* There was a good Maths website he knew that might interest them.

Ms Sally Lovall was actually really busy in the staffroom and had had to have her lessons covered all morning so that she could make an important phone call. It wasn't her fault that the staff Christmas do had been such a disaster this year but she was prepared to give up her time to sort it out. Even with all her planning since September there was no way that she could have planned for Storm Jeanette tearing across the country and making it impossible for anybody to get to the restaurant. Well, that wasn't strictly true. She'd made it into the city centre with the help of Fireman Sam and Shazza had shown resilience getting in for a few drinks too, along with Lynne, Sharon and Sean. It was the very fact that the six of them had managed to get there which meant that nobody could get a refund on their money. It was in the small print apparently. The weather had to be so bad that nobody at all could attend for the restaurant to offer a refund. Well, reading the small print was definitely a lesson for life that she could share with her pupils. And her phone call had not been a total waste of time. Whilst Robin, the nice man she spoke to at The Agaar, could not reimburse every teacher who'd paid for the Christmas do, he did suggest he took Sally herself out for a meal. Having split up with Fireman Sam who'd spent the whole evening talking to Shazza, it did seem to Sally like Christmas really had come early.

Alone in the Headteacher's office with only a bottle of sherry and a mince pie for company Ms Stonehart was also incredibly busy. There was always so much to do before a holiday. Traditionally the school always closed an hour early for the Christmas break but she would have to leave long before that to make sure she didn't miss their flight. Her Deputy Heads could take care of the Christmas assemblies and it was years since they'd had to put on a meal for the old folks from the Cemetery View Care Home.

She pressed the buzzer on her desk to summon the Head of HR and Mrs Spratt appeared at the door in seconds.

"Norma," she said, "you need to have a word with Mr Rojan about the emails that are getting through the filters to me."

"I hear what you say," said Mrs Spratt. "Was it that Swedish company again?"

"No. One of the teachers this time. Mrs Scott?"

"I think she's the new English teacher," replied Mrs Spratt uncertainly.

"Well she's asked if she can leave five minutes early today for her son's Nativity at some primary school. I'm too busy to reply. Just let her know she can't. We're a business not a charity. We'll be inundated with that sort of thing if I say yes."

Ms Stonehart took a sip of her sherry and seemed deep in thought for a moment as she stared at a robin on a branch outside the window.

"On second thoughts, it is the season of goodwill. Tell her she can leave early. She can just take it as a day's unpaid leave."

Mrs Spratt wasn't sure if she should offer to pull the cracker left abandoned on Ms Stonehart's desk. On reflection she decided it was wisest to say nothing and left.

By mid-morning Ms Stonehart was making good progress with her to-do list. She'd already seen Ms Winter and Ms Payne to help her decide which members of staff should qualify for the end-of-term bonus for full attendance. It had always seemed very impersonal just to look at the attendance data and give vouchers for full attendance to the people who hadn't been off at all. Luckily Ms Winter had different data about the workforce that was very helpful. For example, how could you reward people for full attendance if they hadn't completed the after school Fire Safety training? It would also be hypocritical to reward people if they had warnings on their personal file about punctuality. Mr Haddenough on the snow day was a case in point. And, like Ms Winter said, you also needed to consider people like Ms Shakespeare who might have had a day off but contributed enormously to extra-curricular activities and the life of the school. All in all with Ms Winter's help it meant that the process was carried out fairly and transparently. Envelopes with the different amounts in had been put into pigeonholes by breaktime, largely the pigeonholes of the English and Maths Departments and selected other worthy colleagues that Ms Winter had recommended.

Next Ms Stonehart turned to the correspondence that Mrs Spratt had placed in her in-tray earlier that morning. It was disappointing that the telescope she'd ordered wouldn't be delivered till the new year. Still she hadn't needed it when it had been the snow day. As soon as the USA website had announced that their school was closed she had taken the decision to close Wildside Academy straight away. There was also a handwritten envelope which turned out to contain a Christmas card from her daughter. She dropped it straight in the bin. Alice had always taken her ex-husband's side and had been no help when she'd received the divorce papers that Christmas.

When Ms Stonehart opened the next two brown envelopes she again had to call Mrs Spratt through to her office.

"Norma," she continued, "there's a speeding fine here that needs to be paid. Going by the date it would have been when I was leading the SLT brainstorming days. Directed time. Pass it on to Mr Goldbloom to pay, would you?"

She handed her the two envelopes.

"The other one's for Gary," she said. "And ask him not to get personal correspondence sent to work. If he's going to get a parking ticket after all I've done to get everybody a special deal up on Cromwell Road then he deserves everything he gets."

"I hear what you say."

Mrs Spratt headed off to be the bearer of bad news to Mr Wingett, something he looked like he was used to. No sooner had she left her office than Ms Stonehart buzzed her again.

There was just one lesson remaining before classes would be registered and set free on an unsuspecting world for two weeks. Once the mince pies, Christmas cake and chocolates had run out in the Main Office Ms Winter and Ms Payne had decided to go join Mr Kaye in the English Department. There were enough teachers about the place to supervise any pupils wandering between classrooms without the need to be heavy handed at the festive season. Ms Winter stopped at Mr Haddenough's room and barged in to check that pupils weren't making Christmas cards in French. His Year 9 class were all silently completing a Reading assessment in some foreign language. Going by the Learning Objectives on the board it looked like Spanish.

As she got to the English corridor her Head of Department, Mr Billy Kaye, now dressed in a Santa hat and fake beard, was leading the rest of his Department from room to room in a conga. Shazza was trying desperately to hold on at the back, looking a little green. Billy was such a great Head of Department, so good at motivating a team and getting the best out of everybody. Ms Winter was so glad she'd managed to get him an end of term bonus. You were bound to be off for a couple of weeks when you had such a responsible and stressful position.

There were differentiated activities going on in the English rooms with pupils either watching *'Elf'* or completing a Christmas wordsearch. One of the smarter pupils had written on the board that *subordinate clauses are Santa's little helpers!*

"I thought we'd all had enough of *'Lord of the Flies,'* said Billy Kaye as he held the mistletoe up over Shazza again.

Ms Winter smiled. It was the sign of a good teacher to be adaptable to the specific needs of different individuals.

And so, after thirty-eight years of coming in to work at Wildside each day Mr Andy North found himself sitting in the corridor outside the office of the 'Headteacher' one last time. He could still remember the first time he'd waited there when he'd come for the interview. A faulty tap in the washroom had sprayed the front of his trousers moments before he'd been called through and he'd thought he hadn't got a chance. Thirty-eight years ago!

He'd received an email from Mrs Spratt asking him to come down there at the close of business. It was very quiet now. Not a teacher was stirring, not even a mouse. The pupils had all left as soon as the starting pistol had sounded and the office staff seemed to have gone off to The Cock 'n' Bull. A plastic bag containing Mr North's few personal items was on the bench beside him. It was fortunate that he'd not been given any gifts or cards as he'd come in on his bike this morning. His end-of-term bonus for full attendance had probably been posted to his home.

Mr North took a piece of paper from his pocket and quickly read through the speech he'd prepared. Staff hadn't given leaving speeches since Mr Slade had taken it as an opportunity to tell SLT exactly what he thought of them but maybe in Mr North's case the Governors were wanting to thank him personally for all he'd done. To be honest he didn't really want any fuss, even after thirty-eight years of dedicated service without a break.

Twenty minutes later Mr North was still sitting waiting when Stan Lawrence, the Assistant Caretaker, came past with what looked like a table tennis bat.

"You still sat there?" he asked. Even Bob had left ages ago as he'd had a plane to catch. Stan was only here as he felt like he'd been promoted in Bob's absence. "I'm just about to lock up when I've taken this back. Don't know what happened to the other one though."

Contrary to what she said, Ms Stonehart's door wasn't always open. Mr North knocked on it but received no reply. It was the same when he tried Mrs Spratt's office. Even the Christmas lights had been turned off.

Stan was sweeping pine needles up when Mr North went through to the main reception. The chair behind the desk was empty with a red light flashing on the answering machine. Mr North blipped his lanyard pass against the screen as he clocked out of Wildside Academy for the final time. Thirty-eight years without a single day off and the last to leave today.

"I'm off now," he said to Stan. "I've left my keys and lanyard on the desk. Well, Merry Christmas, Mr Lawrence."

"Bye then," said Stan without looking up from what he was doing.

From : JST (Headteacher) - JStonehart@WildsideAcademy
To : AllStaff@WildsideAcademy
CC : TCS - TChambers@WildsideAcademy
*   NST - NSpratt@WildsideAcademy*
*   HR@WildsideAcademy*
*   BED - BEastwood@WildsideAcademy*
*   Office@WildsideAcademy*
*   SLT@WildsideAcademy*
Sent : Fri 21 Dec 10:19
Subject : Have a good Christmas!

Good Morning

As we break up for Christmas I would just like to thank the HR Department and my SLT for all their hard work during a very long term. Under my leadership as Headteacher Wildside Academy continues to go from strength to strength.

My employee of the term recommendation to Mr Chambers is Robert Eastwood who has taken care of every need this year as Head Caretaker. I am sure you will all want to thank Bob for all his hard work when he returns.

Envelopes have already been put in pigeonholes for the relevant teaching staff who I want to reward and I hope that you all have the kind of holiday you deserve.

Can I remind you all that school opens again on January 2nd with a briefing at 8am prompt. You will no doubt be aware that after 544 days since their last visit an Ofsted inspection of Wildside Academy is imminent. I trust that as professionals you will spend the two weeks you are free getting your Lesson Planning folders and data sheets in order. They will need to be handed to your Heads of Department for checking on the first day back. Obviously if we do not get an improved grading at the next Ofsted inspection I will have no option but to review staffing.

On a positive note you will be pleased to hear that the repair men for the staffroom photocopier and the heating system in the main building will be in over the Christmas break to prepare us for an exciting new year.

Tempus fugit!
Merry Christmas!

Ms J. Stonehart, Headteacher, *Wildside Academy,*
Diploma in Human Resources, TGCSEC, CPT, BPB.

Wisdom, **I**nspiration, **L**eadership, **D**etermination, **S**uccess, **I**ntegrity, **D**edication, **E**xcelence.

Sent from my iPhone

Attached : Boarding Cards - Flight TLC2512
Hotel Della Ricchezza, Roma, 7 nights

TERM 2

JANUARY

CHAPTER 21

*"The fool who knows he's a fool is a wise man
but the wise man who thinks he's a wise man is a fool."*

Miss White's Year 7 assembly was all about making New Year's resolutions. As a teacher you got two main chances to make resolutions each year, September and January. For a lot of teachers at Wildside Academy the two resolutions they made didn't really alter much. In September : *It's a new year. It'll be different. I'll do my best not to be stressed this year.* In January : *It's a New Year. It's not going to be any different. I'll do my best to get a job somewhere else this year.*

At the moment Miss Melody White was enjoying working at Wildside Academy. She'd been a member of the English Department for two years and had just taken on the additional responsibility of Head of Year 7. Though she said it herself, she was good at her job.

Larger assemblies took place in the Main Hall whilst for individual year groups they were squeezed into the empty canteen. As she supervised the two hundred pupils and their form teachers making their way in through the only unlocked entrance she reflected that she was in charge of a good group. Mr Ball tended to be a little bit disorganized but other than that they were shaping up nicely as form tutors.

For once her laptop had decided it wanted to join in and the school logo together with the phrase *Tempus fugit!* flickered on the screen at the front ready to display Miss White's PowerPoint. She'd decided against showing Janus, the two-faced God representing new beginnings, as she knew some of the boys would giggle. It had been the same when they'd looked at the planets during Science Week.

She was about to start her assembly when Mr Wingett entered and came across to speak to her. Year 7, still being relatively new to the school themselves, sat uncomfortably on the hard floor and waited quietly.

"You're going to have to leave this," Mr Wingett said to her bluntly, glancing up at the screen. "I'm doing assembly today." He plugged a USB stick into the computer and began searching for a file.

Miss White watched her PowerPoint disappear from the screen and hoped he hadn't deleted it. It had taken a couple of hours in the holiday to put it together. It probably didn't actually matter as she couldn't really re-use a New Year assembly at any other time of the year.

"Right," said Mr Wingett addressing the pupils when he was ready. "The bad news is the holiday's over and you need to get on with some hard work again." It was as close to wishing them a warm welcome back after the festive break as Mr Wingett ever got. "I know Miss White was probably going to talk to you about New Year resolutions but you've all been given your targets so I'm going to talk at you about something more important."

Miss White went to stand further back so that she could see the screen from a better angle. On it were displayed the photos of two comedians from a bygone age which seemed like an odd choice of theme for somebody of Mr Wingett's disposition.

"Now, you'll be looking at this and all thinking the same thing. Who are these two men Mr Wingett's put up on the screen?"

Having not yet studied rhetorical questions in their English lessons a few hands were enthusiastically raised. Unused to working with children in the classroom Mr Wingett was not expecting this response but decided to go with it. Audience participation would be the kind of thing Ofsted would be looking for if they came into an assembly.

"Yes," he said, pointing at a pupil near the front. "No, not you. You, boy! Who do you think these two men are?"

"Is it the Spice Girls?" the boy asked.

At the end of the row his form tutor, Ms Murkett, silently gave him a thumbs up. She knew he'd got it wrong but Corey had had a go and it was good in this day and age that he didn't recognise gender. Girl Power!

"Give me strength!" replied Mr Wingett, deciding to move on.

He pressed a button on the remote and the names of the two comedians appeared along with a brief summary he'd copied from Wikipedia.

- *Sir Norman Joseph Wisdom, OBE (4th February 1915 – 4th October 2010.)*
- *Ernie Wise (27th November 1925 – 21st March 1999.)*

It didn't really surprise Mr Wingett that Year 7 didn't seem to know either of these comedians since as far as he knew neither of them had been on that *Rock Celebrity* thing. It was just disappointing that some of the younger teachers in the room looked like they didn't seem to know them either. What was the world coming to?

"Now, I'll come on to why these two men are up there in a minute. But first I want you to think back to last term. Whilst you were all working here the SLT and myself were also busy, making Wildside Academy an even better place for you to study in. Wildside isn't just the name of our school now, it's what we stand for. What we are!"

With a flourish Mr Wingett clicked the remote and a new slide appeared on the screen, displaying the new school values. Mr Thicke would probably have had an issue with the inconsistent font size had he been there.

> **W**isdom
> **I**nspiration
> **L**eadership
> **D**etermination
> **S**uccess
> **I**ntegrity
> **D**edication
> **E**xcelence

"This is our new list of school values. You'll find them on the screen every time you log on, they're on your classroom walls and you will all say them at the start and end of each lesson. To help you remember them there'll be a series of assemblies looking at each value in turn. So today I'm going to talk at you about wisdom."

Mr Wingett fumbled with the remote bringing up an email from Ms Stonehart before he managed to return to the correct slide in his PowerPoint. Norman Wisdom and Ernie Wise smiled down at him again good-naturedly.

"Wisdom!" he began. "Some people might think of this man when they hear the word wisdom. Norman Wisdom. When they think of somebody wise this might be the face that springs to mind. Ernie Wise. But is that what we mean when we think of our first school value, Wisdom?"

He motioned for the pupils to put their hands back down again. He wasn't foolish enough to go down that route a second time.

"Now you all look at me stood here and see a very successful man," he continued. "Deputy Head at Wildside Academy! The kind of job some of you might only dream about one day. But as I might have told you before, I had a very miserable childhood, growing up in the rough end of Lower Steem on the council estate behind the sewage farm. We were poor. You lot don't know you're born today what with your computer games, your mobile phones and your Faceache. My Dad was unemployed and my Mum worked night shifts as a packer at Grimshaw's. But were we happy?" He didn't even pause to see if there were any hands up this time. "We didn't get Christmas presents. Money was tight. Even before he left my Dad gave us nothing. He was so mean he wouldn't give a door a slam. And I'd go to school and the other kids would have been to see Norman Wisdom at the pictures or they'd be laughing at something from The Morecambe and Wise Show. We couldn't afford a telly. We could barely afford the rent and used to have to hide behind the sofa when the rent man came round. So I never got to see Morecambe and Wise like the posh kids. I just knew there were these two comedians, having a laugh, two inseparable friends…"

He was interrupted by a loud crash at the back of the canteen. Two other inseparable friends had finally arrived, Ms Winter and Ms Payne, late to assembly as ever. Ms Winter shushed her friend and signalled to Mr Wingett to continue while she looked for a seat. Ms Payne clearly wasn't too bothered about listening to Mr Wingett's trip down memory lane as she was busy checking something important on her mobile phone.

Mr Wingett had moved on and was waiting for a video clip to load. The pupils knew what to expect when Mr Wingett played something in an assembly. Unlike the movies Ms Lovall showed them, there was nothing quite like a video of death, destruction or misery to send them on their way on a Monday morning. One time it had been a particularly horrific story about a boy who'd lost an ear during a PE lesson and had ended up addicted to drugs. It came as quite a shock therefore when this particular video clip simply showed a bespectacled man on a stage playing a grand piano in front of an orchestra. He seemed to be arguing with the conductor whilst another man in evening dress stood by them. There were screams of laughter from an unseen audience, a sound that was not usually heard in Mr Wingett's assemblies.

"You're playing all the wrong notes," the conductor was saying.

The man at the piano pulled a face, stood up and pulled the conductor towards him by his lapels.

"I'm playing all the right notes," he explained quietly, *"but not necessarily in the right order."*

His companion nodded wisely as the unseen audience erupted into further fits of uncontrollable laughter.

Mr Gordon, seated at the piano in case he was needed for this assembly, nodded in agreement at the famous line.

Next there was a black-and-white clip of a man giving a toothy grin whilst he played a ukulele in a flat cap and ill-fitting suit. The words of his song were drowned out by the clattering roar of Eric the chef opening up the service hatch at the other side of the canteen. He started to remove a stack of pizzas from the freezer, whistling along to the tune.

"Well, you get the point," said Mr Wingett as he paused the video. "That isn't what we mean by wisdom. You're not going to get anywhere in life by larking about like that. You are at Wildside Academy! This is a school and you're here to acquire knowledge and have the wisdom to apply it. You're not here to enjoy yourselves. And so there you are. That's what wisdom's all about."

Even with the video clips of some of Britain's greatest comedians, it would be fair to say that the pupils had not spent their time enjoying themselves this morning. As wisdom was about knowing how to apply your knowledge Miss White diplomatically decided not to tell Mr Wingett that he'd misspelt the word 'excellence.'

CHAPTER 22

"Don't make commitments that you don't plan to keep."

As part of his Degree in Modern Foreign Languages Mr Ivor Haddenough had spent a year teaching in a French *Lycée* in the sleepy village of Argenton-sur-Creuse in the Loire Valley. It was here as a member of *un club local* that he'd learned to do archery. If he'd learned one thing about hitting a target it was that you were more likely to be successful if you'd chosen to take aim at that target than if you'd had the task forced upon you at gunpoint. So it was with his targets for this year. With a heavy heart he clicked open the email attachment again and read through the goals his *Acting* Head of Department had devised to inspire him.

He'd barely had a chance to read through them again before the door to his classroom swung open and Mr Hamish Buonanulla came in. He was dressed in his cycling gear, having decided this time not only to buy a new bike but a hefty cycle lock as well. He slung his large pink and black saddle bags on the first desk, his version of advertising how much marking he was taking home each night. Mr Haddenough moved his own piles of marking to one side so that there was space for him to sit down. It was going to be difficult to take the meeting seriously though with his *Acting* Head of Department dressed in tartan lycra and a hi-vis yellow cycling helmet and matching gilet.

"So," Mr Buonanulla greeted him in his traditional way. "I've got five minutes before I have to get off so I thought we could just get your Bright Sky targets uploaded too."

The after-school INSET on 'Managing Work-Life Balance' scheduled for the evening had been postponed in favour of two hours reviewing and setting targets for staff. With the car park always empty awaiting the return of the contractors from another job it was difficult to tell who was still here as the clock ticked slowly round to five o'clock. Until Mr Buonanulla had broken the silence Mr Haddenough was beginning to think he was the last person still in the building, except for Bob the Head Caretaker. And Ms Stonehart, of course. As professionals in their own field those two were often the last to leave.

When the training had been announced in briefing the previous day Ms Winter had highlighted that as professionals we were literally all entitled to have a professional dialogue with other professionals about our progress in the profession. It was important at all levels and Sharon and her would be doing exactly the same thing too. Probably down at The Cock 'n' Bull . How had colleagues managed to teach for four months without targets to guide them? It was unbelievable really. Luckily Mr Haddenough had managed to get quite a bit of marking done in the two hours he'd been kept waiting. He wasn't quite sure how this counted as training. Still it was probably better than when Mr Thicke had been his line manager. He'd just printed off his targets and given them to Mr Haddenough to sign without a single word of discussion. The font size had been consistent but the date had been wrong.

"So, Céline and Sarah-Jane's targets took a wee while longer than I thought," said Mr Buonanulla, brushing some stray biscuit crumbs off his sleeve. He started to flick through the emails on his mobile phone. "I've got your targets somewhere here…I don't think I've deleted them…No, that's Céline's. Mine from Lynne…"

"I've got the email here," said Ivor, putting it on the interactive whiteboard for them both to see. He'd already logged into the Bright Sky website and the happy glowing logo filled the screen before he minimized it.

"Oh good. You're always so well-organised. I don't know how you do it. So, if we quickly go through it, we can fill it in on your laptop and then just tick the box."

There did seem to be an element of box ticking to the procedure generally.

Mr Haddenough scrolled down so that his three targets were on the screen. There was an empty box below each one for more detail and a space for signatures.

"Yeah, yeah, yeah, I remember now," said Mr Buonanulla. "Was it all ok? So, let's just fill the rest in then." His mobile phone pinged impatiently several times.

"There was just one thing actually," said Mr Haddenough. "It says that my GCSE pass rate target for this year is 110%..."

"I'd like to hope that we're all giving it 110%," said Mr Buonanulla. "I know Céline and I literally are."

"Right," agreed Mr Haddenough. He was nearly twenty years older than his *Acting* Head of Department but even so basic Maths hadn't changed in that time.

"But 100% is the most you can get."

"Yeah, yeah, yeah," said Mr Buonanulla as if he couldn't believe he had to explain something so simple as this to his colleague. To be fair Mr Haddenough wasn't a Maths teacher even though they'd given him a Year 9 Maths class one year so that he wouldn't have too many free periods on his timetable.

"We're going to increase your class size. Céline's got five or six pupils she wants to get rid of so we're moving them down to your set."

Bigger class size, bigger target!

Mr Buonanulla reached over and typed into the empty box under the first target.

Actions :

1. *Increase class size of GCSE Set 6 in order to help IHH achieve his target.*
2. *HBA to check class lists with CLX and SBN for any other pupils to move to Set 6.*
3. *IHH to liaise with Bob if more chairs are needed in Room 42.*

"So, they've got to be SMART targets you see," Mr Buonanulla explained as he scrolled down to the next one.

The smart thing to do would be to set a target that is at least mathematically possible, thought Mr Haddenough. He himself did the smart thing though and said nothing, knowing that Mr Buonanulla would have lost these targets by this time next year. Anyway they could burn that bridge when they came to it.

"So, just to check," Mr Buonanulla referred to a list on his mobile phone at this point, "Specific, yes, it's different to everybody else in the Department. Measurable, yes, there's a percentage. Achievable, well that's up to whether you put the effort in really. Realistic, goes without saying. Time-based, yes, we'll review it this time next year."

He paused and looked up at the clock as his mobile phone pinged more urgently. Somebody really didn't like to be kept waiting.

"We haven't really got time to look at last year's results if we're going to get all this done. I don't want to keep you…"

"I'm in no rush," said Mr Haddenough just to see the worried look on his *Acting* Head of Department's face. "But I'm sure we can always do that some other time if you like," he added reasonably, once he'd had his fun.

"Yeah, yeah, yeah," agreed Mr Buonanulla, a little unsure what had just happened.

He moved quickly on to the second target.

"So, I thought as you've taught for longer than anybody in the Department, been Head of Department before me, we all ought to benefit from your vast experience of teaching and learning. I thought for your second target you could be in charge of putting some wee MFL displays up about the place maybe?"

Mr Haddenough wasn't sure how this could be measured but as always Mr Buonanulla had the answer. The more displays, the more successful he'd have been.

"So, I want to try and make these targets so that they'll benefit the whole of the Department," said Mr Buonanulla. The storeroom at the back of his classroom for instance should be a good shared resource but it was cluttered. Some mornings when he needed to re-use the previous day's shirt he'd go in there to use the ironing board and have trouble getting it up. Mr Haddenough was well-organised and he might even find a use for all that squared paper that was in there. Mr Buonanulla started to add detail to the second target.

Actions :
1. *IHH to do a full inventory of the MFL stockroom in HBA's room and to co-ordinate with HoD about the purchasing of further Blu-Tack.*
2. *IHH to liaise with Bob for the unlocking of Perspex covers to allow displays on corridors to be changed.*
3. *IHH responsible for producing new displays for all rooms and corridors.*

Mr Haddenough successfully managed to get the wording of the last point changed to *all MFL rooms and corridors in the MFL Department* so that it didn't become too big a task.

"So, that's all shaping up nicely," continued Mr Buonanulla as they worked together. "Now your final wee target needs to be a whole school target. To give you an idea, and I'm sure she won't mind me sharing it with you, as Head of Year 9 Céline's third target is to do a Year 9 assembly every week."

That just sounded like part of the Year 9 job description as far as Ivor could see, for which Madame Loups-Garoux would get an additional responsibility payment. They might just as well give her the target of turning up to work on time every day, although to be honest she might not manage to achieve that one.

"So, maybe for your third target you could run some CPD training for staff after school. Perhaps once a term or so?"

It was a shame they'd already done the stress management training last term or else Mr Haddenough could have volunteered to run that.

CHAPTER 23

"Never send a dog to deliver a steak."

"I can remember when all this was fields," Mr Albert Capstick reflected, looking out at the car park from the staffroom.

Sipping a cup of herbal tea beside him Mr Chang was quietly trying to come to terms with the fact that his masterpiece would soon be gone forever.

Change was definitely in the air and not simply because Mr Capstick had realised he'd have to stop smoking his pipe during working hours if he wanted to keep his job. The contractors had finally returned from the other urgent job they'd had to do and now the maroon vans of Nicholson & Sons blocked the drive again. It looked as if something was bubbling away in vast metal drums, there were drills and machinery everywhere and a steamroller had been left dangerously close to Ms Stonehart's new Jaguar. The front field might be a quagmire bordered by heavy tyre tracks but it had been announced that the staff car park would be open again in a week. Plans to get a member of the Royal Family to snip a red ribbon had not yet been finalized though.

In Bob's absence Stan the Assistant Caretaker had been tasked with repainting the sign at the entrance over the Christmas break. After more than four months of mixed messages clear white lettering on the tarmac finally ordered everybody to STOP. It was a shame that the contractors had taken the sign too literally but they would probably be starting again just as soon as they'd finished their tea break.

Albert Capstick sat down and tapped the remains of his pipe out onto his lesson planning folder. Like Roger Hayes he wasn't far off retirement himself and he couldn't see the point of writing down everything you were going to say or do in a lesson. If he'd had to give advice to young teachers it would have been to *"be spontaneous"* which meant talk about whatever you found left on the board by the previous teacher and *"always present a moving target."* His way of moving out of Ms Winter's sights was to get Ryan Spivey to print out some lesson plans for him from t'internet in return for a good school report. In his mind, any lesson you could walk away from was a good one.

"Not long for either of us," he said to Roger who'd just come into the staffroom.

"It'd come a bit sooner if they'd only try out my system."

Albert had heard the proposal before but was always willing to listen to it again. There wasn't much else to do until the next lesson.

"They just don't like admitting that somebody's got a better idea than them," said Roger. "It's common sense really. Start the school year off in September, same as usual, but don't keep sending the kids home and back every few hours. Get it all done in one go, all out of the way. No weekends, no half terms, nothing. No traffic on the roads all the time, less pollution, less accidents. I know it'd be tough at first but we'd finish the whole school year by mid-October! Just think, over ten months holiday a year!"

"Champion!" commented Mr Capstick through clenched teeth as he re-lit his pipe.

"And as for their argument about the kids getting tired and falling asleep in lessons…"

"Pah! Happens in my lessons all the time, Roger!"

Jules had come in early to make sure everything was ready for the start of the Year 10 mock exam season. He went to the Main Hall where Bob was happily humming a tune that had been in his head since his recent trip to Rome. The wobbly desks and hard plastic chairs were all set out in rows again in accordance with regulations and a large clock was displayed on the screen on the stage. A small heater was plugged in near the fire exit but it had always proved to be about as effective as pouring a kettle of boiling water into the North Sea.

Bob had been in the process of labelling each desk with its own numbered sticker when he'd paused to study some interesting graffiti. Most desks in the school had the names of the young lovers Adam and Sonya scratched into them but he'd found the initials of another romantic pair written on the side of one desk in black marker pen. Was that *JS* or *IS* next to *TC*?

"There's so much to do," Jules exclaimed as he came in, looking round at the hall. "I don't know how I'm meant to fit it all in. You're an absolute darling getting all this set up, Bobby."

He put the box of exam papers on the stage and checked his list. The first exam this morning was Maths without the use of calculators. That would make it easier to administer as the pupils usually didn't have calculators. As the invigilators hadn't turned up Jules started putting the exam papers out on the desks himself.

Turning back to look at his handiwork he'd just realised that he was about twelve exam papers short when there was a commotion out in the corridor. It turned out that Year 9 had come down to assembly, not knowing that the Main Hall was out of action during the exam period.

When Jules looked out into the corridor Madame Loups-Garoux, Head of Year 9, was shepherding the pupils back to their form rooms. Some of the Year 9 form tutors were asking her if assembly was on.

"Allez! Assembly is not on in the Main 'All! Back to your rooms all of you! Dépêchez-vous! 'Ow many times do I 'ave to tell you?"

"Listen very carefully...I shall say zees only once!" yelled a boy called Kyle as he ran off.

Jules went back into the hall, hoping that nobody would set the fire alarm off to add to his problems.

"Bobby," he said. "I'm really sorry to put upon you, but could I ask you a teensy-weensy favour?"

Bob stopped humming his merry tune and looked up uncertainly.

"I've not got enough exam papers and I need to find where the invigilators have got to. And we've got to start on time or there'll be an almighty cock-up for the rest of the day."

The first of the Year 10 pupils were already beginning to arrive in the corridor outside the hall. In preparation for their Maths exam two of the boys were kicking a tennis ball back and forth between them.

"I'd be so grateful," said Jules. He held out an empty cardboard box and a list of names to Bob. "All I need you to do is start getting them in so they're ready for a nine o'clock start."

"What's the box for?" asked Bob, looking inside it.

"They all need to put their mobile phone in it before they are allowed into the hall."

In theory mobile phones weren't even allowed in school but Jules knew there'd be a problem in the exams if he didn't have an amnesty box ready. They could collect them later.

"You're a trooper. A super trooper!" he said, hurrying off towards the nearest photocopier, humming to himself as he went.

When Jules returned shortly after nine, almost every desk in the hall was occupied. As they had been left unsupervised without even their social media for company most of the pupils had got so bored that they'd started looking through the exam paper and discussing what the answers might be. In the absence of any invigilators Bob had diligently stayed with them all but he had had to remain outside the hall where he seemed to be guarding one pupil.

The invigilators hadn't arrived for some reason but Ms Malik, Second-in-Department for Geography, had volunteered and Deirdre the cleaner had said she was free too.

"What's the problem, Bobby?" asked Jules. It wasn't going as well as he'd hoped. Luckily Ms Stonehart hadn't come out of her room to check up on him while the pupils were about.

"You said don't let them in until they've put a mobile phone in the box. This one says he's not got a phone, so I didn't let him in."

Ms Malik took the additional exam papers from Mr Humphreys and opened the door to the hall.

"I thought we weren't allowed mobiles?" said the confused pupil. "My mate had two. Said he'd lend me one if it'd help, yeah?"

So somewhere in the hall is a mobile phone after all, thought Jules as he followed the pupil into the exam room.

"Now, when I tell you to open your exam papers you will have an hour and a half by this clock," said Ms Malik to the Year 10 pupils when they'd finally all settled down. It was nearly quarter to ten. "You may open your exam papers...now!"

The countdown timer started.

"I've always wanted to say that," she said to Jules who was standing beside her.

Deirdre hobbled over to the front of the hall and put her dustpan down on the stage.

"There's a boy over there asking if he can go to the toilet," she reported.

Most pupils had filled in their name, read the introduction and were just about to tackle the first question when the contractors decided they'd drunk enough tea. As an earth-shattering drilling sound broke the complete silence of the exam room, the glass in the windows rattled and any stationery that wasn't nailed down vibrated its way off the desks. Josette's confident smile faded as she realised she would never be able to concentrate enough to find x now.

CHAPTER 24

"The best way to escape from a problem is to solve it."

Whilst Mr O'Brien could quote very little from William Shakespeare the words that had always guided him throughout his life were *"to thine own self be true."* He liked to believe that this principle had led him from his roots in the Channel Islands all the way to his current post as Assistant Head at Wildside Academy. As always he kept himself busy. It didn't matter if the other members of the SLT were rarely on the corridors or spent more time on social media or gambling websites than they did working. It was up to him to do what was right, what was decent. It didn't matter if Janine was more likely to listen to Lynne and Sharon than to his suggestions. He would continue to do what he could to help Wildside Academy go from strength to strength. He would do everything he could to get the school back to where it had been seven years ago when he'd joined. He'd do that for as long as he could, professionally, with a smile on his face, using all the skills at his disposal.

The door to the Assistant Heads' office crashed open and Ms Winter came in, followed by Ms Payne.

"Well that's what Sean says and he should know," Ms Payne was saying as she navigated her way across to her desk without looking up from her mobile phone.

"Brill!" Ms Winter agreed, finishing the last of her raspberry doughnut and licking the sugar off her fingers. "Eric needs to do chocolate ones of them, yeah? I'm having too much fruit these days."

Sam O'Brien looked up from his laptop but the other two Assistant Heads seemed not to notice that he was busy working. It was a shame there wasn't really anywhere else he could go. Although he taught more than all the other members of the SLT put together he didn't have a classroom to call his own, teaching in Mr Milton and Mr O'Reilly's rooms. As senior management it didn't seem the correct etiquette to intrude in the teachers' workroom either. There was a little storeroom next to the Assistant Heads' office but it belonged to the MFL and Geography Departments. Anyway there wasn't room to swing an Ofsted inspector round in it as it was largely full of boxes of blue squared paper or bags of plastic fruit and old clothes for some reason.

Mr O'Brien returned to his screen. The minutes from the Local Headteachers' meeting he'd attended were full of good examples of best practice that he could share with colleagues. There was an attachment about how to improve literacy across the school and fun activities that could be planned for World Book Day.

"Lynne," said Mr O'Brien, looking up. "Sorry to interrupt you. I've just been sent an email with some really good ideas for World Book Day. Do you want me to forward it to you? I know it's not till March but it'll give us all time to plan."

The Literacy Co-ordinator for Wildside Academy paused briefly in her conversation. "Dunno. Don't mind really. Yeah, you could do. Send it to Sharon and I so's we can work on it together, yeah? Brill!"

"So anyway," said Ms Payne, not leaving her friend enough time to thank Mr O'Brien, "they do a sort of special rate on weekends away with a spa treatment…"

Mr O'Brien forwarded the email and opened up the next one. He'd been copied into one from Ms Shakespeare in the English Department. For reasons he didn't quite understand Ms Winter had outsourced a lot of the book scrutinies to other people. In unguarded moments she said it was because she was too busy to do them all herself and that delegation was a good skill, yeah? At other times, after some reflection, she also said it was good career development for younger teachers. Either way it didn't seem professional to sign your emails with the nickname Shazza.

As a Maths teacher Mr O'Brien could spot patterns and could do calculations. Comparing the results on the handful of work scrutinies Ms Shakespeare had attached he could tell that things really didn't add up.

Mr Gordon's work scrutiny for DT had scored a Grade 1, the

top grade, in every category but somehow the overall grade awarded was a 4 with the words *"well unsatisfactory"* added for additional clarity. Mr Cocker's Geography work scrutiny again ticked every top box but clearly the fact that one pupil had not underlined a title for one piece of work was enough to warrant a 4 overall. An old one from Mr Chang's Art lesson had been attached, concluding that there was *"too much drawing and no real checking of spelling, punctuation and gramar."* Perhaps, thought Mr O'Brien, that was just a typo on Ms Shakespeare's part.

He checked over Mr Haddenough's work scrutiny as he knew that Ivor was meticulous in everything he did.

Mr Haddenough (MFL Dept.)	All 1	Most 2	Some 3	None 4	Additional comments
Books scrutinized	Year 8 Set 4 - Ringo Hamilton-Potts.				
Is assessment regular and frequent?	X				
Have pieces of sustained work been marked?	X				
Has self and peer assessment been done?	X				
Have meaningful targets been set leading to subsequent progress?		X			One book out of the 34 had its target sticker stuck upside-down.
Is incorrect spelling, punctuation and grammar corrected using the correct marking codes?	X				
Have pupils evidenced the 8 Wildside Values in their work?		X			
Has Homework been completed in accordance with the School policy and are titles underlined?	X				

OVERALL GRADE : 4 (Unsatisfactory.)
Signed : Ms Shakespeare.

Interestingly the work scrutinies Ms Shakespeare had carried out in the English Department all qualified as Grade 1, Outstanding, no matter which boxes she'd ticked. Mr O'Brien chose Miss Hughes' feedback at random for comparison.

Miss Hughes (English Dept.)	All 1	Most 2	Some 3	None 4	Additional comments
Books scrutinized	Daniel Goodlad, Freya McCann (Year 7, Set 1.)				
Is assessment regular and frequent?			X		Lucy will have given outstanding verbal feedback in class.
Have pieces of sustained work been marked?				X	Longer work will have been done on mini Whiteboards.
Has self and peer assessment been done?		X			Pupils have marked the books well. Most in green pen.
Have meaningful targets been set leading to subsequent progress?			X		This will be more obvious when *Lord of the Flies* is finished.
Is incorrect spelling, punctuation and grammar corrected using the correct marking codes?			X		It would be demoralizing and wrong to correct all of the spelling misstakes. Lucy has the right balance.
Have pupils evidenced the 8 Wildside Values in their work?			X		Sticker on front inside cover of most books. Where missing pupils were absent.
Has Homework been completed in accordance with the School policy and are titles underlined?				X	N/A. Homework is silent reading of *Lord of the Flies* most weeks or learning spellings.

OVERALL GRADE : ONE (Outstanding.)
Signed : Shazza.
All books are being marked to a very high standard in line with guidance from Billy. Well done, Lucy! Cheers for the books!

Mr O'Brien read the additional comments at the bottom of Miss Hughes' feedback. He wouldn't describe himself as a suspicious man but he did wonder whether Ms Shakespeare had mentioned Mr Kaye to justify that she was just following orders if it was wrong. Could the last line imply that Miss Hughes had bribed her for a good report with a drink at The Cock 'n' Bull or was this just the standard way the English Department spoke? Mr O'Brien had an idea.

"Lynne. Sorry to bother you again," he said. "I know how

busy you are."

Ms Winter looked up from the filing cabinet where she was sure she'd put some cans of diet cola.

"Yeah? What?"

"I was just thinking," said Mr O'Brien. "You must be really busy and Victoria's off at the moment, so would you like me to help with a few work scrutinies?"

"I wish I had as much free time as you," muttered Ms Payne as her phone pinged urgently with a message from Sean.

"Yeah," said Ms Winter, peering at Mr O'Brien as she put her glasses back on. "That'd be well brill! I'm bogged down with shedloads of stuff at the mo. Literacy and stuff. I was going to pass these on to Shazza. There's too many for Sharon and I. Cheers!"

Maybe that was indeed how the English Department all thanked each other, thought Mr O'Brien, as he collected the pile of exercise books she'd indicated. The sooner he got these done, the sooner the pupils could work in their books again.

By break time Mr O'Brien had worked his way through all the exercise books. As far as he could see his results seemed a little bit more consistent. He was pleased with Miss White's books but the rest of the English Department was rather disappointing, especially Mr Kay whose language was a little colourful at times.

Mr O'Brien looked at the clock above the door. It would be breaktime soon and whilst it wasn't his day on the duty rota he always liked to go and help out if he could.

He'd be able to scan in the work scrutinies he'd done and send them to the relevant teachers when he got back. He looked down at the last one he'd done. It should help to redress the balance when everybody was looking for something to upload to Bright Sky.

Mr Haddenough (MFL Dept.)	All 1	Most 2	Some 3	None 4	Additional comments
Books scrutinized	Alice Gregfind (Y7), Ringo Hamilton-Potts (Y8), Ashton Bansen (Y9), Kylie Robinson (Y10), Erwin Sloth (Y11), Joe Wettloch (Y11.)				
Is assessment regular and frequent?	X				Marking is of a high standard in each year group with individual motivational comments.
Have pieces of sustained work been marked?	X				Regular pieces of written work have been set and marked thoroughly.
Has self and peer assessment been done?	X				Pupils have marked work and it has also been checked by the teacher.
Have meaningful targets been set leading to subsequent progress?	X				Pupils always respond to the teacher's comments and subsequent progress is evident.
Is incorrect spelling, punctuation and grammar corrected using the correct marking codes?	X				The school policy is followed and the correction of spellings is very beneficial in later pieces of work. Regular vocab tests.
Have pupils evidenced the 8 Wildside Values in their work?	X				Pupils have translated the School Values into French and written a poem about them. Fantastique!
Has Homework been completed in accordance with the School policy and are titles underlined?	X				As well as written HW it is clear that pupils are learning vocab, doing spoken presentations in French and completing online tasks.

OVERALL GRADE : ONE (Outstanding.)
Signed : Mr O'Brien, Assistant Head.

Thank you for your outstanding marking, Mr Haddenough. This is exactly what Ofsted are looking for and as a consistently effective marker you should share what you do with your colleagues.

FEBRUARY

CHAPTER 25

"Great oaks from little acorns grow."

Delores couldn't wait to get home. She was so excited that she sneaked past Darren when he wasn't looking and went up to the zebra crossing by Tangelo's tanning studio instead. Technically it was further but it'd still be quicker. She just didn't want to hurt Darren's feelings.

As she pushed the wheelie bin back into the little yard behind Number 9 Coronation Street a sweet yet sour aroma drifted across from The Golden Dragon nearby. She let herself in by the back door, dumped her school bag by the washing machine and called out to see who else was home. Darwin sauntered into the kitchen, purring to see if anybody would feed him. The tune to *Four in a Bed* was just finishing as her Mum came through from the front room.

"Hello, Princess," she said. "That time already? The day just flies by once you're gone. Your brother back yet?" She started to search for some fish fingers in the freezer. "You had a good day, Princess?"

"It was great. We not only had Science period 1 but Ms Shakespeare was off again so we had Mr Armani for English too."

Two hours with her favourite teacher. She'd even plucked up the courage to tell him about how she wanted to be a vet.

"Can you get something for Darwin, Princess?" her Mum asked as the bag of chips she was holding spilt onto the floor.

"Guess what," continued Delores breathlessly, the cat momentarily forgotten. "I got my end-of-term report!"

"Already?"

"For last term," said Delores. "There was a problem with the printer or something."

She ran to get it from her bag. As she was in Year 7 this was the first summary of how she was settling into "big school" that Wildside Academy had supplied. It was a momentous occasion. The first hint of whether she'd be able to spend her life caring for sick animals was awaiting her in this envelope.

"I don't know if they email it to you as well," she said. "Here it is. Samantha in 7A said the wi-fi was down."

Delores passed the envelope to her Mum and they sat down together on the sofa with a packet of chocolate biscuits. It was what they called MAD : their special Mother And Daughter time in the afternoon.

It was at that point that her brother arrived home.

"That you, Darren?" called his Mum. "Are you wanting fish fingers too?"

Darren Froggett mumbled something about taxis parking on double yellow lines and teachers not crossing over properly and went up to his room. As he slammed his bedroom door the lollipop stick fell over by the washing machine and Darwin made a bolt for freedom. Within moments the incessant mind-numbing screams of Zombie Kombat could be heard upstairs, along with occasional swearing.

Mrs Froggett opened the envelope and pulled out a sheet of paper. *Attendance 100%, Punctuality 100%, Behaviour Points 0.* Delores explained to her Mum that Behaviour Points were a bad thing so zero was actually the best she could get. Mrs Froggett wondered why the school didn't seem to recognise Achievement Points but said nothing as her daughter was still so excited.

YEAR 7 REPORT	*Delores Froggett,* 7X
Form Tutor : *Mr Ball*	*Delores* has made a *good* start to this year. *Delores* has settled in *well* at Wildside Academy and contributes *well* to L4L discussions in form time. He/she *is Assistant Form Monitor.*
Head of Year : *Miss White*	*Delores* has settled in *well* at Wildside Academy. *Delores* is *always smartly dressed* and the pupil's attendance and punctuality are *excellent.* *Delores* is making particularly good progress in *Science.* Well done!
Headteacher : **Ms Stonehart** *HT, DIHR, TGCSEC, CPT, BPB.*	I am pleased with how well *Daniel* has settled into Wildside Academy. I am sure that under my leadership this pupil will go from strength to strength.

As she hadn't ever looked at the school website Mrs Froggett didn't know who Ms Stonehart was but Delores was clearly in good hands. The Headteacher had so many impressive qualifications after her name. She'd met Miss White at the introductory Parents' Evening in the summer term. Delores had enjoyed looking round the school and having a go with some fancy machine that had made her hair stand on end. She'd always loved Science and her Head of Year's comments were very encouraging. It seemed that both Miss White and Mr Ball had got to know her little Princess so well in such a short time. She read through the other teachers' comments.

With the exception of Drama which had been left blank, all her teachers commented on how well *Delores* had settled into English/Maths/Science and so on and how *this pupil* is very enthusiastic and works well. Mr O'Reilly, her Maths teacher, had also commented on her ability to find x with increasing precision. Going by the consistency in her teachers' comments her little Princess was clearly doing consistently well. In the words of this Ms Stonehart she was obviously going to go from strength to strength.

"It's really good, isn't it, Mum?" beamed Delores. "What does Mr Armani say?"

She ran her finger down the identical boxes to find the words that her Science teacher had selected about her.

| Science : | *Delores* has settled into Science *very* well. |
| Mr Armani | *Delores* is *very* enthusiastic and works *very* well. |

Delores found herself wondering which University Mr Armani had studied Science at because ideally she'd like to go there too.

"You've done very well, Princess," said her Mum. "I think this deserves more than just a chocolate biscuit or two. You have a think about what you want to do as a special treat this weekend."

Mrs Froggett put the report down for a moment and gave her daughter a hug. Her little Princess had worked so hard. Reports looked so different from when she had gone to Wildside School in the days when old Mr Abercrombie had been in charge. They'd even changed in the time since Darren had left the school but then it had become one of these Academy things since then so things were bound to be better now. Darren used to get good comments for Drama and that was about it. She could still remember what his Geography teacher, Mr Dowson, had written one year. *"Geography is not Darren's strong point. I am amazed he can even find his way home."* There was some truth in that comment, particularly when Darren had turned up late for his exam and failed Geography GCSE. The old reports had been in black-and-white. Perhaps the fancy coloured boxes all over Delores' report were just for decoration?

"Well done, Princess," she said as she got up to go through to the kitchen. The smoke detector was almost managing to drown out the screams blasting out from Darren's room. "I'm so proud of you."

Delores looked at the target boxes on her report. There were a couple of green ones to show that she was making Outstanding Progress in two subjects. She even had one yellow box to show Satisfactory Progress in French. It was just a shame that the majority of the subjects were shaded red to show Unsatisfactory Progress. If only she hadn't done so well at Primary School the computer wouldn't have challenged her to reach such high goals. Mr Ball had explained that they were called "aspirational targets" and said that he had some too. It was all to do with something called algorithms apparently. Still at least her progress in Mr Armani's lessons meant that Science was shaded in green. He'd be pleased about that.

As her Mum needed to put some more fish fingers under the grill Delores went up to her room to make a start on the Science project she'd been given for homework. She had already decided that at the weekend she'd ask her Mum if her treat could be to go shopping in Berryfield. She wanted to get Mr Armani a Valentine's card.

CHAPTER 26

"Always read between the lines."

Mr Cocker was teaching Geography again. Or, if we're going to be more accurate, Mr Cocker was supervising his Year 8 Geography class as they completed their end-of-unit assessment in complete silence. He was there with them in person but to be honest he was elsewhere, considering his next move in the online chess game he was playing in the evenings. He had no idea who his opponent was in real life but he suspected that they must be a grandmaster as he'd only ever managed to win once in two years. He was awoken from his reverie by a boy putting his hand up on the front row.

"Sir, what do we do when we've finished?"

Mr Cocker mentally replaced his bishop before answering.

"Have you checked through it? Coloured everything in, making sure you haven't gone over the lines?"

Callum nodded vigorously.

"Have you put your name on your booklet?"

Callum checked, added his name and then nodded again.

"Can I read, sir?"

It seemed like a sensible suggestion even though in a GCSE exam Callum would be required to sit in silence if he finished early. There were seven minutes to go till the end of the lesson. He might look like an angel but left to sit in silence for even just seven minutes Callum would soon find a way to disrupt every other pupil in the room. And he couldn't just give him something from *"Exploring Geography Through Pictures and Worksheets"* while the other pupils were still answering questions in case they cheated.

"Please, sir?"

"Of course," said Mr Cocker. "I'll take your answer booklet

in then."

As Callum pulled out a book about the sinking of the Titanic Mr Cocker looked through his completed answer booklet. Having struggled to label most of the countries on the map Callum had just resorted to labelling Australia as *"Down Under"* and everything else as *"Up Over."* For the question where he had to give an example of a country that had changed its name he had decided that *"New Zealand used to be called Old Zealand."* It seemed that Callum wouldn't have scored too highly if he'd attempted Ms Malik's fun quiz about flags either. On the question where he'd had to draw out three flags he'd drawn the Finnish flag looking like the chequered flag used in the Grand Prix. It was typical of Callum's way of looking at the world that although he hadn't got any of the actual questions right he'd chosen to volunteer the observation that *United Arab Emirates*, like *Canada*, was made up of alternating vowels and consonants. Mr Cocker really wanted to give him a mark for that.

"Sir," asked Callum, genuinely interested, "you know how they say everybody can remember where they were when Kennedy was shot? Well, where were you when the Titanic sank?"

With just five minutes to go until the home time bell Ms Winter decided to choose that moment to do a drop-in lesson observation. She made as much noise as if she'd actually dropped in by parachute, startling some of the pupils who were busy concentrating on their final answers. Never far away Ms Payne stayed in the corridor as she had something more important to do on her phone.

"Don't mind me," Ms Winter smiled. A girl near the front of the room started picking up the pencil case that the Assistant Head had sent flying as she'd charged in.

"I'm sure you shouldn't be out of your seat," she snapped at the girl. Going to Weight2Go! each week had probably seemed like a good New Year's resolution when Ms Winter had signed up after Christmas. Unfortunately for everybody else it was having no noticeable effect other than making her more irritable. Shazza had been the same with dry January.

Ms Winter looked at the board and noticed that there were no Learning Objectives on it, proof in itself that the pupils could not by definition be learning anything. Looking through Mr Cocker's planning folder she tutted when she found that some of his planning had been written on the old forms where the school logo still had a grey background. Worse still, the lesson plan for today was simply labelled *"End of Unit 2 Assessment – Countries of the World."* There was no detail to tell her what each question was about, no differentiation, no reference to previous learning, no clue as to where each question fitted into the Scheme of Work. Nothing! Not being a Geography teacher, how was she meant to know what was going on? She threw the folder back on to the desk impatiently and left.

The whole of Mr Cocker's teaching ability would thus be encapsulated by what Ms Winter as Assistant Head in charge of Teaching and Learning believed she had seen in that one minute.

When Mr Cocker received his feedback via email a week later he was mildly surprised that Ms Winter's most vehement attack concerned the fact that a pupil had been sitting quietly reading a History book in a Geography lesson. Her comment that there was *"no place for this sort of thing and it's got to immediately stop at once"* left him wondering whether she was trying to stop people studying History or just reading generally. Tim, being Tim, did send a carefully worded reply to her email explaining why there had been a pupil reading a book in the school.

A week later all staff received an email from Ms Winter. The irony of her concern was not lost on Mr Cocker but for once he didn't reply when he'd read it. He was too busy reading a book entitled *"How to improve your Chess game in thirty easy steps!"*

From : LWR - LWinter@WildsideAcademy
To : AllStaff@WildsideAcademy
Sent : Wed 13 Feb 11:57
Subject : Reading, literacy, books and stuff

Hiya!

Just to let you now that its become obvious to Sharon and I as we've dropped in for drop-in lesson observations this week that the kid's level of literacy isn't as good as what it should be really.

As a school Wildside Academy is going from strength to strength but the kids aren't reading enough books and stuff.

If any of yous can think of ways of getting the kids to read more please could you email your ideas either to Sharon or I. We're thinking of setting up a working party so let us know if you want to be in on that to, yeah? There might also be food too. As Shazza would say - Let's get this party started!

Cheers!
Lynne
Assistant Head i/c Teaching & Leaning,
Literacy Co-ordinator, Advanced Skills Teacher for English.

It didn't come as a great surprise that Ms Winter had received at least one reply by the close of business.

From : MMK - MMalik@WildsideAcademy
To :   LWR - LWinter@WildsideAcademy
CC :   AllStaff@WildsideAcademy
Sent : Wed 13 Feb 12:05
Subject : Working Party

Good afternoon,

I think that sounds like a really good idea. It's so important to help the pupils with their literacy as this will improve their results in all their subjects, not just English and Geography. Please can I help with the working party? My room is free if you need a venue as I'm in there most nights, either marking and planning or teaching revision classes.

Thanks again,
Mina,
Second-in-Department for Geography.

CHAPTER 27

"No two people ever read the same book."

As the Assistant Head in charge of Teaching and Learning, the question of raising the standard of literacy amongst the pupils continued to go through Ms Winter's mind from time to time. Particularly when Ms Stonehart had called another emergency meeting of her SLT. All she'd be able to report back was that the Literacy Working Party had met four times now and had decided that the pupils needed to read more books. That might be enough for Ms Stonehart at this point as she knew Ms Winter was particularly busy at the moment, looking at how to reduce staffing.

As it turned out Ms Stonehart was in a good mood as she'd received an email to say that her telescope was finally arriving that afternoon. She was able to start the SLT meeting with the good news.

"Norma is just finalizing the plans for Professor Brian Cox to come and cut a ribbon to declare the Wildside Academy Telescope officially open," she said. "We should have some good photos for the website, Richard."

"As long as we don't get that Scottish actor," grumbled Mr Wingett. "Bet he knows nothing about the wonders of the solar system!"

"Sean Connery?" asked Ms Payne, only half listening as she quickly switched her mobile phone to vibrate. The last time she'd gone to the cinema was with Sean Devlin and they hadn't really seen a lot of the film.

As the telescope hadn't yet arrived Ms Stonehart had had to resort to Plan B to find out what USA were up to just by looking on their website. As she'd searched amongst the photos of happy people, the inspiring stories and the clearly impossible data, she kept coming across something called Literacy. When she'd checked she found out that not only was it something Wildside Academy should be focusing on but they actually had somebody in charge of it already. As Assistant Head it was part of Ms Winter's job description.

"Now as Headteacher I have a very hands-on approach as you know," she addressed the five members of her SLT. "You've no idea what a responsible job it is but under my leadership Wildside Academy is going from strength to strength. Even so I mustn't deny you the chance to develop professionally and so today I'm going to ask Lynne to lead the discussion on where we are with..." she glanced at her notes, "Literacy."

Having not received an agenda for the meeting Ms Winter was going to have to talk without having the facts to hand but in fairness that didn't usually seem to stop her. Some people talk because they have something to say and some people talk because they have to say something. In situations like this Ms Winter fell into the second category.

"So, yeah, Literacy will mean different things to different people, you know?" Ms Winter began. "But deep down each one of us are a teacher of English, not just Sharon and I. Now I know you should never ever generalize but it'd be brill if we can all work together to make the kids' literacy lots more better than what it is now. And that can be something as simple as checking you don't start sentences with conjunctions, yeah? Or making sure you realise that prepositions aren't something what you're ending sentences with. Double negatives are a no-no too. I could go on but you don't need all the technical stuff. We're very unique as English teachers as we get to speak English literally all day with the kids but there's stuff what you can do even if you're only teaching Maths or PE, you know?"

Mr Thicke and Mr Wingett, having only ever taught Maths, looked like the only time they were interested in the alphabet was when $a^2 + b^2 = c^2$. Perhaps aware of their discomfort Ms Stonehart decided to open the discussion up.

"So what do you all think we can do then?"

The two Deputy Heads seemed quite interested in the grain of the mahogany desk. Mr O'Brien was the first to speak.

"Can I just tell you about the meeting I went to last week?" he began.

Whether it was a rhetorical question or not, Ms Stonehart nodded, allowing him to continue.

"I went to the first of the Local Headteachers' meetings on Thursday evening…"

"To delegate for me," Ms Stonehart clarified hurriedly. "I'm too busy to attend every meeting they want me to go to."

"Thank you for giving me the chance to go," continued Mr O'Brien, diplomatically. His daughter Rosie had had to miss ballet class that evening but she knew how important Daddy's work was. "It's interesting because they were discussing ideas for how they can use World Book Day next month to help pupils improve their literacy."

Ms Winter suddenly remembered that she'd heard something about World Book Day somewhere and had meant to look into it.

"Sorry, Sam, but World Book Day is like one of the options that we discussed about at the Literacy Working Party discussions, yeah? We've already got that one covered."

"Well," continued Mr O'Brien, "it seems a lot of schools have a library and the evidence suggests that if pupils read books it can push all their GCSE results up by a minimum of one grade. Not just in English."

"You know that 87.6% of statistics are just made up though," said Mr Thicke feeling he should add something to the discussion but having no more facts to hand than his colleagues.

Ms Stonehart was trying to do her own calculations in her head. The cost of building and stocking a library balanced against the value that any photos of it on the website would bring to the business.

"I'll have a conversation with Alex," she said, "but I'd say there isn't the funding for a whole library. Maybe a bookcase in one of the English rooms. We've only just finished getting the drive done."

"I was talking to one Headteacher," continued Mr O'Brien, not wanting to refer to Mr Hoskins by name, "who said they've got displays about Literacy. Each teacher has a laminated board on their door where they tell everybody what they're reading. "*Mr O'Brien is reading… 'How to boil a frog'…*", that kind of thing."

"That sounds like a much more economical way of doing things," said Ms Stonehart. "Would that fit in with your thinking,

Lynne?"

"Well, yeah, but what were they suggesting for World Book Day then?" She looked to Mr O'Brien for ideas.

"There were loads of ideas for raising the profile of reading. Dressing up as characters from classic fiction. Teachers giving assemblies about their favourite books to show that adults read too. Everybody off timetable for the last half hour of the day to do silent reading. Competitions where pupils take a photo of themselves reading a book in an unusual place. Book reviews. Peer reading. A creative writing workshop. Poetry recitals. A competition involving making bookmarks. Literary quotes on the website. Guest speakers from…"

Ms Winter was taking notes as quickly as she could.

"Yeah, I don't think there's literally anything what we didn't come up with at my meetings," she said. Ms Payne was looking through the list and nodding in agreement with her friend.

"And there's shedloads of good stuff going on here already," continued Ms Winter. "I did a drop-in the other day and it was really brill that the teacher was letting pupils read books when they'd finished their assessment. I can't remember who it was but it was an utter brill use of time. We've literally got to use every opportunity to improve the kids' literacy and make it better, yeah?"

"Well thank you all for your contributions," said Ms Stonehart. "Let me know what you plan to do on this World Book Day thing. I think we've moved it all on a great deal today."

It was time to finish though as she was expecting a delivery.

CHAPTER 28

"The road to Hell is paved with good intentions."

The resurfacing of the staff car park was finally finished and as nobody famous could be found to declare it officially open after a week it was agreed that staff could now use it. Other than the new STOP sign and the absence of the workmen's rusty vans and equipment it didn't really look any different to how it had before. Never were so many inconvenienced for so long for so little. It had probably cost a lot of money but as a result the school gates now seemed to be permanently jammed open.

As Head Caretaker Bob took his job quite literally and kept himself busy, hoping that he would again win employee of the term. At the moment he was standing all alone in the middle of the front field hammering a sign he'd made into the ground. *"Do not throw stones at this sign!"* was the awkwardly written message. Stan came over to explain to him why the sign really wasn't needed but he was probably just jealous of Bob for having won the award and shown some initiative.

Over by the school entrance two pupils were studying another sign, the road sign that read "Slow Children!" It looked as though they were trying to decide whether it was referring to them.

Mr Chang was glad that he could park his car on the school premises again. Pausing only to look at the spot where his lost masterpiece was buried he optimistically decided to see the new tarmac as just another blank canvas. The possibilities were exciting really. Then he noticed that some other artist had already started adding their mark to the car park before him. The sign that had initially read *"Wildside Academy does not accept any responsibility for anything stolen from vehicles or any damage to vehicles however caused"* had been spray painted over so that it now just announced that *"Wildside Academy does not accept any responsibility for anything!"*

He carefully carried the boxes that his cousin Jimmy had given him inside, making space in his boot for the completed canvases he then brought down from his classroom. He decided to leave *'Crimson Orb'* up in there until he'd worked out why it wasn't popular. There was no accounting for taste.

There were only a few teachers in the staff room as Mr Chang sneaked in quietly and made his way round the corner to the pigeonholes. Nobody had paid him any attention. Ms Grimley was too busy searching through the fridge for her lunchbox, convinced that somebody had already stolen it. Mr Digby was hidden behind a pile of marking in the quiet corner. Brigadier Vernon-Smythe was reading a copy of *"Exchange and Mart"* as he made phone calls. Mr Chang's own pigeonhole was empty apart from a ten-page supplement to Mr Thicke's plans for a paperless office. Looking along the rows of pigeonholes he could see that there was just enough space to plant what he needed in each one for maximum impact. Nobody would probably be going near the pigeonholes for another half an hour so his timing was perfect. He just needed to set everything up carefully and then get out of the way. He'd worked at the school for nearly twelve years and had never ever considered doing anything like this before. Hopefully what he was planning would make people sit up and think about how they treated each other. Mr Chang opened the first of his cousin's boxes, looked round to check that he wasn't being watched, and then carefully and methodically began putting one tiny package into each pigeonhole except his own. As he was often one of the first to arrive at school he hoped that when the dust settled nobody would have the time to work out who was responsible. Mr Chang closed the staffroom door as quietly as he could and made his way down the corridor, convinced that nobody had seen him. He looked at the clock in the canteen as he passed. There were just twenty minutes left...

Oil paints, watercolours, pencils, charcoal and coloured inks had all been used when Mr Chang realised that the bell was about to go and he would have to let the pupils in. *"The Direction of Confusion"* would probably turn out to be one of the best things he'd ever painted but for now it would have to wait.

He opened the door to let his Year 10 class in and began wiping red paint off his fingers with a cloth.

"Ooh, sir! Looks like you've been caught red-handed!" sniggered a tall girl as she came in.

"Morning, sir," said the boy behind her. "Did you see that goal in the second 'alf?

Once Chris Merton had discovered that Mr Chang supported the same football team he always wanted to know his views on every match. Year 10 were working on a project where they had to express artistically what they thought "Freedom" was.

"I want to always make my own decisions," said Grace when Mr Chang went over to look at her work, "but what do you think, sir?"

She had partially completed a painting of a cat making its way through a cat flap, halfway towards freedom.

"There's an excellent feeling of depth in what you're doing there, Grace," he said encouragingly. "I like it."

"Did you know the first cat flap was invented by Sir Isaac Newton, sir?" asked the boy sitting next to Grace. Archie was a mine of information and appropriately he was busy drawing a rocket ship fighting to break free of gravity.

Circulating round the room Mr Chang looked at all the other variations on the theme. The largest was propped up in the corner as its creator, a boy called George, was off today. Clearly a fan of science-fiction films George's creation was made of papier mâché and showed a man who'd been frozen in carbon, his face caught in a scream, his hands reaching out. Mr Chang knew the film well but the more he stood and studied George's interpretation of "Freedom" the more he thought he recognised a different face in it. George had sculpted the features of Mr Taylor, the Headteacher who had mysteriously disappeared when the school had converted to an Academy. It was actually so realistic that for a moment it seemed that Steve Taylor was still here even though Ms Stonehart was now running the empire.

When Year 10's lesson ended Mr Chang found himself once again standing in front of George's project, studying its features. For some reason he couldn't explain he felt a great disturbance. Maybe it was just something he'd eaten? They had had quite a lot last night. He let his Year 9 class into the room and started distributing Keith Haring pictures for them to copy and colour in, keeping within the lines. It was at times like this he felt like a Geography teacher but Mrs Thorne said he either did that or a project on David Hockney.

"Sir, is it true?" asked a girl called Fleur. "Joshua says it's impossible to write on a rubber with a pencil?"

"Course it is, innit?" said Joshua. "Makes sense, yeah? Rubs it out all the time."

The argument wasn't going to be settled however as at that point the windchimes above the door tinkled gently. The door at the end of the corridor had been opened and so the draught had triggered Mr Chang's early warning system. When the door to his classroom opened thirty seconds later pupils were working, Learning Objectives were on the board and he was ready for anybody who wanted to drop in.

To his surprise it wasn't Ms Winter or even Ms Payne who'd arrived but Mr Wingett no less.

"Right leave all this," he said bluntly to Mr Chang, "and follow me."

"Now?" asked Mr Chang, "but I've got Year 9."

Mr Wingett had paused to look at a copy of Munch's "*The Scream*" hanging on the wall that had been painted by Graham Reaper. He seemed to nod before turning back to address the class.

"Just get on with it," he said. "And don't mess with glitter."

"So what's going on?" asked Mr Chang as they made their way downstairs leaving the class unattended.

"Janine wants to see you about what you put in everybody's pigeonhole. We know it was you."

Leonardo da Vinci, one of Mr Chang's favourite artists, once said that everything connects to everything else. There was clearly some truth in this, highlighted by the fact that the phone number of Wildside Academy where Mr Chang worked was virtually the same as that of The Golden Dragon which belonged to his cousin, Jimmy Wong. As they'd shared a family meal the night before to celebrate the Chinese New Year Jimmy had commented on how much extra business they got when people thought they were phoning the school but got the restaurant. A great believer in Random Acts of Kindness Jimmy Wong had suggested that his cousin take in fortune cookies for everybody working at the school and leave them as a surprise. Somebody, perhaps Mr Wingett himself, had worked out that they were from him and now he was being summoned down so that Ms Stonehart herself could thank him in person. He'd be embarrassed if she made him employee of the term but it looked like his fortune cookie last night had been right. *"Recognition of your actions will lead you on the road to fulfilment."* It was always nice when somebody recognised what you did and Jimmy would be pleased that his thoughtfulness had been acknowledged too.

Nobody at Wildside Academy ever saw Mr Lee Chang again. It was as if he'd been airbrushed out. Although no official message was ever issued to explain Mr Chang's sudden disappearance a story did eventually find its way back to the PE Department office via Mr Cocker. According to what he'd heard whilst chatting to Mr Wong one evening, Ms Stonehart had not been impressed by what she'd found in her fortune cookie. She'd taken it very personally and had had Mr Chang escorted off the premises faster than you could say "Happy Chinese New Year!"

"Flippin' 'eck!" exclaimed Jim Fitt as he listened to Tim tell his story. "And what 'ad she got in t'cookie then?"

"The message in Ms Stonehart's fortune cookie," said Tim, pausing for effect, "Headteacher of Wildside Academy, a school that goes from strength to strength…"

"Go on!" encouraged Mike Stringer.

"The message to Ms Stonehart was *"You will have great leadership skills in the future!"* In the future! She didn't like it!"

Ironically the painting *"Crimson Orb"* was sold to a parent who saw it at a Parents' Evening the following term when he turned up expecting to see Mr Chang. The money raised was added to the funds of Wildside Academy.

MARCH

CHAPTER 29

*"If you are not willing to risk the unusual
you will have to settle for the ordinary."*

For Mr Cocker Fairtrade Week was even more exciting than a boxset of *Midsomer Murders* and a family bag of prawn crisps. With the help of those teachers who cared he produced a series of cross-curricular activities each year to highlight why Fairtrade is important and what everybody can do to help. Ms Malik, Second-in-Department for Geography, had even adapted her *"Spot each country's flag!"* quiz so that pupils could label where Fairtrade products come from. The pupils always enjoyed seeing Mr Cocker tottering down the corridor dressed as a giant banana. He'd struggle to get through doorways, stairs were a serious hazard for him and he could never see who was behind him. They loved it.

In the canteen Tim had talked Eric the chef into putting on a special menu for the week with dishes from around the world. The Finance Department had agreed to it without hesitation as Mr Goldbloom had seen it as a justifiable reason to increase the price of meals. The first day had gone well as the chosen country had been Italy and so nobody had really noticed much of a difference to the menu. Pizza, chips, pizza with chips, chips with pizza, extra chips. Today's theme was Mexican food with the Tex-Mex pizza proving to be the most popular choice, followed by *patatas fritas*.

Tim wanted to do something different to raise the profile of Fairtrade this year. As he'd taken his banana costume out of the wardrobe to dust it down at the weekend he'd paused to consider the possibilities. He'd managed to source a large quantity of free bananas that could be handed out in the canteen but now he wasn't sure if that would be such a good idea. After all he'd been the first to hear how Mr Chang's generosity had been repaid when he'd taken gifts in for colleagues. There were rumours that Mr Chang had been dismissed for showing the pupils modern art that Ms Murkett had said was sexist. Tim knew that Lee Chang had once also been accused of being racist. To be fair all he'd said was that all the Julies in the Main Office looked alike to him.

And so it was that Tim found himself squeezed behind a table in the corner of the canteen, still dressed in his bright yellow banana costume. Pupils could help themselves to a free banana, make a donation to Fairtrade if they wished or sign a pledge to try and buy more Fairtrade products in future. With posters created by Mr Cocker's Year 7 IT class stuck up around the canteen, the whole event really was going well. He'd set his laptop up to play the hits of Bananarama on a loop to add to the atmosphere. Adil had even taken a few photos which would hopefully be on the school website when they'd been approved. Having said that, Ms Malik had managed to get herself on to so many of them that it actually looked like she had organised everything with Bananaman as her assistant.

Ms Stonehart had generously agreed that the first day of Fairtrade Week could be a non-uniform day provided pupils made a contribution to school funds. Eager not to be wearing the same uniform as each other they paid their money and all turned up in the same torn jeans and black hoodies. Even staff were allowed to wear what they wanted. Mr Haddenough had found it easier just to put his normal working clothes on. As a result he was probably the only person wearing a tie but he still gave his contribution to school funds as a goodwill gesture. It would help towards another Teaching Assistant.

Mr Haddenough still wasn't sure what he'd done to upset Ms Stonehart but he was getting less and less surprised by the emails he received from her. It was best not to reply to them.

From : JST (Headteacher) - JStonehart@WildsideAcademy
To : IHH - IHaddenough@WildsideAcademy
CC : HBA - HBuonanulla@WildsideAcademy
    LWR - LWinter@WildsideAcademy
FILE : (HR) IHH Personal File
Sent : Mon 04 Mar 13:13
Subject : School dress code policy (male staff)

Mr Haddenough,

    I noticed at briefing in the staffroom this morning that although you were wearing a tie in accordance with Section 4.01(a) of the Staff Handbook the top button of your shirt was, nevertheless, undone.
    Please can you rectify this situation without any delay and ensure that such unprofessional conduct does not happen again.
    Your failure to follow the correct school procedures will be recorded on your confidential personal file in HR once more.

Ms J. Stonehart, Headteacher, Wildside Academy,
Diploma in Human Resources, TGCSEC, CPT, BPB.

Wisdom, **I**nspiration, **L**eadership, **D**etermination, **S**uccess, **I**ntegrity, **D**edication, **E**xcelence.

Tim had managed to get enough bananas for the whole week. All in all he felt it had gone well but today the pupils hadn't seemed as bothered. Either that was because it was the last day or they'd all been more interested in the ambulance that had pulled up on the main drive at the start of lunch.

Tim waddled down to the Finance Office as best he could to hand in the day's donations. Mr Goldbloom had said he'd keep the money safe for him. It was as he was carefully negotiating his way back towards the doors in the Berlin Wall that Mrs Spratt stopped him.

"Mr Cocker," she called out, "Ms Stonehart needs to see you in her office right now."

"Oh. I could do with just popping to the loo," said Tim. It hadn't been easy wearing the banana costume all morning. Keen to promote the cause he'd drunk a lot of Fairtrade coffee.

"I hear what you say," said Mrs Spratt regardless, "but she demands you attend right now."

"Can I ask what it's about?"

"You need to hurry up. She's waiting for you and she doesn't like to be kept waiting," said Mrs Spratt before heading back into her own office.

Ms Stonehart was busy updating her Ofsted counter to 587 days without a visit when Tim knocked on her door. She made herself comfortable behind her desk again, took a leisurely sip of her tea, replaced the cup in the saucer, checked her emails and then commanded him to enter. Tim would have found it hard to sit down even if she had offered him that courtesy.

"Now then, Mr Cocker," she began, "this isn't the first time I've had to summon you to my office. I've just been looking through your confidential file again…"

A large beige folder, bursting with paperwork, lay on the desk before her. Tim could only guess what might be inside it but a sheet of paper sticking out was clearly in Ms Winter's spidery handwriting. He could just see that his name had been crossed out on what looked like a list of names.

"Mrs Ramsbottom is a highly-thought of member of my HR team," Ms Stonehart continued. "The paramedics said she might be off for at least a fortnight."

Tim felt like he'd accidently turned over two pages in the script and hadn't got the foggiest idea what Ms Stonehart was talking about. This wasn't unusual but he felt he ought to say something.

"Mrs Ramsbottom? Irene in Reprographics?" he asked peering out uncomfortably from beneath the yellow latex skin.

"It's no laughing matter," snapped Ms Stonehart.

Tim wasn't actually laughing, no matter how surreal it was that the 'Headteacher' was scolding a giant yellow banana like a naughty child for something he knew nothing about.

"As you well know Mrs Ramsbottom slipped on a banana skin outside the Dining Hall at the start of lunch today. A banana skin that you had brought into the school. Without permission."

Tim hadn't realised he needed permission to bring a banana into school. He'd been eating them at lunchtime for years. More to the point he knew nothing about any accident.

"Now she's off with a broken leg, bruises and possible spinal injuries. The tests also show she has high blood pressure as a result of potassium deficiency." Ms Stonehart didn't seem to see the irony of this but then she did have more important concerns. "I don't know how the photocopying's all going to get done."

"Is she alright?" asked Tim, concerned.

"Well, I suppose there's room for a chair next to the photocopier...As for you bringing unauthorized fruit onto the premises, it clearly states in the Staff Handbook Section 24.8(iii) that..."

She was interrupted by a nervous tap at the door to her office.

"Come!" she commanded.

"I've got that P45 you asked for," said Mrs Spratt, not making any eye contact with Mr Cocker, "but there's a gentleman here wants to see you."

"I asked not to be disturbed!"

"I hear what you say," continued Mrs Spratt hesitantly. "He's not got an appointment but I thought it might be important. He's from *The Wildside Gazette.*"

It was as if the giant banana in the room was suddenly invisible.

"Show him through," exclaimed Ms Stonehart with almost childlike delight.

"I hear what you say," said Mrs Spratt obediently as she left.

When she returned it was with a young man carrying a notepad and a camera. Ms Stonehart motioned for him to sit down before asking him if he'd like a cup of tea. He declined and introduced himself as Fred Bullen, chief features writer on *The Wildside Gazette.*

"It's so good to meet you at last, Ms Stonehart. I've been following your career here, watching Wildside Academy go from strength to strength. It really is quite marvellous what you're achieving."

For once Ms Stonehart almost seemed lost for words. She knew how important it was to keep the press on side when you were running a business like Wildside Academy. She was just wondering where the best place for a photo would be when the journalist turned to include Mr Cocker.

"And this must be the very man I'm looking for."

Somewhat confused, Tim did his best to shake hands with the reporter.

"Mr Cocker?" exclaimed Ms Stonehart incredulously.

"I'd like to do a feature for my editor entitled 'SCHOOL

GOES BANANAS!' I have my sources and I've heard nothing but praise about what Mr Cocker is doing to make the pupils aware of Fairtrade. There are some excellent photos on your website. Very appealing, you might say! This teacher is a real asset to your school, Ms Stonehart. I bet you can't wait for Ofsted to come in and see the great things he's doing."

"Thanks a bunch," smiled Tim.

Ms Stonehart found herself quietly pushing the P45 under the folder and agreeing to have her photo taken beside Mr Cocker. She drew the line at trying to hire a second banana costume for herself though.

CHAPTER 30

"Never judge a book by its cover."

As far as the pupils were concerned the first sign that World Book Day was on the horizon was when laminated boards started appearing in classrooms telling them what each teacher was reading. Some of the titles were possibly genuine (*Ms Grimley is reading... 'Coping with Stress'*), whilst others were probably there to impress (*Ms Malik is reading... 'How to help your pupils fulfil their true potential'.*) Nobody found out who wrote on Reverend James' board in permanent marker. As it read *Rev. James is reading... 'Busty blonde babes'* he had the embarrassment of trying to get a new board from one of the Julies in the HR Department.

Mr O'Brien wasn't sure whether Ms Winter had misunderstood the ideas he'd brought back from the Local Headteachers' meeting or whether she just couldn't read her own scribbled notes. Either way what other schools were doing was getting pupils to celebrate their love of literature by allowing pupils to dress as characters from their favourite book. What was happening in Wildside Academy was that the teachers in the English Department, and nobody else, had turned up in fancy dress.

Ms Winter herself was decked out in a tattered wedding dress with the veil flapping loosely about her unruly hair and a rotting bouquet of flowers in her left hand. She'd even brought along a slice of wedding cake to eat. It was nice that she'd made an effort. Mr O'Brien knew enough about the works of Charles Dickens to realise that she was hoping to look like Ms Havisham from *'Great Expectations.'* Her companion Ms Payne must therefore be the orphan Estella, although the mobile phone was a little anachronistic.

"Break their hearts and have no mercy!" exclaimed Ms Winter as she made her way down the corridor.

Hearing these words Ms Grimley wasn't sure if she was quoting Dickens or preparing for more unexpected lesson observations.

Mr Haddenough had checked that his top button was still properly done up before bringing his form down for assembly. As he was about to follow his class through to the canteen he passed the jilted witch of a woman in the corridor. Ms Winter was accompanied, as ever, by Ms Payne who was also in disguise and Mr Billy Kaye, the Head of English. It looked like he'd been trying to come as Harry Potter but the end result was more like Billy Bunter. It seemed ironic that these three literary figures were accusing Mr Milton of violating the school's dress code simply by wearing a tie with William Shakespeare on it. He probably had his top button undone too. How shocking! At least Mr Haddenough wouldn't be the only one responsible for any drastic drop in GCSE grades this summer.

It seemed appropriate that Miss Hughes, an English teacher as well as the Acting Head of Year 8, should deliver an assembly about World Book Day. She had been going to dust off the one from the previous year but had had to tweak it when she'd been told that she also needed to talk about Wildside Academy's values.

Like her colleagues in the English Department Lucy Hughes had come in dressed as a character from literature. She was Snow White and whilst there were more than enough dwarves around it looked like the evil witch was busy elsewhere.

"Morning everybody," she said as the pupils in her year group shuffled uncomfortably on the hard floor. "Now as we don't have a pianist this morning," she frowned at a boy who was giggling on the front row, "we're going to have to sing acapulco."

The words to *"All things bright and beautiful"* appeared on the screen above her head as the pupils grudgingly stood up. After an unsteady start the majority of the pupils managed to sing some of the words before Miss Hughes decided that the first verse would be enough. The words were a little easier than the original School Hymn, *'I vow to thee, my country'*, but there was no point pushing your luck.

"Thank you, everybody," she said. "Please sit down carefully. You all did very well. It'll be so much easier when Mr Gordon's back. I'm sure, like me, you all wish him a speedy recovery after his accident with the circular saw." As a result of this incident a DT room had been out of action for several days and a supply teacher had taught extra Food Tech lessons in Mrs Carter's room.

Miss Hughes pressed a button on the remote and the new Wildside Academy school values appeared. The pupils probably heard these words more times each day now than they heard their own names.

Wisdom
Inspiration
Leadership
Determination
Success
Integrity
Dedication
Excelence

"Now you'll remember the lovely assembly Mr Wingett gave us all about Wisdom and today we're going to be thinking about our next value, Inspiration. I'm going to start by asking a question. Which books inspire you?"

A few pupils who had been away when they'd covered rhetorical questions in Year 7 raised their hands cautiously.

"And I'm asking that," continued Miss Hughes, "because today is World Book Day. A day for looking at which books are an inspiration to us all."

So with the connection made she could now carry on with her original PowerPoint. The pupils got themselves comfortable, hoping that they were going to be told a story and wouldn't have to keep putting their hands up all the time.

It was at that point that the two Assistant Heads gatecrashed the assembly with Ms Winter shedding a few dusty petals as she made her way down the aisle. Seeing no just cause or impediment to stop her assembly Miss Hughes continued with her presentation.

"Now I asked some of your teachers which books and literary characters inspired them. Here we go. Does anybody know who this is?"

The first slide consisted of two photos. At the left there was a picture of Ms Stonehart, clearly copied from the Wildside Academy website, at the right a character from a novel. It seemed that Year 8 not only didn't recognise the literary figure, they had no idea who the first person was either.

"Is it that Prime Minister woman?" asked a boy near the front.

Miss Hughes smiled awkwardly, looking round the canteen to check who was present.

"Is it the Spice Girls?" called out another pupil without waiting to be asked.

Miss Hughes diplomatically made it clear who everybody on the screen was. "This is Ms Stonehart's favourite book, *'One flew over the cuckoo's nest'* by Ken Kesey and on the right is a character from it called Nurse Ratched. "A cold, heartless, aggressive tyrant" is how she's described." Miss Hughes looked up at the screen. "Nurse Ratched," she added quickly to avoid any ambiguity. Another click on the remote brought up Ms Stonehart's personal evaluation of the novel.

"I first read this book many years ago and found it inspirational. Whether it is in a hospital or in a school setting people need somebody who has their best interests at heart and can lead them from strength to strength. Sadly the film, as often happens, is not as good as the book."
Ms J. Stonehart, Headteacher, Wildside Academy,
Diploma in Human Resources, TGCSEC, CPT, BPB.

There then followed a series of slides from those people who'd replied to Miss Hughes' email request. On the Senior Leadership Team Mr O'Brien was re-reading *'Brave New World'* because he liked books where an individual struggles bravely against an oppressive, dystopian society ; Ms Winter said how much she liked great poetry and had chosen Pam Ayres as her favourite poet ; Mr Wingett commented that his family had been too poor to afford books but this hadn't stopped him from becoming Assistant Head at Wildside Academy. Mr Humble had written how much he enjoyed *'A Clockwork Orange'* whilst Ms Shakespeare's choice wasn't anything from the Bard but rather *'Brigitte Jones' Diary.'* Probably without realising what he'd put Mr Buonanulla had commented that *'How the Eiffel Tower was built'* was riveting. Rather than choosing a book about music Mr Jones was enjoying *"The Secret World of Stenography."* As Head of Maths Mr Milton had chosen *'The*

Mathematical Principles of Natural Philosophy' by Isaac Newton. Some pupils turned to look at Mr Wingett when he laughed at this recommendation. Mr Ash had commented how much he was enjoying *"Exploring Science Through Pictures and Worksheets."* There were even replies from Eric the chef who was inspired by *'Delia's How to cheat at cooking'* and Mr Rojan was enjoying *"Fly Fishing"* by J.R. Hartley. It turned out that Miss Honeywell, the Teaching Assistant, was a big fan of The Mr Men books. Ms Murkett coughed disapprovingly when this last title was announced, particularly as her recommendation of *'The Female Eunuch'* had not been mentioned. She had hoped that the assembly rota would include International Women's Day this week but it was probably Thicke or Wingett who had put the schedule together. She would have to write a strongly-worded email as soon as assembly finished.

"Well, it looks like there's lots of ideas to keep you busy," said Miss Hughes. "Perhaps over the Easter holidays you might ask for a book rather than an Easter egg?"

"I know which I'd rather have," said Ms Winter to her best friend beside her. Having long since given up on her New Year's resolution all she'd learned from it was that fun-sized chocolate bars shouldn't really be described as "fun."

"Now to celebrate World Book Day," continued Miss Hughes, "we are launching a competition! All you have to do is take a photograph of yourself reading a book in an unusual place, email it to the English Department and you could win a prize. And the top prize, generously donated by Ms Stonehart, is a £20 Nando's voucher."

Mr Haddenough wondered why the World Book Day Competition prize wasn't a book voucher. Having said that if nobody could spell 'excellence' correctly then maybe literacy wasn't that important after all?

CHAPTER 3.14

*"Life is like Maths. You need to be able to convert
negatives into positives."*

There was some disappointment in the staffroom when people
realised that World Pi Day had nothing to do with food. Perhaps
the lesson had been learned after Fairtrade Week and people
certainly didn't mention Mr Chang's fortune cookies anymore.
After the English Department had celebrated World Book Day it
was almost as if the Maths Department just wanted to show that
numbers were important too.

Mr Milton, the Head of Maths, had emailed resources to all
staff, fun activities that could be done in form time and now he too
was talking about Pi with his own Year 10 form. Some colleagues
had thanked him for sharing his resources whilst Mr Wingett had
commented that there were better things they could be doing with
form time. He'd suggested he looked at what Mr Devlin did with
his class.

"As you'll remember from your Maths class," Mr Milton began
once he'd done the register, "Pi is an endless string of numbers that
is usually just shortened to 3.14. And that's why we celebrate it
today, the third month and the fourteenth day."

He pointed to the date on the board, March 14th, for extra
clarity.

"So it could have been the 31st of the 4th month and that would
have worked too then, wouldn't it, sir?" suggested a girl on the
front row.

"Possibly," said Mr Milton, diplomatically, "except April only
has thirty days, Faith."

Faith seemed a little unsure of this and started reciting a rhyme quietly to herself.

"Isn't it a bit American doing it that way though," asked a boy near the board, "'cos I'd say the 14th of March and that'd make Pi 14.3!"

"Actually back in 2015 it was called 'Super Pi Day', Tom," continued Mr Milton, "because if you wrote the date as 3/14/15 then at 9:26:53 precisely you had the first ten digits of Pi. But you made a good point there, Tom."

For no apparent reason a few of the pupils were starting to look interested so Mr Milton pressed on.

"Pi is what we call an irrational number. Who knows what irrational means?"

"You'd better ask her," grunted Adam who, for probably the first time ever, was not sitting next to Sonya. Sonya ignored him and Adam spent the rest of form period staring out of the window.

"An irrational number," explained their form tutor, "is a number that can't easily be written as a simple fraction. The nearest is probably 22/7…"

"So that would make it the 22nd of July but that'd be when we're on holiday," said Faith, "so is that why it's in March, sir?"

"Well, let's leave the date on one side for now," said Mr Milton, not wanting to go off at a tangent. "What does the number Pi actually represent? Anybody?"

"Is it something to do with circles?"

"That's right, Jess! Pi is the ratio of a circle's circumference to its diameter, like you say. And no matter what size the circle is, Pi is always the same. Let's say 3.14."

"March 14th!" exclaimed Faith. "I think I get it now."

"Pi is seen as an endless string of numbers containing the digits 0 to 9 in every possible combination. So all your phone numbers, bank account numbers, passport numbers, every number you can think of is in there somewhere…"

"Woah, that's got to be against all the data protection stuff," said Kevin indignantly. "What if somebody got hold of this Pi thing? They could nick all us money, do identity theft, all that stuff, yeah? I'm not jokin', sir, you gotta tell somebody!"

"Don't worry, Kevin. It's perfectly safe."

Kevin didn't look like he was convinced.

Mr Milton decided to press on.

Also if you were to convert all the numbers to letters, 1 is A, 2 is B and so on, you'd find every book you'd ever read was in Pi too."

In Kevin's case that might not amount to too many books.

"And just watch this," continued Mr Milton enthusiastically.

Adam was still more interested in the outside world. To be fair he was on task in a way as he was watching Bob create crop circles on the front field with the sit-on mower he'd got for Christmas.

Mr Milton wrote 3.14 on the whiteboard, took a small mirror and held it up beside the number. The reflection read PIE. Faith nodded enthusiastically as if it had all fallen into place.

"And that wouldn't work with other dates, would it?" she concluded.

"And here's another interesting fact if we're talking about dates. Albert Einstein was born on March 14th and Stephen Hawking died on March 14th..."

"What are the chances of that!" exclaimed a boy called Kane.

All in all, Mr Milton thought it was best not to get into discussing probability too. He'd learned his lesson when a pupil had told him that the chances of winning the Lottery were 50:50. You either won the Lottery or you didn't!

CHAPTER 32

"Only in the darkness can you see the stars."

There was no more logical place for the Wildside Academy Telescope to be but on the top floor of the Science Block. Ms Stonehart had initially had it positioned in her office but all she could really see through it were the holly bushes outside her window. She'd had the shock of her life one morning when she'd peered through it to see what had to be a pupil from Wildside Academy grinning back at her as he'd been caught short coming into school. Angling the telescope away from him she'd been able to see Bob diligently putting a new sign up on the front field. It was facing away from her so she couldn't read it but as employee of the term Bob would be doing just what she wanted. It occurred to her that if she got CCTV fitted throughout the school, rather than just on the executive car park, she could keep an eye on everything without leaving her office. It was something to look into. There would be enough money for it as it was a safeguarding issue and that was very important to Ofsted.

There was a knock at the door and Mr Wingett came in on her command.

"Norma said you wanted something," said Mr Wingett bluntly.

"Yes. Come in, Gary. It's about the Science Department."

"Richard's the SLT-link for Science," he began quickly. "If it's about the Van de Graaff..."

"No, Mr Goldbloom's following up on that. I just need to go over to Science to check up on the Telescope and I thought you might like to come too?"

They always say there's safety in numbers.

When the Science Block had been built it had been named after a famous scientist and for reasons long since forgotten the physicist Erwin Schrödinger had been chosen. It seemed appropriate as nobody was really sure what was going on in there, good or bad, until they looked inside.

"We could do with changing this," said Ms Stonehart looking up at the scientist's name above the entrance. A stray cat glanced at her with disdain as it wandered past on its way to the wheelie bins. "It's been like this since before we became an Academy. Look into it, would you, Gary? Some suggestions on my desk by close of business. Not that Brian Cox though after he failed to reply."

Trying desperately to punch the correct code for the outer door, Mr Wingett grunted and made a mental note to ask the Acting Head of Science for suggestions. He just hoped Miss Skellen didn't try and turn it into another of her Science Department Competitions that she was so fond of. If it were left to the kids they'd probably end up with 'The Victor Frankenstein Science Block'!

"Just look at that," commented Ms Stonehart as they entered the building. She pointed at a poster informing everybody that "STEM Club" met in LAB-1 every Tuesday lunchtime. "What would Ofsted say if they saw that? Literacy's the big thing at the moment and spelling mistakes just aren't acceptable. Anyway I would have thought a club about Lower Steem would be more appropriate in the Geography or History Departments. Get it sorted, would you, Gary?"

Mr Wingett said he would tell Miss Skellen what she had said.

The Science Department was on three floors which were theoretically devoted to Physics, Chemistry and Biology. In practice very few classes carried out the sort of experiments that had been commonplace in the old days of Wildside School. Most pupils in Mr Armani's class now had their heads down, silently copying out extracts from the textbook *"Exploring Science Through Pictures and Worksheets"*. If ever Mrs Ramsbottom's photocopiers all broke down at once the solution could probably be found in these laboratories. In theory they could eventually recreate the entire works of Shakespeare if they stayed long enough and Mr Armani did like to keep them back after school.

Heading past the Biology rooms where Mr Campbell was inspecting what looked like brains in glass jars, his face bathed in an eerie green light, Ms Stonehart and Mr Wingett made their way up to the top floor. Here was the latest addition to the school, the long-awaited Wildside Academy Telescope. Ms Stonehart smiled and stepped forward to look through the eyepiece.

Blurry at first, the enemy slowly came into focus. Upper Steem Academy. USA! She could feel her blood pressure rising as she thought back to that disastrous Open Evening. Moving the telescope a little to the left she was pleased to see that their car parking facilities were no better than those at Wildside Academy. There weren't any Jaguars or Mercedes parked there either! With another slight adjustment she was looking in through the classroom windows. It looked like Science Laboratories where pupils, wearing safety goggles and no doubt smiling, were doing something with Bunsen burners.

"Tell Miss Skellen I want to see her in my office at close of business and tell her to bring all her Schemes of Work along too," said Ms Stonehart, still peering through the telescope. "And she needs to do a full inventory of all the chemicals and equipment in the Science Prep Room before she comes…"

Mr Wingett took a pad out of his inside pocket and started writing a list of all the things he had to tell the Acting Head of Science.

As the telescope swept over Upper Steem Academy Ms Stonehart let out a sigh that was only just audible. She could see right into the Headteacher's office! There was that dreadful man, Hoskins! She adjusted the telescope to make the image a little clearer and she could see him with that irritating black beard sitting at his desk. What was he doing? Something on a computer? Maybe it was data about Literacy? It was all so annoying! This was meant to be the best telescope money could buy and she still couldn't see a thing! Moving the telescope a little to the left only meant that she had to track down his office window again. Second from the right… No! It was definitely the right window but in the brief time she'd been searching Hoskins must have closed the blinds!

She looked up to check Mr Wingett was still there.

"Remind me to see Mr Goldbloom about ordering some blinds for my office," she said, before continuing her stake-out of Upper Steem Academy.

Their front field was full of boys playing rugby whilst beyond the staff car park girls were making their way to the all-weather pitch. Ms Stonehart swung the telescope right round to study the sporting facilities of Wildside Academy. Nothing of any merit was going on there. The front field was deserted apart from Bob who was dragging what looked like a broken sign back towards the main building.

"Gary! Get down to the PE office at once! Mr Greenfield needs to get some of our boys running around out there and the same with Mrs Mower and the girls."

It was only when Mr Wingett had hurried off to sort out all these issues that Ms Stonehart realised she would have to get all the way back to the safety of her office unaccompanied. She took out her mobile phone. Perhaps Mr Humble might like to come across and see the new telescope?

CHAPTER 33

"You're never too young to change the world."

Nobody knew why Mrs Thorne had been put in charge of the PGCE students who came from The University of Wildside Teaching Foundation each year but to be fair nobody else wanted the paperwork.

There had been a lot of emails from the University about the student teachers and a lot of forms to print off and complete. She still found it hard to think of the old Wildside Polytechnic College as a proper University like where she'd studied Fine Art and Architecture. Mind you, she was now Head of Department in a school that was run by somebody who hadn't even trained as a teacher!

"Hello," said a young man cheerfully as she entered the reception area. With long curly black hair and round tinted glasses, this must be Dylan Cooper, the trainee Music teacher. He even appeared to be wearing exactly the same blue suede jacket, frilly shirt and bow tie as the photo on his file, as if to make identification easier.

"You must be Dylan," said Mrs Thorne. "I'm Mrs Thorne. Ursula. I'm Head of Art and I'll be your Teaching Mentor while you're all here."

She looked behind Dylan but there were no other student teachers to be seen.

"The others are on their way," explained Dylan. "I cycled in." He started to remove the cycle clips from his ankles, putting them in his jacket pockets, having first removed a banana. "They shouldn't be long. I think they're aiming for the space next to that Jag."

Mrs Thorne turned a little pale, perhaps fearing that they would scrape Ms Stonehart's car.

"That's reserved for police," she said even though Bob had never labelled the parking space with his traditional white lettering. It probably wouldn't look too good on school publicity photos.

To her relief the other four student teachers appeared in the doorway at that moment, blinking and yawning in the early morning sunshine. Mrs Thorne looked at the photos on their files as she tried to identify each one. The young man who looked about twelve and was muttering about sharing the cost of the petrol must be Gareth Worral, the Science trainee. Beside him were the Geography student teacher, Alex Tennant, and the English graduate, Kimama Akinyemizola. The lady at the back wearing a black beret and long flowing silk dress was obviously Holly Phillips who would be joining the Art Department.

"Welcome to Wildside Academy," said Mrs Thorne once she'd introduced herself again for the latecomers. "I'm sure you'll all be just as happy here as we are. Now we just need to get your lanyards sorted and then we can go through."

Unfortunately the Julie on the reception desk was too busy to operate the camera and laminating machine that created the lanyards. She smiled politely as she slowly explained that with Mrs Ramsbottom still off after the incident during Fairtrade Week they'd all had to take on extra responsibilities. It was a very busy time for all of the office staff and everybody would just have to be very understanding and patient. She went back to the magazine she'd been reading as she waited for the phone to ring.

Mrs Thorne operated the equipment herself and was relatively pleased with the results. For some reason all the lanyards ended up with a large red 'L' printed on them, inadvertently highlighting how inexperienced the PGCE students were. Miss Phillips' photo was upside down and Gareth's lanyard labelled him as Mr Wirral, but other than that everything had turned out fine.

"Now you'll need your lanyard to blip in and out each day," explained Mrs Thorne as though they'd never come across a similar system before, "but the code to get through here is easy. It varies each week but it's always the same digit repeated. This week it's three fives."

She entered the code as Julie watched. The light on the keypad remained red and nothing happened.

"The code's changed again," said Julie helpfully.

Mrs Thorne started to ask the inevitable next question.

"It's three sixes this week."

She thanked her and the PGCE students entered a school for the first time since they'd sat their A Levels.

Mrs Thorne always found it was best not to introduce Ms Stonehart to people who were training to be properly qualified teachers. They'd only be on this initial placement for a few weeks and would be able to pass through without disturbing her. She hurried them past the Student Welcome desk without a word of welcome, pausing only to emphasize that they were not to think of using the photocopiers in there under any circumstances. Until Mrs Ramsbottom returned they could try the machine in the staffroom if they needed to copy anything.

The Music student, Dylan, had started to eat his banana before Mrs Thorne noticed.

"I'm sorry but we tend not to eat bananas in this school after Fairtrade Week," she said. "Just make sure it ends up in a bin, won't you? Right, I'll take you to your different Departments then."

Safely beyond the Berlin Wall they were about to be treated to a guided tour of Wildside Academy in action.

They passed the Main Hall where a variation of *'All things bright and beautiful'* drifted out and a man in a very smart suit yelled at the pupils to put more effort into their singing. From a distance it sounded like the pupils were commenting that *'all creatures grunt and smell.'*

"That's Mr Armani's Year 10 assembly," said Mrs Thorne. "He's Science so you'll be meeting him later, Gareth."

They went past the canteen where Bob the caretaker was sweeping up and tidying chairs.

"Looks like Year 9 assembly's been cancelled again," she informed them.

The PGCE students were struggling to think of questions they could ask Mrs Thorne as they trailed along behind her.

"Is this the English Department?" Ms Akinyemizola finally asked as they turned onto a corridor displaying posters the pupils had made of *'Lord of the Flies.'* "It looks just like when I was at Berryfield Academy."

"That's right," said Mrs Thorne. "I think this is the period when Mr Kaye teaches. You can sit in on the end of his lesson."

When she opened the door Mr Billy Kaye, Head of English, was perched on the end of a desk with his back to them. According to the whiteboard his Year 10 class were actually studying something called *Lord of the Files*. Other than those four words there was no clue as to what anybody was trying to achieve in this hour. Nobody even seemed to have a copy of the novel. Ms Akinyemizola spotted a copy of *"Exploring English Through Pictures and Worksheets"* on the teacher's desk. A boy sitting near the front was clearly still trying to sort something out in his own mind.

"So, sir, why is the word abbreviation so long then?"

"I don't know, Washington," smiled Mr Kaye, "I really don't! It just is!"

"Sorry to interrupt you," Mrs Thorne said. "This is Ms Akinyemizola, the PGCE student? I sent you an email about her joining us till just before Easter?"

"Right," said Mr Kaye who tended not to read emails. "Well the more the merrier. Cheers! Has anybody got anything they'd like to ask Miss?"

"Yeah," said Washington straight away. "You know what I don't get, yeah? We did about palindromes the other day. So why isn't palindrome spelt the same backwards?"

Mrs Thorne closed the door quietly, leaving Ms Akinyemizola to the idiosyncratic wonders of the English language in the capable hands of Mr Kaye.

Next they made their way outside and across to the Music Block. The clocks in the school seemed to work as though Wildside Academy was spread across various time zones and so some of the pupils had already been let out for break by mistake. They were standing round a couple of scrawny pigeons near the bins and trying unsuccessfully to get them to eat some of the leftover food from the school canteen.

"They 'ate the burgers here too!" said a ginger haired boy.

"Too right!" agreed his mate.

The PGCE students were a little alarmed as they turned a corner and found the white chalk outline of a body marked out on the black tarmac.

"Has there been... Has something happened?" asked a

concerned Mr Worral, the Science trainee.

"That'll be Graham in Year 9 again," sighed Mrs Thorne. "He's very good at Art but his family are the Reapers, the Funeral Directors up on the main road? He's a bit, erm, obsessed, shall we say? You'll probably meet him later today, Holly, in Art."

The shrill sound of *Greensleeves* welcomed them as they went through into the Music Block where Mr Jones was finishing his Year 8 lesson. It was the kind of sound that would have had people clutching their heads in agony in a low budget science-fiction film.

"It looks like a big Department," said Dylan, putting his banana skin in a bin as he gazed at the Music practice rooms that lined the corridor.

"There's only one teacher. Mrs Jones was…" Mrs Thorne wasn't sure how to phrase it. "There's just Mr Jones, Head of Department."

A door swung open and Year 8 came pouring out, the sound of their recorders replaced by their squeals of delight that the canteen was open. The PGCE students quickly moved back out of their way.

"Ah," said Mr Jones, "these must be the student teachers. Lovely!" A slight hint of his Welsh accent could be heard in his enthusiastic tone. "It'll be good to have some company again since…"

"How is Cathy?" asked Mrs Thorne.

"Not good. Trying to keep herself busy really." Mrs Jones had loved being the other half of the Music Department, working with her husband Huw every day. "She's tried organizing a music festival but there's not much call for it in Lower Steem. Not like back home. She's teaching piano to one of the neighbours for an hour a week…" He looked across at the piano gathering dust in the corner. Nobody had touched it since November and some sheet music for Grieg's Piano Concerto in A Minor was still there from the last time it had been played.

It was as if the spark was going out of Mr Jones. He rarely came in the staffroom now. Mr Wingett had explained to them both that Wildside Academy could not afford two Music teachers and would have to let one of them go. Rather than go through the redundancy process, competing against her husband, Mrs Jones had resigned. The duet had become a solo. Had it not been for the mortgage, they'd both have walked out together.

"Well, this is Dylan Cooper," continued Mrs Thorne after an uncomfortable pause. "He's here for a few weeks."

"So what do you play?" asked Mr Jones. "Strings, brass, woodwind, percussion? I bet it's the piano! We need a pianist now. You can do assemblies till Mr Gordon's back, eh?"

Dylan Cooper looked at the floor to avoid the smiles of the other PGCE students as they left. From having shared a flat with him they knew what his particular musical skills were.

"I was thinking I could start a Recorder Club?" he ventured.

In the Geography Department Ms Mina Malik had volunteered to mentor the PGCE student because she was after all the Second-in-Department for Geography. It was important to share best practice and help trainee teachers as they started out on their career and it would ease her Head of Department's workload. It was also one of her Bright Sky targets.

As Mrs Thorne came into the Geography classroom Ms Malik was finishing off her Year 10 lesson. From the Learning Objectives on the board it was obvious that in a clearly differentiated way the group had been developing their map reading skills. Now in the plenary stage of her three-part lesson Ms Malik had tested the pupils' progress and was just checking if they had any final questions.

"So, Miss," asked the girl who was collecting the atlases back in, "if people from Poland are called Poles, shouldn't people from Holland be called Holes?"

"I'll tell you what I'll do," replied Ms Malik calmly. "I've already put your homework on 'S'Cool!' but I've got a quiz sheet about flags that should answer that for you. I'll attach it. Due in on Thursday."

"Thanks, Sophie!" shouted a boy at the girl who'd got them all extra homework.

"Stay behind, Shane," said Ms Malik pointing at a poster that stated in large bold letters *"We do not shout out in Ms Malik's class!!!"*

The second the bell rang on the Geography corridor Ms Malik's lesson came to an end and she dismissed the pupils in an orderly fashion, one row at a time. As Mr Tennant, PGCE student for Geography, was left alone with just Shane and his teacher he knew that he could learn a lot from Ms Malik.

"Now Miss Skellen's off again today," said Mrs Thorne as she reached the Science Block with the two remaining PGCE students. "So Mr Armani's said he'll sort you out, Gareth."

Break was ending and Mrs Thorne hurried to grab the door before it closed and left them stranded in the playground. She was distracted by a group of Year 11 girls noisily doing the conga on their way to PE and when she turned back the door had closed. The code from the main reception entrance was clearly different to that of the Science Block.

"Schrödinger," the trainee Science teacher read out from above the entrance. "Wasn't he the one in the Snoopy cartoon like?"

By chance the door opened again and two Year 9 pupils in white coats and safety goggles ran out screaming. As Mrs Thorne couldn't stop them she smiled awkwardly and ushered the two student teachers inside.

"Do yous have a STEM club here?" asked Gareth.

Dave Ross, the lab technician, was busy fiddling with dials on a metal box when they looked into the Science Prep Room. It could have been an oscilloscope or he may simply have been trying to tune his radio in for the racing results. A pungent odour filled the air.

"We're looking for Calvin," said Mrs Thorne hopefully.

"Eh?" said Dave, without looking up from the workbench.

At that moment the connecting door to one of the classrooms opened and Mr Armani appeared, silhouetted by the bright neon lights behind him. Removing his spotless white coat he was dressed in an immaculate and clearly expensive suit, a silk handkerchief to match his tie, every hair in place. Even after a morning spent demonstrating chemical reactions to Key Stage 3, he was still a vision of sophisticated style. He carefully hung his white lab coat up on a hanger.

"Calvin, you're looking after our new PGCE student with Karan off, aren't you?" began Mrs Thorne.

"Indeed," said Mr Armani. He went over to shake hands with Miss Phillips, holding her hand a little longer than was really necessary. "It'll be a pleasure. I'm Calvin. And you are...?"

"This is Miss Phillips," Mrs Thorne replied. "She's joining us over in the Art Department. And this is Gareth our Science trainee."

"Welcome to Wildside Academy, Mr Wirral," said Mr Armani as he read the lanyard. "So why did you want to be a Science teacher?"

"Well, erm, there was this advert about becoming a teacher on the telly like. Showing kids how to use a Van de Graaff generator…"

Mr Armani took an instant dislike to Mr Wirral. There was something that reminded him of Darren Froggett. In no time at all he was recounting some of the things he'd witnessed over the years just to see how much he really did want to be a teacher.

"…and when they'd mopped up all the acid all they found was a single eyeball and a scorched school tie…"

Mrs Thorne closed the door and started to lead Holly away to the safety of the Art Department. She really hoped Mr Armani didn't upset the PGCE students. Her Bright Sky target depended on them giving her a good report.

CHAPTER 34

"He who has no charity deserves no mercy."

Unlike other teachers it never actually occurred to Ms Lovall that being summoned to Ms Stonehart's office usually wasn't a good thing. She'd seen teachers waiting nervously outside the Headteacher's office, awkwardly checking their top button was done up, their shoes polished and any paperwork they had was in order. Sally didn't have a top button on her Greenpeace t-shirt, her Doc Martens were fine and anything she needed was stored on her laptop. She really didn't know why some people seemed not to like Janine.

"Hiya!" she began enthusiastically when Ms Stonehart summoned her into her office and welcomed her to sit down. She even offered her a cup of tea but Ms Lovall declined, asking whether she had any dandelion and burdock instead. Ms Stonehart buzzed through to Mrs Spratt, asking her to track the drink down, even if it meant going up to the corner shop.

"Now then, Sally," began Ms Stonehart pleasantly, "you've only been with us a short while but I've been impressed with what I've seen. Lynne says your teaching's outstanding, there's the L4L lessons you plan, the staff training, the work you do with Ms Murkett on Women's Rights… Some of the other teachers could do with following your example."

"Cheers!" smiled Ms Lovall wondering if verbal feedback counted against Bright Sky targets.

"I've asked you to pop in because I'd value your opinion on what to do about charity, Sally."

"Charity Adebowalé in Year 10? Well I only teach her for RE but if she revises properly…"

"Charity, Sally. Collecting money, taking photos for the website, sponsored walks, that kind of thing."

Ms Stonehart had no idea who Charity Adebowalé was but she

did remember that Year 10 was your ninth year in the education system.

"Oh, yes. Fab! That sort of charity. Like in the Bible. Got you."

"I'll be frank with you," Ms Stonehart confided. "I don't have a lot of time for Mr Cocker. He's a thorn in my side, to be honest. But I had a reporter from *The Wildside Gazette* saying how much he liked the Fairtrade Week we did and it got me thinking. The school needs to do more for charity. We've got nothing on the website and there was an article in the paper last week about USA pupils doing something called a charity bag pack? Did you know Mr North's no longer with us? Never mind. I've decided to make you Charitable Promotions Developer and I want you to come up with a plan of how we can support a charity with the maximum impact in the most economical way. Your choice. Maybe something to do with children? I don't really care which charity as long as it looks good."

"Wicked!" exclaimed Ms Lovall.

At that point Mrs Spratt entered the room, a little out of breath, carrying a can of dandelion and burdock and a glass on a silver tray.

"Arrange cover for Ms Lovall's lessons, would you?" said Ms Stonehart. "There'll be people free. Don't use that supply agency."

"I hear what you say," wheezed Mrs Spratt out of force of habit as she went back to her computer.

Ms Lovall was about to comment that since charity begins at home maybe she'd be best working from home on her plans. She didn't get a chance to make her suggestion however as Ms Stonehart brought the meeting to an end.

"I'll need your ideas about which charity by close of business," she concluded, pouring herself a fresh cup of tea.

Mr Haddenough had been given an emergency cover to plug the gap in an otherwise full day's teaching. He was sure he'd seen Ms Lovall in the canteen earlier. He just hoped she'd left some cover work for the lesson this time. He'd stood in for her so many times this year that some pupils were beginning to think of him as their regular teacher and would often ask him what they were doing in RE next. As always he was punctual, getting to Ms Lovall's room in time for the start of the lesson. A sticker on the door of Room 7 had rechristened it "7th Heaven" and a laminated poster informed everybody that *'Ms Lovall is reading...Random Acts of Kindness.'* After five minutes of watching the corridor empty of pupils with nobody arriving at Ms Lovall's door he began to think something was wrong. He checked the slip of paper Mrs Spratt had sent him.

FAO : Mr Haddenough (IHH) Emergency Cover for Ms Lovall (SLL) Period 3, Room 7, Year 11, 11A/L4L. Urgent!

The door at the end of the corridor opened noisily and Ms Murkett appeared. As she drew nearer Mr Haddenough stepped forward to speak to her.

"Morning. Sorry, you don't know where Year 11 might be, do you? I've got a cover for Sally, Room 7?"

"No," said Ms Murkett, continuing on her way without even making eye contact with him.

"Thanks anyway," called out Mr Haddenough as she disappeared, leaving him alone in the empty corridor once more.

He hadn't really expected much assistance from Ms Murkett who had never liked him from the day she'd joined Wildside Academy. This was quite a long conversation they'd had just now. She'd never really spoken to him since calling him a "sexist dinosaur" one time he'd held a door open for her.

Mr Haddenough decided to see whether there was any other information on the staffroom noticeboard. Perhaps there'd been a room change? There were very few people in the staffroom, perhaps fearing that this wasn't the safest place to be if emergency cover slips were being handed out. He did however find Ms Lovall who was busy having a coffee with Ms Shakespeare in the central area that seemed to be reserved for English teachers and their guests.

"Well, I said to him," Ms Lovall was saying, "if your idea of a good night out is just going to the same restaurant every time I might as well've stayed with Fireman Sam, yeah?"

"You've not got any paracetamol then?" asked Shazza. "Still feeling a bit fragile. I shouldn't be in really."

"We're just too professional at times."

"Sorry to interrupt, Sally, but I've got a cover for you? Room 7 but there's nobody there?"

Ms Lovall looked up.

"Yeah. No, they'll be in Room 15. There's only four of them so we did a swap at the start of the year. Norma's maybe not updated SCAMS. Anyway, they're lovely and they know what to do. Fab!"

Four pupils. Mr Haddenough had thirty-four in each of his

GCSE classes.

When he found Ms Lovall's class, who had decided that actually they'd prefer to be in Room 18 today, Ms Winter and Ms Payne were already there. Mr Haddenough had been observed so many times in the last fortnight that he was starting to think he should just add Lynne and Sharon on to the end of his register.

Ms Winter put her can of diet cola down, checked the time and marked something off on her clipboard. There was no work left on the teacher's desk, no instructions on the board and the pupils were all staring at him with a look of mild bemusement. The copy of *"Exploring Sport Through Pictures and Worksheets"* on the desk seemed to have no relevance to the lesson he was covering.

"Ms Lovall said you know what you're getting on with?" he ventured as SCAMS finally loaded on his laptop. The register for this class did not appear on his screen. Knowing Ms Lovall there was probably a video on the shared area somewhere that they were meant to be watching.

"Do you have exercise books?" he asked.

Four faces looked at him as if he had spoken in Chinese. Ms Winter had already crossed off that he had not put Learning Objectives on the board. A starter exercise had not been done. It wasn't looking good. As Mr Haddenough realised that these seemed to be the only four pupils in the school that he didn't teach he knew this lesson would not score highly for differentiation.

"Sir," said one of the two girls helpfully, "Miss said we were going to be thinking about why we have rules in society."

"Ok. Thank you," said Mr Haddenough, feeling he was now getting somewhere. "Who'd like to start the discussion?"

A boy at the front chewed his pencil thoughtfully before speaking.

"Sir, last lesson Miss said that there's an exception to every rule," he said. "So is there an exception to that rule then?"

"I thought Miss said we'd be doing about Essex today," interrupted a boy near the front, looking like he'd wandered into the wrong classroom.

One of the girls pointed out that the topic had actually been 'Ethics.'

Chances are Ms Winter and Ms Payne won't stop to observe the whole lesson thought Mr Haddenough as he tried to come up with a suitable answer.

By lunchtime Ms Lovall felt she'd had a very productive morning. As Carol Underwood, the Cover Supervisor, had been free all morning they'd bounced ideas off each other over a hot chocolate. They'd even managed to come up with ideas for an end-of-term staff do to make up for the Christmas party wash-out.

Ms Lovall had trawled the internet to help her narrow all the possible charities down to just one. The stickers on the lid of her laptop had been a big help but in the end it was still a difficult choice. Perhaps an art therapy project for children in Africa? There were so many issues that she felt so strongly about. On the plus side she had got herself quite a bargain on a pair of shoes on eBay.

Glancing up at the staff noticeboard Ms Lovall saw a greetings card pinned there that she'd never noticed before and got up to see what it was. It turned out to be from Mr North, wishing everybody well and saying he was sorry he'd not got a chance to say goodbye to everybody before he'd retired. The back of the card announced that all proceeds from it were going to The Dyslexia Trust. This was very unusual and she wondered who'd put it there. Usually when people disappeared they were never heard from again. Mr North had not been replaced and the Teaching Assistants had been left to organise the School-Home Intervention Team as best they could. Somebody really needed to be promoted to take over that important rôle, thought Ms Lovall, the newly-appointed Charitable Promotions Developer and Lessons For Life Co-ordinator.

Opening up her laptop again Ms Lovall researched The Dyslexia Trust. It took her a couple of attempts as she kept typing their name in wrongly, but then she was looking at their website. Ironically The Dyslexia Trust was based in Reading but it was very keen to work with schools to raise money and awareness for the vital work they did. Wildside Academy could work with The Dyslexia Trust to raise awareness, supporting a charity with the maximum impact in the most economical way. This would be ideal.

So that was decided then! Ms Lovall looked at the clock at the other end of the staffroom. There were only fifty minutes of last lesson remaining so it didn't make sense to disturb whoever was covering her lesson. She'd finalise her plans, have another hot chocolate and then go see Janine before close of business. She'd even volunteer to do a charity parachute jump for The Dyslexia

Trust and get everybody to sponsor her. It was something she'd always wanted to do.

From : LWR - LWinter@WildsideAcademy
To : SLL - SLovall@WildsideAcademy
CC : SPE – SPayne@WildsideAcademy
Attached : BS-Lesson Observation SLL/LWR
Sent : Wed 27 Mar 14:08
Subject : BS Lesson feedback

Hiya!

Sharon and me popped in to watch a bit of your lesson as we were free this morning and didn't have anything to do. We've decided to grade it as "Outstanding" even though you wasn't there as we know what you're normally like and the planing would of been fab as always, yeah?
It's a shame Ivor made such a cock-up of doing what you'd planned but we've sent him his lesson feedback and if he's got a problem he can see Sharon or I.
I've attached your feedback for Bright Sky.
Brill! See you in the pub later?

Cheers!
Lynne
Assistant Head i/c Teaching & Leaning,
Literacy Co-ordinator, Advanced Skills Teacher for English.

APRIL

CHAPTER 35

"Integrity is doing the right thing even when nobody is watching."

Senior Moment (noun) : *An action performed or a decision made by a member of the Senior Leadership Team that is so unbelievable that they are unable to recall it later and everybody else is supposed just to forgive and forget about it too.*

There are some events in life that you always remember where you were and what you were doing at the time. This was the case with what happened at Wildside Academy on April 1st. Despite the date it wasn't some kind of foolish prank. It actually happened.

Whenever anybody mentioned that day, glancing round first to check that it was safe to speak, it was always to say whether they had or hadn't read the Email. It was so significant that you could almost hear the capital letter if the Email came up in conversation. When it was mentioned it was either with a feeling of excited disgust at what you'd seen or annoyed dismay that you'd missed out. There were rumours that some people had thought to forward or print it before it disappeared. If it did still exist in the real world nobody was suicidal enough to bring a copy into school. Enough people saw their careers ruined by it without there being further casualties.

It had all begun pretty much like any other Friday morning. Things had been taught and hopefully lessons had been learned. As a result of the school commandment *"Thou shalt not read emails whilst teaching"* most teachers did not even get to open the Email. If they did see it sitting in their inbox just as they were about to go for lunch they left it unopened as they had more important things to do. To be fair it looked pretty dull. An email from Mr Wingett entitled *Developing accurate flightpath target data for KS3 with calculations.* There were only a few teachers who took the time to open the Email and scan through the data in the document and fewer still who stayed awake long enough to open the attachment as well.

News of the Email's content spread through the staffroom in less time than it takes experts in education to invent new acronyms. It was always believed, though never proved, that it was Ms Malik, Second-In-Department for Geography, who went to report to SLT that Pandora's Box had been opened. Mr Lazenby, Head of IT, was the one who brought the news down to the staffroom and that could possibly explain why he mysteriously disappeared a few days later.

"Have you read your emails?" he asked when he sat down in the corner of the staffroom with his packed lunch. He trusted the group of teachers he always sat with if he was free at dinnertime.

"Don't tell me," smiled Tim Cocker. "Rowena's lost her favourite mug again?"

"You've not seen it then? The Email, I mean?"

Mr Digby had his laptop in its case beside him. He opened it up and began to log in. He typed his details in carefully a second time and then tried again.

"I can't log in, Alec," he said. "Oh, hang on a mo'." A message popped up on the screen. "It says I don't have permission to access anything. That's weird. I've just put all my data onto SCAMS."

Tim Cocker tried logging in with his details and got a further message saying that the laptop should be returned to the IT Support Department of Wildside Academy. A moment later the laptop turned itself off with what seemed like a contented sigh. The weekend had come early.

"I'm no expert," said Tim as he opened a bag of prawn crisps, "but that's not right. Is it?"

"It looks to me like somebody's authorized a total system lockdown," said Alec. "That never happens. It'll be chaos. Like the Millennium Bug. Somebody really doesn't want us to read that Email."

"And I'm guessing," said Mr Ansari, lowering his voice and checking who was sitting nearby, "you've read it? Go on, Alec."

Instinctively the small group of teachers moved a little closer together as Mr Lazenby began.

"I was free last lesson," he said, "so I went on my emails. There was one from Gary that he'd sent to all staff about how he's changed how he wants today's data put on SCAMS. Now he's sent that but he must then have attached the wrong file. Not one about *Dev*eloping data but one meant for *Dev*lin in Maths!"

"So what's he sent us all then?" asked Mr Haddenough who'd been too busy to open his emails before lunchtime. He was teaching a full day and would have to put the data on before he went home for the weekend.

"He's only gone and sent us all his thoughts on Jim," said Mr Lazenby, "obviously based on conversations he's had with Sean Devlin. Written on Monday. Now you know me, I'm no prude, but this was the most foul-mouthed character assassination of a person I've ever read. I mean really personal and uncalled for. Vicious!"

By Jim he meant Mr Milton who'd been Head of Maths at the school for over ten years.

"I don't know what those two have got against Jim," said Mr Eccleston. "They're always running him down in meetings. Decent bloke and they always get amazing results in Maths."

Alec glanced round the staffroom. It was fairly empty, there were no members of the SLT present and Ms Malik was on playground duty.

"We just all need to watch out," he advised quietly. "The second part of what Gary had sent to Sean Devlin was his plan for how they could get rid of Jim as Head of Maths. Making stuff up against him. Nobody's been safe here since Steve left."

There was an eerie silence in the corner of the staffroom as the implications of the Email sank in. The silence was eventually broken by Ms Grimley, over by the fridge, complaining loudly that somebody had taken her sandwiches again. Miss Honeywell, the Teaching Assistant, looked up from her copy of '*Wuthering Heights*' and wondered whether to tell Ms Grimley that she'd seen her eating her sandwiches at breaktime.

The chaos that afternoon was, as Mr Lazenby had predicted, unprecedented even by Wildside Academy's past record. Trevor Rojan had been ordered to shut down all the computer systems straight away and now Adil needed to go to every single room in the school to check that the Email was not inadvertently displayed on any frozen whiteboards. Trevor would remain in the IT Support office where his computers were the only ones still in operation apart from Ms Stonehart's. His first task would be to go through the photocopying log for the last two hours meticulously checking whether anybody had sent the Email to print. Then he would have to check every file that had been downloaded to USB or forwarded via email. He could forget about his sandwich as Ms Stonehart wanted any information by the end of lunchtime. Then their next assignment would be to go through every single employee's computer account and re-set every password before assigning them each a new email address.

"I'm guessing this is going to take us a while," said Adil to his boss as he set off on his quest.

"Erm, yeah, I think so," sighed Trevor.

The pandemonium in the canteen was worse than ever. Nobody could log in to collect money for meals and Mr Goldbloom had come along to insist that pupils were not to be given food for free. Ms Malik, Second-in-Department for Geography, was trying to take a list of pupils' names and the meals they were trying to purchase.

"And do you want fries with that?" she found herself asking over and over again.

It was hopeless.

As the bells were regulated by the computer system they failed to signal the end of the lunch break and most pupils just chose to stay out of earshot at the far end of the field. It was decided that the job of herding them all up and shepherding them back into lessons was really the responsibility of Heads of Year rather than SLT. Eventually, once pupils realised that they could no longer get a signal on their mobile phones, phones which theoretically didn't even exist in school, they got bored and came back inside to see what was happening.

Some of the younger teachers found themselves totally rudderless without a computer and an interactive whiteboard. After two weeks of preparation the PGCE students were not able to deliver the five-minute starter they'd all planned. In some Departments though it was pretty much business as usual. In the Science Department pupils continued to copy pages out of their textbooks, maps were again meticulously coloured in for Geography. The Music classrooms echoed to recitals of *London's Burning* and in the English Department pupils were pressing on with '*Lord of the Flies*'. The Maths Department were not so desperate that they needed to blow the dust off the slide rules and log tables. Unfortunately the lockdown created problems for the office staff who could not log on to get the cake rota for the following week. Jules was just glad that the fire alarm was disabled.

And because everything needed to carry on as normal Ms Winter and Ms Payne continued to do their drop-in lesson observations for the chosen few on their hitlist. As teachers could not access the online materials that formed the very backbone of their courses there was naturally only one thing they could conclude. Lessons were *"unsatisfactory because they did not use the full range of resources needed to demonstrate differentiation and meet the needs of every pupil"* in the five minutes that they had observed.

Nobody wanted to miss Monday morning's briefing and the only two people noticeable by their absence were Trevor and Adil. As they had had to work right through the weekend, resetting the entire computer network of Wildside Academy, Ms Stonehart had agreed that they didn't need to come in till morning break on Monday.

"Nothing from me," she announced to her hushed audience, "except to thank my SLT and the HR Department for keeping everything running so smoothly during the events of last Friday afternoon. Gary?"

All eyes turned to the Deputy Head. Was the Email really going to be addressed? Somebody's text ringtone broke the silence with the sting from *The Good, the Bad and the Ugly* but the moment went unchallenged.

"I'll be brief as it is a briefing," said Mr Wingett who'd either spent his weekend thinking up that opening line or had got somebody else to write it for him. "It's one of our school values, Integrity, and that's what we're talking about here. Integrity. My definition of integrity has always been "doing the right thing even when nobody is watching." Now on Friday, as some as you will know, the integrity of our school's computer system was breached. Hackers got in, did all sorts of dreadful things, including identity fraud and corrupting important files. It was only down to the integrity of the SLT and the hard work of Trev and Adil in IT Support that the whole thing wasn't a lot worse. No money was actually stolen from the business you'll be pleased to hear. But I want you all to think about that word, Integrity."

He paused for effect, trying to look as many teachers as he could squarely in the eye. Ms Malik was sitting on the edge of her seat, no doubt believing that she'd be mentioned in dispatches.

"Were you there in the canteen or helping to get pupils back in to lessons? Were you out on the corridor between lessons or at the gates at the end of the day, keeping things calm? Where were you when you were needed? And did you put your data onto SCAMS before the deadline in the way I'd asked? Integrity. Doing the right thing even when nobody is watching….Some of you need to remember that."

Mr Lazenby felt that he was looking at him. Mr Haddenough surreptitiously checked that his top button was done up.

"And I'll just also add," Ms Winter butted in, "that somebody *was* watching. Those of you what had lessons observed by Sharon and I will be getting feedback. It wasn't good enough."

"Now the system's up and running again," continued Mr Wingett and as if to prove it the bell for registration rang out. "When Trev's back in after break he'll send you all an email showing you how to log on to the new email system. Those of you who didn't get your data on SCAMS in time in the format I said can also expect an email from Mrs Spratt."

"If we're going to continue to go from strength to strength," said Ms Stonehart, startling those teachers who'd forgotten she was still there, "we need Integrity. It's what Ofsted are looking for. Like Gary says, doing the right thing when nobody's looking and that's why I've decided we need more CCTV. "

In what might be called the aftermath of all this nobody at Wildside Academy ever saw Mr Jim Milton again. Perhaps appropriately for the Maths Department it really was a case of divide and conquer. Within a week Mr Devlin had been promoted to Acting Head of Maths just to fill the gap. It came as no surprise that after the Easter break even the word *Acting* had been removed from his job title.

The following term, without even a hint of irony, Mr Wingett went on to deliver an assembly on Integrity.

CHAPTER 36

"The past was once the future."

Much to Mrs Thorne's relief, the placement for the PGCE students would soon be coming to an end. With no classroom base to call their own they had assumed squatters' rights on the main row of computers in the workroom adjacent to the staffroom. Here they had spent their days, occasionally leaving to watch a lesson being taught in their Department, but mostly working on their 80,000-word essays or catching up on social media and funny cat videos. The more diligent trainees had planned their five-minute starter PowerPoint activity which was going to be their only hands-on teaching experience in the four week placement.

Even though the student teachers clearly misunderstood the label *"the quiet room"* most teachers tolerated their presence in there. They were about the only people who could help with logging on to the new email system that Trevor Rojan had set up after the incident that had become known as EmailGate. Most of the staff had done just enough INSET about online security to know that an email with the phrase T.Rojan in it was probably a virus. The PGCE students were generally very helpful in unblocking the photocopier too.

"So there I was," said Mr Eccleston, making the most of his free period to chat to the young trainees, "Period 5, Friday, thirty-two Year 9 pupils, eight Ofsted inspectors in and I'm dangerously low on worksheets. Then this one kid, Craig, notorious throughout the school as a chucker, throws up all over my desk just as…"

At that moment Mrs Thorne came in, looking a little concerned that her protégés were mixing with old school teachers again. They were like moths to a flame, eager to hear stories about teaching although this had twice led to Gareth saying he didn't want to be a teacher anymore.

"I think Norma was looking for you, Pete," she said to Mr Eccleston. "A Drama cover or something next lesson."

Mr Eccleston made his excuses and promptly left.

"Run for your life!" he smiled as the door closed behind him.

"How are you all doing?" Mrs Thorne began, a little relieved. "The final PowerPoint presentations all ready? If you need any help, just let me know. I'm sure you know I'm always here to help you."

Glancing at Gareth Worral's screen she'd seen that he'd started filling in the PGCE Student Voice Assessment of how well she and Wildside Academy had done. He was Mrs Thorne's main concern as she knew he had not really enjoyed his time in the Science Department. The other four trainees would give her a good report. Alex Tennant absolutely idolized Ms Malik, Second-in-Department for Geography ; Dylan Cooper had enjoyed being in Recorder Club ; Holly had clearly appreciated having Mr Chang's old Art room to work in ; Mr Kaye had said Kimama Akinyemizola had fitted in so well that there'd be a job for her in the English Department when she finished her training. Provided she bought him a pint! Four out of five would count as a success for her Bright Sky target.

"Ah, Mrs Thorne," said a quiet voice nervously behind her.

She turned around to find Mrs Spratt holding out a slip of paper.

"You've got an emergency cover next lesson. Mr Humble in the Drama studio?"

"I thought Mr Eccleston was down for that..." Mrs Thorne began.

"I hear what you say but he says he's got a meeting with Miss Skellen about Bright Sky or something."

And without any further discussion Mrs Spratt was gone, back to the safety of her policies and her filing cabinets behind the Berlin Wall. Reluctantly Mrs Thorne had to leave the trainee teachers to their own electronic devices, hoping desperately that they wouldn't speak to Brigadier Vernon-Smythe.

"So what are you doing for the assignment?" asked Holly.

Alex, PGCE student for Geography, looked up from his screen.

"I've got about half of mine done. '*The pedagogical impact of the transition from chalk to talk in twenty-first century child-centred learning.*' Mina's given me some great ideas."

"You've done well loads," said Kimama, looking at his monitor. "I bet it's brill! Read us a bit, Lex, pretty please."

"*According to Adamson, Barber and Conti in 'Every Child Matters' (2017),[1]*" Alex read out, "*child-centred learning significantly encompasses pedagogical methods of learning that shift the focus of largely didactic instruction from the teacher over to the learner with the aim of developing greater learner independence and cognitive autonomy…*"

"Not bad," said Dylan, standing up to look over Alex's shoulder. "I'm doing the one about *'The cross-curricular benefits of a holistic approach through Phenomenon-Based Learning as a multidisciplinary constructivist form of pedagogy.'* PhenoBL's not what I thought it was though. To be honest there's so little time I'm thinking of just copy-and-pasting bits of it off the internet."

"I can't do that again like," moaned Gareth, the Science trainee. "My tutor said last time that I plagiarize too much. Her words, not mine."

"Have you noticed," said Dylan, "that you only ever hear the word 'cohort' in schools?"

"True," said Alex.

"Do you ever wonder if these assignments have any relevance to what goes on out there?" pondered Holly, looking out of the window towards the nearest block of classrooms.

"I know what you mean," added Dylan. "If actions speak louder than words why do we have to write 80,000 words then?"

There was silence for a moment, broken only by the thump of a boy whacking the glass before running off screaming.

"They must be important," said Alex. "They wouldn't have us sitting in here typing away like monkeys unless…" The thought had sounded better in his head. "Actually, I might ask Mina if I can observe another of her lessons. Just to check before I do my starter exercise next week." He opened a copy of *"Exploring Geography Through Pictures and Worksheets"* hoping to find some inspiration amongst the monochrome pages.

Dylan Cooper had decided that if he was to look at cross-curricular themes in his assignment then the best thing to do would be to speak to teachers from other Departments. Writing down what they said surely wouldn't be plagiarism if he'd done all the research himself? He opened the Welcome Pack they'd all been given at the start of the placement and scanned through the staff list for possible victims.

"Holly," he said, without looking up, "Mr Chang in your Department, what's he like? Would he give me some ideas for my assignment?"

Holly had to think for a moment and then she remembered.

"He doesn't work here any longer. That's why I've got his room. He mysteriously disappeared about a couple of months ago."

"What like Mr Lazenby and Mr Milton after that Email?," said Dylan, looking round the room.

"That was when the Head of RE resigned, wasn't it?"

"I can't believe how few Heads of Department there are. Have you met the *Acting* Head of MFL! I don't think he'd be able to help me."

Dylan found he was quietly humming the *Marseillaise.*

"It's weird how many teachers are *Acting* but only one Drama teacher like," commented Gareth. "Jamie. CBA? What does that stand for anyway?"

"I heard that there were originally two Drama teachers but the one that ran the course in mime was never heard from again one day."

"And what's an Executive Head of Department?" asked Holly but nobody knew.

"Who's Fraulein Schadenfreude?" asked Kimama, looking at the list. "If that's how you pronounce it."

Foreign languages were not her strong point. In fact she even felt her grasp of English had gone downhill in the short time she'd been with Billy and the girls at Wildside Academy.

"Huw's mentioned her. She used to teach German apparently," said Dylan. "I don't think this has been updated. He said she was a right old battle-axe!"

It was purely coincidental that Ms Grimley came into the quiet room at that point and told them all to be silent. She'd not been observed for two days and she needed a quiet space where she could check over her lesson planning folder again. Grabbing his salad box Dylan decided that he could just as easily carry out his research in the staffroom. After a moment with Ms Grimley the other PGCE students decided to join him.

As they left the workroom the phone in the corner started ringing. Fearing a cover lesson Ms Grimley ignored it but Mr

Abbott bravely took the call.

"You're looking for a what?" he asked, looking shocked. "A pianist? Oh, right. Sorry, I misheard you."

Mr Cocker greeted the trainee teachers like long lost friends when they came through to the staffroom. Even though the lunchtime bell had just sounded the room was still fairly empty as most teachers had now found other places they'd rather eat. In about ten minutes the English Department would raucously fill up their usual places and the little clique of diners who sat at the breakfast bar would block off the kettle and the microwave again. Ms Grimley raced through from the workroom, opened the fridge, then glared at the other teachers.

"Have any of you taken a red sandwich box?" she demanded, storming off to the canteen when she got no joy.

Mr Cocker invited the PGCE students to join him and the other teacher he was with. Ms Akinyemizola declined, preferring to sit and wait for the other members of the English Department.

"So how's it all coming along?" asked Tim, opening a second bag of prawn crisps. "You'll be finishing soon."

"Not too bad," said Alex Tennant who'd already watched one of Mr Cocker's Geography lessons. "Up to our eyeballs in essay writing."

"We never had to do all that in my day," said the man sitting next to Mr Cocker. He paused from the carrot he was nibbling. "All we ever did was teach. Reciting verb tables."

"Sorry, what is it you teach?" asked Holly politely.

"I used to teach Latin," said Mr Bland, "but then they reorganized it all. I teach Maths now."

It had been Mr Thicke who had reviewed the school's curriculum that year. In his opinion dead languages were even more useless than German. Alphabetically Maths was probably the nearest thing to Latin and Mr Bland still had a mortgage to pay.

"Quis erit, erit!" said Mr Bland philosophically, returning to his salad.

"You what, Malcolm?" said Tim.

"Que sera, sera."

"Right!" Tim nodded, none the wiser. "Well, it is what it is."

"You speak a lot of languages for a Maths teacher," commented Holly.

"All the main ones," said Malcolm proudly. "French, German, Mandarin Chinese, Welsh, you name it."

"Ĉu vi parolas esperanton iel?" asked Dylan, a cherry tomato on a plastic fork paused in mid-air.

"Mi ne kredas ĝin!" exclaimed Mr Bland smiling, a tear in his eye. "Mi ĉiam sciis, ke mi trovos iun alian ol mian familion, kiu parolis esperanto!"

"And for those of us who don't speak Klingon like?" grumbled Gareth Worral, the Science trainee.

"Malcolm's our Esperanto specialist," explained Tim. "He speaks it like a native."

"Is there much call for Esperanto in Lower Steem?" asked Gareth without thinking. "You could do with a STEM club like."

"More to the point," said Holly, "where did you learn Esperanto, Dylan? You kept that quiet. "

"Too busy on that recorder at all hours!" grumbled Gareth.

"I lived in Vietnam for a year," said Dylan. "I learnt it there. Se vi ne komprenas min, Holly, uzu vortaron!"

Malcolm Bland smiled at their private joke, knowing that if Holly spoke Esperanto she wouldn't actually need a dictionary.

"You must come along to the Esperanto Club I run here. My son, Melvyn, would love to meet you."

In truth Melvyn was the only member of the Esperanto Club. It gave him something to do at lunchtime rather than just sitting on his own reciting Latin verbs. Not having a television or computer in the Bland household meant that Melvyn often felt he had little in common with his peers. He didn't know what this *Celebrity Academy* thing was. His fellow pupils had no idea how delightful it was to visit National Trust properties and they would probably be terribly envious of his collection of teapots.

"I bet you like crosswords too," continued Mr Bland, picking up a copy of *The Times* from the seat beside him. "It's a shame they don't do this in Latin. *Quidquid latine dictum sit, altum sonatur!*"

"No idea what you're on about, Malcolm," smiled Tim.

"Whatever is said in Latin sounds profound," explained Malcolm with a smug look on his bearded face. He took a look at the first clue.

1 Across :
Swindler escapes down prison wall, of course! (13 letters.)
"*Condescending!* That's just a big word for patronising, meaning

when you talk down to people," Malcolm explained.

1 Down :

A satisfying feeling when I catch rat (9 letters.)

"*Cathartic!*" replied Malcolm without hesitation.

"Like writing your memoirs about working at this place?" added Ivor Haddenough who had sat down to join them. "We could tell some stories, couldn't we, Tim?"

"But would anybody believe us!"

"Cathartic?" queried Gareth.

"It's an anagram," explained Malcolm

"Malcolm's the anagram expert, you know," said Tim as he put his crisp packets in the bin. "Along with Huw."

Malcolm glared at him.

"So what would Dylan Cooper be as an anagram?" Dylan asked.

"Corny old ape!" said Malcolm without hesitation.

"Back of the net!" exclaimed Gareth. "I'm going to call you that! Corny old ape!"

"Can you make up anagrams for anybody's name?" asked Holly.

"Of course. It's not difficult."

"What was that one you made up for Janine when we had to do the Fire Safety training again?" pondered Ivor.

Malcolm glanced round to check that the staffroom was still empty before continuing.

"Well, I know it's a bit naughty but I worked out that *Janine Stonehart* is *Another INSET, Jan?* There are other ones like *Janine Northeast* and a rather surreal one about that stuff she drinks, *Jan's ten rhino tea!*"

It was a shame that Malcolm was so engrossed in his wordplay with the students that he failed to notice Ms Mina Malik coming in to the staffroom. When he got summoned to Ms Stonehart's office he probably didn't get a chance to explain that he was discussing anagrams of the words *Wildside Academy*. Taken out of context the phrases *"mildew aids decay"* and *"decide dismal way"* might possibly sound like he was criticizing either the facilities or her leadership. He didn't even get the opportunity to agree that Wildside Academy was indeed going from strength to strength.

Dylan Cooper never got to attend the Esperanto Club and found himself attempting *The Times* crossword on his own from then on.

CHAPTER 37

"A leader knows the way, goes the way and shows the way."

Madame Loups-Garoux had chatted to the other Heads of Year as this wasn't just any assembly she was delivering, it was the one her Bright Sky target was based on. She'd learned that the way the new Wildside Academy values were being wheeled out would mean that she had to include the theme of "Leadership" in her assembly. Mr Heinz, the Head of Year 11, had jokingly commented that SLT wouldn't be covering that theme as they'd be seriously out of their comfort zone. Shortly after making this observation Steve Heinz had gone off on long term sick, suffering from stress. Jamie Humble had quickly been promoted to the post of Acting Head of Year 11, his next stepping stone towards the Senior Leadership Team itself.

"Merci beaucoup for 'elping me so much," said Madame Loups-Garoux to her Acting Head of Department.

"Yeah, yeah, yeah, no trouble, Céline. It was the least I could do, after all you've done for me," said Mr Buonanulla, checking that the leads were correctly attached to the laptop.

There was a brief buzzing sound and then the PowerPoint they had made together appeared on the screen above their heads. The first slide, in the corporate colours of Wildside Academy with the designated font size for assemblies, proudly announced that today's theme was "Leadership."

Madame Loups-Garoux looked round the empty canteen where Bob had set out chairs for Year 9. She'd arrived early and had a quiet word with Eric the chef, asking if he could leave the serving hatch closed until her assembly was finished. It had cost her the price of a drink down The Cock 'n' Bull but it was worth it for her Bright Sky target.

Mr Buonanulla ran through the different slides of the PowerPoint for her to check that everything was in order. They'd decided against a starter exercise asking the pupils to rearrange the letters in the word "Dealership" and so end up with the key word "Leadership." If anything had been learned from Mr Bland's disappearance it was that witty anagrams were not appreciated, particularly ones that could make the school sound like a second-hand car business.

As Acting Head of Department and Head of Year it hadn't taken them long to compile a list of the key characteristics of a good leader. Between them they had a lot of free periods to search the internet together for ideas. Words like vision, communication, creativity and accountability were generously sprinkled across the slides, always in the corporate colours and font.

"So, what I really like about this," said Mr Buonanulla, returning to the initial slide, "is the link between the theme of Leadership and the Leaders of Language scheme you run."

Learning Foreign Languages is genuinely a worthwhile thing to do. It improves your vocabulary, increases empathy and awakens parts of your brain that might otherwise remain dormant. It improves your performance in other exams, your employment chances and your foreign holidays. All this is true but for Madame Loups-Garoux there was a more important concern.

About two years ago she'd discovered an association called Leaders of Language and as soon as she'd read what they did she signed up immediately. As a Co-ordinator of LoL she'd been given a week off timetable to go on a residential training course, allowing Mr Haddenough to cover her lessons if he was free. Returning with a colourful certificate she then had the skills to identify the top ten linguists in the school and give them an instruction pack about how to teach Modern Foreign Languages. Now when Madame Loups-Garoux felt too tired to teach or Mr Buonanulla had a wee migraine a pupil on the Leaders of Language scheme could step in to teach the topic for them. There were days when they'd pile into the minibus with all the Leaders of Language from each year group and go teach Primary School pupils how to say *Bonjour* or use translation software properly. It was also good as it allowed Miss Brown and Mr Haddenough to develop their leadership skills in the absence of the rest of the Department.

"I'm 'oping the Leaders of Language will be 'ere any minute," said Madame Loups-Garoux, a little concerned. "I did tell them all to turn up at least ten minutes before assembly. Zut alors!"

She turned as the door at the back of the canteen squeaked open. But instead of her little helpers Mr Gordon looked in.

"Do you need me this morning?" he asked cheerfully. "I can even play the *Marseillaise* if you want!" He wriggled his fingers to show that he was fit for work again after his accident in the DT Department.

"Dean!" exclaimed Madame Loups-Garoux. "I didn't know you were back! We've decided against a song this morning."

It certainly wouldn't have been the *Marseillaise* which hadn't been heard since the night of that Open Evening.

Mr Gordon's face sank when he found he was redundant, realising that he'd have to spend half an hour's registration with Ms Shakespeare's Year 8 form rather than happily tickling the ivories. Still it could have been worse. He could have been made redundant in a more permanent sense!

A minute later the door opened again and a boy and a girl entered, two of Madame Loups-Garoux's Leaders of Language.

"But where are the others?" she demanded without a word of thanks that they'd turned up. "M'enfin!"

"We just came to check it was today. With you telling us about it in French, we weren't sure if it were Thursday, Madam Lewd-Gerroux."

"Loups-Garoux," Mr Buonanulla corrected them quietly.

"I definitely said *mercredi*," insisted his friend. "Mine are always the Wednesdays. Usually. See if you can find the others, d'accord? Vite! Allez!"

The two pupils turned and left. She heard Chloe mutter the word *mercredi* as the door closed again. Her French was definitely improving if she was starting to use slang now.

With just two minutes left until all her form tutors would arrive with their classes Madame Loups-Garoux gave everything one final check. The chairs were all out, ten chairs positioned at the front for her ambassadors, the PowerPoint was quietly humming in readiness and it seemed that Eric had gone to have a quiet cigarette. Absolument parfait!

When the bell finally rang for the start of first period Madame Loups-Garoux stood up and looked round the empty canteen.

A figure appeared at the side door coughing.

"Alright if I get the pizzas ready now is it?" asked Eric.

Madame Loups-Garoux waved him on impatiently and looked over to her Acting Head of Department who was sitting alone near the laptop, rubbing his temples. Even her Leaders of Language, the *crème de la crème* had not turned up for her assembly. The ten large cards that they would have held up to spell out the word 'L-E-A-D-E-R-S-H-I-P' lay untouched on the row of chairs at the front.

"I don't understand where everybody is," said Madame Loups-Garoux.

"You never get the wrong day," said her Acting Head of Department. "You're always so well organised. I don't know how you do it."

Over the years they had genuinely both forgotten about that disastrous trip to Cafard-sur-Mer. Madame Loups-Garoux had run the trip abroad with Year 10 because it had been the cheapest way for her to take Hamish to meet her family. Unfortunately she'd misread the date on the return tickets and when they all arrived at the Calais ferry terminal the boat had already left the day before. Luckily it had all been sorted out with a quick phone call to Ivor back in England with the added bonus that they'd been able to blame him for the whole thing afterwards.

"You lookin' for Year 9?" Eric called out as he went to open the shutters. "They're all in the Sports Hall with Whingey."

Mr Buonanulla was thumbing through his phone, carefully checking his emails.

"So, there's an email from Gary here. He's cancelled Year 9 assembly. There's a list of all the kids he wants to see after some incident on the school bus last night."

Madame Loups-Garoux looked up at her PowerPoint. It had frozen on the slide about communication being a key part of effective leadership.

"Well, 'e could 'ave told me!" she said. "This was my Bright Sky assembly."

"Don't worry," Mr Buonanulla assured his friend. "I'd already filled in the paperwork as I knew it'd be good. We put a lot of effort into it."

He handed her the form to sign. All the boxes were ticked, all the criteria had been met and her assembly had been 'outstanding.' The first of her Bright Sky targets had been passed with flying colours.

"So, I won't be able to get it scanned in till later."

"Oh, 'ave you got a class now? You work too 'ard."

"No. I'm free till this afternoon. I'm not sure what I'm going to do with Year 7 though." He pulled another blank form out of a folder. "I think I'll to go watch Ivor teach. See what he's doing with Year 7. I've not observed one of his lessons for a couple of days now."

CHAPTER 38

"It's not over till it's over."

It was at times like these, thought Ms Stonehart as she glanced at her schedule for the day, that the tremendous burden of being a Headteacher was all worthwhile.

The Easter break was just around the corner and with the real exams imminent it was a case of everybody mucking in together, making sure that Wildside Academy went from strength to strength and all the pupils got what they deserved. It was for that reason she hadn't booked a holiday abroad over the Easter break. It would be a lot easier for her staff to contact her if she spent the two weeks in Cornwall. As long as she wasn't in some sleepy little village somewhere that didn't get a signal.

To start the day she had instructed Eric the chef to lay on a special breakfast for the Prefects and her Senior Leadership Team. As Mr O'Brien was on playground duty she'd invited Ms Lovall in his place. The four Prefects together with the Head Boy and Head Girl entered Ms Stonehart's office with some trepidation, the only pupils ever to have gone in there in a very long time. Having pointed them in the right direction Mrs Spratt returned to her office and her policies.

"We really do have some lovely youngsters here at Wildside Academy," said Ms Stonehart as the pupils took their seats at the large conference table. "I really don't understand it when some teachers claim their classes are unruly and disruptive."

"Aww, they're wicked!" agreed Ms Lovall.

"Yeah," commented Ms Winter briefly as she helped herself to another bacon and sausage butty. There was a time for talking and

246

a time for eating and she knew which this was.

At the other end of the table Mr Wingett and Mr Thicke looked like they could think of a million other places they'd rather be. As for Ms Payne, she was trying to hide her phone under the table while she texted Sean.

"Please, help yourself," said Ms Stonehart, indicating the steaming plates of bacon butties, sausages and cheese toasties that Eric had placed on the table.

"Daniel, isn't it?" she continued, turning to the Head Boy. She'd checked on his SCAMS profile that morning to make sure.

"Yes, Miss," said Dan, politely. Nobody had called him Daniel since Year 7 and under the circumstances it took him unawares.

"And what do you enjoy most here at Wildside?"

"Maths, Miss," said Dan, pausing in his attempts to get ketchup out of a bottle.

"Maths? So why do you like Maths so much, Daniel?" continued Ms Stonehart. It was important that everyone saw how well she got on with young people. They weren't unruly or disruptive for her. It was a gift really. You couldn't be taught it. You either had it or you hadn't and she was full of it.

"I just like the way Mr O'Reilly teaches it really, Miss. He just makes it relevant to real life I suppose."

Dan glanced nervously at Mr Thicke who'd taught him Maths in Year 7. He could still remember his school report from him that year saying that he'd *never really amount to much.*

"That sounds so interesting. Tell me more," encouraged Ms Stonehart.

Looking at the food laid out before them all prompted Dan to tell her about the fascinating conundrum of three people going for a meal in a restaurant and leaving a tip for the waiter. Not being a Maths teacher, or indeed a teacher, Ms Stonehart had found the calculations a little hard to follow. She had, however, been so keen to understand Daniel that she had even got her purse out so that he could demonstrate it with real money.

At the other end of the table her two Deputy Heads seemed to be arguing. Mr Thicke was asserting that each person had actually paid nine pounds thirty-three and a third of a penny recurring infinitely. Mr Wingett's point seemed to be that you shouldn't have to give waiters a tip. Nobody had ever given him a tip just for doing his job.

"Well, Maths all seems to have changed since my day," Ms Stonehart concluded, putting her purse away without thinking. She moved on to the other pupils to give them a chance to tell her why Wildside Academy was such a great school under her leadership.

When the breakfast treat came to an end the pupils breathed a sigh of relief, knowing that their friends wouldn't believe they'd met the Headteacher. Sinead, the Head Girl, made a point of looking at the name plate on the door as she left so that she could tell her Dad who it was they had met.

Once the pupils had left Ms Stonehart turned to her apprentice.

"So, tell us, Sally, how's this charity thing coming along? Have we got something good for the website to replace that Fairtrade thing?"

"You know what, it's not as easy as I thought it'd be," said Ms Lovall. "It's fab we've got The Dyslexia Trust as our charity but I asked form tutors to get their classes to make some posters to promote it…"

She rummaged in her laptop bag and pulled out a handful of loose sheets of paper.

"The trouble is most of the kids can't spell dyslexia," she continued. "These were about the best posters I got and I don't think we can put them on the website."

Instead of *dyslexia* one pupil had designed a poster that looked more like it was about knife crime with the words *yields ax* on it in large red letters. The only comment she made about the second poster was that she was glad Sonya hadn't done a drawing to go with the words *daily sex*.

"I got Mr Bland's Set 1 pupils to design a new logo for *The Dyslexia Trust* but they must have misunderstood it and came up with the words *Thursday Textiles!*"

Ms Stonehart's left eye twitched involuntarily at the mention of Mr Bland's name.

"I must admit I'm a little disappointed," Ms Stonehart said. "If you let me know which teachers you asked for the posters I'll send them an email. I can probably guess who it was. It's not good enough. They've let us all down."

"Yeah, but on the plus side I've organised my parachute jump for over the Easter holidays. It'll be wicked!"

Ms Stonehart thought for a moment.

"We may have to try a different charity. There's no point doing all this for a charity if there's nothing to put on the school website." She glanced out at the front drive where Bob was sweeping up. "It's a shame about the dyslexia thing. I just hope we haven't spent too much on it. Did you have any other suggestions?"

Ms Lovall hadn't really had enough time to come up with other ideas. She glanced down at the papers in her hand. On top of the posters was a handwritten letter from a parent explaining why her daughter had been absent. After twelve crossed out attempts at the word diarrhoea, the Mum had just decided to write that Emily had had "the runs."

"I was thinking that we could go with *Children With Diarrhoea*," suggested Ms Lovall. "And with that cause in mind it'd be good to get everybody off timetable for a Fun Run? But not get anybody making posters this time. I mean dyslexia was a fab idea but some of the kids were making fun of it. You know, like saying DNA stands for the National Association for Dyslexics."

Ms Stonehart looked puzzled.

"Deoxyribonucleic acid, isn't it?" said Mr Thicke after a moment, surprising everybody.

"Well, anyway," Ms Stonehart concluded. "Good luck with the parachute jump."

It took Ms Lovall a moment to realise she wasn't needed at the meeting any longer. Much as Ms Stonehart liked her, Sally needed to be reminded that she wasn't actually a member of her SLT. Yet.

"If you need to be off timetable to plan for the new charity just see Norma. I'm sure you'll have a lot to do. Don't let us keep you."

The penny dropped faster than a faulty parachute.

"Cheers for the butties!" she said, getting up. "Wicked!"

"Now there are a few things I want to talk to you about," Ms Stonehart continued once Ms Lovall had closed the door behind her, "like integrity."

Mr Wingett sat forward a little in his seat, looking a little uncomfortable. "Integrity?"

"Yes, integrity. One of our school values. You spoke to the staff about integrity, Gary, and I have to say I was impressed with how you phrased it. What was it again?"

"Doing the right thing even when nobody is watching," said Mr

Wingett.

Ironically it was a phrase that he'd first heard Mr Milton use when he'd been observing one of his form periods.

"That's it!" said Ms Stonehart. "I like it and it got me thinking. You remember the Literacy thing Lynne's working on? We need inspirational quotes like that around the school. Words that will stop the pupils in their tracks when they're going up and downstairs and make them think."

She'd noticed on the USA website that the walls of their rival school were decorated with similar words of wisdom. It would be so much cheaper than building a library.

"Any thoughts, anybody?"

Without thinking Ms Payne had got her mobile phone out and was searching for ideas.

"*Your life should be your message to the world. Write inspiring words and your name will live forever,*" she read out.

"I like that," said Ms Stonehart. "Who said it?"

"Oh," replied Ms Payne. "It's anonymous!"

"Well, you get the idea," continued Ms Stonehart. "We've got plenty of money set aside for this kind of project and Alex says Vernon-Smythe's brother's a painter who could do the job at a reasonable rate. I'm calling it '*Project WOW!*' Words of Wisdom, you see?"

She handed them each a floor plan of the school with the words '*Project WOW!*' printed across the top.

"I want you all to come up with quotes for each of these areas by close of business tonight. Make them relevant to the subject taught there. I'll choose the best ones so we can get started after Easter."

"What about the ones on the MFL corridor?" said Mr Thicke, annoyed that this project didn't seem to involve a few days at the Premier Inn. "None of us speak foreign languages. Should we get the MFL Department to do it?"

"Certainly not. Haven't you heard of translation software?" said Ms Stonehart, emphasizing the importance of Modern Foreign Languages at Wildside Academy.

"And speaking of Literacy, Lynne, I'll be wanting those photos in after Easter so I can choose the winner."

"Yeah, it'll be brill," commented Ms Winter who'd totally forgotten about the competition. She made a mental note to remind Melody to sort it out before Easter.

"Totes WOW!" added Ms Payne as though she'd won the Nobel prize for Literature. "Dead brill!"

"And one last thing," said Ms Stonehart, handing them all another sheet of paper. "Speaking of nobody watching. We're getting that CCTV fitted over the holiday. Bob's got two weeks' leave and he'll be away down south. I can't really just leave it up to Stan and IT Support to sort it all out, so I've drawn up a rota. As there's five of you it'll only mean two days each and you'll probably be wanting to come in to supervise Year 11 revision classes anyway. I'll give you the number of where I'm staying in case you can't get me on my mobile. But only in a real emergency, please. You've no idea how tiring it is being a Headteacher."

She opened her purse to search for the little card that had the details of where they were staying. It was a good job she did as she realised she needed to go to the bank to withdraw some money for the holiday. She'd thought she had about thirty-five pounds on her.

From : JST (Headteacher) - JStonehart@WildsideAcademy
To : Allstaff1@WildsideAcademy
CC : TCS – TChambers1@WildsideAcademy
Attached : Rota of voluntary Year 11 revision sessions (two week schedule.)
Sent : Fri 12 Apr 11:59
Subject : Easter plans

Good Afternoon

As we break up for Easter I just wanted to take this opportunity to remind you of all the improvements that my SLT and HR teams have made this term. The new staff car park is a vast improvement and the telescope is a welcome addition to the Science Department.

As you come in for the Year 11 revision classes over the Easter holiday you will notice other work being carried out to make Wildside Academy an even better place for you to work in. CCTV will be being fitted throughout the school which will work in conjunction with SCAMS (SLT only.) Whilst you do not hear of staff here being assaulted by pupils like at USA, as your employer we take your personal safety very seriously.

A team of painters will also be preparing the walls throughout the school which will see my "Words of Wisdom!" (WOW!) Literacy project begin after the break. A big thank you must go to the SLT who have come up with so many good quotations for our walls. The pupils' Literacy will improve enormously as a result of my Words of Wisdom! Under my leadership as Headteacher Wildside Academy really is going from strength to strength!

My employee of the term recommendation goes to Ms Lovall who has worked tirelessly to set up the school charity. I am sure you will all want to sponsor Sally with the parachute jump she is doing over Easter. Please email Alex Goldbloom if you would like your donation to come directly out of your salary.

Can I remind you all that school opens again on April 29th with a briefing at 8am prompt. As the real GCSE exams are imminent I know that as professionals you will be coming into school most days to help Year 11, even if your name is not on the attached rota. In my absence Mrs Spratt will be keeping a list of those teachers who attend over Easter. You will be aware, I am sure, that an Ofsted inspection cannot be far off as they have not been in for 612 working days. Obviously if we do not get an improved grading at the next Ofsted inspection I will have no option but to review staffing. The list of who has attended the voluntary sessions over Easter will help to inform my decision and make sure that everything is done in a transparent manner.

To end on a positive note, you will be pleased to hear that the repair men for the heating system in the main building will be in looking at how to turn it off now that the warmer weather is here and exams are starting.

Tempus fugit!
Happy Easter!

***Ms J. Stonehart, Headteacher**, Wildside Academy,*
Diploma in Human Resources, TGCSEC, CPT, BPB.

Wisdom, Inspiration, Leadership, Determination, Success, Integrity, Dedication, Excelence.

TERM 3

CHAPTER 39

"By words we learn thoughts and by thoughts we learn life."

If you had time to read all the Words of Wisdom that were appearing on the walls all over Wildside Academy you might conclude that the painters had probably bitten off more than they could chew. Either they wanted to get the job done quickly before the kids returned or else they had simply painted what they'd been told to paint. For whatever reason the first slogan that greeted you in the main reception announced that *Wildside Academy is a school where every child mutters.*

Following on from Ms Stonehart's encouraging email there seemed to be almost as many teachers in school over the Easter break as there were on a normal day. Ms Malik, Second-in-Department for Geography, could regularly be heard commenting that it was a wonderful opportunity to help the pupils achieve their full potential. Most of Year 11 on the other hand had decided that if any extra revision was needed it could best be done in the comfort of their own bedroom. What they didn't know now, the saying went, they probably wouldn't ever know. Ms Malik made a point of being the first to clock in and the last to leave each day since effectiveness is clearly measured by the amount of time you spend in a building.

Surprisingly some teachers did not spend any of their holidays in school. Mr Hayes, for example, said that it would invalidate his calculations for how long he had till retirement. As it turned out, the fact that he was quietly made redundant two weeks after the Easter break meant that his calculations had always been wrong. Mr Buonanulla saw two weeks in the south of France as professional development, leaving it to Mr Haddenough and Miss

Brown to come in and prepare students for their speaking exams.

Returning refreshed for the new term, Ms Stonehart looked at the words she had chosen to have painted above her office door.

"The task of the leader is to get their people from where they are to where they have not been."

She had chosen her words wisely. Not only was she leading the school from strength to strength on a daily basis, she was confident that the GCSE results in the summer were going to be like nothing Wildside Academy had ever seen before.

She was keen to see all the work that had been carried out around the school in her absence but as the pupils were already in the building she didn't want to disturb them. When Mrs Spratt brought through her first cup of tea of the day she was disappointed that the scones were nowhere near as tasty as the ones they'd had in Cornwall.

"I'm afraid I've had to get the scones from the KwikShop," apologized Mrs Spratt. "We had to let Mrs Carter go before the holidays and Eric says he can't do scones. Sorry."

To be honest Eric had problems with the recipe for ice cubes.

"Well, look into finding a better supplier, would you?" grumbled Ms Stonehart. This was not a good start to her day. "Has all the CCTV been installed? I don't want to be disturbed by drilling when I'm concentrating."

"I hear what you say," said Mrs Spratt, obediently. "I believe there's just a little bit left to do at the far end of the Main Hall and on the MFL corridor. Other than that I think the system's pretty much up and running."

"Excellent! Send IT Support in straight away, would you? I want to see it all in action."

Ms Stonehart's computer was probably the best-equipped one in the whole school and loaded up SCAMS without the usual twenty-minute wait for essential updates.

"So I'll be able to see everything that's going on in the school from here?" she asked excitedly. In many ways this would be even better than the telescope.

"Erm, yeah, I think so," confirmed Trevor, fiddling with Ms Stonehart's mouse for a moment.

The screen showed a mosaic from sixteen of the cameras that

were now positioned the length and breadth of Wildside Academy. With over four hundred cameras to choose from this would be even better than watching television at home.

With so many choices it was easy to overlook the fact that none of the cameras covered the IT Support Department.

"I want to see what it all looks like out there," she said. "Let's start with the staffroom."

Trevor adjusted a setting so that one small piece of the jigsaw now filled the entire monitor screen. The newly-painted quote could clearly be seen running the full length of the back wall : *"Choose a job you love and you will never have to work a day of your life."* She had had another wall covered in the eight Wildside Academy values whilst quotations from Ofsted and targets to lead them to victory covered all the remaining space. Her staff would be able to read all this while relaxing and having their lunch, rather than having to strain their eyes on computer screens all the time. Staff well-being was important to her. She could see that most of the teachers in the staffroom were pointing at the new displays, clearly appreciating what she had done for them.

"An excellent start, Trevor. Let's have the guided tour now."

Trevor moved the mouse over different images, clicking to enlarge them before moving on a few moments later. At the centre of her web Ms Stonehart would be able to see nearly everything that was going on without having to move from the comfort of her office. Ofsted would praise her for her efficiency.

The first screen she looked at showed the canteen. How useful that would be, making sure she could attend every assembly, even when she had more important things to do. Trevor demonstrated how to pan the camera around, allowing her to see all the new quotations. The one above the tills had been Alex Goldbloom's suggestion. *There is no such thing as a free lunch.* Eric the chef had recommended that pupils should *Be a legend in your own lunchtime!* He had explained to her why that was funny apparently.

Moving on to the corridor by Ms Lovall's Lessons For Life room she discovered that *It's nice to be important but it's more important to be nice.* As she watched Mr Gordon getting the pupils into the room she realised he must be doing a cover. Norma had said that Ms Lovall wouldn't be in for at least a week while her leg was still in plaster.

Upstairs on the Geography corridor were the reassuring words that *Wherever you go, that's where you are.* Across in the DT block was the advice that *You cannot hang everything on one nail.* It really was looking good. She could almost hear the sound of GCSE grades sailing even higher.

Like the teachers in the staffroom pupils were beginning to stop and look at her Words of Wisdom which must have appeared as if by magic. She could be lenient if pupils were a little late to lessons today as they stopped to read the writing on the wall. She could only imagine the impact she was having on their education. It would be lovely to hear the pupils' voices, to find out what they were saying about it all.

"Can we get sound on this too?" she asked as Trevor clicked on to another area of the school.

"Erm, yeah, I think so," he replied, adjusting the volume setting.

The screen showed the English corridor where Miss Hughes was discussing one of the new wall slogans with a pupil from her year group.

"For the millionth time, Robin," the Head of Year was saying, "don't exaggerate."

"Sorry, Miss, but it's true."

"Hard work never hurt anybody!" Miss Hughes read out again, pointing at the words.

"It's just that I don't want to take the risk, Miss. It's like that one there too."

He pointed at the other wall and Trevor carefully moved the camera round.

"It's never too late to start."

"So can I leave today's homework until next week, Miss?"

Ms Stonehart was wondering whether the quotations were too difficult or whether the pupils were deliberately misunderstanding them. The ones she'd met before Easter didn't seem like they'd have any difficulty with them. Perhaps it was the teachers' fault if the pupils didn't understand?

"Show me another one," she commanded. "That one."

The main doors to the playground filled the screen. A large group of pupils seemed to be blocking the exit and shouting across to one of the teachers. She didn't recognise him but thought he was probably one of the new Science teachers.

"Teachers will open the door for you," read the lettering above the

exit, *"but you must walk through it for yourself."*

That had been one of the most inspiring quotes she'd been given, encouraging independence and a love of learning.

Sir, come and open the door for us!" the crowd of pupils were all shouting at him at the top of their voices. "Please, sir! We can't do it ourselves!!!"

"I think the volume controls might be faulty," was Ms Stonehart's response. "Let me have a go."

This time she found herself inside a classroom. She felt a little bit disorientated for a moment.

"Remember no man is an island," read Miss Armitage to her class, looking at the words that had appeared above her whiteboard.

"Sorry, Miss," interrupted a girl on the front row. "What about the Isle of Man?"

Well, it was a Geography lesson.

It was probably as well that the CCTV cameras weren't yet ready in the MFL Department.

"Oh, mon Dieu! Merde alors!" exclaimed Madame Loups-Garoux when she turned the corner and saw what had been daubed on the corridor by her classroom. She ran to tell Mr Buonanulla straight away.

Mr Buonanulla hadn't actually noticed the words when he'd arrived that morning. His usual morning struggle getting his bike upstairs and safely into his storeroom had taken up all his attention. Now as he looked at the five incriminating words, black on white with the strip light drawing attention to them like a work of art, he could feel one of his wee migraines coming on.

"So, I knew they were going to put something," he said, "but Gary said he didn't need any help. He said he'd be fine using translation software."

Some of the pupils from the class Mr Buonanulla had abandoned had appeared at his door and were practising their listening skills.

"Sir," said one of them. "What does *Ma patrone est une ordure* mean?"

The pupil had a good French accent but then Mr Buonanulla only ever taught the top sets.

"It means *My school is extraordinary*, Noah," replied Mr Buonanulla quickly. Perhaps this was what Mr Wingett had meant to put. "Back inside now, everybody. I don't expect this from a Set 1."

He hurried his pupils back into the classroom, telling them to finish the wordsearch, before turning back to his friend.

"Et alors? Are you going to say anything?" she asked.

"Those meetings with Janine are bad enough without me calling her that," he replied, looking a little pale.

"I've got it!" exclaimed Madame Loups-Garoux after a moment. "You told me that Ivor's Bright Sky targets include the displays on the corridors, non? Well, this is a corridor. Bof! It is 'is responsibility, n'est-ce pas? 'E was the one in over Easter, not you. Pas de problème!"

"You're right, mon amie," agreed the *Acting* Head of MFL.

Ms Stonehart was beginning to tire of her new toy by lunchtime but luckily she had other important tasks to do. For this reason she had summoned Ms Winter to her office and as always Ms Payne had come along too.

"Time for me to judge the photo competition," she said. "What with my Words of Wisdom on every corridor and now this, I'm beginning to wonder if we actually need a Literacy Co-ordinator."

"You're far too busy to do all the Literacy stuff," said Ms Winter, automatically switching to self-preservation mode. "We need you as our Headteacher, guiding us from strength to strength."

"Too right," agreed her friend.

Ms Stonehart studied the two Assistant Heads for a moment as though she'd missed something. She was too busy with everything she had to do but she liked her SLT to remember that they weren't indispensable.

"So the challenge was to take a photo of yourself reading a book in an unusual location?"

"Yeah," agreed Ms Winter opening up her laptop and clicking on a folder.

There were less than a dozen photos in the folder. Perhaps reading a book was unusual enough in itself for most pupils with the strange location just adding an extra level to the challenge.

"Is that all of them?" Ms Stonehart asked, somewhat surprised. About half of them were from staff. She herself had emailed a lovely photo from Cornwall.

"We had to get rid of a few," said Ms Payne. "It turns out Bailey Greenwood reads while he's on the loo. We couldn't have that on the website!"

"Well, I think there should be a pupil and a staff prize," pondered Ms Stonehart. "This one first I think."

She pointed to a photo.

"Brill! That's Graham Reaper, Year 9," said Ms Winter.

The photo showed a tall boy with his jet black hair sleeked back from his long gaunt face. He was dressed in a morning suit reading a copy of *Dracula* by Bram Stoker. The most unusual part of the photo was not what he was wearing but the fact that he was lying in a coffin surrounded by bunches of lilies, the whole scene flickering in the light of two tall candles. It looked like an odd advertisement for the family business.

"He's really thinking outside the box with this," said Ms Payne without thinking.

The photo beside it showing Delores Froggett on a park bench with her cat and a James Herriot novel was not quite as impressive.

"For the staff prize," continued Ms Stonehart, pausing only to look closely at a picture of Mr Fitt reading a book whilst swimming, "it has to be this one."

And so it was that a former Employee of the Term also won a Nando's voucher in the Literacy competition. Bob's photo showed him reading a Dr Seuss book sitting out in the Easter sunshine whilst eating a Cornish cream tea. If you looked carefully, the person who had taken the photo was just visible too, reflected in his sunglasses.

CHAPTER 40

"Fall down nine times, get up ten."

Year 10 assemblies, as run by Mr Armani as Head of Year, were unlike any other assemblies in the school. They were carried out with military precision from the very moment the pupils first entered the canteen in complete silence and took their places in alphabetical order. Even Ms Winter and Ms Payne always arrived at Mr Armani's assemblies on time. This morning only Ms Lovall arrived a little late but then she was on crutches with one foot in plaster.

Mr Armani was not a particularly religious man, he was a Science teacher, but his assemblies always began with an act of collective worship. It wasn't something that Ofsted checked up on but Mr Armani didn't do things just to please Ofsted. There had been prayers and hymns with Mr North when Calvin had been a pupil at the school and so there would be the same now that he himself was Head of Year. There was a higher power looking down on him, watching over everything he did. He could just see the red light flashing on the nearest CCTV camera.

"Thank you, Mr Gordon," said Mr Armani as the echoes of *'All things bright and beautiful'* were replaced by the clatter of Eric taking the bins out as he went off for a cigarette. "That was just slightly better than last week's attempt but there's always somebody who thinks they don't have to sing, isn't there? Skinner, Ashworth and Warzowski!"

As Mr Armani was one of the few teachers who chose to address pupils by their surnames, it did sound like he was calling out for a firm of lawyers. There was no way they would ever amount to that! *'My client refuses to confirm whether he has or has not completed the homework that was set on the eighth of last month...'*

"On your feet now, you three!"

Three boys near the back shuffled awkwardly to their feet, looking down at the floor and remembering not to put their hands in their pockets.

"That was abysmal!" shouted Mr Armani. "If you know what that word means. Abysmal! My gran could sing better than you three!" The canteen remained deathly quiet. Year 10 knew better than to laugh. "Go wait outside my lab. I'll deal with you after assembly."

Although they'd never admit it, deep down the vast majority of pupils actually liked the fact that there were rules. It gave them some sort of structure or something to rebel against. They could break the rules and take the consequences, but at least it was their choice to break the rules. Those pupils who wanted to get on with their work appreciated that Mr Armani made it possible for them to do that. If pressed even Skinner, Ashworth and Warzowski would admit that Mr Armani was their favourite teacher. He was, in their words, *100% ripe banana,* firm but fair.

"Now I am sure you will have noticed," Mr Armani began, "as we said the school prayer this morning that actually two of our eight school values are mentioned in that prayer."

It was only in Year 10 assemblies that the school prayer was ever heard. Whilst the pupils recited all the school values at the start of every lesson, most would have been hard pushed to say which two occurred in the prayer. They couldn't even phone a friend for help with mobile phones being banned in the school. None of them would forget what had happened to Mr Smith when his phone had pinged in Mr Armani's assembly at the start of the year.

Mr Armani pointed to a girl on the front row, putting her on the spot as to which two school values had been mentioned.

"Erm, Wisdom?" she guessed, remembering a short video about a man playing a piano. "Success?"

"Inspiration and Determination!" thundered Mr Armani. "And it's the second of those, Determination, that we're looking at today. Determination!"

The girl on the front row shifted uncomfortably on her seat. She felt she had let her Head of Year down.

Mr Armani's assemblies often revolved around Science and Ryan Spivey in 10Y was running a clandestine sweepstake as to whether the assembly would be about Physics, Chemistry or

Biology. It was unclear whether Mr Armani knew that betting was going on or whether he secretly tolerated the enterprise as a way of getting pupils interested in his subject.

This morning's assembly would be classified as Biology and specifically it was about the lifecycle of butterflies.

Even those pupils who claimed not to be interested in Science would listen attentively as Mr Armani told them stories and showed them colourful pictures. The textbook they always used in class, '*Exploring Science Through Pictures and Worksheets*', seemed to have been printed before the invention of colour.

Today Mr Armani's passion for Science brought the magical metamorphosis of butterflies to life. They watched a short video of a colourful one emerging from its cocoon to begin the next exciting part of its journey. At each stage of the process he drew comparisons with the pupils from their first arrival in Year 7 right through to Year 11 and their eventual emergence into the adult world, fully-formed and ready for anything. He spoke of the caterpillars that tragically failed to do what they should during the feeding process, somehow making it sound like he was talking about Skinner, Ashworth and Warzowski without actually mentioning them by name.

You could have heard a pin drop. You couldn't have heard a phone ring, of course. Not in one of Mr Armani's assemblies.

"What has this to do with our school value, Determination?" asked Mr Armani, rhetorically, after a brief pause. "Let me tell you a story."

There was a slight ripple across the canteen as the pupils made sure they were sitting comfortably. Whilst it might not have been effective for any other Head of Year, Mr Armani found that treating Year 10 like they were still at Primary School did the trick.

"There was once a man camping in a forest," he began, "when he noticed a butterfly's cocoon on a tree branch. As it was a lovely day, the sun was shining and the birds were singing, he decided to stop and watch this incredible transformation. He watched for hours as the butterfly tried to force itself through the tiny hole in the cocoon." He paused for effect. "And then the butterfly stopped. It was stuck."

You could hear a sharp intake of breath from his audience. Miss Fullilove, the Assistant Teaching Assistant, looked worried.

"The man decided to help the butterfly. Taking his penknife out of his rucksack he carefully cut the cocoon open in a way that would not hurt the emerging butterfly."

The flow of his narrative was interrupted only by the need to remind pupils that Wildside Academy has a zero-tolerance policy on knives. It was one of the school's few good policies.

"But as the butterfly finally came free of the cocoon," he continued, "its little body was swollen and its wings were shrivelled and weak. The wings never did develop properly and the butterfly never ever flew. It just crawled about a bit and then that was it. Dead! Stone dead!"

Somehow the assembly seemed to have developed into one of Mr Wingett's stories, full of upsetting death and needless destruction.

"But there's a moral to this story," concluded Mr Armani. "The man thought he was doing the right thing, helping the butterfly. It wouldn't have to persevere in its struggle to get out of the cocoon. But it was his very actions that stopped the butterfly from developing strength! The determination needed to break free from what held it back. Sometimes, Year 10, you can't let others do it all for you. You have to show determination and struggle if you are going to succeed."

Ironically Mr Armani always liked to tell Year 10 what his assemblies were about. They'd probably struggle to understand them if they were left to work it out by themselves and then they'd get it all wrong. Especially Skinner, Ashworth and Warzowski!

CHAPTER 41

"Be not afraid of greatness. Some are born great, some achieve greatness and some have greatness thrust upon them."

Much of the planning that went on in the English Department took place in The Cock 'n' Bull on a Friday night but very little of it ever got written down. If it had been chronicled, the Head of Department had no doubt, they would have been as successful as J.K.Rowling writing in an Edinburgh café.

As always Billy Kaye was keeping the members of his Department entertained, this time by telling them anecdotes about his previous school. All the usual gang were there although Sharon Payne had wandered off to have a game of darts with Sean Devlin. Having agreed to teach her how to play golf at some point the two of them were now sitting in the snug, making arrangements to play a round.

"And I'm not joking there really was a teacher called Richard Head! Richard Head! You couldn't make it up!" Billy was saying. "You can imagine what the kids called him but the other teachers never mentioned it once. Not once. I think that made it worse for him 'cos he must have known we'd all realised! Then we also had this Deputy Head, Roland Morley, who was always getting things wrong in front of the whole school in assembly. And I don't just mean the wrong name, I mean amazing spoonerisms."

He took another swig of his pint and then realised that the other members of the English Department looked like they didn't recognise the technical term.

"You know!" he said. "Roland would be like doing assembly and mean to say *"God is a loving shepherd"* and he'd come out with *"God is a shoving leopard"*, you know?"

"Oh, I get you," said Lynne Winter, concentrating on putting her empty glass back on the table, "funny 'cos it's all swapped round."

Victoria Shakespeare looked up, hearing the word 'round.'

"And then one day he's handing out these certificates for something in assembly," Billy continued, "attendance or achievement or something, I don't know. And one of them is for a quiet little girl in Year 7 called Nicola Tipple. And he gets her name wrong…yeah?"

He finished his pint, waiting for them to join the dots and supply the punchline.

After a minute there were screams of raucous laughter from the other English teachers to show that they'd caught up. Billy was so funny, so experienced, such a fantastic Head of Department.

"Cheers everyone!" said Jamie Humble as he came back with the next round of drinks. "So what're we chattin' about then?"

"Billy was just telling us about funny names of kids he's taught," said Victoria reaching for her next drink. "Like Jenny Taylor."

"'Ere, your name's a bit of a good 'un," commented Jamie, "for an English teacher, eh, Shazza? Shakespeare!"

"Why's that then?" asked Lynne.

It was only as Ms Shakespeare was making her way towards her classroom on Monday morning, convinced that she really shouldn't be in if she felt like this, that she found the beermat. It was in her pocket along with something that looked like the lanyards other teachers wore and a phone number on a scrap of paper. Pausing to read what was written on the beermat she discovered it was the English Department's revised Scheme of Work for the next half term. It was then that the conversation in the pub drifted back to her.

The mention of the name Shakespeare had reminded Billy that he'd heard from a teacher at another school that as well as reading 'Lord of the Flies' all pupils were meant to be studying Shakespeare. It turned out that none of the English teachers who were there had ever read a Shakespeare play since being at school themselves although Lucy Hughes had seen a film of Romeo and Juliet. As she'd left before the end of the film she didn't feel confident teaching it at GCSE level. And then with a sinking feeling in her stomach, caused not only by the previous night's wine, Ms Shakespeare remembered that she had been elected to teach Shakespeare. Elected probably wasn't the right word. She just happened to have gone to the loo when the decision had been taken. As she was called Shakespeare, so the argument went, she was the ideal person to teach about the Bard. As she entered the classroom she couldn't help wishing that Jamie had been barred from The Cock 'n' Bull for bringing the subject up in the first place!

Although she'd been off ill and so not taught this class for two weeks most of her Year 10 pupils still seemed to recognise her. Her bright red hair was, in the words of Ms Winter, very unique. Most of the pupils had their copies of *'Lord of the Flies'* out ready. She got the pupils to recite the Wildside Academy values largely because it would give her time to look for resources about Shakespeare on the computer. She clicked on the PowerPoint that looked the most promising and the name William Shakespeare appeared on the whiteboard, followed by the dates 1564-1616.

"Right, Year 10," Ms Shakespeare began. "Who can tell me what we're doing today?"

This was how she usually began her lessons but this time the pupils had something on the screen to help them.

"Chapter two of *'Lord of the Flies'*?" came the safe answer.

"Something about your Dad, Miss?" asked one of the girls pointing at the board. "I'm guessing that's not his real phone number, right?"

"Today we're starting on the plays of Shakespeare," said Miss Shakespeare, ignoring their suggestions. "Who can give me a famous quote from Shakespeare?"

There was silence.

"Ok. Who knows how many plays Shakespeare wrote?"

The silence continued.

"Right. Well, who can name one of Shakespeare's plays?"

It was still early on Monday morning.

"Ok. Hands up if you've heard of Shakespeare..."

It was a reasonable show of hands but maybe some of them just recognised the name of their teacher. She clicked on the next slide.

"Right. Rather than hit you with an entire play I thought we'd start with some of Shakespeare's most famous quotes."

> All the world's a stage,
> And all the men and women merely players ;
> They have their exits and their entrances ;
> And one man in his time plays many parts.

"So, Miss," said a boy near the window, "where would the audience sit then? No, but if all the world's a stage then where would the audience sit? They'd have to sit on the stage too! That's not right."

Ms Shakespeare was just reading the lines again when a girl questioned another part of the quotation.

"I don't get it, Miss. It says *exits and entrances*, yeah? Well, surely you'd have to come out onto the stage first before you can exit? Like on *Celebrity Love Rock Star Academy*. Did you see it on Saturday, Miss?"

"But you can't come out onto the stage," continued the first pupil, "because there isn't anywhere to come on from. There isn't anywhere else. *All the world's a stage*, so where would you be to make your entrance. It don't make sense, do it?"

"Too right!" agreed a ginger pupil near the back of the classroom.

"Can we do '*Lord of the Flies*' again, Miss?"

If Billy expected her to study sonnets with them after this, thought Ms Shakespeare, things really would go from Bard to verse!

CHAPTER 42

"Start by doing what's necessary, then do what's possible
and suddenly you are doing the impossible."

"Sean absolutely thrashed me last night," said Ms Payne. "Although he says I've got a lovely double top."

"Go on, show us," said Ms Winter.

Even though Mr O'Brien was working quietly at the other side of the Assistant Heads' office Ms Payne went over to the dartboard near the door and retrieved her darts. She'd got Bob to hang it there after the last Ofsted inspection and it was a credit to his workmanship that it was still in place after more than two years. The tattered photo of Jeremiah Grimes, the Minister for Education, still clung desperately to the wire framework.

"One hundred and eighty!" Ms Winter bellowed out as the darts thudded into the board and the nearby wall, startling Mr O'Brien from his calculations. "Brill! Me next!"

Glancing across from his computer Mr O'Brien could see that Ms Payne hadn't actually got the top score. As the canteen wouldn't be open for another thirty minutes his two colleagues were probably at a loose end, tired of doing lesson observations. Luckily he wouldn't be disturbing them in about ten minutes as he'd taken the unusual step of making an appointment to see Ms Stonehart.

An hour later Mr O'Brien was still sitting outside the Headteacher's office. Even though she claimed her door was always open, it rarely was but he'd taken some marking along to do as he knew he'd be kept waiting.

"The task of the leader is to get their people from where they are to where they have not been."

Mr O'Brien smiled to himself as he read the words above her door. Those words were certainly true, he thought. Maybe it was a good omen, a sign. Who knows? He wasn't superstitious but that was typical of Taurus apparently. Mr O'Brien had been too busy to read all the Words of Wisdom that had been painted throughout the school. Now, as he sat waiting, he read the quotation on the HR corridor above Mrs Spratt's office and wondered who had chosen it.

"Who controls the past controls the future.
Who controls the present controls the past."

He was drawn back from his thoughts by a sound further down the corridor, the clattering of a stepladder being set up. He expected to see Bob but to his surprise he saw that the figure in the paint-spattered overalls was none other than Mr Thicke, a paintbrush in one hand, a pot of black paint in the other.

Then he remembered what Alex Goldbloom had told him. Apparently Mr Thicke had upset the painters by complaining that the size of the lettering was not consistent in what they were painting. There had been some heated discussion about whether the painters would actually get paid, leading to them leaving the job unfinished. In fairness they had added an additional quotation above Mr Thicke's door at no extra cost : *"Nobody ever builds a statue to honour a critic!"* followed by two words and a drawing that Bob had painted over with the last of his white paint.

Ms Stonehart had insisted that it wasn't up to Bob to finish the incomplete lettering and that was why Mr Thicke now found himself balancing a tin of black paint whilst stretching to reach the wall. Now that it was up to him to do the task he found it wasn't actually as easy as he'd thought. He looked at the next one that needed to be finished .

"Always plan your time so that you can finish what you st…"

Mr O'Brien decided that the kindest thing was to let Mr Thicke get on with the job without passing any comment. He remembered a quotation that he'd suggested should be somewhere in the school but for some reason Ms Stonehart hadn't wanted to include it..

"Kindness is a language which the deaf can hear and the blind can read."

Mrs Spratt happened to come out of her office at that point.

"Sorry, to bother you, Norma," said Mr O'Brien, "but I had an appointment with Janine for quarter to ten?"

"I hear what you say," said Mrs Spratt as she hurried past. "You're late and she really is very busy this morning. You'll just have to wait. Sit there."

On principle Mr O'Brien did not sit down but went to look at the paintings of Mr Chambers, the Chair of Governors, near the Main Hall. A moment later Mr Wingett's door opened and the Deputy Head looked out.

"Sam," he called out gloomily. "Have a look at this, would you?"

He passed him a pile of papers.

"Janine's asked me to go through the last Ofsted report and just tidy it up a bit so that we can update what's on the website. It's a bit long. Nobody wants to read all that. She wants it by close of business. What do you think?"

Mr O'Brien could understand where the quotation on the HR corridor had come from when he looked at the carefully edited résumé of the Ofsted comments. Mr Wingett had deliberately chosen genuine phrases such as *"clear vision by the Headteacher"*, *"decisive actions from SLT"* and *"significant impact on pupil progress"* but had made it sound like this was what Wildside Academy had, rather than what it lacked. The phrase *"SLT are taking the school into areas they haven't explored before"* seemed particularly poignant.

Fortunately Mr O'Brien was spared the dilemma of wondering how to comment on Mr Wingett's creative writing as it was at that point that he was summoned through to Ms Stonehart's office. She didn't like to be kept waiting.

Mr O'Brien had to be careful in his choice of words when he told Ms Stonehart what he'd come to see her about. He was fairly confident that she'd agree with his proposal, it was just that you never quite knew how she'd react when she heard the name Hoskins.

"Thank you for agreeing to see me," he began carefully. "I've got something I wanted to tell you about and I didn't think a full SLT meeting would be the right forum for it."

"You sounded very intriguing in your email, Sam," she said, pouring herself a fresh cup of tea. "Something about Ofsted?"

"It's more about the Local Headteachers' meetings at the Town Hall," he said. "Thank you very much for letting me go in your place by the way. I think they've been very useful. There was another one last week and something came out of it that I think could be a big help. I know how much you've been trying to keep an eye on what USA have been up to and the telescope and checking their website have been a unique way of doing that. Going from strength to strength under your leadership, you might say."

"Go on," said Ms Stonehart, warming to the topic.

"Imagine if there was no need to second-guess what they're up to at USA or read about it after the event. What if we had somebody working there, high up on the management team, who could see what's going on there first-hand?"

"How do you mean?" asked Ms Stonehart, putting her teacup down and leaning forward.

"Just between the two of us, there's a job coming up at Upper Steem Academy. A pretty high up one. If I were to apply and got it, I could let you know what's really going on there. And if you kept my job open, six months later it'd be possible for me just to hand my notice in there and come back here."

Ms Stonehart went and looked out of the window as she considered the proposal. Beyond Grimshaw's Glue Factory USA was a constant dark shadow hanging over her kingdom. It might just work.

"Do you think you stand a chance at interview?"

It did cross Mr O'Brien's mind that that question could have been phrased better but he carried on regardless.

"Well, I did speak to Mr Hoskins and he said he thought I was a very strong candidate for the post."

Ms Stonehart's left eye twitched involuntarily at the mention of Mr Hoskins' name.

"The only thing is," continued Mr O'Brien, "I'd really need a reference if I'm going to do it."

Under Ms Stonehart Wildside Academy had adopted a policy of refusing to supply references when colleagues went for interviews, claiming that they were too busy to write them. It was good business sense really. If they didn't want to lose an employee there was no point helping them to leave by writing a glowing reference. If they wanted to get rid of an employee there were more effective methods. Mr O'Brien, on the other hand, was a special case.

"I like your scheme," concluded Ms Stonehart as she resumed

her seat, "but we'd better not mention it to anybody till you get the job. Till then only you, me and the Governors will know about it. It'll be our secret. I said to Mr Chambers you'd go a long way. At least we won't really be losing you though, will we?"

She fiddled with the cactus on her desk for a moment.

"We could do with a secret name for this scheme. Any ideas?"

It was the telescope all over again.

"How about *Operation Cuckoo?*" suggested Mr O'Brien.

"Like the bird you mean?"

"It doesn't build its own nest but lays its eggs in…"

"In a clock!" added Ms Stonehart. "Ok. We'll go with that. I like it. Laying our eggs in Hoskins' school. Perhaps you'd like to jot down what you think would be the most effective reference under the circumstances and I'll look over it. Shall we say by close of business?"

"I don't think either of us will regret this," smiled Mr O'Brien as he was dismissed.

That was the hard part done, he thought as he left Ms Stonehart's office. Cuckoo! After that the application form and the interview should be a piece of cake.

MAY

CHAPTER 43

"A bend in the road is not the end of the road unless you fail to turn."

It turned out that there were areas of Wildside Academy that weren't actually covered by Ms Stonehart's all-seeing CCTV cameras, places where she'd have to venture out of her office if she wanted to know what was going on there. It was in these places that certain conversations took place, although it was still customary to check who was nearby first before offering any opinions.

There was no CCTV coverage behind the Main Hall as the contractors were probably waiting for the GCSE exams to begin before they started drilling again. Eric's traditional haunt for a quiet cigarette had got a bit busier since cameras had been installed everywhere else. There was no CCTV coverage of the staff car park either as apparently this was not the school's responsibility. It was safe to talk in the staff toilets, provided you could remember the code for getting in there. Mr Buonanulla had taken to talking to Madame Loups-Garoux in French a lot more and the Teaching Assistants had adopted their own version of sign language. Harry Greenfield just put a rugby jersey over the camera in the PE office whilst in the IT Department Dave Benson was a little more inventive. He'd rigged up a looped video of him teaching an outstanding all-singing-all-dancing lesson that he could transmit every day instead of the live coverage. Once Ms Stonehart noticed a glitch in the video footage it was the last anybody saw of Mr Benson, apart from a brief clip that found its way onto social media.

Whilst there were no cameras around the IT Support Department Adil was good enough to share with Dean Gordon a little trick for making the staffroom safe if he wanted to go in there. For some unknown reason whenever the staff microwave was being used it overrode the nearby CCTV cameras. There was a sudden increase in microwaveable meals being brought in and cups of coffee that needed to be re-heated.

And when teachers found isolated areas of sanctuary in Wildside Academy, what did they talk about? There were the usual daily grumbles, of course, like why the photocopier never worked but one topic of conversation kept coming up time and time again. Unlike Adam and Sonya in Year 10 whose romance was carved into desks and scrawled on walls throughout the school, Janine Stonehart and Bob Eastwood genuinely believed that nobody knew about their secret liaison. Whenever anybody had been told about the relationship their reaction had always been the same : disbelief that the Headteacher and the Caretaker had got it together. When they were spotted snogging on an escalator in a clothes shop in Berryfield any doubts were finally dismissed. Some said they must have hooked up because they shared a sense of humour. Bob would definitely have had to share his sense of humour with Janine as she didn't have one. It was said that behind closed doors Ms Stonehart had shortened Bob Eastwood's name to give him the nickname "Beast" and the Head Caretaker certainly did seem to take care of the Head's needs!

When Janine and Bob split up then it became a major topic of whispered conversations. It apparently happened over the Bank Holiday weekend. Nobody knew who'd dumped who but whatever happened Bob managed to keep his job at Wildside Academy with his title changing to Senior Ground Maintenance Supervisor. Ms Stonehart became more like a Victorian monarch in mourning, dressing in black and rarely coming out from her office at all. Few people noticed any difference. Ms Payne inadvertently let slip that she'd heard Janine had a new boyfriend and that he was a policeman. Whether that was true or not Bob became rather grumpy and introverted.

"And this next request is for Maureen who's celebrating twenty-five wonderful years of marriage to hubby Ian. She'd like me to play 'Love is all around' *from the smash film* 'Four Weddings…'"

Seeing Bob standing motionless as he pulled in at reception Jim Fitt hurriedly reached over to turn his car radio off.

As he was coming back out from signing in Jim noticed that Bob was still standing there, watching a snail slowly making its glistening way across the black tarmac in front of him. Suddenly he stepped forward and crushed the snail under his boot leaving a sticky cracked mess on the white STOP sign. Jim had never seen such aggression from Bob in all the time he'd known him.

"Ay up!" he said. "You alright there, Bob? What's thee laikin' at?"

"I hate that snail," said Bob. "It's been following me about all week."

"What y'up to t'day then, our kid?"

"You see this broom?" said Bob. "I've had this broom since I started here. It was my Dad's before that when he worked here. Mr Abercrombie gave it to him. He was a proper Headmaster, Mr Abercrombie. Treated people right. Like Mr Taylor. Proper Headteachers don't mess people about."

He paused, looking across at the police car parked beside Ms Stonehart's Jaguar again. He'd considered repainting the 'Headteacher' sign as 'Head Cheater.'

"Ay, it's a champion broom," Jim said encouragingly.

"It's been in my family for generations," commented Bob, "and the only part that's ever needed replacing is the broom head. Oh, and the handle, of course. Don't need a new broom to sweep clean."

He leant on the broom again, motionless, deep in reflection once more. Jim Fitt could see he was busy.

"Well, I can't be late," said Jim, getting back into his car. "She's got cameras all over t'shop now. There's now't we can do now without them checking up on us, tha knows."

"The way I look at it," commented Bob philosophically, "if I'm little more than an odd job man then I'll look at the list and just do jobs 1,3,5,7 and 9!"

"You're dead right. Any road, look after y'self, Bob."

As Jim drove off Bob smiled when two magpies made a mess on the two vehicles parked at the front of the school. One for sorrow, two for joy.

It was clearly being economical with the truth to say that Ms

Stonehart was a "person person" whose door was always open. At the moment she wasn't even socializing with the HR Department, spending lunchtimes alone in her room with a mug of soup while she watched the CCTV footage from around the school. Bob looked like he was as busy as ever. All in all the summer term was failing to live up to her high expectations. It was probably a good thing that she didn't know how Mr O'Brien was getting on at the interview he'd gone for at Upper Steem Academy today. He'd ring her when he had something to report.

There was a quiet knock at the door. Mrs Spratt came in when she was summoned, managing to appear even more nervous than usual. Things hadn't gone well that morning when she'd brought Ms Stonehart her mid-morning tea only to be told she never wanted to see a tray of Cornish clotted cream scones and jam in her office ever again.

"Sorry to disturb you," she began hesitantly. "I know you're busy but there's a visitor here who…"

The School Police Liaison Officer pushed past her.

"That'll be all, Norma," said Ms Stonehart, smiling.

"I hear what you say," said Mrs Spratt quietly as she left them to whatever it was they were up to. She needed to go get Mr Eastwood his new lanyard.

"Maybe it's not such a bad day, after all," said Janine, putting her mug of soup back down and switching off the CCTV.

CHAPTER 44

"The time is always right to do what is right."

Even before the installation of CCTV cameras throughout the school Ms Grimley had always acted as if her lesson was about to be observed at any minute. Each morning she would return all her exercise books to the shelves in her classroom, making sure that the three best books for a work scrutiny were on the top of each pile. She put a lot of effort into her exercise books, sometimes spending over an hour trying to predict which ones Ms Winter was most likely to take. She'd make sure that her lesson planning folder was in order with copies uploaded onto the computer network. After much thought she'd devised some Learning Objectives for her whiteboard that were suitably generic that she didn't need to change them every hour yet they still seemed like they'd been written specifically for the current lesson. She was particularly pleased with *Be able to outline the events that led to this conflict*. It had felt like she was doing lines as a punishment having to change her Learning Objectives at the start of each lesson whilst also standing at the door to meet and greet her pupils with a starter activity. In her view the pupils no more needed to understand the mechanics of a lesson than she needed to know how her car engine worked.

It came as no real surprise then when the door to her classroom crashed open and Ms Winter and Ms Payne barged in.

"You don't mind if we sit in, do you?" asked Ms Winter as if she was offering her a choice.

"Let's not stay too sodding long," said Ms Payne to her friend as she looked idly around the classroom. History didn't really interest her. It was boring. She preferred to live for the moment rather than look back all the time.

The Assistant Heads' unexpected raid had been announced by a staccato rapping on the glass as Ms Winter had spotted a boy she thought wasn't giving the lesson his full attention. The door had then crashed open with all the force of a bomb falling during the Blitz or the subtlety of a visit from the Gestapo. It was perhaps appropriate that Ms Grimley's Year 9 class were busy studying the Second World War. Today they were presenting the talks that they'd been researching in the ICT rooms for the last two weeks. It had seemed like a good idea at the time, an effective way of reducing her heavy workload whilst also ticking the box for peer assessment. In truth the talks hadn't been particularly good so far and she did wonder whether they'd just been playing that Zombie Kombat thing while she'd been trying to catch up on all the paperwork.

The best presentation had probably been by Graham Reaper who, as always, had taken a great delight researching the statistics behind the number of people who had died in battle. He'd made a PowerPoint with some particularly gruesome pictures, lest we forget, and said that he was sorry for our loss. Nathan Briggs had given a talk that seemed to be based on a Hollywood war film he'd watched at the weekend. Orphelia Strang appeared to have copy-and-pasted her entire talk from the internet and had mumbled her way through it as best she could, struggling with some of the German names. Makenzie Sheriden-Smythe had refused point blank to talk in front of everybody else and had just folded her arms and burst into tears. It wasn't going well but Ms Grimley decided to let Logan Cholmondeley do his talk as it'd give her time to plan the next part of the lesson observation.

"For my talk on the Second World War," Logan began confidently, "I've decided to focus on the German leader, their Führer, Adolf Hitler." He held up a picture he'd printed off in case anybody was unsure who he was talking about. "Adolf Hitler was born in the same week as Charlie Chaplin but where Chaplin made millions of people laugh, Hitler was a very evil man who killed millions of people. I hope you enjoyed my talk and thank you for listening."

Logan went back to his place and after a moment the form applauded the effort he had put into his work over the last fortnight. Ms Grimley asked the form to write down their scores for Logan on the peer assessment sheet and then welcomed any comments on his presentation. With Ms Winter and Ms Payne peering at them all and constantly writing things down on a form, the class decided to say nothing.

"Well, perhaps you could make your talk a little longer next time, Logan," commented Ms Grimley.

Ms Winter wrote something else down on her form.

"Now, as you know from your research, a lot has been written about the World Wars," Ms Grimley continued, clicking on a PowerPoint. "I want you to read through these words that were written by a German vicar, Martin Niemöller…"

"It's not in German, is it, Miss?" asked Orphelia Strang, anxiously.

"No, this version's in English. I'd like you all to have a read through it with me and then tell me what you think it's about."

> First they came for the Communists
> And I did not speak out
> Because I was not a Communist.
>
> Then they came for the Socialists
> And I did not speak out
> Because I was not a Socialist.
>
> Then they came for the Trade Unionists
> And I did not speak out
> Because I was not a Trade Unionist.
>
> Then they came for the Jews
> And I did not speak out
> Because I was not a Jew.
>
> Then they came for me
> And there was no one left to speak for me.

Even after she had read it aloud a second time not a single hand had been raised to pass comment on the poem. Then, hesitantly, one boy near the front put his hand up. It was Melvyn Bland.

"Yes, Melvyn," said Ms Grimley encouragingly. "What do you think the message of this is?"

"Well, Miss," he began slowly, "as it was written about the War I think it deals with the themes of persecution, guilt, repentance and responsibility. It illustrates what happens when people turn a blind eye to the evil things that are going on around them as if it's just somebody else's problem. It's about being strong enough to stand up for what's right even if nobody else will."

Much as Ms Grimley had never really liked his Dad, Melvyn himself was her star pupil, a pleasure to teach. He studied a lot and could always be relied on to contribute in class. She really hoped he'd choose History for GCSE rather than Geography.

"That's right, Melyvn," said Ms Grimley, looking to see if Ms Winter had noticed how well her pupils responded to her questions. She was busy looking at a poster about motte and bailey castles.

"I first came across it in an Esperanto book my Father gave me," Melvyn continued. *"Tiam ili venis por mi Kaj restis neniu Por parole por mi.* It reminds me of all the teachers I've had here this year. Mr Chang for Art, Mr Milton for Maths, Mr Lazenby for IT, Reverend James for RE, then…"

"Yes, thank you, Melvyn," said Ms Grimley hurriedly, realising where this particular train of thought was taking them. "That's not what we're talking about."

She looked at her lesson plan, flustered and hoping that Ms Winter hadn't been paying attention. Luckily Ms Payne was back on her phone again.

"So, well, coming back to Charlie Chaplin and Adolf Hitler. Chaplin actually made a film called '*The Great Dictator*' in 1940…"

She breathed a sigh of relief once Ms Winter and Ms Payne had left, having decided they'd seen all they needed to see. Perhaps Melvyn Bland would choose Geography for GCSE after all, she thought, as she searched in her bag for her tablets.

Later that week everybody in the History Department received the same email from their Head of Department.

From : HFD – HFord1@WildsideAcademy
To : HistoryDept1@WildsideAcademy
Sent : Fri 03 May 14:19
Subject : History Dept Meeting this afternoon

Afternoon Team!

I just wanted to give you a heads up that we've got a Department Meeting this afternoon in my room. I'll give you a copy of the new agenda at the meeting but I just wanted to highlight item 36 which is about the new Schemes of Work that you've all been working on. Ms Winter said she may pop in to the meeting.
Lynne has said that when she passed the lesson observation feedback forms on Janine was not happy with some of the content we are teaching. I believe she said it was "subversive and revolutionary" and that she did not want pupils thinking like that in her school.
As a matter of priority we must not use the poem by Martin Niemöller under any circumstances and we will spend part of the meeting going through the Schemes of Work to remove any other inappropriate content.
We will also need to go through the lists of Year 9 pupils who have chosen History as a GCSE option next year.
Also, item 42 on the agenda, we're going to look at how we might make Department Meetings a bit shorter. I was thinking we could get into pairs for ten minutes to discuss possible ideas and then brainstorm back at the end. I'll aim to do it as quickly as I can as I know you'll be wanting to get away for the weekend.

Thanks, Harry.

One change that Ms Grimley made straight away was to alter the Literacy poster on her classroom wall. She wondered if the Thought Police would notice that it now said *"Ms Grimley is reading...Nineteen Eighty-Four."*

CHAPTER 45

"One language sets you in a corridor for life.
Two languages open every door along the way."

Once when he had been covering a Year 7 RE lesson for Ms Lovall Mr Gordon had overheard a snippet of conversation between two girls that had stuck with him ever since.

"So if he does exist, what do you think he would look like then?"

"I dunno really. I suppose I've always thought of him as an old man. With long white hair and a beard. With a really calm voice and really wise. And, like, just wanting what's best for us all I suppose, you know?"

"Well I don't think he exists. That's just for when you're a little kid at Primary School. I mean, if he is real how comes we never see him? And if he wants what's best why do bad things happen, like homework and school dinners?"

It was the next part of the conversation that stopped Mr Gordon in his tracks and made him smile.

"Well, he's probably busy. My Mum says he'll have his work cut out for him taking us from strength to strength."

"All I'm saying is, Chelsea, I don't believe it."

"Well my Mum and Dad do. They said there was a Headteacher when they were at school."

"That was ages ago! So yeah, he's like immortal then?"

"Well, he could be. And all-powerful. Watching over us all the time!"

Mr Gordon smiled to himself and returned to his marking. He wondered whether these pupils would ever get to see Ms Stonehart in the five years they would spend at Wildside Academy.

That possibility was even more remote this particular week

as Ms Stonehart had gone off on a five-day residential training course in the Cotswolds. According to the PE Department it had been organised by the School Police Liaison Officer with a view to fostering closer links. Tim Cocker said they'd probably gone to Feelem-on-the-Hill and as he taught Geography he should know.

By Monday dinnertime Ms Winter and Ms Payne were complaining that it was too noisy in the Assistant Heads' office with Mr O'Brien doing whatever it was he did all day. It would be a shame to leave such a lovely office as Ms Stonehart's empty all week. The two of them would pop down and keep it warm for her. And just in case Ms Stonehart decided she didn't want to be the Headteacher for ever it would be helpful if they tried her big chair out for size now. And really, to get the full picture, they needed to get one of the teachers in and drill down into their performance. Ms Winter got a piece of paper out of her pocket and started looking at the list of names on it.

"I know," said Ms Payne looking over at the possible victims. "I've done a work scrutiny of some books in the MFL Department. I know exactly who we should get in. It'll be a right fracking laugh."

She'd chosen books from the MFL Department as those were the classrooms nearest to the Assistant Heads' office.

"A meeting with you and I should be done proper, yeah?" said Ms Winter gravely. "I'll get Norma to send an email."

Miss Brown had taught Modern Foreign Languages at Wildside Academy for just over three years. She'd taken the job because she'd been promised that she'd get to do lots of teaching in the Sixth Form, an area that really interested her. Instead Madame Loups-Garoux had been given all the Sixth Form classes and then the Sixth Form itself had closed in order to make more office space. She'd found herself with a timetable that was only surpassed by Mr Haddenough's in terms of large class sizes and low-ability pupils. Each year, for reasons that were never explained, Mr Buonanulla had given himself and his best friend the *crème de la crème*. She and Ivor were given pupils who were proud of the fact that they could shrug in four different languages.

As an outstanding teacher Miss Brown had expected to move up the pay scale quite quickly when she'd joined the school. She hadn't managed to work out whether it was her Head of

Department's incompetence with paperwork or Ms Stonehart's desire to save money that was holding her back. Perhaps the summons to the other side of the Berlin Wall meant that she was going to be told her pay rise had been granted?

Ms Winter and Ms Payne had kept Miss Brown waiting so long that they suddenly realised the meeting wouldn't be able to last long if they were going to get to the canteen before the lunchtime rush. They came straight to the point once they'd ordered Miss Brown to sit.

"We've been looking at your performance, Sarah-Jane," Ms Winter began, peering over the top of her laptop. "Analysing the data and I'm well not happy with the homework what you're setting for them kids, yeah?"

Sarah-Jane was not sure what she meant. She set homework for all her classes, made sure it was differentiated, appropriate and handed in on time and she always marked and returned it promptly. What more could she do?

Ms Winter turned her laptop around to show her the screen.

"I'm not sure what you mean, I'm afraid," said Sarah-Jane politely as she looked at the data displayed on the *'S'Cool Homework!'* website. All the recent homework she'd set was displayed there as green blocks stretching across the calendar page.

"You're setting too much homework!" Ms Winter gestured towards the points where classes appeared to have two French homeworks set on the same day.

"Oh, I see. No. That's just the way your page is set up. Can I show you?"

A few clicks on the mouse pad reconfigured the page to show the data filtered by *"Date homework set."* Now it was clear that Miss Brown had set just one MFL homework for each of her pupils each week.

"When I set pupils a longer project to complete, like say preparing their spoken answers for GCSE, I give them a little longer to do it. On here it ends up overlapping with the following week's homework. But it's just one homework every week."

Miss Brown seemed to know a lot about computers. A moment later she had clicked on a setting that had brought up the homework schedule for Ms Winter.

"I think *'S'Cool!'* sometimes glitches," said Sarah-Jane. It had been far better when pupils had taken responsibility for their own learning by writing their homework down in a planner. Now they could just claim they couldn't log on to *'S'Cool!'*

She looked closely at the screen.

"Like here. It's only showing two of your classes," she said to Ms Winter "and saying that you've only set one homework all month."

"We're not here to talk about me," snapped Ms Winter, turning her laptop back to face her. "Anyway, I'm an Assistant Head. I could be called out of a lesson at any moment to deal with some emergency."

"But it should still show up on *'S'Cool!'* so that whoever's covering your lesson can tell the pupils…"

Miss Brown realised where her helpfulness was leading her and drawing on her knowledge of several languages she stopped talking.

"Your problem is you can't take constructive criticism," concluded Ms Winter. She unwrapped a chocolate bar as Ms Payne took over the interrogation.

"And we've been looking over your marking too," she said, picking up an exercise book. It was Anton Grawlix's book. So that was why he hadn't had his book when she'd collected them in for marking this morning.

Ms Payne opened the book at his last homework, a page of creative writing on the topic of holidays. Anton had had to use the superlative to write a piece entitled *'Hôtel de rêve ou hôtel de cauchemar?'* Which hotel had he enjoyed staying in and which one had been a nightmare? The two Assistant Heads remembered little of any French they'd been taught at school but Ms Payne prided herself on being able to swear in four different languages. Amongst all the French words she did recognise in his homework, such as *'weekend'*, *'hôtel'*, *'train'* and *'camping'*, she had spotted a rude word!

She drew Miss Brown's attention to where Anton had written the sentence *'L'hôtel à Torquay où nous sommes restés l'année dernière était complètement merde parce que le patron était fâché tout le temps!'*

"He's written *merde!*" exclaimed Ms Payne as if she'd never seen the brown word before. "We can't have the bloody kids writing words like that in their sodding books! I'll have to inform Janine when she's back in. This is a safeguarding issue."

"I've not even seen that piece of work yet," replied Miss

Brown, a little exasperated.

To be honest if Anton had written that sentence in the actual GCSE the examiners would probably have been impressed by a long list of achievements. His perfect use of the past tense, the subordinate clauses, the inclusion of opinions, his faultless spelling and the correct use of accents to name but a few. The use of colloquial, everyday French would probably have ticked the box for cultural awareness too rather than actually giving them a heart attack.

"Well, we're going to have to end it there," said Ms Winter, looking up at the clock. "But all this will go down on your file and just remember that we're watching you."

Later as Miss Brown was doing her voluntary lunchtime duty in the canteen Ms Winter and Ms Payne came past, heading back to their new office with their trays of food. Anton Grawlix was asking her when he'd get his French exercise book back. She was just telling him that she'd have it marked for tomorrow when the Assistant Heads paused to join in her private conversation.

"There were too much bloody swearing in your book," said Ms Winter.

"Yeah, it were well shit," agreed Ms Payne.

Then they headed off, leaving Miss Brown to try and explain it all to the confused Year 10 pupil in front of her. Even though she was quite a popular teacher thanks to Ms Payne's use of the brown word the pupils sitting nearby now had a new nickname for Miss Brown.

When Ms Stonehart returned the following week the two Assistant Heads would find themselves having to explain to her why Miss Brown was absent. They showed her the sick note that she had sent in from her doctor who had signed her off for two weeks suffering from "work-related stress." Under the circumstances her absence could genuinely be described as French leave.

CHAPTER 46

"A man who knows two languages is worth two men."

There are many similarities between doing your French speaking exam and taking your driving test, not least the fact that it's just you and the person testing you alone together. Just as what people do on their driving test bears little resemblance to how they later behave on the road, the oral exam is nothing like what you experience abroad in the real world. It is perhaps for that reason that exam requirements change on a regular basis, hoping to make the experience of learning a foreign language more authentic.

In the early days there had been very little spoken work as though the only contact you'd ever expect to have with foreigners would involve writing formal letters to prove that you could conjugate verbs. Over the years the skills needed to pass the exam had changed to include the ability to regurgitate a prepared foreign speech the length of a Shakespearean play whilst still making it sound spontaneous. For some reason examiners see spontaneity as commendable in MFL although for pupils studying Music it is different. They are never expected to act like they've only just picked up a trumpet for the first time in their lives on the day of the exam. In fairness the current format of the spoken exam is clearly very relevant to young people in the twenty-first century. It is almost impossible to visit a foreign country nowadays if you haven't developed the rôle plays skills needed to see yourself as a Mediterranean fisherman or you can't discuss the problems of global warming. Who knows what skills the next specification would require?

With Miss Brown still off sick Mr Buonanulla had made provision for her GCSE pupils to sit their speaking exams as planned. Supply teachers rarely returned to Wildside Academy and good MFL teachers were hard to find. Many people who might have gone on to study and teach foreign languages had been put off by the trauma of their own spoken exam and the low marks exam boards had awarded them for all their efforts. As Mr Buonanulla was too busy acting as *Acting* Head of Department and Madame Loups-Garoux had a lot to do as a Head of Year, the abandoned pupils would be tested by Mr Haddenough. It made sense really as he had also been teaching Miss Brown's classes since her disappearance.

As always Mr Jones had been forced to vacate the Music practice rooms to allow the MFL speaking exams to take place. The recorders would fall silent for a week whilst pupils worked their way through the textbook *"Exploring Music Through Pictures and Worksheets."* A few years previously he had found himself playing a much larger part in the outcome of these exams. That was the year that Mr Buonanulla had read on social media that it was a lot easier to pass MFL exams using the Welsh Exam Board and so had arranged for the school to change from the exam board it had always been with. It was only when the security seals were broken on the packets of exam papers that arrived at Wildside Academy that Mr Buonanulla found he'd ordered the Welsh-language version rather than the English one. It was fortunate for him that Huw Jones spoke a second language and could translate them all for him.

Carol Underwood, the Cover Supervisor, had turned up late to supervise the preparation area, getting the whole thing off to a disorganized start. Pupils each had an exact time to turn up for their exam and if this went wrong the whole thing collapsed like a house of cards.

"I thought they'd be up in the Languages rooms," she said. "I've been waiting there for ages. It's not my fault. It just says *"MFL Speaking Exams"* on my cover list for today."

"No, it's too noisy to do the exams near the Assistant Heads' office," said Mr Buonanulla. "So, let's see if everybody's here."

The only two pupils who had turned up were Richard Broadbent and Dawn Bywater from Miss Brown's class. They both looked incredibly nervous waiting by the piano clutching their French exercise books. According to the schedule there should have been eight pupils present at this point.

"So," said Mr Buonanulla to the two of them, "do either of you know where everybody else is? So we should have Leo Axmiles, Agnes Belviahula, Lief Husk, Bertie Kiddieserf, Abdul Merrilee-Gaol and Chris Mumremes?"

"Sir," I don't think any of them will be in today," said Richard hesitantly.

Mr Buonanulla raised an eyebrow quizzically. "Oh? Whyever not?"

"It's just that Zombie Kombat 360 came out at midnight, sir. They said they were staying off to play it, sir."

Madame Loups-Garoux muttered something in French that wasn't the kind of language that normally got recorded in the exam.

"So," continued Mr Buonanulla, trying to remain calm, "I'll go see if they're actually in school today and have just forgotten. Céline, could you pop to the staffroom and make a few phone calls home please. And Ivor, you might as well get started with these two."

Chloe Jessop chewed the end of her pen as she read through the Rôle Play card Mr Haddenough had given her to prepare. The instructions to candidates informed her that she was *"working in the French Ministry for the Environment in Paris"* and that *"your teacher will play the part of your friend."* That was an encouraging start. She'd already been to Paris on holiday and it was nice to have a friend with you when you were starting a new job. The instructions then told her that *"When you see an exclamation mark (!) you will have to respond to something you have not prepared."* That would be the spontaneous element Mr Haddenough had talked about in class. Chloe had deliberately made sure there were whole sections of the syllabus she had not even looked at so that she would score highly on spontaneity. The final line advised her that *"When you see a question mark (?) you will have to ask a question."* She'd already decided that at that point she was going to ask Mr Haddenough how to say 'global warming' in French. For a moment she pondered what kind of person would be taking the exam if they had to have it explained to them what question marks and exclamation marks looked like. She was ready now but as she still had ten minutes' preparation time left she decided to read the details that were written in French below the instructions. Mr Haddenough must have known that Chloe wouldn't need all the preparation time as he'd also left her a nice photo to look at. It too had a question on it *"Qu'est-ce qu'il y a sur la photo?"* Chloe could only assume it was one of those rhetorical questions that they had done about with Miss Hughes. She'd also been given some paper in case she wanted to pass the remaining time doodling. Mr Haddenough knew she liked to decorate the borders of her work with flowers.

Vous travaillez pour le Ministère de l'Environnement à Paris.

Vous parlez avec votre ami(e.)

- Votre opinion sur les problèmes de l'environnement.
- !
- Comment sauver la planète. (Trois details.)
- ?
- Le réchauffement climatique et le sens de la vie.

Mr Haddenough had conducted four of Miss Brown's speaking exams when he noticed that Madame Loups-Garoux had started doing hers. As the exams were only recorded rather than videoed she was doing exaggerated hand gestures and mimes to help her pupil with the answers. Looking through the glass Mr Haddenough could only assume the Rôle Play was about working on the runway at Charles de Gaulle airport. It turned out that Mr Buonanulla had delayed his spoken exams until the afternoon as he was suffering from one of his wee migraines again. There was no sign of Mrs Underwood in the preparation room.

He'd never taught Mohammed Mistry before but he remembered Sarah-Jane saying he was better at Listening than Speaking. As the oral exam continued he realised that what she'd really meant was that Mohammed couldn't speak French. It wasn't just that he didn't know words or that he chose the wrong ones. He could clearly understand everything he was asked in French and replied promptly but for some reason he replied in English with an accent that he seemed to have picked up from watching *'Allo! 'Allo!* Mr Haddenough wasn't even sure if he knew he was doing it.

"Et maintenant, Mohammed, on va parler des vacances. Où est-ce que tu passes tes vacances normalement?"

"Normalee ay spend zee 'olidayz een Fronz wif ma famylee. Ah preefair to stay een a notel becors there ees often a bitch neer buy."

As the regulations did not allow him to interrupt the recording Mr Haddenough just had to avoid making eye contact with Mohammed and carry on.

"Et qu'est-ce que tu aimes manger en vacances, Mohammed?"

"Eef eets 'ot ah weel 'ave the playzeer of a nice creem. When there ees a boulangerie ah a door a pain oh chocolate or piss off cake too."

There were always difficult questions in exams but the hardest one came right at the end.

"So, sir, how do you think I did, innit?" asked Mohammed enthusiastically as the recording ended. "Fantastique?"

Ivor could only comment that it was in the top five he'd done that morning.

Ivor had had high hopes for the next of Miss Brown's candidates as he had taught Lucy Scott when she had been in Year 7. Whilst she was clearly good at French he could tell that she was not going to score very highly in the spoken exam. She had chosen to answer each question truthfully leading to short monosyllabic answers that sadly did not show how good she really was at French.

"Alors, Lucy, tu as des frères ou des soeurs?"

"Non."

(Ok. No siblings. No follow-on questions there.)

"Tu as un animal à la maison, Lucy?"

"Non."

(And no pets. Right, where next?)

"Tu aimes les films?"

"Non."

(Not much of a cinema-goer then. Only another four minutes left...)

Jack Spivey had said very little during his spoken exam for very different reasons. The trouble had started as soon as he'd sat down at the preparation desk and looked at the documents laid out there including a photo showing various factory roofs. It was actually a Photo Card on the topic of unemployment but Jack didn't know what the French said.

"I don't know nothin' about that!" exclaimed Jack, standing up again indignantly. "If lead's been nicked off the roof again then it'd be our Ryan. I was at home on Tuesday doing my homework. You ask me Mum!"

It only got worse when Mr Haddenough took him through to the little Music practice room and started recording their conversation.

"I don't have to say nothin' to you!" Jack shouted out. "I'm phoning me Dad. He'll sort you out."

As Mr Haddenough patiently tried to explain to Jack that mobile phones weren't allowed in school and certainly not in exams, there was a crack of thunder outside the window followed by heavy rain. When he played back the recording later it just sounded like a case of police brutality as they tried to force their suspect to answer.

Mr Haddenough had managed to get through all of Miss Brown's pupils by the end of the day and felt like he had just completed the Tour de France. Once he'd tidied up the little room he'd been using he found that Madame Loups-Garoux had already gone home and Mr Buonanulla was obviously checking his candidates had recorded. As his *Acting* Head of Department wasn't conducting exams it'd be alright to knock on and just let him know he was going back to tidy up his classroom.

"There, Matthew. That bit. Yeah, yeah, yeah. You need to say what I've written there next!" he heard Mr Buonanulla's voice whispering.

"Oh, right, sir. Le réchauffement climatique est un grand problème de nos jours pour tout le monde. Was that OK, sir? What next?"

"And on the Rôle Play card it's une pizza. Feminine. If you say un pizza nobody will know what you mean..."

Only at that point did his Acting Head of Department realise that he was not alone. He hurriedly switched the recording off and smiled nervously.

"So, all done for today then? Everything go alright?"

"Not too bad. I don't really know Sarah-Jane's class but I think I got the best I could out of them. They weren't too sure about the stuff on homelessness and unemployment. How about you?"

"Yeah, yeah, yeah, they both did really well. So there was a problem with Matthew's and it didn't record so I'm going to have to get him back in to do it again tomorrow."

"That's a shame. He'll have to do a different Rôle Play and

everything and you'll have loads of paperwork to fill in for the Exam Board."

Mr Buonanulla said nothing and there was a moment before he looked away.

"So, anyway, you can leave me to lock up," he said. "I've got a meeting with Lynne later anyway so I'm not heading off just yet."

Mr Haddenough went back to his classroom which looked like it had been hit by a small bomb. Gathering together the books he needed to mark from today's cover lessons he headed out to the car park. It had been so much fun today he could hardly wait to conduct Miss Brown's Spanish exams tomorrow. After that he could start on his own groups.

CHAPTER 47

"The road to success and the road to failure are almost exactly the same."

"Well, I've got some bad news and some worse news."

It had fallen to Mr Wingett to run the morning briefing as Ms Stonehart was tied up with the School Police Liaison Officer again.

"Some of you will have heard that Ofsted are working in the area at the moment. They were at Berryfield Academy last week and downgraded them from *'Outstanding'* to *'Inadequate.'* We could be next. It's all down to what you do in the classroom."

Those teachers who kept up to date with this kind of thing on social media knew that Mr Wingett was again not telling the whole story. The teaching and learning at Berryfield was still outstanding and probably always would be. Unfortunately the lady on their reception had just welcomed the Ofsted inspectors through without checking any credentials, meaning that the school automatically failed for lack of adequate safeguarding. The teachers probably had lesson plans, Learning Objectives and everything.

"With this in mind Heads of Department are going to be checking your lesson plan folder at the start of each day and Richard has a pupil progress checklist for each of you. We need you to pay particular attention to any pupil who has an acronym after their name on SCAMS. OK? Richard?"

Mr Thicke handed out the new flight paths he'd made for each pupil that would allow them to succeed at GCSE if only they would do what he'd calculated. After two weeks of printing off all this colourful data it meant that Mrs Ramsbottom could now focus on other photocopying and rumour had it that the repair man would be coming to fix the machine in the staffroom.

Finally Ms Winter announced that staff would have the opportunity to show how successful they were being as it was time for the mid-year review of Bright Sky targets with Heads of Department. Ms Payne contributed to the briefing by saying she agreed with Ms Winter.

With Mr Heinz, Head of Year 11, still off on long-term sick Mr Humble had been organizing the assembly rota for the year group each week. Usually he would tell them touching stories about his Mam and how tough it had been growing up in Sunderland after his old man had been arrested. He would often coax somebody else into doing the assembly simply because he knew that delegation was a skill he would need to develop if he expected to join the Senior Leadership Team.

The theme for the latest assembly was 'Success' so he had looked to the PE Department for ideas. Harry Greenfield, the Head of Boys' PE, had said that he didn't want to come all the way over to the canteen and Jim Fitt had happily become his substitute. However when Ms Murkett heard of his plans she had insisted that it would be sexist if the Girls' PE Department were not involved too and so Mrs Mower and Miss Marsh found their names added to the team sheet. Alison Mower wanted to talk to Year 11 about golf but Jim Fitt pictured the pupils trying to beat the school's keepy-uppy record. In the end Lisa Marsh diplomatically suggested a table tennis match, boys versus girls. They had just enough table tennis bats somewhere. Ms Murkett said she'd come and offer her support and Jim managed to talk Bob into setting up the hall for the tournament.

"Now then, listen up Year 11," began Mr Fitt as the tune of *"All things bright and beautiful"* faded away. He'd wanted to sing something they sang on the terraces but Jamie had reminded him that Ms Stonehart was probably listening in. The screen above his head was blank but Mr Fitt didn't need a PowerPoint here any more than he did for his pre-match pep talks out on the field.

"As we're thinking about success today," he continued, "let's kick off with a big round of applause for Under-16 rugby team who played Coal Hill this weekend. By 'eck what a crackin' match that were! I'd go t'foot of our stairs it were that good. They're a tremendous group o'lads. Like I always tell 'em, it don't matter if you win or lose and we didn't lose. We came second. It were champion, proper champion! Well done, lads! Now, how good are you all at the old ping pong?"

Ms Stonehart muted the monitor in her office as the constant echoing tap-tappetty-tap of ping pong balls was beginning to get on her nerves. Eddie, the School Police Liaison Officer, had just left but he'd been very helpful. He'd agreed to do a stakeout at her house to try and solve a mystery that had been puzzling her ever since she and Bob had split up. Every Thursday morning she'd put her bins out before heading off to work and every afternoon she'd find that her bins had not been emptied even though those of her neighbours had. It was as if somebody was moving her bin out of the way before the lorry arrived so that it would never get emptied. Bin bags were beginning to stack up at the back of her house. But who would do such a thing? Who could have a grudge against her? Eddie said he'd get to the bottom of it.

In the light of what had happened at Berryfield the previous week he'd also shown her how to use the CCTV cameras more effectively. Now when Ofsted came the SLT would be able to track their progress around the school and send texts to warn teachers of their imminent arrival. Under her leadership they would continue to go from strength to strength. Perhaps it might be worth doing a dummy run before Ofsted actually arrived?

She was just changing the Ofsted counter on her wall to 622 days when Mrs Spratt turned up with Mr O'Brien as instructed.

"Well, Sam, straight to business," she began as soon as the door had closed. "How did you get on with the interview at…How did it all go?"

It was as if she couldn't actually bring herself to say the words Upper Steem Academy.

"It was a pretty rigorous process," Mr O'Brien explained. "There was the usual tour of the school, I met some of the other teachers there, then had to give a presentation about what makes a good leader. To be honest, I just thought about how you lead us all here at Wildside as I answered that part. There was a data exercise followed by an interview with a panel of pupils…"

"Pupils?" exclaimed Ms Stonehart. "What do pupils know about running a school?"

"Exactly! You could run rings round them. And then after all that they narrowed the nine candidates down to just three and I was one of the ones who got through to the interview stage in the afternoon."

"And I bet they asked a lot of ridiculous questions knowing that lot. So what did they ask you?"

Ms Stonehart looked like she was about to take notes.

"It's hard to remember everything they said really. There was one about how would a leader motivate people and I ended up thinking about your Words of Wisdom. I don't think we've got it in the school but I've always liked that one by Antoine de Saint-Exupéry about building a ship. I'd have to get Mr Haddenough to say it in French."

With no knowledge of foreign languages, Ms Stonehart just looked puzzled.

"It's something like *'If you want to build a ship, don't drum up people to collect wood and don't assign them tasks and work, but rather teach them to yearn for the endless immensity of the sea,'* I think," said Mr O'Brien.

"That'd be the kind of daft thing they'd like there," replied Ms Stonehart, thinking he was joking, "like getting the kids to run the interview! I mean imagine asking your staff what they'd like to do? Ridiculous! Tell them what to do and sort them out if they don't do it!"

"The Wildside Academy way," commented Mr O'Brien.

"Exactly! Well, never mind, Sam, you tried your best. It doesn't surprise me your plan didn't work if you had to deal with rubbish like that! There's not much you can do if you're talking to an idiot."

"Tell me about it!" said Mr O'Brien. "But I did it. I got the job. I can start next term."

"Really? That's excellent news," said Ms Stonehart. She seemed to be thinking for a moment. "You know what, the sooner you start there, the sooner we'll find out what they're up to and beat them. Ofsted have been into Berryfield you know. In fact, thinking about it, if I were to ignore your notice period you could probably start next week? I'll have a word with the Governors and Norma can start sorting out all the paperwork."

She pressed the buzzer to summon Mrs Spratt.

"And even though I know you're not really leaving us I think it'd be best if we got you a leaving present. Actually if you're going at the end of the week it might be easiest if Alex just takes donations straight out of everybody's pay. By the way you never said what your job title is going to be?"

It was at that point that Mrs Spratt came through from her office. She'd brought with her two tickets that Eddie had dropped off for the Policeman's Ball. Not being a teacher Ms Stonehart never realised that she hadn't actually got an answer to her final question. She was too busy planning for the weekend. It didn't really matter. She'd find out Mr O'Brien's new job title soon enough.

DAVID ADAMSON

CHAPTER 48

"History will be kind to me for I intend to write it."

"I wouldn't believe anything you read in there," mumbled Mr Wingett, passing *The Wildside Gazette* back to Ms Stonehart. "It's all doom and gloom anyway. I only look at it for the Lottery."

"It's just a biased rag!" said Ms Stonehart. "There was no mention of our new telescope, was there? Too busy writing about that other place sending their pupils to the moon or something!"

Actually Upper Steem Academy had organised a school trip to NASA but Mr Wingett knew better than to correct the Headteacher.

Ms Stonehart's day had actually started out so well too. The local paper was running a feature about schools, perhaps because Ofsted had been sniffing around the area lately. Her cup of lapsang souchong had tasted even more delightful than usual as she'd perused the article about Berryfield Academy. How any school could fail to have all its policies in place was beyond her. Policies were probably the most important thing in any school. Along with profits, of course. But then it had all turned a bit sour. Somehow the reporter who had phoned her the week before had got it all wrong. She'd been misquoted!

"Ms Stonehart, there's a reporter from The Wildside Gazette on the line. Should I put him through or tell him you're busy?"

"Put him through, Norma. It's probably that Mr Bullen who wrote that nice article about us last term. Tell Mr Buonanulla to wait."

"I hear what you say. Putting him through now, Ms Stonehart."

"Hello, yes? You're speaking to Janine Stonehart. Is that Mr Bullen?"

"*No, no. Mr Bullen's moved on to The Walkbridge Echo. I'm Terry Morgan, social affairs reporter with The Gazette. I've only recently moved back up north. I know very little about your school, other than what Verity, that's my sister, has said about it. I was hoping to talk to the Principal of Wildside Academy?*"

"*I'm the Headteacher here. We don't have Principals here.*"

"*No principles. Ok. And I can quote you on that, Ms...?*"

"*Stonehart. Ms Janine Stonehart. S-T-O-N-E-H-A-R-T. Headteacher of Wildside Academy. Headteacher, Diploma in Human Resources, TGCSEC, CPT, BPB. Did you get all that, Mr Morgan?*"

"*It all sounds very impressive.*"

"*When would you like to send a photographer to the school?*"

"*There's no need for that, Ms Stonehard. We've got photos on file we can use. I was wondering if I could ask you a few questions about staffing, pupil progress and how money is being spent in the school?*"

"This is slander!" Ms Stonehart exclaimed throwing the paper back down on the table in front of Mr Wingett. "It starts by saying that I said the school has no principles and then just gets worse! And he's spelt my name wrong too!"

The photo they'd used was not particularly flattering either.

Standing to the side of them Mrs Spratt continued staring at the floor, wishing she'd never brought the morning papers through in the first place. Technically it would be libel rather than slander, she thought, but in this case it would be best if she heard what was said but said nothing herself.

"I should put you on a written warning for this!" Ms Stonehart continued, glaring at her Head of HR. "You should have known better than to put that reporter through to my office! The policy is that if we have anything to say we release a press statement. Why do we pay for lawyers?"

She wouldn't actually put anything on Norma's file as she needed her to help sort this mess out. Letting her think her employment was coming to an end would certainly improve her performance though.

"You may go, Norma. I'll summon you when you're needed."

Mrs Spratt had definitely heard what she said today.

Somewhere in the distance a bell tolled.

"Have you actually read it?" demanded Ms Stonehart,

turning her attention back to her Deputy Head as the door closed. "It says that parents weren't happy with the closing of the Sixth Form, that we're haemorrhaging staff, cheating in exams and not spending money wisely! This is an outrage! We should sue them. I just hope Mr Chambers hasn't seen it…"

The portrait of the Chair of Governors seemed to be watching her.

"I'm a good judge of character but he was so convincing, that reporter. I thought the article would be like the one last term. Where are they getting this information from? Half of this didn't even come up in conversation. He's been talking to somebody else. Somebody's got a grudge!"

Mr Wingett suspected that she was going to ask him to come up with a list of suspects by close of business. It'd be quite a long list too.

"Would you like me to draft a press release?" he offered instead, hoping to derail her train of thought. "I suppose I could use some of the summary of that Ofsted report I prepared. We could focus on how the plans we have in place have the potential to move us from *Inadequate* to *Requires improvement* ?"

When you're at *Inadequate* the only way is up.

"That would be helpful, Gary. But run it past me first, of course. Close of business today will be fine."

Ms Stonehart glanced down at the photo of Berryside Academy again. The photo showed the Acting Headteacher, Mr Hardial, looking very sad under the headline *'Failure can often be the highway to success, says inadequate Headteacher."* She smiled. Maybe things weren't as bad as she'd thought.

"I'm afraid there's some worse news," said Mr Wingett with impeccable timing. He turned the page to the centre spread. Both pages were devoted to the enemy, Upper Steem Academy. Ms Stonehart could barely bring herself to look at the full-colour photo of Hoskins surrounded by happy pupils and staff. She started to read the article.

Roads were blocked and parking spaces were at a premium this week as it seemed that everybody wanted to go to Upper Steem Academy. This is, of course, not an unusual occurrence for this high-performing and over-subscribed school as witnessed by the crowds turning up

---

for its Open Evening last October. "I was one of the lucky ones who got to go to USA!" said Zayne Medley, winner of this year's *Celebrity Love Rock Star Academy*. But the crowds weren't coming to hear Zayne sing this time. They'd come to say a fond farewell and thank you to Mr Niall Hoskins, Headteacher at Upper Steem Academy, who officially retires this week.

Upper Steem High School, as it was called when Mr Hoskins joined thirty years ago, used to be an underachieving school with a lot of problems and very poor exam results. Under Mr Hoskins' guidance Upper Steem Academy has gone from strength to strength. Mr Jeremiah Grimes, the Minister for Education, thanked Mr Hoskins publicly, commenting that he should be recommended for an OBE for his services to education. With his usual self-effacing modesty, Mr Hoskins praised the hard work of his staff and spoke of the pleasure of working with such amazing young people.

The feeling is obviously mutual and over the last few months pupils in Year 9 have spent many hours after school converting an unused area of ground at the side of the school into an outstandingly beautiful garden. The Niall Hoskins Remembrance Garden as it will be known will be used by residents of a nearby nursing home, Sunnyview Meadows.

Mr Hoskins went on to comment that he believed the School was in safe hands following the Governing Body's recent rigorous interviews. When asked about his own plans for the future Mr Hoskins replied that the Prime Minister had asked him to become a lead Ofsted inspector and that he was particularly looking forward to visiting the other schools in the local area.

"Going from strength to strength!" exclaimed Ms Stonehart, dropping the newspaper. "I said that to him about Wildside Academy!"

"It does sound like you," agreed Mr Wingett.

He picked the paper up, bravely turning it over so that she could see the second page of the feature. He might be no good at choosing his Lottery numbers but he could safely predict that she wasn't going to like the end of the article.

So will Mr Hoskins be a hard act to follow? We spoke to Mr Samuel O'Brien, the new Headteacher of Upper Steem Academy.

"I've been a great admirer of Mr Hoskins for years," he said, "and have enjoyed working with him and other Headteachers at the regular Local Headteachers' Meetings. I know everybody will be very sad to see Niall go but we'll all try our very best to make him proud of us. The pupils at USA are unbelievable, showing a real thirst for learning, the staff are just so committed, always going the extra mile and the SLT work amazingly well together as a team. I just know that together we are a school where everybody matters and together we will continue to go from strength to strength.

I'm sure that Niall will be keeping himself busy in retirement but he'll never be too busy to keep an eye on us here. It's like one big happy family at Upper Steem Academy. As a former French teacher Niall will no doubt be spending time in France but he has promised to come back in July to present the new award we've set up in his honour, the Niall Hoskins Award for MFL."

Like his predecessor Mr O'Brien is not one to sing his own praises. Having worked with him in a previous school, the Head of the Maths Department at USA, Mr James Milton, commented that he would be a first-class Headteacher. Back home in the Channel Islands Mr O'Brien's family said how proud they were of him but perhaps the final word should go to his daughter Rosie, aged 6. She can't wait till she's old enough to go to Daddy's school. She'll have to wait for that place but with Mr O'Brien hoping to be here for many happy years to come the time will no doubt fly by. As they say, *Tempus fugit*!

Straight away Ms Stonehart ordered Mrs Spratt to check the paperwork that O'Brien had signed. There was no mention of him coming back in six months! She read the reference she'd given him and discovered she'd actually recommended him for the post of Headteacher! What did he know about being a Headteacher? Then, with a sick feeling in her stomach, she got Mr Goldbloom to check that they weren't still paying this Judas. Luckily they weren't but he'd had a very generous leaving present! In desperation she told Mr Thicke to check whether Wildside Academy held the copyright on the phrase *Tempus fugit!* It turned out they didn't, nor did they own the phrase *"going from strength to strength."* Finally she did something she thought she'd never ever do.

The looped recording of '*Simply the best!*' when she phoned Upper Steem Academy was even more irritating than the sound of the ping pong balls so long ago. Eventually she got through.

"Good afternoon, Upper Steem Academy," said a female voice that she thought she recognised. "You're through to Verity Speke, the Headteacher's Personal Assistant. How may I help you, please?"

"Oh, hello," said Ms Stonehart, trying to place the voice, "I'd like to speak to Sam. Mr O'Brien. It's Ms Stonehart. Headteacher of Wildside Academy. He'll be expecting me."

"One moment, please, Ms Stonehard. I'll see if he's available."

Holding the phone at arm's length, Ms Stonehart continued to ponder where she'd heard that voice before. It seemed ages before the voice replaced the tune.

"Sorry to have kept you waiting, Ms Stonehard. I'm afraid Mr O'Brien's door is usually open but he's in a meeting at the moment. Would you like to leave a message?"

"Just tell him to phone me back. Wildside Academy. He knows the number."

"Sorry, what was the name again, please?"

"Ms Stonehart. Janine Stonehart. He'll know who I am."

"Stonehard? Sorry how are you spelling that?"

"I'm spelling it like it's spelt! S-T-O-N-E-H-A-R-T."

"Sorry, I didn't catch that. There was a bit of a whistling sound on the line. Could you repeat that, Ms...?"

"Stonehart! S-T-O-N-E-H-A-R-T!"

"Thank you, Ms Stonehard. I'm sure Mr O'Brien will phone you back when he's available. Shall we say by close of business?"

As she was replacing the receiver Ms Stonehart thought she heard somebody laughing. Where *had* she heard that voice before?

Even though Ms Stonehart didn't like to be kept waiting she stayed in her office until long after close of business that day sitting by the phone. Mr O'Brien did not return her call. He was probably too busy, doing all the things you had to do when you're the Headteacher of a high-performing and over-subscribed school. As it turned out she never heard from him again, in spite of instructing Mrs Spratt to keep calling him on a regular basis. Never again did Norma get a chance to tell him that she heard what he said.

For his part Mr O'Brien was true to his word, keeping his old boss informed about what was happening at Upper Steem Academy. The USA website was regularly updated with stories and the school's successes rarely seemed to be out of the local press. When Ofsted visited them, Upper Steem Academy was still judged to be *"Outstanding"*. She found the comment that *"the new Headteacher, Mr O'Brien, is taking the school from strength to strength"* particularly hard to swallow.

As she sat in her darkened office that cold May afternoon waiting for the phone call that never came she found herself thinking about that voice again. What had she said she was called? Vanessa? Vicky? No, Verity, that was it! Verity something. It was a good job that she was a "person person" who was good with names. With time to kill Ms Stonehart idly started browsing through the old staff lists on her computer. Eventually she found her! It had been about five years ago. Of course! Verity Speke had been the HR Assistant to somebody called Kirsty. She couldn't remember much about Kirsty but Verity Speke had been trouble. She'd started criticizing procedures in the Finance Department and had threatened to go to the press with her allegations. Actually she just hadn't been very good at her job and they'd had no choice but to let the spiteful woman go. Mrs Speke could go blow her whistle somewhere else. It served O'Brien right if he had to work with Verity Speke!

Ms Stonehart had decided to call it a day and was just

getting into her Jaguar when her mobile phone pinged. It would probably be O'Brien at last. He did have her personal number.

She wouldn't reply straight away.

She'd keep him waiting.

She wouldn't even look at the text until she got home.

She closed the car door and looked at the text.

> Janine
> Sorry. No idea about the bins but this
> is not how I want to spend my time.
> It's not working out with us.
> Don't want to see you again.
> Eddie.

Just as she was getting out of the car to examine the flat tyre it started to rain.

CHAPTER 49

"It's not about being the best it's about being better than you were yesterday."

In the good old days before Wildside School converted to Academy status there had been two separate PE offices. Now, for financial reasons, the teachers of both Boys' and Girls' PE shared the same one. It was only because they worked so well as a team that this system was possible with each one of them finding their own place in the limited space.

Perhaps understandably the office was a little cluttered but in spite of Miss Marsh regularly bringing in air fresheners the smell of sweaty trainers still drifted in from the nearby boys' changing rooms. On the back wall stood the trophy cabinet that had been made by Brigadier Vernon-Smythe many years ago for a very reasonable price. It contained the cups and shields that were awarded at the annual sports day, although to be honest they hadn't actually seen the light of day in over six years. There was also the pride of Year 10, a small cup that they had won in a table tennis match against Brewery Road Primary School. It had become known as 'The BURPS Cup.'

However cramped it was, the office was a comfortable place for PE teachers to relax between and sometimes during lessons. When they found out that the microwave could block out the CCTV system it became a safe place for conversation again.

Mr Harry Greenfield, the Head of Boys' PE, rarely ventured out of this office. A lot of pupils simply knew him as a disembodied head that would appear at the window, shouting for them to run round the cross country circuit one more time. He himself would spend most of the working day in front of the portable television in the corner of the office. Whilst he couldn't get any of the proper sports channels he had found one that repeated classic Wimbledon tournaments all day. He was currently re-watching the 1977 Ladies' Semi-Final and nothing would tear him away from that sad day.

The chairs on either side of the cluttered desk belonged to the two teachers who were most likely to use the phone. Jim Fitt had regular football and rugby matches to arrange with other schools whilst Alison Mower, the Head of Girls' PE, often needed to phone the golf course or the hair salon. The old sofa by the window was used by the other members of the PE Departments : Mike Stringer, Marcus Deeside and Lisa Marsh. Placed incongruously beside the fridge was a brightly striped deckchair. The Fairtrade logo on its fabric advertised that it belonged to the honorary member of the Boys' PE Department, Mr Tim Cocker. Today he was recovering in it with a bag of prawn crisps after a particularly strenuous session on the rowing machine.

As the door to the office swung open Marcus set the microwave going for another twenty minutes. Mike had been over to the staffroom to collect all their planning folders as Ms Winter had insisted on seeing everybody's lesson plans even though the two Heads of Department had already checked them. Mike would have got back sooner had he not stopped to do star jumps with some Year 10 pupils in the yard.

"Frosty knickers says we all need to put something called SPAG into our lessons, whatever that is" said Mike, checking that the microwave was on. "Sounds like somebody's been on a course."

"I think she sent an email about something," said Alison.

"SPAG?" said Tim Cocker through a mouthful of crumbs. "One of the kids told me about that in my IT lesson. Spelling, Punctuation And Grammar. We couldn't work out why the word "and" was worth a capital letter. You know what I said? I said that at Wildside if we don't use a capital letter we'd probably get punished for it. Capital punishment! "

"Ay up, Tim," said Jim Fitt. "You've told us that one before. Tell us summat new, mate. Like how we're meant to practise grammar while running round t'pitch."

Jim Fitt wasn't a big fan of grammar. To him the word conjured up images of his teams being beaten at posh Grammar Schools that had much better facilities than Wildside.

"So, 'ow do you think she'll cope without O'Brien t'run the shop? I'd love to 'ave seen look on her faces when she worked it out!"

"We'll go from strength to strength, of course," quoted Marcus. "I mean we've still got Thick Rick, Whinger and the Gruesome Twosome to help her."

"It's not all about Ofsted!" quoted Alison Mower in her best impersonation of their esteemed Führer.

"He was alright, Sam O'Brien," said Tim. "The only decent lesson observations I ever got were from him. Did you ever notice he was the only member of the SLT to wear a lanyard?"

He laughed. To keep himself sane Mr Cocker often played his own version of I-Spy during the working day. The number of points you could score if you saw a member of SLT wearing a lanyard or carrying their laptops in a case was quite high. You got extra points if they were also telling an ordinary teacher off for not having a lanyard or a laptop case.

"And do you remember that INSET video he did?" he continued.

It had been the first day back in September one year and at the last minute Mr O'Brien had been landed with running the training day even though he himself was out on a course in Leeds. Rather than waste a day for the rest of the staff he'd gone to the trouble of recording a video of himself with all the instructions for the INSET day. In a change to his usual formal appearance though he'd put on a loud Hawaiian shirt and sunglasses, filming it in front of a greenscreen whilst sipping a colourful drink from a tall glass. Whilst most people appreciated the effort he'd gone to, Ms Grimley had genuinely thought he was in the Seychelles or wherever while she was busy working. Mr Thicke just wasn't happy that he was drinking during the school day. Like the annual Summer Fair, good-natured moments like this soon disappeared under Ms Stonehart's leadership.

"You heard what happened with Deirdre, didn't you?" said Alison.

Deirdre had wanted to send a card to Mr O'Brien from all the cleaners to say that they were sorry he was leaving and wish him good luck. He was the only member of the Senior Leadership Team who had ever noticed they existed, other than Mr Thicke who would complain about the amount of litter on the field.

"So, Deirdre asked at the Main Office if she could have Mr O'Brien's home address for the card," continued Alison "and she gets told she can't have it because of data protection."

"Knowing them they'd probably shredded all the stuff with his name on it," added Jim.

"Well, while she's cleaning Thicke's office she asked him if he could pass the card on to him for them. When she empties his bin the next day she finds he's just torn the card up."

"Why couldn't it have been Thick Rick that left instead of Sam?" pondered Lisa Marsh quietly.

"Or the Gruesome Twosome," added her Head of Department.

"So the question is," said Mike, "who's next?"

On the wall beside Mr Fitt's team sheets was a long list of all the people who had mysteriously disappeared from Wildside Academy over recent years. Apart from the spidery handwriting in felt-tip it did make you think of the names on war memorials remembering those who had died in battle.

"I've just thought of one you've missed off," said Tim as he studied the list. "What was he called? In RE? Mr Kane. They got rid of him on capability."

Given that he always got outstanding exam results it had seemed like somebody was having a laugh with that one. A teacher of RE called Kane who was not able to teach well enough?

"Oh yeah," said Mike, adding the name to the list. "I'd forgotten about Adam Kane."

"And the kids found out his first name was Adam and they'd say *'I don't Adam 'n' Eve it, sir!'*" added Tim.

"Oh yeah. It doesn't change the odds though, pal."

In keeping with the British way of coping with catastrophes Mr Stringer was running an illicit sweepstake about staff disappearing from Wildside Academy. Mr Cocker was a little worried that the odds against him weren't good. The favourable publicity he'd got the school during Fairtrade week had only bought him a little time.

"My money's on Dean Gordon," he said.

After the accident with the circular saw Mr Gordon wasn't as quick on his feet as he had been and Ms Winter was constantly checking whether he was a few seconds late to lessons.

"Look at the odds you've got on the office staff going,"

said Marcus. "You could retire on your winnings if one of them was sacked!"

"Best one was Roger," said Mike grimly. "I'd based it on how long he'd said he had left."

"He used to peel those little stickers off his apple each dinnertime," said Tim, "and keep a tally count on the edge of his desk. You know the cleaners have never got rid of them? Leaving it all just the way Roger left it when he was taken from us before his time."

Tim had lost quite a bit of money on the sweepstake when Roger had disappeared prematurely.

"Do you remember that time O'Brien came over 'ere and saw all this?" said Jim, pointing towards their noticeboard.

There was still a sheet of file paper pinned up on it listing *'Things you'll never hear in Wildside Academy!!!'* It had been written in response to Ms Stonehart's Words of Wisdom. Top of the list of impossible quotations was *'You all know so much more about teaching that I do!'* attributed to Ms Stonehart followed by *'That was such an amazing lesson, Mr Milton. Thanks for all your hard work!'* from Ms Winter.

Mr O'Brien had looked at the list, the sweepstake and the photo they had chosen for their dartboard before smiling and quietly telling them to be careful. It was like he was part of the rebel alliance. Luckily once the vending machine was removed from the Sports Hall entrance, again for financial reasons, there was little chance of Ms Winter coming over to bother the PE Department.

"You 'eard Cruella's split up with her fella?" said Jim. "First time in months I've been able to park at front of school."

"Oh dear," said Tim, smiling, "she's not really having a good time of it at the moment, is she? All those bad reports in the press, the only decent one on SLT digs an escape tunnel out of here to leave her right in the brown stuff and now her boyfriend's dumped her!"

"My heart bleeds for her," said Marcus.

Harry Greenfield looked up.

"She really deserved better than that!" he said. "Much better, poor woman."

There was a shocked silence for a moment as his colleagues struggled to understand how he could possibly have any sympathy for Ms Stonehart after all she'd done. Rather than going from strength to strength they'd all watched her take Wildside Academy from *'Outstanding'* all the way down to *'Inadequate'* with many casualties along the way. Then, noticing that he was gazing up at his precious signed photo of Sue Barker, they all realised that he hadn't been listening to a word they'd said.

"Harry!" exclaimed Alison in an exasperated tone. "It's at times like these I'd rather be playing golf."

The bell was ringing to signal the end of break and Year 9 were already beginning to queue up outside the Sports Hall.

"Ah, well," said Harry, "back to reality. Must press on with it. Busy morning."

He opened the window and bellowed at the boys to get started on a cross country run.

CHAPTER 50

"Always expect the unexpected..."

It didn't seem like such a momentous email when Mr Haddenough first opened it at the start of his lunch break. It was nothing like the infamous Email of April Fools Day. The importance of it only really sank in much later in the early hours of a sleepless night. At the time it was no more unsettling than most of the other emails that were fired at them from beyond the Berlin Wall.

Mrs Spratt had "invited" him to a meeting that afternoon, thirteen minutes into the final lesson, without any mention of what the meeting would be about. All he knew was that it was taking place in the interview room, Room 101, and that Ms Winter and his *Acting* Head of Department would be present. It mentioned BS in the subject line of the email but that could stand for any number of things at Wildside Academy. Guessing that it would be something to do with his Bright Sky targets and surprised that anybody could still remember them, Mr Haddenough carefully worded an email reply to HR.

From : IHH – IHaddenough1@WildsideAcademy
To : NST – NSpratt1@WildsideAcademy
CC : LWR – LWinter1@WildsideAcademy
    HBA – HBuonanulla1@WildsideAcademy
Sent : Fri 17 May 12:24
Subject : BS Meeting period 5 today

Accept ~~Decline Rearrange~~

Good afternoon,

Thank you for letting me know about the meeting period 5. I would be delighted to attend but will need cover as I have Year 9 Spanish Set 5 at that time. I will prepare some work for them to do.
    Please could you let me know what the meeting is about?

Thanks,
Ivor.

Although Mrs Spratt's email invited him to *Accept / Decline / Rearrange the Meeting* he knew that whilst this might look like Multiple Choice there was only one correct answer.

Once he had prepared suitable work for the abandoned class he made his way down to the staffroom for what little was left of his lunch break. Mr Buonanulla was sitting at the breakfast bar with Madame Loups-Garoux where he had made them both cappuccinos to accompany the dish he'd prepared. Mr Haddenough politely interrupted them, hoping to find out what the impromptu meeting that afternoon was about.

"So, I've no idea," he claimed, mixing the last of the pesto sauce into the rigatoni with roasted potatoes, shrimps, squid and feta cheese.

"I think it might be about Bright Sky?" Mr Haddenough suggested.

"Yeah, yeah, yeah. That'll be it. Yeah."

Mr Buonanulla would have checked on his mobile phone but he really didn't want his garlic bread to go cold.

When Mr Haddenough opened his emails after dinner Inhuman Resources had been too busy to respond. He just had time to click on the cheery Bright Sky logo and look at his targets again before the bell went and his pupils arrived outside Room 42 with their usual enthusiasm. Once he'd made sure the Learning Objectives were on the board, the register had been taken and he'd got everybody started, Mrs Underwood, the Cover Supervisor, turned up.

"I can take over now," she said, seeing that the pupils were settled. "It'll be right. I went to Torremolinos once."

Mr Buonanulla was already in Room 101 chatting happily to Ms Winter when Mr Haddenough arrived. He knocked on the door, entered when he was told and sat down where he was instructed. Seated opposite the Assistant Head and his *Acting* Head of Department, the blinds behind them as firmly closed as their hearts, Mr Haddenough felt there should be a bright lamp shining directly into his eyes. Also conspicuous by her absence was Ms Payne. The thought crept across his mind that he'd never seen one female Assistant Head without the other. It felt somehow unnatural. Not for the first time he reflected that it was a shame Mr O'Brien had gone.

"At last! Right, let's get on with it," began Ms Winter impatiently even though he'd managed to get the lesson started and still arrive three minutes before the time the meeting was scheduled to begin. "We've been sat here for ages, yeah?"

"So, let me just move that out of your way," said Mr Buonanulla helpfully, removing a plate from in front of Ms Winter. There was a faint smell of pesto and garlic and something that looked like squid hung from her chins.

"Yeah, that was utter delish, Hamish," said Ms Winter. "Thanks for sharing that with Sharon and I. Brill!"

Perhaps Ms Payne had gone home with food poisoning?

Mr Buonanulla returned to his seat at Ms Winter's side as the meeting he said he knew nothing about began.

"How can I help you?" asked Mr Haddenough amiably.

At that point the door behind him opened and Ms Payne joined them. As she kicked the door closed behind her the bag of doughnuts she had brought along fell from the laptop she was using as a makeshift tray.

Taking the empty seat at Ms Winter's right-hand side she tore open the paper bag.

"The last four!" she exclaimed. "Eric saved them just for me. Let's get this party started!"

She chose a raspberry doughnut, gestured for Mr Buonanulla to help himself and Ms Winter took the remaining two. Clearly the prisoner wasn't getting one.

"I've called this meeting because I'm well not happy with how things are working out with you and Mr Buonanulla workwise," said Ms Winter. "Hamish is literally the best Head of MFL we've got and if you can't get along with people it's you what'll find you're in a precarious position…" She peered at Mr Haddenough over the top of her glasses.

Mr Haddenough wasn't sure what he was meant to have done to upset his *Acting* Head of Department but he needn't have worried because Ms Winter was about to tell him.

"The offensive emails you've sent him are all on your file," she began.

Mr Haddenough genuinely had no idea what she meant. He'd never seen the infamous Email Mr Wingett had sent but he himself was always very careful to be professional in his correspondence with anybody. It took him ages to type things so he always took the time to check them thoroughly before pressing send. The cleverest emails were those from Mr Jones.

"I don't know what you mean," he said. "What emails? Can you show me, please?"

Mr Buonanulla started searching through his mail on his mobile phone.

"So, I've got them here somewhere…"

Ms Winter put her hand on Mr Buonanulla's arm to stop him searching further. As she did so the little piece of squid fell to the floor.

"You don't need to," she said. "They're literally on his HR file. Like this one what you sent to Mrs Spratt today." She looked down at her laptop. "It's sarcastic, patronizing and it's not for you to question the actions of your superiors! Norma was dead upset by it, yeah?"

Mr Haddenough wasn't aware that he'd been any of those things but in the absence of any minutes being taken he made a mental note to read his email again later.

"And clearly you hadn't planned your lesson or you wouldn't of needed to find some work for the kids at the last minute. And that's not the first time neither."

Ms Winter started to demolish the other doughnut so Ms Payne took over the interrogation. It was the old bad cop/bad cop routine.

"It's not just about your bloody language in sodding emails," she began, "there's also the matter of your capability in the classroom." She'd wiped the excess sugar off the keyboard of her laptop and opened up the Bright Sky website. Her face took on a sickly yellow glow as she looked at the screen.

"Your progress towards your targets this year is proper rubbish!" she said. "The SCAMS data flight path prediction reckons your GCSE group is only on about 96% pass. And that's after Hamish and the rest of the MFL Department have done a wicked job of trying to help you and all."

Whilst you were never allowed to take somebody else into meetings like this with you, Mr Haddenough did feel he could have done with an interpreter. Somebody who could interpret their version of reality, a world in which he could still reach his 110% target if he tried harder. It was a shame Mr O'Brien was no longer here.

It would be interesting to know how well the groups he didn't teach were doing but that would obviously mean breaching the Official Secrets Act.

Ms Winter looked at the second target.

"Hamish tells me that the storeroom in his room is just as untidy as it was at the beginning of the year and as for the displays, yeah?"

"Can I just say there wasn't an awful lot of Blu-Tack in any..."

"You could have used your initiative," countered Ms Payne. "Bought some yourself. It's not like it costs a bomb!"

Having never asked any school to supply him with even a solitary red pen, Mr Haddenough had actually gone out and bought his own Blu-Tack and used it to put the displays he'd created up in every MFL room. Apart from Fraulein Schadenfreude's old room, of course, which had been closed off since last summer when it was found that mice had made the floorboards unsafe.

The trouble with doing something right the first time was that critics didn't appreciate how difficult a task was.

"*IHH responsible for producing new displays for* all *rooms and corridors,*" Mr Buonanulla read out. Clearly he had not saved the correct wording of the target for whatever reason and now Mr Haddenough, as he'd feared, found himself criticized for not having decorated the whole school.

Ms Winter tutted at this point. She actually tutted.

"You were meant to be running a CPD training session for staff each term," noted Ms Payne, moving on to the final target, "but you did nothing in the first term."

"But the target wasn't set until January," said Mr Haddenough not unreasonably.

"Sounds like excuses to me," said Ms Payne, going back to her mobile phone.

"Then I ran the CPD training on improving your memory but nobody turned up because they forgot."

"Yeah, well anyway, this is literally an information giving session," said Ms Winter. "We don't want to waste our time listening to excuses. That's not why we're sat here. You don't need to say nothing. We know anything you could possibly think of saying. We're proper experienced in this sort of thing, Sharon and I. You just literally need to shut up and listen."

He had the right to remain silent in a way that just wasn't right.

She turned to Mr Buonanulla.

"Anything what you also want to add further, Hamish?"

"So, I just think Ivor needs to work harder and be more respectful to me as his Head of Department. It's because of him that I get these wee migraines all the time."

Acting Head of Department.

"How's he doing markingwise?"

Having first demanded his silence Ms Winter had now obviously forgotten that Mr Haddenough was even still there. He was the irrelevance in the room.

"I picked up one of his books on the way down to the canteen," said Ms Payne. She opened it to show that other than today's date there was nothing in it. No work, no marking, no Next Steps comments with advice on how to improve, no group work or peer assessment. Nothing!

"I literally don't even have the words to describe how bad

your marking is!" said Ms Winter. To be fair she wasn't what you'd call a walking thesaurus.

As she closed the exercise book Mr Haddenough could see that it belonged to Connor Strang in the Year 9 class he would have been busy teaching had he not been summoned to Room 101. He'd given him the new exercise book today before heading off to the meeting. Connor had clearly only had time to write his name and the date before Ms Payne had snatched it off him to do a work scrutiny.

Five minutes into its life this new book, naked without even a target sticker on its cover, was meant to represent the generations of other books he marked every week of the year, day in, day out.

"It's well disgusting," sneered Ms Winter. "Even the cover's a mess."

Mr Haddenough could have explained why the exercise book was covered in greasy, sugary fingerprints but he wasn't allowed to speak.

At this point he noticed the list of names on the desk in front of Ms Winter. As an experienced teacher Mr Haddenough was good at reading upside-down and he could see that Mr Chang's name had been crossed out at the top, followed by Mr Milton and Mr Lazenby.

This is how it begins then, he thought.

Mr **Haddenough** (MFL Dept.)	All 1	Most 2	Some 3	None 4	Additional comments
Books scrutinized	Connor Strang (Year 9.)				
Is assessment regular and frequent?				X	
Have pieces of sustained work been marked?				X	
Has self and peer assessment been done?				X	
Have meaningful targets been set leading to subsequent progress?				X	
Is incorrect spelling, punctuation and grammar corrected using the correct marking codes?				X	
Have pupils evidenced the 8 Wildside Values in their work?				X	
Has Homework been completed in accordance with the School policy and are titles underlined?				X	

OVERALL GRADE : 4 (Unsatisfactory.)
Signed : Ms Winter/Ms Payne.

CHAPTER 51

"The best time to repair the roof is when the sun is shining."

"You know what I think?" said Ms Winter to Ms Payne, not really expecting her to list the sum total of her knowledge even though they had time.

"Probably," said Ms Payne, looking up from her mobile phone.

They were sitting in the Assistant Heads' office taking a well-deserved rest and planning what they might do together in the half term break. Perhaps today's sunshine would carry on into the following week?

"We're on the same wavelength me and you," said Ms Winter. "What it was was I was just thinking about O'Brien. I could of told Janine that he were no good."

She looked across at the empty desk. Luckily for Mr O'Brien he was one of the few teachers who had not been subject to Ms Winter's regular judgements.

"She should of got rid of him like ages ago. Called himself an Assistant Head but he wasn't a team player like you and I, was he?"

"Yeah. Do you remember when we had that darts tournament with Sean? O'Brien just sat over there with his head in a pile of books and didn't join in. He was always scribbling things down or messing about on his sodding laptop."

"I don't think I ever saw him down The Cock 'n' Bull neither."

"Well, he's gone now," said Sharon. "Don't miss him. His loss."

"Too right," agreed Lynne, "but have you seen what Trev's done?"

"Erm, yeah, I think so!" mocked Sharon as she leant forward to look at her friend's laptop screen.

Regardless of any data protection considerations Ms Stonehart had instructed Trevor Rojan to forward all of Mr O'Brien's school emails straight to Ms Winter's inbox.

"Janine is expecting me to sift through all these emails and pick up anything what needs doing. As if I've not got nothing else to do neither!"

"How many times can Rowena lose a fracking mug?" exclaimed Sharon, distracted by one of the regular messages. "I thought she was off on mat leave anyway."

"We've got to talk Janine into getting a replacement who she'll replace O'Brien with," said Ms Winter.

"Fat chance," said Ms Payne without really thinking. "She doesn't trust outsiders after what happened. I think she's only just forgotten about that whole thing with, what was she called now, that bloody secretary, Verity Speke?"

Ms Payne thought about the problem for a moment. She'd read something on her mobile phone that might help them.

"I think I've got an idea," she said eventually.

Like they always said, there was a first time for everything.

"You should just be able to share any work out between the four of you," said Ms Stonehart when they were finally granted an audience. "I mean there's only one of me and you never hear me complaining about how much work I have to do. And you don't find me running to those Local Headteachers' meetings for help every five minutes!"

"Absolutely. I was just saying to Lynne how extra busy you must be now," nodded Ms Payne, "continuing to take Wildside Academy from strength to strength. And with only four of us to help you now. I'm sure what they're saying on social media isn't aimed specifically at this school. Well, we'd better not keep you from your work. Thank you for seeing us."

Ms Stonehart looked up and told them to wait. It had been a risky manoeuvre on Ms Payne's part heading for the door when she had not been told they could go, but it looked like it might pay off.

"What are they saying?"

"I'm sure it's nothing really. There were discussions about

how big the SLT needs to be in a school to be really effective, to go from strength to outstanding. There were comments from people saying that Ofsted are looking for schools to have at least five members of SLT. Maybe even six or seven. I'm sure they didn't know what they were talking about. A lot of people don't."

During the silence Ms Payne wondered whether she'd been chancing her luck a little there. She'd hate the school to lose two members of the SLT in so short a time.

It would be a momentous occasion if they managed to get Ms Stonehart to change her mind on something. When she had first become Headteacher she had decided to stamp her mark on the place by getting all the pupils to walk on the right rather than the left. This had caused horrendous congestion on the corridors as the doors were not designed to open that way. In the end though rather than get her to change her decision it had been easier just to get every door in the school rehung.

"I've just had an idea," said Ms Stonehart, glancing up at the counter on her wall displaying the fact that it was 631 days since Ofsted had last visited the school. It was at that point that Ms Payne knew she had taken the bait. "You look at Nelson, for example. He didn't go off into battle without enough troops. We've got rid of the deadwood and now we need new blood."

If Ms Winter had known what a mixed metaphor was she still wouldn't have mentioned it at this crucial point. Also she knew Ms Stonehart was a big fan of Nelson Mandela.

"I would like the four of you to come up with a job description for a new Assistant Head," she informed them.

Somebody she could trust this time rather than somebody who tried to pull the wool over her eyes.

The task of writing a job description turned out to be more problematical than the SLT had thought and soon their list contained more than two hundred and thirty-five different responsibilities for the new employee. It was as if the current members of the SLT had quietly moved their own responsibilities over to the new job description.

"Perhaps we could just sum their new rôle up with the phrase *forgive and forget*?" commented Mr Thicke. The other members of the SLT ignored any further suggestions he made, particularly when he criticized the font size of what they'd typed.

As she had no plans for the holiday Ms Stonehart decided to take their suggestions home to look over. If she liked what they had come up with Mrs Spratt could put the advertisement in *The Times Educational Supplement* as soon as the school re-opened after the half term break. She would not be putting it in the local press.

All things considered it was a pity she didn't read through their suggestions before close of business on the Friday.

JUNE

CHAPTER 52

"The best time to plant a tree was twenty years ago.
The second best time is now."

It was only when Mrs Spratt tried to place the advert for a new Assistant Head that she discovered there was a problem.

"Hello, is that the TES Recruitment Department? This is Mrs Spratt from Wildside Academy. Lower Steem. I'd like to place an advert. We're looking to employ a new Assistant Head to start straight away."

"Well, that is most unusual."

"Yes, it is, isn't it? We've a very strong SLT here at Wildside Academy. They don't often move on. In fact this is actually the first time I've had to do this."

"I thought you must be new to it. It's just you've missed the end-of-May deadline."

"But the school year doesn't finish until July. The six weeks' holiday?"

"Yes, Mrs Spratt. I mean you can place your advert if you like, we'll happily take your money, but teachers have to have resigned from their current post by the last day of May. The only applicants you'll get will be PGCE students looking for their first post or teachers who are currently resting between jobs shall we say?"

"Ah. I hear what you say. Oh dear. Ms Stonehart isn't going to like this."

Learning from past experience Mrs Spratt had a quiet word with Alex Goldbloom in the Finance Department. He was able to convince Ms Stonehart that it'd be more economically beneficial to the business to recruit somebody who already worked at Wildside Academy, rather than spending all that money on adverts. Like Ms

Stonehart said, if they were to employ outsiders you never really knew who you could trust.

And so it came to pass that the only three people who wanted a place on the SLT at Wildside Academy found themselves sitting outside Ms Stonehart's office the following Monday morning. There were actually four teachers waiting there initially but after an hour Mr Buonanulla was told that his regular weekly meeting with her had been cancelled. Ms Malik had bought a new suit for the interview, Ms Lovall had polished her Doc Martens and Mr Humble had bought a few extra rounds at The Cock 'n' Bull the previous Friday.

Interviews in schools are unlike any other interview in the real world, not least because the candidates all have to sit together on the same day and try and make polite conversation with their rivals. Ms Malik, Second-in-Department for Geography, was not comfortable with this situation. She did not do small talk at the best of times, even about the weather which was odd for a Geography teacher. She just needed to run over the answers she'd prepared and learned during the previous week. The field trip the day before had cost her valuable preparation time. It was too important an opportunity to forget some of the acronyms or all the metacognitive ability differentiation strategies she'd memorized. Jamie Humble and Sally Lovall were chatting away, laughing about previous interviews they'd been at.

"So it got to the end of the day," continued Jamie, "and we're all sitting in reception, the six of us, waiting to find out who's got the job, yeah? And the Head's secretary comes out, not making eye contact with anybody except this one bonnie lass and asks her back through to the Head's office."

Sally got up to put her empty can in a bin.

"We all start getting our stuff together, of course, ready to go and then this lass from Liverpool says *'I wonder who'll get the job like?'* We just looked at her. It turns out she thought they were eliminating us one by one like on *Rock Star Academy*! Whoever's still standing at the end gets the job!"

"You're joking, Jamie!" exclaimed Sally.

"But then she thinks about it for a minute and says *'But I bought this suit specially like! It cost a bleedin' arm and a leg!'* What a canny day that was though but."

"Why would you buy a new suit for an interview?" said Sally. "I got a new outfit for Rowena's wedding but that's a bit different."

"I went to one school where a bloke turning up for an IT interview crashed all the school's computers during the interview lesson!"

Ms Malik tried to block out the sound of their voices as she ran through Wildside Academy's values again and how she would demonstrate each of them in her leadership when she got the job.

"Good morning everybody and welcome to Wildside Academy," said Mrs Spratt, looking down at the notes on her clipboard. Realising that she'd been looking at her original interview plans she turned the page and hurried on. "You're going to be going alphabetically, so Mr Humble, you'll be first."

"Away man," said Jamie enthusiastically as she led him through into the Headteacher's office, "let's get this show on the road."

Sally wished him good luck whilst Ms Malik studied the quotations on the wall.

For once Ms Stonehart was not sitting on her throne behind her vast mahogany desk. As it was such an important occasion Toby Chambers, the Chair of Governors, had taken her place. Ms Stonehart had been relegated to his side and the four current members of the SLT made up the remainder of the interview panel. Ms Winter gave Jamie a smile and a thumbs up signal as he sat down.

"Good morning, Mr Humble," began Ms Stonehart "and thank you for showing an interest in the position of Assistant Head here at Wildside Academy. Please make yourself comfortable. Now I'm going to ask Ms Winter to start the questions."

It reminded Jamie of the staff briefings on a Monday morning. He'd be surprised if Janine spoke again during the interview.

"So then, Jamie," grinned Ms Winter, "I know when we was talking about this down the pub last week you was saying how much you like working at Wildside Academy. How do you think you'll feel when we appoint you as an Assistant Head here?"

"Brill!" said Sally when it was her turn to be led through for her interview.

"Good morning, Ms Lovall," began Ms Stonehart "and thank you for showing an interest in the position of Assistant Head here at Wildside Academy. Mr Chambers, you said you'd like to ask the first question?"

"Indeed, love. Now, Sally, is it? I like to have women in key positions in my business. I see from your application that you're already the Lessons For Life Co-ordinator and the Charitable Promotions Developer. Well done, dear. Now my question is if I were to appoint you Assistant Head how good would you be at delegating things? I wouldn't want it all to be too much for that pretty little head of yours, my dear."

Ms Malik had just been going through everything in her mind one last time when her turn came. She quickly put her revision cards away, straightened down her suit and followed Mrs Spratt through into the dragons' den. She'd gone through every possible interview question she could find on the internet, swotted up on all the latest educational jargon and practised her answers enough to make them sound spontaneous. *"My weaknesses? Oh, I think I'm just too much of a perfectionist really. I don't care how many extra hours I put in so that everything is just right. I can't help but give everything 110%."* She was ready for the safeguarding question. They always asked one on safeguarding. To make it a fair process they always asked everybody the same questions.

"Good morning, Ms Malik," began Ms Stonehart "and thank you for showing an interest in the position of Assistant Head here at Wildside Academy. Sit down. Now Ms Payne perhaps you'd ask the first question?"

"Cheers! So, Ms Malik, why on earth do you think Wildside Academy would want to employ a Geography teacher in the important rôle of Assistant Head? And specifically, why would we ever think of choosing you?"

The three candidates had been ordered to wait outside Ms Stonehart's office while the interview panel deliberated on their decision. Eventually Eric and the catering team wheeled through various trolleys hiding delicious smelling dishes that were never found on the standard canteen menu. There was even the sound of corks being popped although Mr Thicke would be insisting on orange juice.

Jamie and Sally had been keeping themselves occupied during the long wait. What had started as a simple game of I-Spy had led to them trying to remember all the winners of *Celebrity Love Rock Star Academy* from season one onwards. They had both got stuck on the question of who had won four years ago. Jamie was certain it had been Danni Wong but Sally was sure Amber Riley had won. Ms Malik was just considering asking if she could go back to her room to teach her bottom set Year 9 group when the door to Ms Stonehart's office finally opened.

Toby Chambers was heading off. A decision must have been made and those golf balls would not find their own way round the course. It wasn't all about Ofsted. Ms Malik shifted uneasily on her seat. Like a jury returning with a guilty verdict the Chair of Governors did not make eye contact with her. His cheery goodbye, a little slurred perhaps, seemed to be aimed at either Mr Humble or Ms Lovall. How on earth could either of them be an Assistant Head? If she had found the questions hard they must have been ten times more difficult if you hadn't done any preparation.

They all waited for the door to open.

By the time the day's final bell went Jamie and Sally had agreed that Danni had won season six and Amber Riley had been the winner two years before Zayne Medley.

The door opened.

Mr Thicke and Mr Wingett came out and glanced briefly at the three teachers waiting outside before heading off to their offices.

The three candidates watched as the shutter came down on the Student Welcome desk, signalling the official close of business. Once the office staff had made their way out to the car park the silence behind the Berlin Wall was only broken by the unusual sound of laughter coming from the Headteacher's office.

Eventually Mrs Spratt ventured out of her office.

"Mr Humble, Ms Lovall, if you'd like to go back in Ms Stonehart will see you now."

"Brill!" said Sally as the two of them went back into Ms Stonehart's office together, closing the door behind them. The sound of laughter greeted them.

Ms Malik really hoped that they were eliminating the candidates one by one before announcing who had really got the job.

From : JST (Headteacher) - JStonehart@WildsideAcademy
To : Allstaff1@WildsideAcademy
CC : TCS – TChambers1@WildsideAcademy
Sent : Mon 10 June 16:18
Subject : SLT appointment

Good Afternoon

Following a very rigorous series of interviews I am pleased to announce that we have now appointed a new member of the Senior Leadership Team today.

We had two very strong candidates for the post and as a result I have decided to appoint Jamie Humble as Assistant Head. He will continue to fulfil his rôle as Co-ordinator of Behaviour and Attitudes as well as Acting Head of Year 11.

Mr Chambers was also particularly impressed with Sally Lovall and so it was decided that she will take on the post previously held by Mr North, the Co-ordinator of the School-Home Intervention Team. She will continue to fulfil her rôle as Lessons For Life Co-ordinator and Charitable Promotions Developer.

I know that you will all want to congratulate both Jamie and Sally on their new positions. Their continual hard work, planning and dedication will help me to continue to take Wildside Academy from strength to strength.

Tempus fugit!

Ms J. Stonehart, Headteacher, *Wildside Academy,*
Diploma in Human Resources, TGCSEC, CPT, BPB.

Wisdom, Inspiration, Leadership, Determination, Success, Integrity, Dedication, Excelence.

CHAPTER 53

"The truth is more important than the facts."

"Integrity" quoted Mr Wingett, "is doing the right thing even when nobody is watching."

He was conducting one of the last assemblies that would take place in the Main Hall before it became off-limits and covered in individual exam desks once again. The contractors were scheduled to come back in any day now and start fitting the last CCTV cameras in the corridor outside the Main Hall. Tutors would find themselves in lockdown with their forms for an extra half hour every morning unless they were fortunate enough to be on Mr Thicke's litter rota.

Today Mr Wingett was addressing Key Stage 4 pupils. Year 11 found themselves looking forward to one of his usual tales of death and destruction as it would make their forthcoming GCSE exams seems a little less depressing. As always with Mr Wingett's assemblies they ran the risk of being disappointed.

"Right," said Mr Wingett to start his assembly. The piano had already been moved out of the Main Hall and he hadn't been prepared to listen to them singing without something to drown out their voices. "The bad news is that this will be your last assembly for a while. And with our school value of "Integrity" in mind you all need to sit up straight and watch this video."

As the cartoon started an American voice told them a story…

There was once an ancient Emperor who knew it would soon be time to name his successor and yet he had no children. Calling together all the children in his Empire he gave each one of them a tiny seed. The children were then instructed to take their seed home, water it, care for it and return with the results a year later.

As the months passed a young boy called Ling found that nothing had sprouted in his pot of soil despite all the care he had lavished on his seed each day. All his friends told him how beautiful the shrubs and bushes were that had come from each of their own tiny seeds.

When the day came to return to the mighty palace Ling was so embarrassed that nothing had grown for him that he nearly didn't go. But courageously he took his pot of soil to the Emperor who inspected it along with all the other children's successful plants. When he was asked about the empty pot he explained how he'd tried his best every day but he felt like a failure.

Calling the boy forward to stand beside him the Emperor explained that far from being a failure, Ling would be the new Emperor. The seeds he had given to everybody had been boiled first so that they would produce nothing. Unlike the other dishonest children Ling had shown integrity, determination and courage. He was the only one with the qualities needed to rule the Empire!

"Integrity!" repeated Mr Wingett. "Doing the right thing even when nobody is watching! But people *are* watching. You are always being watched here even when you might think you're not. We're here to keep an eye on you. How often do you use school computers to try and play that Zombie game or search that *Celebrity Rock* thing you're all obsessed with? Everything you do on a Wildside Academy computer is logged on your SCAMS profile! Every key you press, every site you visit, every message you send."

He pointed towards the nearest of the three CCTV cameras above the stage.

"We have CCTV everywhere. Next time you're thinking of dropping that crisp packet or leaving a half-eaten slice of pizza on the stairs, think again! We can see you. And for those of you who were thinking of trying to cheat in your exams, you lot need to have another think about that too! With or without integrity, we're watching you!"

This was turning into the kind of assembly they all expected from Mr Wingett. All it needed now was a true story about a girl who'd slipped on a discarded piece of pizza, spending the rest of her life in a wheelchair, her dreams of being an Olympic athlete in tatters.

"Very soon you'll all be doing exams in this very hall and there'll be no cheating from any of you. These exams will decide the whole of the rest of your life. Everything. That's how important it is that you revise and show integrity. If not, you could end up like a lad called Tom from my last school who thought he'd just copy his exam coursework. Go down past the railway arch and you'll find him there in all weathers. A homeless, penniless drunk, addicted to drugs sleeping rough in a cardboard box with the rats! That could be you!"

Mr Wingett could never have got a job writing the verses for greetings cards. He ended by reading out the list of pupils he wanted to see after assembly. It might have been quicker to name the pupils who hadn't been spotted breaking a school rule whilst in range of a CCTV camera.

When Mr Armani had told them the same story about the Emperor in the previous week's assembly it had not had the same downbeat ending. Nevertheless the pupils felt a warm feeling of security now that Mr Wingett's assemblies were back to their usual tone again.

CHAPTER 54

"In the book of life, the answers aren't in the back."

Trevor Rojan had been instructed by Ms Stonehart to block the Upper Steem Academy website from every computer in the school except hers. She had also had him reconfigure her computer to notify her whenever Wildside Academy was mentioned on the internet. Unfortunately this had not been too successful as she had received a message every time anybody referred to any version of the song *"Walk On The Wild Side."* She also got emailed unsolicited offers to purchase various medical products at a discount rate. One time she accidently clicked on a link to the Wikipedia page about the 1956 novel of the same name by Nelson Algren and found herself reading the following paragraph.

> Algren noted, "The book asks why lost people sometimes develop into greater human beings than those who have never been lost in their whole lives. Why men who have suffered at the hands of other men are the natural believers in humanity, while those whose part has been simply to acquire, to take all and give nothing, are the most contemptuous of mankind."

She didn't really understand what it meant and instructed Trevor to return her computer to its default settings. She had originally started looking at the Upper Steem Academy website only to remind herself how right she had been to sack O'Brien. It had been Toby Chambers who had employed him before she'd even joined Wildside Academy. It was nothing to do with her.

She'd shown she was a good judge of character by choosing Jamie Humble to join the team alongside Lynne Winter and Sharon Payne. With her SLT now as it should be she would take the school from strength to strength again. She did not need O'Brien getting in the way.

She'd just have one more look at the USA website before close of business, just to see what kind of ridiculous things they were up to now.

Almost as soon as he'd taken on the position of Headteacher at Upper Steem Academy Mr O'Brien had started posting a weekly video message to parents on the school's website. Usually it was all so sickeningly sweet about how wonderful everybody was at his school that Ms Stonehart found she couldn't watch it more than five times. It was typical of him pushing himself forward all the time when he was little more than a glorified Maths teacher with big ideas. Videos to the parents! She should have sacked him when he made that daft video in that Hawaiian shirt.

She clicked on the new video he'd posted that morning. The USA slogan *"Working with the stars of today for tomorrow!"* faded to reveal Mr O'Brien's smiling bearded face.

"Hello again and I want to start this week with a big thank you to everybody here at Upper Steem Academy who made our talent show such a great success last week. What amazingly talented people we have here at Upper Steem Academy. It's an honour to work with them all and thank you for your continued support as parents and guardians.

My video message would be incredibly long this week if I were to mention everybody by name but you'll find all our superstars listed below. I'm also really proud of our Young Film-makers Club who have put together a video of the highlights of our first Upper Steem Academy Talent Show for those of you who couldn't make it last Saturday. It proved to be so popular that I think we're going to have to run it over two nights next year! As a special treat for you our Young Film-makers have also managed to get a brief interview with Zayne Medley from Celebrity Love Rock Star Academy who got the evening started, of course.

A big thank you to our Head Boy and Head Girl, Andrew Brodie and Gill Cresswell, who did a sterling job as compères throughout the evening and of course it was lovely to see Mr Hoskins back as our Chief Judge. Who would have known that he could juggle? As always the staff here have gone the extra mile to make all this possible and it would be remiss of me if I didn't embarrass a few of them by name. Mrs Illingworth, Head of English, for organizing the whole event, Mr Chang for creating such an amazing stage for us, Mrs Jones and all of the Music Department…"

Ms Stonehart paused the video and clicked on the one below it labelled USATS. She thought it had something to do with the tests she'd seen when she'd worked at Berryfield Primary School but it turned out to be the video of the Upper Steem Academy Talent Show. After a couple of minutes watching pupils doing gymnastics, magic tricks and reciting poems in some foreign language Ms Stonehart decided she had seen enough.

She buzzed through to Mrs Spratt.

"Norma. Find Sally Lovall at once. I need to see her urgently."

She hurriedly replaced the receiver before Mrs Spratt was able to confirm that she'd received the instruction.

"Sally," said Ms Stonehart, indicating that Ms Lovall could be seated. "I've been thinking about how we market the business and as Promotions Developer I want you to come up with some ideas."

Ms Lovall noticed that her title had changed slightly but didn't correct Ms Stonehart. It wasn't simply that people didn't correct the Headteacher, it was the fact that whatever she was proposing would make a change from sorting out the School-Home Intervention Team cupboards.

"We've got the website, of course, and our social media accounts," continued Ms Stonehart, "but we need more publicity if I'm to take Wildside Academy from strength to strength."

Even though the Upper Steem Academy website was blocked in school there was nothing to stop Ms Lovall from going on it on her mobile phone. She'd seen Sam O'Brien's videos and was astute enough to realise that it wouldn't be long before Ms Stonehart would want something similar. It was never mentioned but they all knew what had happened with Mr O'Brien. Janine wouldn't just want to copy what Upper Steem Academy were doing though. She'd want something better and Ms Lovall thought she had just the thing.

"I know exactly what we need," she said with all the confidence of youth. "It'll be brill! A promotional video!"

"That sounds expensive."

"We can do it ourselves," explained Ms Lovall. "I've got a

friend down at Steem Amateur Dramatics & Operatic Society, Barry, who could lend us any props or costumes we need."

"What about music? You're not suggesting the Recorder Club or Mr Gordon on piano?"

"We won't need anything like that. The craze at the moment is to mime over the top of a song. No singing needed. It'll be wicked!"

Ms Stonehart stood up and looked out of the window. Jim Fitt was struggling to get a group of boys all to run round the field in the same direction. Two of them had already fallen over.

"It's a nice idea, Sally," she said, "but I don't think the children would be able to do it. I don't want something embarrassing."

"Yeah, no, I should have said. It wouldn't be the kids. It'd be us. The staff. And Jamie's Drama, he'd help me sort it. Nobody else has got a promotional video on their school website. It'd be fab!"

Upper Steem Academy didn't have a video like that on their school website. Ms Stonehart found herself warming to the idea.

"So what song would it be?" Ms Stonehart wasn't really in touch with the latest top of the pops.

Although it was the most popular choice for businesses Ms Lovall had heard '*Simply the best!*' on the USA website and knew that it wouldn't do for Wildside Academy.

"I've got an idea," she said after a little more thought. "We need something upbeat, funky. A song that will show how all the pupils are supported here, how we're always there for them and what a friendly school it is. I know just the tune. It'll be wicked!"

Ms Stonehart didn't know the song she played her and had never even heard of *The Rembrandts* but since Ms Lovall had been her choice she knew she could trust her to do a good job.

When the Wildside Academy promotional video entitled *"Goin' from strength 2 strength!"* got its official première in morning briefing two weeks later it got a round of applause and a standing ovation. Ms Lovall had managed to get almost everybody involved from Ms Stonehart herself right down to Bob, the Senior Ground Maintenance Supervisor. Those teachers who had refused to take part in it because their contract didn't require them to sing and dance after school as part of their teaching duties received a sternly worded email from Ms Stonehart about not being a team player. They were replaced on the video by supply teachers, something that would probably happen soon enough in the real world too. The video ended with a still of Ms Stonehart and her new improved SLT striking a pose, all friends together.

When the video appeared on the Wildside Academy website it got some very pleasing comments like the one from Ms Malik. *"It was great fun making the video. We're so lucky working at Wildside Academy with such an amazing SLT."* There were always going to be people who wrote unpleasant things on the internet just as there were with the printed press. Trevor had said he thought there was a way to remove the comment that said *"You'd think teachers would have something better to do in the run-up to GCSE exams like helping us revise!"*

It was probably as well Ms Stonehart never saw the alternative version of the video that was posted on social media by somebody calling themselves *WASurvivor365*. With clever use of editing software and footage from the very mobile phones that were banned on the school premises, this video had a different message. There was still the same friendly tune but the new video showed what really went on at Wildside Academy every day of the year. All the usual suspects were there : Ms Stonehart getting out of her shiny Jaguar, Ms Winter shouting at pupils and teachers alike, Ms Payne too busy on her phone to notice a fight, Mr Wingett trying to manoeuvre the school minibus stuck in second gear, Mr Thicke sending a class out to collect litter in the pouring rain. Somehow Ms Stonehart's hair wasn't quite as scary in black-and-white as it was in its usual colours. As the video came to an end the original credits had been replaced with a silent list of all the teachers who had mysteriously disappeared from the school recently. The final shot still showed Ms Stonehart and her new SLT but the caption had been replaced with the word FIENDS.

CHAPTER 55

"Never ask a penguin how to fly but listen when it tells you how to swim."

As one of the first duties in his new rôle Mr Humble had been told he had *carte blanche* to improve the Parents' Evening system. Once Jamie discovered that this phrase meant he could do whatever he liked, he felt like a proper member of the Senior Leadership Team. Ms Stonehart's only requirements were that it mustn't be too expensive, that it mustn't involve the local press and that it must be better than whatever they did at that other excuse for an Academy down the road. It was a good job he could get the USA website on his mobile phone.

He'd often noticed people pointing at the banners that ran along the perimeter of Wildside Academy and so suggested that this might be the best way to advertise the forthcoming event. Together with Ms Lovall he'd brainstormed a lot of possible names to replace the title 'Parents' Evening' after Ms Murkett had pointed out that the phrase wasn't politically correct nor even necessarily accurate nowadays. The proposed phrase 'Alert Evening' had seemed a little intimidating particularly as there were fewer and fewer adults coming each time as it was. Equally the promising words 'Action Evening' could prove problematical under the Trade Descriptions Act.

In the end Ms Stonehart had agreed to the term 'Review Time' and banners were ordered to announce the first of the Wildside Academy Review Times. As the school had bought banners from them before the printing company offered to make the capital letters luminous at no extra cost. This had helped Mr Humble to sell the idea to Ms Stonehart as well as the fact that they would be able to reuse the banner in subsequent years. Everybody had forgotten that there was already a banner in a storeroom in HR somewhere that they had been hoping to use again. Just as soon as there was another February 29th. And it fell on a Monday. And there was a Year 8 Parents' Evening on that night.

When Mr O'Brien had been in charge of organizing Parents' Evenings they had always been well-attended, unless there was something more urgent on the television or it was raining. Mr Humble could still remember what his predecessor had said to him when he'd turned up for his very first one. *"Always remember, Jamie, when a Parents' Evening seems to be going on late into the night after a long day spent in the classroom, remember that this is the 'after-sales service' of the teaching profession. We should consider ourselves honoured that parents entrust their precious children to us and want to know what we think. You wouldn't get that privilege if you were a plumber."*

Jamie had commented that you would probably get paid a lot more as a plumber.

Now, to keep Ms Stonehart happy, Mr Humble was trying to make sure that his 'after-sales service' was different to what had gone before. With Bob and Stan both refusing to work after close of business he'd pressganged a group of pupils into helping him set up the Main Hall. He'd even set the promotional video to play on a loop in the main entrance and it was getting a lot of interest as if people had never seen it before. None of the other members of the SLT had any parents to see and it wasn't long before he regretted organizing a table at the front just for himself and Ms Stonehart. In the absence of anybody else to talk to she would keep asking him questions where it wasn't clear how she expected him to answer.

"I was thinking about ways we could improve the grades that pupils get at GCSE," she continued. "What do you think about us changing the title 'Heads of Department' to 'Curriculum Leaders' maybe?"

He knew what the sensible answer would be but found himself wondering what middle management were called at Upper Steem Academy. Was it a trick question?

As luck would have it he was saved from his dilemma by an echoing crash as one of the older chairs collapsed, leaving one of the older parents in a confused heap on the floor. Even if the Science teacher she'd been talking to, Dr Whittaker, had been a real doctor, Jamie would still have taken the opportunity to go over. Ms Stonehart stayed where she was in case there were any parents who wanted to talk to the Headteacher.

As Mr Humble was reluctantly making his way back to another inquisition he paused to take in what had to be described as Wildside Academy's most successful Review Time evening so far. The whole of school life was there before him, snippets of conversation reaching him as he moved proudly between the tables.

"Well, I was saying to you, wasn't I, Terry? Maths has changed so much from when we was at school. You can't keep up with it! Now it's not just square roots, is it, but you've got your circular roots, triangle ones, yeah? We just can't help our Kayleigh with it at home these days."

"No, don't worry, Mr Hall. If his mate goes to another school he may well be studying different set texts. It is what it is. You have my word as Head of English that if Tom knows 'Lord of the Flies' like the back of his hand and the Shakespeare quotes we're doing at the moment he'll just proper smash the exam. No sweat, yeah?"

"Now when you're writing about established historical facts, Mark, you mustn't exaggerate. I've told you that a million times this week already. I mean, you're a good student, Mark. You should be doing History at University. Like me you've got a fantastic memory. I can't remember the last time you forgot something. Now what was I saying?"

"Looking at her individual Flight Path, Caitlyn's Target Grade for Geography is a 7B with her Aspirational Target being a 7A and her Floor Target being a 7C. In her last assessment she achieved a 5C, her classwork qualifies as a 6B and her homework scores all average out at a 4A, just two marks off a 5C. So that would make her current Working At Grade a 5B, possibly working towards a 5A and her WAG could go up to a 6C overall, of course, when we take into account the fieldwork project she's just handed in today. Maybe even higher. She should be aiming at a 7A."
"So, erm, what does that mean exactly, Ms Malik?"
"Well, to put it in layman's terms, Caitlyn's Target Grade for Geography is a 7B with her Aspirational Target being…"

"I'm very proud of how Jennie's got on since she's joined the school. It's never easy joining a new school mid-way through the year. She's settled in very

well, made friends, joins in with everything. Excellent attendance and punctuality, always smartly dressed. A rôle model for the younger pupils. Very promising work in class and homework is always done on time. She's a pleasure to teach, a great addition to the form and a credit to you. Was there anything either of you would like to ask?"

"Not really. Thank you, Mr Haddenough, for everything you've done. Erm, would you just be able to explain to us what these numbers on her Geography report mean?"

"I've just been looking at the past paper you did last lesson. You've just got to make sure that you do everything that you're asked when you sit the real exam, Mickey. You've got to be in it to win it, you know? If you don't write anything on the paper you definitely can't get the marks. I mean, is there anything worse than unanswered questions?"

"You look a bit lost. Can I help you? Which teacher were you looking for?"
"It's his Maths teacher, love. I think it's Mr Milton?"
"Oh, right. Mr Milton doesn't work here any longer, I'm afraid. It might be Mr Devlin now?"
"And we couldn't find Mr Chang?"
"Oh, right."
"Don't worry, love. Thanks anyway. We'll go see his IT teacher."
"Not Mr Lazenby, is it?"
"Mr Benson?"

"But why are his marks so low, Miss Grimley? Nathan spends ages on his homework, always doing research on his computer and stuff. He loves his History."
"To be blunt, Mrs Briggs, I don't think he always listens in class. His last homework was an essay on Brexit. He wrote about breadsticks."

Mr Humble could see that Ms Stonehart was still waiting for somebody who needed to talk to her. It looked like she was deciding whether painting the walls a different colour would have a positive impact on exam performance.

"Señor Buonanulla, Santiago dice que tienes un acento de español muy bueno."
"So, it's probably best if we speak English in front of Santiago and his

Mum, Mr Gomez."

"Está bien, Señor Buonanulla. Mi esposo me enseñó a hablar español como nativo."

"Yeah, yeah, yeah, Mrs Gomez, but it's not fair on everybody else around us if we speak in Spanish...."

"Well, I know how much you teachers in the Geography Department must like travelling, Miss Armitage. No, trouble at all. It's amazing how many photos you can store on it. Where was, I? Oh yes, that was the airport, the coach to the hotel and this one's got the Eiffel Tower in the background behind that man's head…"

"Mum! We need to move on!"

"Sorry, no, Mrs Chesterfield, when I said that Kyle's work was still outstanding I meant that he hasn't handed any of his work in this term…"

"No, I'm afraid Ms Shakespeare can't be here tonight. I'm Mr Wilson. Yes, I've been covering some of her lessons lately so let's see how I can help you. And it was Stacey Millington? Ah yes, here's the right print-out. Stacey's Target Grade for English is a 5C with her Aspirational Target… No, sorry, that's Sara Miller's Flight Path. Right…"

"Thank you, Mr Cocker. He's a bright lad really just not good with computers and stuff. Like his brother Nero. D'you remember Nero? You should see him now! Who'd have thought it? Handling financial transactions for a multi-billion pound global organization every day. We're so proud he got the McDonald's job."

"If I had a pound for every piece of work he leaves unfinished in my lessons I'd…"

Mr Humble managed to slip out of the side door and down to the empty staffroom. Forty minutes later, after three cups of coffee, he felt he really should return to his seat beside Ms Stonehart. It would be best to enter the hall by the far door just so that he could check whether any of his colleagues needed his support as Assistant Head.

"Like fourteen out of every twenty-eight people she often overcomplicates things. And sometimes in her writing she'll use phrases that she doesn't

understand and vice versa…"

"No, Mum, Mr Hurndall was my Science teacher last week. This week it's Miss Doolittle but she's not in tonight 'cos she's part-time. Let's do English next. Ms Shakespeare…"

"If you want the hatchback I could probably do it for a few hundred less and I'd throw in some floor mats as well."
"Nice doing business with you again, Monty. I'll give you a ring in the week. Set up a game of golf too. How's he doin', by the way?"
"Stephen? Nothing to worry about. First class chap."
"I'll leave you to it then. Cheerio. Love to Elizabeth."

"I'd been hoping to have an audience with Reverend James about how well Graham is doing in RE but I've been informed that he's passed on to some other school? I'd be mortified if Graham ended up in some dead-end job with no qualifications at the end of everything."
"Don't worry, Mr Reaper. I've been teaching Graham this year and I've been amazed at how much he knows. He's very enthusiastic. Really throws himself into his work."
"Bless you. That's most kind of you, young man. RE will be very important if he's to go into the family business eventually. Sadly in these difficult times we only have a skeleton staff at the moment. A most grave state of affairs."

"Just remind me when your appointment was so that I can tick you off my list…?"
"Seven-fifty. It's Lydia Drew's Mum. Sorry we're five minutes late. There was a bit of a queue for her IT teacher."
"Ah, yes. Of course. Hello, Lydia. Just find my notes. Now, looking at Lucy's individual Flight Path her Target Grade for DT is an 8C…"

"So, how's our Clint doing, Mr Armani? He loves your lessons by the way. Thinks you're smashing."
"Mum!"
"Let's just say that if procrastination was an Olympic sport Clint would probably think about maybe competing in it later. It's sometimes like he's made a mental note of everything and then can't remember where he's put it. You just need to show a bit of initiative at times, Clint."
"Oh he does have initiative, Mr Armani. He just needs to be told when

to use it."

"Well maybe he just needs to be a bit more spontaneous then."

"Cheers, sir. I'm planning on being spontaneous tomorrow."

"No, you don't actually teach her. It's just that I can see the car park from here. Her Dad said he'd pick us up about five and twenty past. You've not got the time on you, have you, love?"

After another hour spent strolling round the hall Mr Humble knew that he could not delay returning to the empty seat beside Ms Stonehart much longer. He had hoped that some parents might sit and talk to her but unfortunately this had not happened.

"It all seems to be going well," he commented as he resumed his place. "Lots of happy parents though but."

"I was just considering whether Ofsted might prefer that those were the down stairs and the ones by English the ones for going up?" continued Ms Stonehart as if he hadn't been away. "What do you think?"

Jamie was wondering how best to reply when something drew his eye over towards where the English teachers were sitting. Excusing himself and hurrying over he found that two Mums were about to start World War Three.

"I've been sat here over twenty minutes," said the first woman. "My appointment were for quarter past!"

"Well, my appointment's five past!"

"But you've only just got 'ere! You should of got off y'backside and got 'ere on time! I've been sat here twenty minutes, I 'ave!"

The situation wasn't helped when Mrs Smith pointed out that it should actually have been *"sitting here"* or even *"seated here."* Her colleague would also have corrected the phrase *"would of"* had Mr Humble not interrupted her.

"I'm sure we can sort this out amicably," said Mr Humble, quoting a phrase he'd heard Mr O'Brien use very successfully many times. "Would you mind if I saw your appointment slips, please, ladies."

He studied the two computer print-outs for a moment.

"Ah, I see," he said. "Mrs Cooke, your appointment for five past is with Mrs Smith. And Miss Riley, your appointment at quarter past," he indicated the teacher sitting or seated beside Mrs

Smith, "is with Mrs Smythe. Is that Ok then?"

"Well, it's a ridiculous system," said the first Mum without a word of thanks. "Utterly ridiculous! Why don't you just get little tickets like on deli counter?"

"Yeah, good idea, Jayne," agreed the second Mum. "It were never like this with that Mr O'Brien. They need to get it sorted like *Gazette* says. How's your Tracey doing these days by the way? I've not seen her in ages. She still workin' down at KwikShop?"

"Yeah, but I think they should change their slogan when she's on till!"

'KwikShop : Where there's never a queue!'

With the crisis averted Mr Humble started to make his way slowly back to his seat. He paused by a group of teachers he didn't immediately recognise. That happened often in Wildside Academy as supply teachers came and went but these teachers looked vaguely familiar. Then he realised who they were. It was the PE Department but dressed in suits! Even Harry Greenfield had turned up.

"I didn't recognise you with your clothes on," he joked but they were too busy to acknowledge him. He was part of the SLT now.

There was a long queue of young Mums waiting to speak to the teachers in the Boys PE Department whilst at the next desk Ms Lovall looked like she was taking part in speed dating.

"He just seems to have poor concentration skills," he heard Doug Digby saying to one Dad as he went past. Unfortunately the man seemed to be more distracted by a wasp that was buzzing about just behind the teacher's shoulder.

He stopped and watched the Maths Department play the game they always amused themselves with on occasions like this. A little like Bingo, it was something Mr Devlin had started as Head of Department as a way of encouraging team spirit. Each teacher came up with five random words and a list of all the words was given to each member of the Department. The first person to work all the unusual words into their conversations with parents was the winner. Last time the word *'coconut'* had turned out to be a particularly difficult word to work into the evening's discussions.

"So unless he wants to spend the rest of his life trekking across the Sahara with a lawnmower..." he heard Mr O'Carrob say, "he's going to have to improve his algebra."

As the boy's parents nodded wisely, Mr Humble assumed Ben O'Carrob had just added another couple of points to his score.

Heading back to his seat again the new Assistant Head consoled himself with the fact that there were only about twenty minutes left until the Review Time evening officially ended. There were only so many questions Ms Stonehart could ask him in that time. Looking at the long queue of parents still waiting to see Mr Cocker it looked like he was settling in for another hour of discussions at least. The English Department had already left but Jamie would be able to catch up with them at The Cock 'n' Bull soon enough. It was at that point that he saw an old lady, perhaps somebody's grandma, approaching the table where Ms Stonehart had waited patiently, alone, for over three hours. Her moment had come!

Ms Stonehart saw the woman heading towards her and cleared her dry throat, ready to answer her first question of the evening. Whatever she wanted to know, she was talking to the right person, the one who was taking Wildside Academy from strength to strength. Norma had printed off all the data she'd need and she'd brought along a copy of Mr Wingett's Ofsted résumé. This was it. Here we go. I can do this! Deep breath!

"How can you help me?" she asked the old woman. She coughed nervously. "Sorry, I mean how can I help you?" She paused expectantly and tried to smile.

"Excuse me, love," said the old lady. "Are there any toilets nearby?"

CHAPTER 56

"Live every day as though it were your last."

It had become something of a tradition at Wildside Academy that in the run-up to their GCSE exams Year 11 would always be told, quite categorically, that they would not be getting study leave but would be staying in school. Mr Wingett's annual announcement to this effect was as eagerly anticipated as a certain department store's Christmas advertisement. According to the Deputy Head the pupils would not revise if they were at home and then a week later this was always exactly what they would be sent home to do. It was as if the time in between was there simply to give them the opportunity to buy packets of flour and boxes of eggs.

It always seemed strange that with only a couple of days left in school Year 11 would invest in a new uniform when they'd been promising to replace their trainers with school shoes for over six months. Every year without fail the latest fashions were displayed on the catwalks between classrooms but the fashions never really seemed to change. For the girls, the short skirts and stockings would not have looked out of place at St. Trinian's. As for the boys it was a lot easier, simply a matter of untucking the shirt if it wasn't already hanging loose and repositioning the school tie around the forehead. Trainers or high heels were essential whilst all other accessories were optional. Sometimes the easiest way to create your own *fin-de-collège* style was simply to read what was banned in the school dress code and act accordingly. *Detention for a breach of the dress code? When would that be, Ms Malik?* Whatever was chosen you had to wear a clean white shirt for your last day at secondary school. Where else could you write farewell insults to your mates, declarations of undying love and friendship or quite simply draw those amusing diagrams like the ones in *"Exploring Biology Through Pictures and Worksheets"*?

Anybody who had bought a Leavers' hoodie from Mr Goldbloom was allowed to wear it and so a splash of colour punctuated the normally monochrome uniform. As this was their last day none of the pupils complained that the school had ordered hoodies with the wrong year on the back. Keswick McBride was particularly proud of the fact that his hoodie had nothing on it at all apart from the phrase "CHOOSE TEXT HERE" on the back.

At the Monday morning briefing in Year 11's final week staff were always told, quite categorically, that the pupils would not be getting study leave but would be staying in school. It was business as usual. There would be no wordsearches and Wildside Academy was not a multi-screen cinema. At the end of the briefing staff were reminded that pupils' exam performance rested on what they learned in these last few days, in the same way that the job security of staff depended on the subsequent exam results. Having said that, the English Department would obviously need to show the video of *Lord of the Flies* one last time.

Over in the Science Block Mr Ian Campbell, one of the longest serving and most successful teachers in the history of Wildside Academy, had found an amusing way of saying goodbye to his Year 11 pupils. He'd finished and revised the syllabus, they were all going to get outstanding results and any further attempts to cram any more in would only confuse them and possibly lead to lower grades. Despite what the Headteacher had told them in briefing, his professional judgement as an experienced teacher told him that you shouldn't really revise the night before an exam. Still, he would do as he'd been told. There would be no wordsearches and no videos. He'd even typed up a lesson plan.

"Good morning, Year 11," he began, his gentle Scottish tones catching the pupils' attention straight away, "and today we're going to do something a bit different before you all go. These wee tests you've got coming up, and that's all they are, tests, just people asking you questions about things you know, well, they can be stressful. But only if you let them be stressful. So we're going to do an investigation that won't come up in the Biology paper, but I think you'll enjoy it. Learning should be enjoyable. And I just wanted to say, by the way, you're a great bunch of lads and lasses and I've really enjoyed teaching you all. Even you, Denver."

Denver Bernstein cheered and punched the air.

He'd taught Denver since he'd joined in Year 7 and those five years seemed to have flown by. It didn't seem five minutes since that first lesson when Denver had asked him why some elements in the periodic table were letters that weren't even in their name. He was still showing an enquiring mind in Year 11, like asking whether you could dilute water.

Even though it probably hadn't been said by Albert Einstein, the quotation pinned on the noticeboard had a lot of truth in it. *"Everybody is a genius but if you judge a fish by its ability to climb a tree, it will live its whole life believing that it is stupid."*

Today Mr Campbell explained that they were going to study how the stick insects in the glass cabinets behaved throughout the lesson. How much do they move? Do they eat? Does sunlight affect them? Basically, what behavioural patterns do they display?

And so for the best part of an hour Mr Campbell's GCSE group sat quietly and calmly watched the glass cabinets, often with arms folded and heads down. It was truly peaceful as the sunlight refracted through the glass to cast myriad colours across the bench tops. Their only conclusions at the end of the investigation were that stick insects didn't really do anything but were very soothing to watch. One pupil said it reminded her of primary school days when they were encouraged just to close their eyes at the end of the day while Mrs Major read them a nice story. It certainly was a very pleasant way to end their time at secondary school in the company of one of their favourite teachers.

"Well, good luck with the exams all of you," Mr Campbell called to his pupils as they left his laboratory for the last time. A couple of the boys wanted to shake hands with him while the girls insisted on a photo on the phones they didn't officially possess. Mr Campbell was genuinely touched when Denver saluted and gave him a 'Thank You' card they'd all made for him. It was so big that it made Delores Froggett's Christmas card to Mr Armani look like a note to the milkman.

"Och, you shouldn't have," he said quietly as he put it on the shelf beside the framed caricature a colleague had done of him before disappearing off to do jury service.

As Denver moonwalked out of the classroom one last time he shared a final observation with Mr Campbell.

"Sir, you know how Neil Armstrong was the first man on the moon? D'you realise that *Neil A* backwards is *Alien?*"

Then the room was empty again. Mr Campbell took a moment to check his emails before he left for break. There was just one new one, a short email from Ms Winter telling him that she thought the lesson she'd observed yesterday wasn't good enough. He deleted it straight away, knowing that he'd never need it. She was entitled to her opinions, wrong though they were. The phrase 'bright sky' would mean something different to him in future. His application to work in an international school in Dubai had been accepted that very morning and by September he would no longer be at Wildside Academy. These would be his last Year 11 pupils.

Just as he was about to switch the lights off he paused and went back to the glass cabinets near the window. Removing all the little twigs that he had gathered up on his way into school that morning, he put them in the bin. They had served their purpose. His pupils were ready for the exam and would do well, calmly, without any last-minute panic attacks.

"Are you alright there?" he asked the boy who was standing outside Mr Armani's Science lab as he locked up.

"Yes, thank you, sir," said the boy politely. "Sir said I'm in detention and told me to wait here over break."

"Och, what are you in detention for?"

"I don't know, sir. I couldn't find which room I was in for Science and when sir asked me which set I was in, I told him. And then he said I'd got a detention. I don't know why, sir."

Mr Campbell didn't recognise the boy. He wasn't a pupil he'd ever taught in all his years at Wildside Academy.

"And which set are you in then?"

"4Q, sir."

As the SLT were all having a meeting to decide when to release Year 11 back into the wild it was up to the other teachers to supervise them over break. Einstein said that time is relative and when you're patrolling the yard or the canteen break time certainly seems longer than any other twenty-minute period in the school day. As he'd come out of the recently-renamed José Delgado Science Block Mr Armani had spotted Robinson Morgan smoking behind the bins. He started to walk over to him. When Robinson picked the missile up on his radar he panicked. Rather than throw the cigarette away where his Head of Year might find it he hurriedly stuffed his hands into his pockets without thinking and tried to look innocent. It was hard to say which was more uncomfortable, the cigarette that was slowly burning through his trouser pocket or having to make polite conversation with his Head of Year for ten minutes. As the smoke started to drift out from Robinson's trousers Mr Armani smiled and quietly informed him that he had a detention.

Over by the bike sheds Mr Kaye was sharing a joke with some Year 11 girls whilst signing their shirts. Leaning beside him Ms Shakespeare had felt well enough to come in today and collect the bottles of bubbly parents had sent in to thank her. Jim Fitt and Mike Stringer had come out of the PE office to organise one final burst of star jumps with the Year 11 boys but it had soon developed into a conga around the perimeter of the school field. Elsewhere Year 7 pupils were fearlessly dodging the flour bombs and rotten eggs thrown by Year 11 whilst Ms Malik, Second-in-Department for Geography, wondered if her attempts to stop them had been noticed. The fact that her new interview suit would need dry cleaning would definitely be noticed.

When the bell tolled to announce close of business one last time those Year 11 pupils who hadn't already left through a gap in the perimeter fence found themselves drifting towards the main school exit. Most wandered off, either in silence or shouting loudly at the brave new world that was opening up before them. But there were always others for whom the novelty of a lie-in each morning or an endless game of Zombie Kombat suddenly seemed a little flat. With nothing looming on the horizon except their GCSE exams, the security of school routine had been abruptly pulled out from beneath them. They had been told, quite categorically, that they would be staying in school! Amongst the hugs and tears, their ink-covered shirts fluttering in the wind, it was as if an invisible forcefield were stopping them from leaving. Much as the pupils claimed to have hated every minute of their time at Wildside Academy this was no different to the Stockholm Syndrome that convinced many staff they liked turning up to work there every day. For Year 11, like Mr Campbell, the page was going to be turned and a new exciting chapter was about to be written.

The messy combination of flour and eggs covering the cameras meant that there was limited coverage of the day's events from the CCTV. When Ms Stonehart finally ventured out of her office to go home she had no way of knowing who had let down all of her tyres. She suspected it had been some of the pupils as they'd left. But she couldn't be sure.

CHAPTER 57

"Always remember that you are all as unique as everybody else."

The School-Home Intervention Team had been largely overlooked since Mr North had retired at Christmas. On the plus side nobody had thought to fit CCTV into the Learning Support Department rooms. So when Ms Lovall took on her new rôle she found she was in charge of four people who'd just got into the habit of working whichever way suited them best. With no actual timetables to follow the Teaching Assistants would turn up at classrooms with all the certainty of a Lottery win.

There was actually only one Teaching Assistant, Miss Penelope Honeywell, but she had an assistant, Miss Lorna Fullilove, which made her job title the Assistant Teaching Assistant. They were both assisted by Judith, an older lady who seemed to spend most of her time sitting in the corner studying street maps and bus timetables. She didn't appear to have a job title as such but it turned out that she was in charge of carrying out any home visits to meet the special needs of absent pupils. Unfortunately she didn't drive, didn't know the local area and had no sense of direction. Miss Honeywell had told Sally that there was also another member of the team, Zoe Foster, the Trainee Assistant Teaching Assistant. She had gone to get some more biscuits from KwikShop about three weeks ago and had not been seen since. Mr Cocker was something of an honorary member of the Department. On wet lunchtimes he would often turn up with his bag of crisps and his chess set rather than trudge across to the PE Department in the rain.

Ms Lovall had managed to get her lessons covered to give her time to sort out the cupboards and organise the resources. She'd had a productive morning making a list for Alex Goldbloom of everything she wanted to order. Mr North had been rather old school in his choice of materials but Ms Murkett had been very helpful with suggestions as to how the Department could be updated. As a result she had even found time to put together a display for the new school charity. There wasn't any space left for it in the Learning Support rooms and as Miss Fullilove had only just completed her Christmas display in the corridor she didn't really like to ask her to take that down. Instead she'd found there was just enough room to put her "Children With Diarrhoea" display on the noticeboard by the canteen entrance. She was particularly proud of the photo of her charity parachute jump and the picture of the hospital.

Tim Cocker had decided to join the Department for lunch today and whenever he did he always began with the same joke.

"Is Zoe in today?" he asked "or has the TATA said tata?"

At first he'd had to explain to Miss Fullilove that TATA was both a Trainee Assistant Teaching Assistant and an informal farewell. After a week or two Miss Fullilove had commented that she thought Tim was very funny.

"Weather's awful out there," said Tim, sitting down on one of the colourful beanbags and opening a packet of prawn crisps.

"I saw Orville once, you know," said Judith without looking up from her bus timetable. "At a show in Blackpool. Near the pier."

Nobody was ever sure if Judith was a little bit hard of hearing or was too busy concentrating on her paperwork to contribute fully to their conversations. Half her audience were too young to know who the little green bird was anyway.

"Cool!" said Sally. "I love Blackpool. I'm just gonna pop over to the canteen if anybody wants anything, yeah? Keep an eye on things would you, team? I don't know where everybody is and the kids'll be down here soon."

"Zoe's not in today," said Miss Fullilove a little anxiously, "and I don't know where Penny's got to either."

As if on cue the door opened and Miss Honeywell tottered in. She propped her dripping umbrella up and went to stand by the radiator.

"We thought you weren't coming," smiled Tim.

"I was over in DT with the Brigadier and Year 9," she said.

Glancing down she realised she must have laddered her stockings on a nail. "He thought one of the saws had gone missing so he wouldn't let us out till he found it."

"That'd make him a saw loser," chuckled Tim.

"So what happened?" asked Miss Fullilove, concerned.

"It turned out Monty had miscounted. There was actually one less saw than he thought there was."

"Well, I'm sure success with Ofsted doesn't depend on a saw," reflected Tim. Having finished his crisps he came to sit next to Miss Honeywell to see what she'd brought in to eat. It turned out she was on a diet again and so had only got one tomato rather than two today and a bottle of mineral water.

"That wouldn't feed a rabbit," he said.

"It's OK. I'm off out with my daughter tonight. A trip to the theatre and then we're going to try that new Italian in Berryfield. *Leonardo's*. I think it must be named after Leonardo da Vinci. It's got the Mona Lisa on its all-you-can-eat menu."

"Like in *Titanic*," said Judith, looking up from her bus timetable for a moment.

"I saw that film twice," added Miss Fullilove. "Somebody spoilt it for me the first time by telling me the ending though."

"So why did you go see it again then?" asked Miss Honeywell.

"Well, I didn't think they'd make the same mistake again and hit an iceberg twice."

Their conversation was interrupted by the door crashing open and a small boy tumbling in. He gave them all a thumbs up signal by way of a greeting. This was Eamon Nuttall who came down every lunchtime to join in with the Games Club that was held in Room 2. It was thought it would help him with his social skills.

"Miss!" he began, breathlessly looking to Miss Fullilove for attention. "They won't let me play chess with them. They say I don't know the rules but I think it's because I'm well better at throwing a double six to start than them."

"Don't worry, Eamon," said Mr Cocker. "I'll come and give you a hand."

"Are you sure?" asked Miss Honeywell.

"No problem," said Tim. "I love chess. I've even brought my own pieces. Anyway you're halfway through your lunch."

As often happened neither Miss Honeywell nor Miss Fullilove

got a chance to finish what they were eating as pupils soon turned up wanting help with their homework.

Judith had got her coat on, picked up the umbrella by the door and was about to leave.

"I think there's a bus at half past that goes near Steem Junction," she said uncertainly. "And then it should be a two-minute walk past the police station on Letzby Avenue to Downside Way."

"Who are you off to see today?" asked Miss Honeywell.

"Will Jennings," said Judith, searching in her pocket for her glasses case. "Just like his brother Brian. School refusal. I keep telling him the first five days after the weekend are the worst. Then I should be able to catch the number 13 by the sewage works to go see Washington Makenzie's Mum. She wants him home schooled. Says he's gifted and that Mr Devlin picks on him."

"Miss!" The voice came from a small Year 7 girl sitting at one of the computers. "Miss, why don't autobiographies end with the person writing a book?"

"Remember to clock out this time," called out Miss Honeywell to her departing colleague.

Judith closed the door and left them to the endless string of questions that always punctuated the tranquility of their lunchbreak. With the large school gates refusing to open she could just see her bus heading slowly off in the direction of Grimshaw's Glue Factory.

"Miss! Mr Armani's put us a project on 'S'Cool!' about smoking. But I've looked it up, yeah? It says people often die from smoking."

"That's true, Albert," agreed Miss Honeywell. "People do often die from smoking."

"Yeah but, Miss, my grandad smoked a lot and he only died once. I don't get it, Miss."

"Miss, for Geography, yeah, is Spaghetti Junction that bit where there's a big fork in the road?"

"Miss, if we say forty-four when it's two fours, why isn't eleven pronounced onety-one?"

"Miss, this question's asking us if we can imagine a world without hypothetical questions? I don't get it, Miss."

"Miss, is XL the Roman for forty because that's how old they are when they have to buy bigger clothes?"

"Miss, does condensed milk come from really small cows?"

"Miss, if 75% of accidents happen in the home why don't more people move house?"

They say a little knowledge is a dangerous thing. It was often the case that the more the pupils worked independently on the computers the less likely Miss Honeywell and Miss Fullilove were to finish their lunch. Just as Miss Honeywell had dropped the squishy remains of her half-eaten tomato into the bin Ms Lovall returned from the canteen, ready to take up the challenge.

"Miss Lovall," said a boy near the window before she'd even had a chance to sit down. "Could you help me with the RE homework you've set us on 'S'Cool!', please?"

The homework had been on for a week and was due in tomorrow but as always Tom Bleasdale had left it till the last minute.

"Yeah," she said, putting her vegetarian pizza down on her laptop. "What are you stuck on?"

"Well, it's the stuff on death," said Tom. "I did ask my mate Graham, but he wasn't much help. He just said he was sorry for my loss. So what I can't work out is, what happens if you get scared half to death twice? And also do you spend all eternity in heaven in the clothes you died in or with a broken leg in plaster? And then if people go to heaven and get wings, if birds go to heaven do they get arms? And hell, yeah? If heat rises wouldn't hell be really cold? I don't get it!"

"Miss, I've looked that bit up and it's says Hell is in Norway, near somewhere with the letters crossed out," said the girl beside him.

Ms Lovall looked at them both for a moment while the benefits of home schooling drifted across her mind. She decided the best thing to do to encourage a thirst for learning would be to direct them towards websites about death. Provided Trevor hadn't blocked them all. Looking at her cold slice of pizza twenty minutes later she decided that maybe it'd be a good idea not to run the homework club until Zoe was back in?

Miss Fullilove had gone off to find an English lesson as she wanted to know how 'Lord of the Flies' ended and Miss Honeywell was busy counting the chess pieces in Room 2. There had been an awkward moment when she'd popped her head round the door to say she thought Mr Cocker had left his pawn with the children's board games. With Miss Honeywell now on a mission to track Mr Cocker down and return his stray chess piece Ms Lovall could quietly go through the paperwork she'd inherited.

She smiled when she saw the contents of the first box which contained letters and leaflets from the days before the internet. What a strange world that must have been, having to write everything out on paper. There was a monochrome flyer announcing training courses that had been available in 2007. She couldn't help thinking that the one entitled 'Boys behaving badly' sounded particularly intriguing. Nowadays anger management courses were all the rage. There were also handwritten notes from parents that must have been sent when Mr North was a form tutor. She chose one at random.

> 26, Greenmeadow View,
> Lower Steem,
> Wildside,
> M66 0MG.
>
> Tuesday, November 23rd.
>
> Dear Mr North,
>
> I'm sorry that Sarah is not wearing her correct school uniform to school today. She left it in her Dad's car after netball practice last night and he's gone to work in it.
>
> Best wishes,
> Mrs Penhaligon.
> (Sarah's Mum.)

The next file she opened proved to be more useful. It contained the minutes of all the meetings Mr North had attended along with some handwritten notes for how he'd been planning to take the School-Home Intervention Team from strength to strength. Sally was just pondering whether this was where Ms

Stonehart had acquired her favourite phrase when one particular suggestion caught her eye. A Pupil Voice! Asking the pupils what they thought of everything like the anonymous feedback form on that hotel programme. She could see why Mr North might have been hesitant to suggest it but if she chose the right random pupils to interview the results could be quite promising. As she was off-timetable for the next two days it would give her something to pass the time.

By the end of the week she had managed to speak to all the pupils on the list she'd drawn up. It had meant taking them out of lots of different lessons, of course, but the disruption was worth it if the results were going to cover the full breadth of the curriculum. She'd even found some comments from parents in Mr North's paperwork that she thought were worth adding to the Pupil Voice. They would have been pupils once. And what a Pupil Voice it was, she thought as she read through her summary again. Her last thought before she went through to the Headteacher's office was that Ms Stonehart would be so impressed she'd probably add a whole new page to the school website.

Wildside Academy – Pupil Voice.

"I really love our Geography lessons. The sixty-page booklet we were each given about the destruction of the rainforests was really colourful and made me think about the damage we are needlessly doing to the planet."

- **Katy, Year 10.**

"I think 'Lord of the Files' is a brill book and I hope we get to read another chapter next year."

- **Nabil, Year 9.**

"Mr Fitt is really good as our football coach. He has taught us that it doesn't matter if you win or lose and I think that will be important in later life as I want to be a professional footballer with Accrington Stanley when I'm old enough."

- **Josh, Year 7.**

"Mr O'Reilly really explains Maths well. I feel really confident about finding X now whenever I might need to."
- **Josette, Year 10.**

"When I joined the school I couldn't speak any foreign languages but I can now count to twenty in Spanish thanks to Mr Buonanulla. Hasta la vista, baby!"
- **Matthew, Year 11.**

"Until I started learning Geography at Wildside I really, really thought the world was flat."
- **Yolanda, Year 8.**

"Mr Armani is the best teacher in the world!"
- **Delores, Year 7.**

"I was really worried that my son Jack would be picked on for being different when he started 'big school.' He really enjoys Wildside as the L4L lessons have taught him that it's alright to be straight."
Comment received from the parent of a Year 7 pupil.

JULY

CHAPTER 58

"A question always has more than one answer."

Differentiation is one of those things that trainee teachers are told about, something magical that can score you double points on a lesson observation. It's like going to a restaurant and finding that although the chef has neither the time nor the ingredients to make something different for absolutely everybody he's expected to have a go. You might have to wait a long time to be served and then you'll be given something that you didn't really want anyway. And after all this differentiation in the classroom, you'll still all just find yourself with exactly the same exam paper anyway.

There is differentiation in the exam hall but perhaps appropriately it's a bit different. There are those pupils who turn up in good time and those who think the exam is next week. There are those who have revised thoroughly and those who believe that spontaneity is the key to success. There are those who come prepared and those who just 'borrow' a pen from Mr Patel's lottery counter on the way in to school. There will always be those who claim that Einstein failed Maths as though that somehow justifies their own performance. After the exam there will always be somebody who got 351,965.74 as an answer when everybody else got 7.

For the last ten years Brian Hawksworth had been a chief exams invigilator having taken early retirement as a teacher on the grounds of failing eyesight. He probably wasn't the only teacher who'd ever had trouble with his pupils. Brian was proud of his trusty eagle-eyed team. Nothing ever went wrong during his exam supervisions and nobody ever cheated, as far as he could see. With the exam papers all correctly waiting on the exam desks, the pupils all seated at their designated places and the crates of confiscated mobile phones secured, everything was as it should be. The other three invigilators took up their positions to stop anybody leaving and waited, knowing from experience how Brian would get the pupils' undivided attention. Even though he no longer taught, he knew what he was doing, a black belt at the ancient art of Tea-Ching.

"Hello!" he boomed, splitting the silence and startling some of the pupils who were all seated the regulation distance apart. "Makes you notice, doesn't it? A little bit of distance, refines the senses, focuses the mind. It's time to sit your English exam with no distractions, no sudden ringtones, no glaring screens, no talking. So, stay in your seats, remember everything you've been taught and just do your best. When I tell you to start you will have three hours by this clock." He paused to savour the moment before delivering what he liked to think of as his catchphrase. "You may open your exam papers...now!"

The countdown had started.

Erwin Sloth wrote his name into the gap at the top of his English GCSE paper. So far, so good. He then carefully wrote out the date, feeling that words would be more appropriate than numbers in this case. It wasn't a Maths exam after all. As he wrote it he couldn't help thinking that the word 'Wednesday' had probably been created by the same person who had thought up the spelling of 'February.' Then he realised that the date was written on the board at the front below the clock. Good, he'd got that question mostly right. The next question was an easy one too. Next to 'Centre Name' he carefully wrote out his middle name, Lewis. With all the questions completed, he carefully checked through them before turning the page.

He was aware that other pupils had put their hands up, startling the invigilators so early on in their vigil. Erwin watched the three other invigilators return to the one who had made the announcement as though they needed some clarification from their leader. Then the man made his way out of the hall, his shoes squeaking across the polished floor with every step. A while later he returned, followed by Mr Kaye, the Head of English.

Mr Kaye had decided that his words would carry more weight if he made his announcement from the stage but unfortunately he tripped over a tray of exam papers that had been left on the steps.

"Now, listen up, Year 11!" he began once he had got his breath back. "It turns out there's a bit of an issue with the exam papers. It looks like the Exam Board has sent us copies that have been printed wrong. Typical! As some of you have already spotted, yes, thank you everybody, they've only gone and missed off the questions from *'Lord of the Flies.'* I know! You just can't get the staff, can you? Well, it is what it is. So, no sweat. I'll go to the staffroom and phone the Exam Board. You just get on with the Shakespeare question and the poetry and stuff while you're waiting, yeah?"

As a parting gesture he walked across to the clock at the front of the hall and moved it back half an hour.

"There. Extra time as it's not your fault."

It was as if he was mocking the words on the plinth, *'Tempus fugit!'*

Mr Hawksworth watched the Head of English leave and reflected on the fact that the exam had now started twenty minutes before the pupils had even entered the hall.

In the absence of any questions about *'Lord of the Flies'* Erwin pondered whether he'd write about *'Animal Farm'* or *'Of Mice and Men.'* He'd not read either of the books but the fact that he had a small white mouse as a pet seemed like a good omen. He carefully read through the first question.

'Of Mice and Men' by John Steinbeck.

Question 1.

Choose a character who you think is a victim of loneliness because of the society in which he or she lives. Write about this character, explaining the reasons for your choice.

Erwin couldn't believe his luck. This question was a gift. He carefully read the question again to check that he hadn't misunderstood it before starting on his answer.

> My name is Erwin and in answer to the question I think that my grandad is a victim of loneliness, particularly since my grandma died three years ago. After she passed on he found it very difficult to look after himself and he now lives in the Cemetery View Care Home near my school, Wildside Academy. I love my grandad as he used to play football with me when I was little. As not many people visit him I try to be very conscientious and

He paused and studied the word '*conscientious*.' Was that the correct spelling? He remembered Ms Shakespeare saying when she'd been in one time "*I before E, except after C.*" That was weird really. It didn't seem very scientific. He found himself scribbling down the words '*weird*' and '*scientific*' in the margin to see whether Ms Shakespeare's rule worked. Ah well, Ms Lovall had said there was an exception to every rule. As Erwin watched his original train of thought steaming off over the horizon he decided to move on to another question. He could come back to this one later. They still had over three hours left.

Unbeknownst to Brian Hawksworth the other invigilators felt something of a feeling of resentment towards him as chief exams invigilator. As the title was largely an honorary one with him being paid just 17p an hour more than them their resentment never lead to anything like a power struggle within the little tribe of invigilators. It simply explained why the three of them filled the endless hours of boredom with their own amusing games, usually while Brian was polishing his glasses. Sometimes Hilda would just get on with some knitting she was working on or Neville would watch the seagulls landing on the front field. Malcolm always had a book of Sudoku with him if things got really dull.

One game they played a lot, largely because Brian always complemented them on how well they patrolled the exam room, was based on that old favourite, Battleships. With the pupils all seated in a strict grid pattern it was a simple enough matter to mark off your chosen 'ships' on your seating plan before going to stand behind a pupil you thought your opponent had chosen. The game could happily last quite a while, particularly as pupils insisted on interrupting it with requests for extra sheets of paper or trips to the toilet.

As a variation on Battleships Neville had made up a similar activity to help pass the time. Quite simply he would come up with a title such as *"the one most likely to fail this exam"* and the other two invigilators would go stand behind the pupil they nominated with Neville then picking the winner.

Ultimately this had led to something that they only did with pupils who'd been particularly uncooperative for them in previous exams. One of them, usually Hilda, would quietly patrol up and down the rows as expected before pausing to read a pupil's answers over their shoulder. There would then be a sharp but audible intake of breath, followed by a sympathetic smile when the pupil looked up. It was a look designed to say *You've made the worst mistake I've ever seen in an exam in my life and I'd really like to help you but I'm so sorry but I'm not allowed to.* If the pupil didn't then start scribbling out answers, left, right and centre, it was time for the second part of the plan. Hilda would return to the pupil bringing one of the other invigilators or sometimes both of them, depending on how difficult the pupil had been in the past. On one occasion the three invigilators had shaken their heads in disbelief so much that the victim had crossed out all his answers before checking the spelling of his own name. It was a game that was best played to coincide with Bryan Hawksworth delivering his other catchphrase.

"You have two minutes left, everybody!"

Even with just two minutes left Mr Kaye never did come back to the exam room to tell the pupils what to do. Afterwards Erwin and his mates decided to go tell him how they'd got on as Ms Shakespeare wasn't in school again. They found him in the canteen chatting to Ms Winter and Ms Payne.

"Miss said we had to make sure the words we write increase the value of the paper we write on," said Erwin's friend, Freddy.

"Mine will have done," said Erwin relieved. "I used a really expensive pen."

"Hey, don't worry," Mr Kaye said when the boys mentioned

'Lord of the Flies', "you'll have proper smashed that exam, believe me. No sweat."

"Yeah, this man's literally the best Head of English what there is," Ms Winter added. "Although you'd still have passed with Ms Payne or I 'cos we're all brill teachers us."

Ms Payne looked up from her mobile phone where the Upper Steem Academy website filled the screen.

"Just think yourself lucky that you don't have to go to USA. They've gone and had their kids revising two whole Shakespeare plays when all you actually need is them quotes that Miss S gave you."

"Anyway," said Mr Kaye as he picked up his next slice of pizza, "the Exam Board will have to sort it all out because it's their fault. You just wait and see on results day, Erwin. I bet you'll be surprised!"

CHAPTER 59

*"The two most important days in your life are the day you were born
and the day you find out why."*

Amy Sinclair had been patiently sitting halfway down the stairs each morning just waiting for the letter to come. When it did eventually fall on the mat she snatched it up before Lizzie, their enthusiastic white Scottie dog, had a chance to tear it to pieces. This one was too important to become a dog's dinner. She ran through to the front room with it to find her parents.

"It's come!" she called out so enthusiastically that her Mum nearly spilt the cup of tea she was drinking.

Her parents looked at the envelope with a feeling of trepidation. It was franked with the intricate crest of Wildside Metropolitan Borough Council Education Authority. *"To the parents and / or guardians of Amy Sinclair..."* That was them! Here it was, the moment they'd all been waiting for.

Her Dad opened the letter and started to read it out with all the suspense of a game show host announcing what the contestants could have won. Please, let it be her first choice. She really didn't want to go to that dreadful Academy down the road. Fingers crossed...

"Dear Parents and / or Guardians of Amy Sinclair," her Dad read out, *"Congratulations! We are delighted to inform you that your son/ daughter has won a place at Wildside Academy for the forthcoming academic year, starting on September 1st. Please find enclosed..."*

The rest of what he read was drowned out by the excited screams of both Amy and her Mum. Even Lizzie wandered into the room to find out what was happening as though she knew she was living through momentous days.

"Listen to this," continued her Dad. "It says there's a special evening event for us to meet your form tutor and everybody."

"We need to order you a school uniform," said her Mum, practical as ever. "And PE kit and all your pens and everything. Do you think they still use slide rules?"

"That letter's going in the memory book, our Amy," said her Dad, smiling.

"Can I go round and tell Delores, Mum? Please? She'll be so chuffed that we're going to be at school together."

As she watched her little girl disappearing out of the back door, all grown up and ready for big school, she was so glad she hadn't ended up at that dreadful Upper Steem Academy.

Amy had enjoyed her time at St Damien's Primary School but Thursday, July 4th was marked off on her Zayne Medley calendar as "independence day", her first visit to Wildside Academy. Even though they were only going for some sort of a talk and to meet Mr Gordon, her form tutor, Amy felt nervous as they walked down Cemetery Road to the school. It was even worse than when she'd had to go up on stage to get her certificate for full attendance from Miss Tetley. That was the time Gavin Doyle had been sick in assembly sitting right next to her. She noticed that her parents seemed a little nervous too. Her Dad was wearing his best suit and had started chattering on about how much he loved the gothic architecture of the cemetery gates beyond the school. Her Mum had had her hair done and was unusually quiet as they walked into the school reception.

"There now, I said we'd made the right choice," said her Dad, looking up at a sign in the entrance. "It's got something in Latin on it and look what it says, *Wildside Academy is a school where every child matters.*" He was just re-reading the sign when a lady called Julie handed him a glossy brochure. There was a picture of the Headteacher on the front.

"Look at all the letters after Ms Stonehart's name. She must be very clever," commented his wife quietly.

Mr Sinclair looked at the brochure and wondered what all the letters stood for. Beneath the photo of the Headteacher there was a caption that informed them that the school was going from strength to strength and that their GCSE results were even better than the previous year. That's what Debby Froggett had told them and her daughter always seemed very happy when she came home from school.

The lady offered the two of them a glass of sparkling wine and orange juice for Amy. A nice man in a suit introduced himself as Mr Thicke and pointed out that orange juice was available for the adults too. As they followed all the other parents through to the Main Hall, looking at all the framed photos as they passed them, the Sinclairs knew that they had made the right choice. If it was half as good as Delores told her Amy knew how lucky she was to have got a place at Wildside Academy. She would not let anybody down.

"This is a lovely hall," commented Mrs Sinclair as they sat down near the front. "I wouldn't want to polish all that wood panelling though."

"Gives the place a bit of class though, doesn't it?" added her husband. "And those velvet curtains."

"There's that phrase again," said Amy, looking up at the stage.

There was a row of teachers sitting on the stage to the left of the plinth, some of them looking as uncomfortable as Mr Sinclair felt. The young lady sitting on the right must be Amy's new Head of Year.

"What does *Tempus fugit* mean, Dad?"

Amy was still at an age where her parents were the fountain of all knowledge but luckily for her Dad the phrase had been the tie-breaker in his pub quiz recently.

"*Tempus fugit?* Time flies."

"Why would you want to do that?" asked Amy. "They move so quickly."

Maybe it was something to do with Science? Delores had said something about stick insects. Her thoughts were interrupted by a man talking loudly on the row behind them.

"Can't even get their meetings started on time!"

Mr Sinclair happened to glance in the man's direction and immediately wished he hadn't. It was Billy who worked in the garage where he had the van serviced. He always tried to avoid Billy if he could as he was a man who always seemed to have a glass that was half empty. Particularly in The Cock 'n' Bull .

"Tony!" said Billy as soon as he spotted him. "I was just saying to Paula, it's not a good sign if they can't even start on time, is it? We were hoping our Orla would go to USA but we've ended up here. Typical! We've put in an appeal you know."

Mr Sinclair could only assume that Billy hadn't actually looked through the brochure to see how good a school Wildside Academy was. He was the kind of man who probably read '*The Wildside Gazette.*' Luckily any further complaints from him were silenced as a teacher at the front stood up and tapped his baton on a music stand. A leaflet inside their brochure said that the Recorder Club were going to perform a medley and this must therefore be Mr Jones, the Head of Music. Apparently the teacher accompanying them on the piano was Amy's new form tutor, Mr Gordon. He quietly pointed him out to Amy as the music started.

Mrs Sinclair was no music expert but she recognised some of the tunes they were playing, starting with an enthusiastic if slightly jarring rendition of everybody's favourite, '*London's burning*'. It was as they were ploughing their way through an imperial march that the doors at the back of the hall swung open. Three figures entered the hall and walked purposefully down the central aisle before mounting the steps and taking their places on the stage.

"Blimey!" exclaimed Billy. "The force is with us. Where's her cape then?"

Mrs Sinclair had read in the brochure that Wildside Academy was a modern, forward-thinking school. That would probably explain why the Headteacher wasn't wearing fuddy-duddy, old-fashioned academic gowns just to show off her qualifications.

The Headteacher stepped forward to the microphone stand, glanced down at her notes on the plinth and coughed.

"Good evening everybody, parents and erm, children. This is our school, Wildside Academy, and you're welcome to it. I'm Ms Stonehart, Headteacher, and I'll now pass you over to my Deputy Heads, Mr Wingett and Mr Thicke."

She sat down. Mrs Sinclair approved of people coming straight to the point. It was the sign of an educated and ordered mind. Amy would get a good education here with Ms Stonehart as Headteacher. She'd been in charge of the school a good few years so she must know what she was doing, unlike at USA where they had a Headteacher who was new to it all.

The man who had recommended the orange juice then proceeded to show them a series of graphs and charts that illustrated the progress pupils would make over their five years at the school. It was all very complicated but the Deputy Head assured them that they would do better here than at any other school. Apparently it was all worked out scientifically, something to do with something called base line data, target grades and, if she'd heard him right, flight paths. It seemed to have something to do with music as he kept mentioning something about algorithm. Anyway he clearly knew what he was talking about. There were lots of different colours on his PowerPoint even if the size of the lettering made it difficult to read in places. He promised that reports on pupil progress would be sent home fortnightly with Review Time Evenings every half term. It was all very reassuring.

As this was clearly a lot to take in Mr Thicke's presentation was followed by a display of the school uniform and the PE kit. Amy recognised Dominic Harrop from Primary School as he paraded with the other immaculately-dressed models across the stage and back. Mrs Sinclair commented on how quickly the First Aiders came to help him when he fell down the stairs. It was all very reassuring. Behind her Billy was not impressed by the fact that the uniform was only available from one supplier in Berryfield. No doubt Wildside Academy would be taking their cut of the profits. Mr Sinclair shuffled uncomfortably in his seat, hoping that people didn't think he was the one talking in assembly.

"I've got the graveyard shift," said the other Deputy Head as he took his turn behind the microphone. "A hard act to follow after the catwalk."

He seemed a little surprised that parents smiled at his comment as though he'd been trying to be funny.

"I'm Mr Wingett," he continued "and I'm going to talk you through what your sons and daughters will be experiencing during their five years at our outstanding school, Wildside Academy."

Mr Wingett then proceeded to read each slide of his PowerPoint to the parents even though the same information was included in the glossy brochure, word for word. Whilst Mrs Sinclair smiled and commented on how thorough they were, Mr Sinclair was pleased to see Billy disappearing off in search of another glass of sparkling wine.

"Here at Wildside Academy," began Mr Wingett, "we believe that pupils should follow a broad and varied curriculum that will prepare them for life in the twentieth century. At Key Stage 3 all pupils study a range of subjects including English, Maths, Science and ICT. At Key Stage 4 pupils will be guided by the Senior Leadership Team to the subjects that best fit the timetable. All students will have one hour per week of Learning For Life, L4L as we call it, which is organised by Ms Lovall…"

As his monologue continued pupils could follow his words on the screen to discover what was taught in each subject.

ENGLISH

Pupils study a broad and varied range of literary works, starting with the poetry of Pam Ayres in Year 7. At Key Stage 3 pupils will study extracts from *'Lord of the Flies'* in readiness for the GCSE course. We also celebrate World Book Day with a range of fun educational activities.

Head of Department : Mr Kaye.

MATHS

Pupils will be able to buy a calculator from their Maths teacher (batteries not included.) Log books and slide rules are no longer needed under the National Curriculum. We also celebrate World Pi Day with a range of fun educational activities.

Head of Department : Mr Devlin.

SCIENCE

The Science Department provides a broad and varied range of written activities to complement the textbook *"Exploring Science Through Pictures and Worksheets."* Pupils in Set 1 may use the Van de Graaff generator under supervision. We are the only school in the area with its own telescope.

Acting Head of Department : Miss Skellen.

IT

Wildside Academy has several ICT suites and access to the World Wide Web. Pupils will learn how to use Windows Vista, make a short interactive game and produce a PowerPoint for their final assessment. The Computer Club runs after school on Thursdays but please note that Zombie Kombat is banned.

Executive Head of Department : Mr Rojan.

DT (aka Woodwork etc.)
Pupils will design and produce a mobile phone holder and learn how to cook a croque monsieur. There will be an additional charge for everything produced to cover the cost of materials along with our fund to repair the circular saw.
Head of Department : Brigadier Vernon-Smythe MFI, DIY, MDF.

GEOGRAPHY
The Geography Department offers a broad and varied range of lessons looking at clouds, rocks and the flags of the world. To complement the textbook *"Exploring Geography Through Pictures and Worksheets"* some pupils will go on the Iceland trip which visits the Berryfield branch.
Head of Department : Miss Armitage.

HISTORY
Pupils look at the history of History teaching under the umbrella title "Does History have a future?" From prehistoric cave drawings through the crimes of Jack the Ripper to the question of Brexit every period of history is covered. We use the newly-updated textbook *"Exploring History Through Pictures and Worksheets"* to offer a broad and varied range of lessons.
Head of Department : Mr Ford.

MODERN FOREIGN LANGUAGES (MFL)
Using the online courses *"Bof! On est français!"* and *"Aturdir España"* to complement the textbook *"Explorer les Langues à travers des images et des fiches de travail"* pupils will learn all the foreign words they will ever need when travelling abroad. Pupils may also apply to join Mme Loups-Garoux's Leaders of Language scheme.
Acting Head of Department : Mr Buonanulla.

ART

Pupils will learn to copy the artwork of Keith Haring and colour it in, keeping within the lines. In Year 7 some pupils will visit Saltaire Mill to see the David Hockney masterpieces. There will be a charge for this trip to cover costs.

Head of Department : Mrs Thorne.

RE

Our new Scheme of Work studies the life and works of Charles Darwin and the words of *'All things bright and beautiful.'* Pupils going on to study RE at GCSE will learn the words of the school hymn. (Ms Lovall's group only.)

Acting Head of Department : Mr Livingstone.

LESSONS FOR LIFE (L4L)

The L4L Programme of Study offers a broad and varied range of lessons to prepare pupils for everything in life. The course is made up of five themes :

Year 7 : "Who am I?"

Year 8 : "Who are you?"

Year 9 : "Where are we?"

Year 10 : "What's happening to me?"

Year 11 : "What next?"

Every term each Department will deliver themed lessons covering diversity, how to spot the signs of bullying and safety near reservoirs. Year 11 will also have a lesson on how to write a CV with a follow-up lesson on coping with unemployment.

A special lesson on *'What to do in the event of an Ofsted inspection'* will be taught as needed.

Head of Department : Ms Lovall.

MUSIC

Parents are advised to see Mr Jones for details of the peripatetic instrument lessons (at very reasonable rates.) School Choir meets every Monday lunchtime with Recorder Club after school on Wednesdays.

Head of Department : Mr Jones.

THE SCHOOL-HOME INTERVENTION TEAM

Please contact Ms Lovall if your child has any Special Needs, including special dietary needs.

Homework Club is available in the Learning Support Department including individual support for logging onto the 'S'Cool Homework!' website.

Head of Department : Ms Lovall.

THE PE DEPARTMENT

Exercise is good for you. Laziness is not.

Pupils must wear the correct kit and will need to bring their own table tennis bats.

Heads of Department : Mr Greenfield and Mrs Mower.

"That looks like Sue Barker," whispered Mr Sinclair to his wife looking at the pictures on the final slide.

"I bet they have all sorts of celebrities popping in to open things and help out," she replied.

"You know all this is just for Ofsted's benefit, of course," said Billy behind them choosing to join in their private conversation again. "That's why they haven't mentioned Ofsted once. Free drinks and glossy brochures because they know Ofsted send us a survey about what we think. Parent Voice!"

"We wanted our Orla to go to USA," added his wife.

"We've put in an appeal you know."

Mrs Sinclair smiled politely and read through the Pupil Voice comments that were included at the back of the brochure.

The final part of the evening gave parents a chance to talk to the form tutors informally. It felt like the new school year had already started as a younger teacher with a Geordie accent read out the register for each form, directing everybody to the correct form tutor. It transpired that Amy and Orla were going to be in the same class. They had to wait a little while before Mr Gordon could join them, much to Billy's evident annoyance, as Mr Wingett was having a quiet word with him first. Amy thought Mr Gordon was very nice whereas Orla wasn't really bothered as she was going to transfer to Upper Steem Academy anyway when her appeal came through. She was going to the school Zayne Medley had gone to.

"We liked your piano playing," said Mrs Sinclair when they

got a chance to speak to Mr Gordon.

"Thank you. I'm glad somebody did," smiled Mr Gordon.

Amy smiled back at him.

As they happily made their way towards the exit Mrs Sinclair asked her husband whether they should speak to Ms Stonehart herself.

"Just to introduce ourselves," she suggested. "We'll be seeing a lot of her over the next five years. And you never know, there might be work here too. People will always need plumbers, Tony."

Her husband looked round a little nervously.

"She'll be very busy, love. She's the Headteacher. We can always make an appointment to see her at the next Review Time Evening when Amy's been here a little while. What do you think, our Amy?"

"I can't wait to come here, Dad! Thank you!"

As the Sinclairs happily made their way out into the cool evening air Ms Stonehart was indeed being kept busy with all the questions parents needed to put to her.

"Excuse me, love. Are there any toilets nearby?"

CHAPTER 60

"If you want to be the best and you want to beat the rest,
dedication's what you need!"

Madame Loups-Garoux was late for her own assembly. She knew it wouldn't be in the Main Hall as the GCSE exams were on but when she got to the canteen Mr Armani was already in there with Year 10. Ironically he was doing an assembly about punctuality. He must have gone straight to his sermon now that the school did not have a pianist. As she hurried back down the corridor towards the staffroom she saw Mr Cocker and decided, against her better judgement, to ask him if he knew where her assembly was meant to be.

"Team!" she called out to him in case any pupils didn't know his first name. "Team! Do you 'appen to know where assemblies are 'eld en ce moment? Mine seems to 'ave disparu!"

Céline Loups-Garoux had a tendency to drop French phrases into her speech whenever she got stressed and her gallic accent would become stronger. Even at the best of times she had trouble pronouncing Mr Cocker's first name. There clearly was no 'i' in Tim. He was no use though, simply joking that when he'd worked at an Academy sponsored by Ikea assembly had taken ages.

When she looked on the noticeboard in the staffroom the assembly rota had disappeared. Noticing that the Girls PE Department were both here she wondered whether assemblies were being held in the Sports Hall.

"Alison, " she called over to the Head of Girls' PE, "do you know if assemblies are on in the Sports 'All?"

"There's nobody over there," replied Mrs Mower, "but I think Calvin's in the canteen with his year if that'll do?"

"No, I am looking for my Year 9s."

"I was going to ask you," continued Alison, putting her coffee cup down, "my club are playing in an international golf tournament in the summer. We're going to a place called Cafard-something in France. You don't know it, do you?"

"Cafard-sur-Mer? But of course! I was born and raised in Cafard. My family still live in the centre-ville."

Much as Madame Loups-Garoux knew she should be out looking for her flock she found herself sitting with the Girls' PE Department for ten minutes and singing the praises of her hometown. The fish market in particular was worth a visit.

Over in the PE Department office Mr Cocker poured himself a black coffee and set the microwave going for twenty minutes to allow them to talk freely.

"I managed to delay her," he said. "I told her how it's not as bad as when I worked at an Academy sponsored by Ikea…"

"Yeah, assembly took ages," finished Jim Fitt. "Don't you 'ave any new jokes, our Tim?"

"Tough crowd," smiled Tim. "Anyway, as I've said before I never ever repeat myself. Hey, did I tell you about when I went out with a girl called Simile? I don't know what I met 'er for!"

"Text from Lisa," interrupted Marcus Deeside, much to everyone's relief. "They've managed to keep her talking in the staffroom. There's only fifteen minutes left. We should be OK."

"They shouldn't be putting assemblies on in our Sports Hall," said Harry Greenfield, not for the first time. "They never remember to take their shoes off. Ruins my floor."

"I've set up equipment for an assault course and a beep test even if they do get in," said Jim.

"And someone's nicked the table tennis bats again."

Marcus eased two of the slats open on the blinds and looked out towards the main school buildings.

"No sign of anybody," he reported. "Just Bob chasing a pigeon."

"SLT think they can just do whatever they like here," repeated Harry as he returned to Wimbledon.

"Speaking of which…" said Mike Stringer, passing an envelope over to Tim.

"What's this?"

"Your sweepstake winnings. Rollover last week as nobody was sacked. It would've been double if you'd chosen Jones as well."

Mr Gordon had got his marching orders after playing the imperial march to announce the arrival of Ms Stonehart and her troops at the New Year 7 Evening. As conductor Mr Jones had also disappeared for 'conduct unbecoming'. Even under interrogation neither of them had confessed as to who had chosen the music that evening.

It seemed wrong somehow taking the money as Dean and Huw had been very popular colleagues but this was just the British way of getting through dreadful situations. Noticing that the odds had now increased next to his own name Tim decided to keep the money as he might be needing it before too long.

With the blinds all closed and the only illumination coming from the microwave and Harry's television the PE Department office should appear unoccupied to the outside world. As a precautionary measure they'd also locked the door from the inside which would over-ride the entry panel. Nevertheless a few of the more eager Year 9 pupils had now turned up for assembly.

"I'll get it," said Marcus. "Hang on."

Unlocking the door he popped his head out into the rain and, sounding like his Head of Department, told them to go for a run round the front field. The first one back would be in detention.

Madame Loups-Garoux was feeling quite homesick as she left the staffroom. It was a shame they no longer ran trips abroad. She'd prepared her assembly on the school value of 'Dedication', focusing on the dedicated French citizens in her country's history. She had been going to ask Ms Grimley to help her research it but Thora had been off for a few weeks now due to stress. She was pleased with her PowerPoint which covered just about everything including Joan of Arc, the French Revolution, Napoleon, the French Resistance, the student riots of 1968 and the regular strikes at French airports. Reminiscing about Cafard-sur-Mer had made her realise that she should have included her *grandpère* to add a personal touch to her PowerPoint.

As she passed the Main Hall she remembered that it was the French GCSE exam that morning. Looking in she could see that her pupils had all turned up, even though Sam Tyler looked like he'd already fallen asleep at his desk.

"*Question numéro treize,*" the exam recording competed with the bin lorries doing their collection outside the hall. *"Pour moi, les problèmes de l'environnement sont très importants. Et toi, Sophie?"*

That was good. She'd told her group that there'd be a question about the environment in the Listening exam.

Back in the Sports Hall the PE teachers were trying to guess what the letters after Ms Stonehart's name actually stood for. It had started when Jim Fitt had noticed that Harry Greenfield had 2,311 unread emails on his laptop. In the end the prize of a packet of KwikShop chocolate biscuits went to Mike Stringer's suggestion.

"TGCSEC stands for Two GCSE Certificates," he suggested. "CPT is obviously the Cycling Proficiency Test you do at Primary School. And BPB has to be the good old-fashioned Blue Peter Badge!"

The worrying thing was, all joking apart, when they searched it up they couldn't find anything else it could be.

"Miss," called out a pupil as Madame Loups-Garoux made her way towards the playground, having decided to check the Sports Hall after all. It was one of her Leaders of Language Ambassadors.

"Miss, do you need us for assembly as it's *jeudi?*"

"It's *mercredi*, Chloe, and no I don't. I don't think assembly's on today because of the exams."

"Okay-dokey," said Chloe, heading back towards her form room.

With little more than five minutes left Madame Loups-Garoux arrived at the Sports Hall to find it locked. There was just a pile of bags by the door and an art folder that had spilt its contents out into a puddle. She spotted Bob busy checking that the bins by the Science Block had been emptied and went to see if he could unlock the Sports Hall. Maybe her Year 9 pupils were all inside, neatly seated cross-legged in rows and patiently waiting for her. In all honesty it wouldn't be the first time they'd got to assembly before her.

As Senior Ground Maintenance Supervisor Bob had so many keys that it was always going to take him a while to find the right one.

"It's always the last key you try that opens the door," he said good-naturedly.

"Obviously," said Madame Loups-Garoux without a word of thanks. "You're not going to find the right key and then try a few more after that, n'est-ce pas?"

The bell for first lesson sounded out as Bob opened the door to the Sports Hall to reveal that there wasn't a single pupil inside, not even Adam and Sonya.

"Hiya, Madam Lewd-Gerroux," said one of the Year 9 pupils as they came back to retrieve their bags. "See you after break."

"C'est la vie! L'enfer, c'est les autres! " said Madame Loups-Garoux to herself as philosophically as Sartre as she watched everybody hurrying in out of the rain. It was true : *Hell is other people!* She may not have got to do her assembly on 'Dedication' but she'd definitely displayed dedication in her attempts to do so.

CHAPTER 61

"If you want to get somewhere, know where you are going."

As always there was a lot going on in the Main Office. The kettle was bubbling away, the cakes had been organised for the busy day ahead and Jules was standing on a chair putting up a banner.

"Am I straight?" Jules called down to the others.

"Needs to be up your end a bit," replied Julie. "That's it! Perfect!"

Jules climbed back down to admire his workmanship. The long colourful banner read *"Welcome back, Julie!"* and was the first thing she'd see when she returned to work after all this time.

"Quick everybody!" announced Judy as she raced in to the office. "She's just signing in. Julia's keeping her talking. Hide!"

In seconds the Main Office looked like the *Marie Celeste* with mugs of steaming coffee abandoned on desks, phones ringing and the photocopier churning out blank paper without any assistance.

"Hello?" called out Julie to the empty office as she came in and looked around for her colleagues. She'd kept in touch with them all on social media while she'd been off on maternity. They knew she was coming back today. Had she missed a fire alarm?

"Surprise!" exclaimed her colleagues appearing from out of the kitchenette and from behind the photocopier. There was a moment of panic when Jules found he'd got himself stuck in the stock cupboard but it was a memorable way of introducing himself to Julie when he finally came out.

"Welcome back to the madhouse!" said Juliette. "I hope you've brought loads of photos of her."

"What have you called her?" asked Jules as Julie passed round her mobile phone.

"Julie-Anne," said Julie, "after her grandma."

"Aw, bless! She's an absolute poppet!" exclaimed Jules when he saw her.

He passed Julie the tin of fairy cakes he'd made. They probably wouldn't get much work done this morning but they'd soon catch up now that there was another pair of hands to help them.

Judy had suggested that Julie should just have light duties in the first week to ease her back into the world of work. It seemed best that she took over from Julia on the main reception desk as by mid-morning it really only involved chatting to the postman and re-directing calls to The Golden Dragon. On this fine July day though it was different. This was the day that Ofsted inspectors finally returned to Wildside Academy!

Julie looked up from her phone as the doors opened with a sigh and two men and a woman strode purposefully towards her desk.

"Welcome to Wildside Academy," she said politely. "How may I help you?"

"We're from Ofsted," said one of the men, smiling. "We're here to see the Headteacher, Ms Stonehart."

"Certainly, sir. I'll just need to get the laminating machine so that I can make you some passes. Just give me a moment, would you, it's my first day back. It's here somewhere."

The three of them waited patiently for a minute before deciding they'd been kept waiting long enough.

"We'll see ourselves in," said the second man, tapping a code into the door panel.

As Julie watched the three of them disappear towards the Headteacher's office she could only assume that this wasn't the first day of their visit if they knew the door code. As Ms Stonehart must be expecting the Ofsted inspectors she could happily return to looking at her photos.

"Sorry to bother you," said Mrs Spratt. Luckily the door to Ms Stonehart's office was actually open for once. "I believe your visitors from Ofsted are here."

After all this time Ms Stonehart felt ready for this visit and she smiled warmly as they entered. As she always said, it wasn't all about Ofsted. They got to sit in the three most comfortable chairs and Mrs Spratt soon hurried back with tea and coffee in the best cups and a selection of the luxury chocolate biscuits. Introductions took no time at all and as soon as the plan for the day had been agreed her three guests headed off to see what Wildside Academy had to offer, accompanied by Mr Humble.

"Norma," said Ms Stonehart as she returned to her office, "I need Trevor and Sharon without delay!"

Five minutes later Ms Stonehart was sitting in front of her computer screen with Mr Rojan and Ms Payne either side of her. Mrs Spratt waited in readiness with a mobile phone and a list of numbers. A plan of the school was spread across Ms Stonehart's desk like this was a military operation. A random chess piece marked the current location of the enemy just beyond her office.

"What if the Ofsted inspectors go in different directions?" Ms Stonehart thought out loud. It wasn't something they'd considered before. "Will we be able to track all of them?"

"Erm, yeah, I think so," said Trevor.

He tapped at the keyboard and the picture on the screen divided to show both the current location of the group with Mr Humble and the next area they were walking towards.

"Maths!" exclaimed Mrs Spratt excitedly as she studied the plan of the school. "They're heading towards the Maths Department."

This was the most excitement she'd had in years. Trevor was so good with computers.

As she read out Mr Devlin's phone number from her list she realised that she should probably have brought her reading glasses with her. There was no time to go back and get them. They'd be arriving at the Maths Department any minute now unless Jamie could delay them on the corridor.

"There's no answer!" said Ms Payne shaking the phone she'd been given. "I don't even think that's the right number. It just beeps. Hang on."

She passed the school phone back to Mrs Spratt. She had Sean's number on speed dial on her own mobile phone.

"Sean? It's Sharon."

"Sharon! Hello, love. Listen, about last night…"

"Sean. I'm on speakerphone in Ms Stonehart's office.

Operation Nostradamus! It's go, go, go! About to arrive at Maths in two minutes, yeah? Action stations! See you later."

"About eight? In the usual…"

Ms Payne ended the call.

As she waited for them to return to her office at the end of the day Ms Stonehart found herself wondering why on earth she'd been so worried about an Ofsted inspection. She was glad she'd dumped Eddie but his advice had been useful and the visit had gone a lot better than expected. She herself had had quite a relaxing day in her office, knowing that there was nothing more she could do at this stage, and nobody had come to seek her help. She'd let Ms Payne and Mr Humble join her in her office as she knew they'd feel less nervous with their Headteacher there to support them. She phoned through to Mrs Spratt. It was time for the post-mortem.

As the three of them came through, their verdict was hard to read on their faces. They silently sat down opposite Ms Stonehart and the members of her Senior Leadership Team.

"So what are your conclusions?" she asked, coming straight to the point.

"We have seen every single Department in the school, except for Drama," said the first man. "We've observed lessons, looked at pupils' work and watched how pupils behave in school. We've looked at all the data on SCAMS. I think you'll find we've been as thorough as you would want us to be. But there's some good news and, of course, some bad news."

He paused and looked to his colleagues for their observations.

"I noticed," said the man beside him, "that whilst all lessons had Learning Objectives on the board and flight path data clearly displayed in classrooms, the font size was not always consistent on every slide of PowerPoint presentations. In addition I spoke to one pupil who could not immediately tell me his Aspirational Target grade without checking the front of his book first. And I found some litter."

"Yeah," said the woman sitting beside him. "Well, what I spotted was that there was some kids that didn't know the first thing about grammar. They didn't have a scooby-doo! You could just tell, yeah, as soon as they opened their mouth to speak to you or I."

"But the school is going from strength to strength, isn't it?"

interrupted Ms Stonehart. "You've seen my Leadership and the SLT? Did Mr Humble tell you that we're thinking of changing the title 'Heads of Department' to 'Curriculum Leaders'? Did you see the Words of Wisdom on our walls? That was my idea. What about our telescope? USA haven't got a telescope! Or a new car park or a helipad."

She was starting to sound rather desperate and the so-called Ofsted inspector was beginning to feel a little uncomfortable with his boss showing how insecure she really was.

"Don't worry," said Mr Wingett. "If this had been a real Ofsted inspection then they'd have come to the same conclusion as us. No doubt about it. The good news is that Wildside Academy is an outstanding school as far as we can see. Under your leadership we are continuing to go from strength to strength."

"The kids just need to work on their grammar though, yeah?" agreed Ms Winter.

"And the teachers their font size," added Mr Thicke.

"It was well brill that. I enjoyed it."

"Mind you, there's always the bad news," Mr Wingett continued. "And the bad news is, if real Ofsted inspectors had just been let in as easily as we were, without any checks, it'd be like at Berryfield. In fact, knowing our luck, we'd probably be graded worse than inadequate!"

CHAPTER 62

"Today is the first day of the rest of your life…"

Operation Nostradamus! had shown that Wildside Academy was actually an outstanding school whatever Ofsted might say but there was still room for improvement. The teaching staff seemed to fall into two categories. One group, largely the teachers that Ms Payne had phoned during the dummy run, had displayed a welcoming attitude and outstanding teaching. The rest had just looked surprised when four members of the SLT had unexpectedly arrived at their door to judge every aspect of their lessons. If anything the actions of the SLT had just reinforced what Toby Chambers said at the Open Evening. There were people employed at the school who did nothing worthwhile and as a result some teachers would have to go. Fortunately Ms Winter still had her original list and any unfinished business could be completed in the final two weeks of term. Like Alex Goldbloom had remarked, there was no point paying people over the summer break just to have to let them go in September.

In the case of the first two teachers it was almost too easy. Mr Capstick didn't have a leg to stand on as he was still continuing to smoke his pipe during the working day. His argument that he would always leave his classroom to go stand in Cemetery Road when he lit up did not work in his favour. Mr Ash, the last of a long line of Science teachers who had been employed throughout the year, disappeared after a pupil commented that he had been *"looking at me in a funny way."* The fact that she meant Mr Ash had been looking at the class with his eyes closed whilst explaining how the eyelid functions was not seen as important.

"This is getting well easy," said Ms Winter. "It's almost boring!"

She'd sent an email to Mrs Spratt to demand more supply teachers and was now enjoying a hot drink with Ms Payne in the staffroom after a busy morning. The other teachers who'd been working there had left, perhaps concerned that they were under observation even having their lunch.

The new staffroom photocopier had finally arrived a few weeks earlier and everybody had been issued with their own six-digit PIN. Ms Payne was multi-tasking, printing off the boarding cards and hotel reservations for her summer break whilst drinking her coffee and checking her social media.

"I've got a wicked idea," she said as her last colour copy slid silently out of the machine. "Time to get creative."

"Brill!"

"Trevor! Adil! How're you doin' down here?"

Ms Payne greeted the IT technicians like old friends when she and Ms Winter went to see them. Neither of the men looked impressed by the amount of things the two Assistant Heads had knocked over as they'd squeezed into their tiny cupboard of a room.

"It's like the centre of everything down here," smiled Ms Payne, "keeping everything running smoothly, protecting us all from nasty cyber attacks and millennium bugs. You two are the unsung heroes of Wildside Academy. Well done, you."

Only the week before Trevor had sent out a spoof email to see whether the internet safeguarding training staff had done after school had been effective. Some teachers had paid attention but then overcompensated by ignoring any email containing the phrase t.rojan in case it was a virus. Many of the staff had come down to reception to collect the Scrabble set the email claimed they had won online. About the only teacher who didn't respond to the junk email was Ms Lovall who, ironically, had actually ordered a Scrabble game for the Learning Support Department.

On the wall was a picture of Trevor sitting by the canal fishing. This was how he normally spent his weekends but as he worked in IT Adil had added an amusing caption.

"Gone phishing! Catch you later!"

"Yeah, it's well cool down 'ere," added Ms Winter as she looked round. "All these computers and screens and stuff. Is that the spaceship off of *Brief Encounter*?"

"We were just wondering if you could settle an argument," continued Ms Payne.

"Between Sharon and I," added Ms Winter for clarity. "We don't usually argue but it's about that new photocopier and PIN numbers."

"Well I can settle that argument straight away," said Adil. "It's just PIN. Not PIN number. Otherwise that'd be Personal Identification Number number. OK? Does that settle it?"

He started to pick up a pile of keyboards that had toppled over again. Ms Winter looked like he had been talking to her in some sort of alien computer language.

"No, that wasn't it, thanks," continued Ms Payne pleasantly. "I was just saying there's no way of knowing what somebody's photocopied on that machine and Lynne thinks you can find out."

"Like, take Sharon and I, yeah?" said Ms Winter. "If I put my PIN number in then it'd be like being on SCAMS or 'S'Cool!', yeah, I could get up all of the data wotsits for what she's copied too?"

"You couldn't get the data on the staffroom copier," said Adil, "but we could see it all here. Isn't that right, Trev?"

"Erm, yeah, I think so," Trevor contributed to the discussion.

"No way!" exclaimed Ms Payne. "That'd be a massive job, wouldn't it? It'd take you like forever."

"Literally forever and a day," agreed Ms Winter.

"Well, we'd better not keep you from your work," smiled Ms Payne employing her usual tactic. "They're so busy, Lynne. It's like you were saying. Janine should be giving them a pay rise. They're such a big help to everyone."

"Name a teacher," said Adil.

"Oh, I don't know," Ms Payne seemed to ponder. "Tim Cocker?"

It took Adil less than a minute to print off a log of everything Mr Cocker had photocopied since the new machine had been installed.

"I said it could be done," said Ms Winter to her friend. "Wicked! You owe me a pint!"

"Well, it is what it is. Cheers!" agreed Ms Payne.

With no need to remain in this untidy, smelly cupboard with these two sad losers a moment longer Ms Payne took the computer print-out and left without a word of thanks. As Ms Winter slammed the door behind them the fuse box sparked, leaving the two men in total darkness.

"That was well brill!" exclaimed Ms Winter to her friend when they were back in the Assistant Heads' office.

"It's like Sean says. In this job you've gotta box clever if you wanna stay on top. I think them two are friends with Cocker. They'd have said this couldn't be done if we'd just asked for it."

"That's 'cos they're not team players like you and I."

"Well, Team Sharon, you can come and help me sort through it all, now we've got it."

"I'll just grab us some doughnuts from Eric, yeah? Looks like it could be a big job this."

As it turned out it took them most of the afternoon to go through the log of what Mr Cocker had been photocopying lately. They were beginning to think they wouldn't find anything incriminating but the devil was in the detail and eventually they found what they were looking for. Hidden between worksheets on oxbow lake formations and how to make PowerPoints, there they were, things he really shouldn't have photocopied! Things nobody else in the school would have printed. There was no way Mr Cocker was going to wriggle his way out of this one with a few Fairtrade bananas!

It was ironic really that Tim Cocker was queuing for the photocopier when they came for him. As always he was in a cheerful mood, looking forward to getting home to his family and watching more of the *Midsomer Murders* boxset they'd got him for his birthday.

"Sorry, was that a 1 or a 7 at the end?" he joked as Mr Ansari typed in his six-digit PIN for the photocopier.

"You know what," smiled his colleague, "I was going to ask if you wanted to go first but seeing as it's you, I just need to copy all this. Enlarged, back-to-back, stapled, thirty of each page! Won't be too long, mate."

He held up a thick, dog-eared copy of *"Exploring Design*

Technology Through Pictures and Worksheets" before stepping back to let his friend go first.

"Mr Cocker," said a voice nervously behind them as he reached to type in his own code. "You're to come with me. Mr Wingett wants to see you. At once. Bring all your things with you."

It was Mrs Spratt.

Instead of going to Mr Wingett's office and then having to wait in the corridor for twenty minutes Tim found it more worrying that he'd been taken straight to the interview room, Room 101. Mr Wingett allowed the condemned man to sit down as Mrs Spratt immediately started taking notes. Sitting over in the corner, as though keeping as far away from him as possible, she didn't make eye contact with Tim once.

"How can I help you?" asked Mr Cocker amiably.

"Well, there's some bad news and some worse news," Mr Wingett began in his usual way. "You'll be aware that we did a mini-Ofsted recently? We were very thorough and as part of that inspection we looked at how the new photocopier in the staffroom is being used. It cost a lot of money and you've been issued with Mr Thicke's policy on reducing photocopying costs. I think you know what I'm leading up to?"

Tim genuinely had no idea where the conversation was going so Mr Wingett continued.

"You realise that you photocopy more on that machine than any other teacher in the school?"

"Well, I've got a lot of classes," Tim began reasonably, "and Mrs Ramsbottom said that after that unfortunate incident with…"

"You regularly infringe copyright laws by photocopying more than the allowed 10%," continued Mr Wingett as though Tim hadn't even spoken. "You've even made photocopies for your own personal use."

Ms Payne had highlighted a returns label that Tim had printed out. He'd actually been sending back an unused Geography revision book he'd bought online out of his own money.

"The main reason I'm seeing you today is far worse," added Mr Wingett, opening a large black folder with Mr Cocker's name and staff code on it.

He spread some colour photocopies across the desk as though Tim was being accused of murder in his favourite crime drama.

"Do you deny that you photocopied this…material?"

Tim looked down at the sheets of paper picked out on the desk by the harsh strip lights above his head. He looked up at Mr Wingett, unsure what he was meant to say.

"Stuff like this has no place in a school like Wildside Academy," sneered Mr Wingett. "Personally I find it hard to understand somebody who promotes this kind of thing to be honest. I'd say it's a bit extreme myself."

"It's just something I've always been in to," said Tim. "I think we should be encouraging more of it. A lot of the kids really come round to it when you talk to them. They love doing it."

Mr Wingett passed two sheets of paper across the desk to Tim. One had the school crest and the words *Tempus fugit!'* at the top and the second sheet was on headed notepaper from the school's lawyers, Webber, Maddox & Douglas.

"You just need to sign each one at the bottom," he said without giving Tim time to read either of the sheets of paper. "Just for our records. You'll be paid up to the end of the month which is very generous if you ask me. If it were up to me you'd at least be paying back what you owe us for photocopying. You should be thanking us all that we're not taking it further really. Getting the authorities involved. Misuse of school resources is a serious business. You just need to return your lanyard, laptop and keys. Then you'll be escorted to your car and off the premises."

Although Mr Wingett's words were, like the Deputy Head himself, very simple, they still took a moment to sink in. This is what it must have been like for all the others, thought Mr Cocker as he looked down at the Fairtrade leaflets on the desk in front of him.

"But we're a Fairtrade school," he said, still failing to understand the situation.

"We *were* a Fairtrade school," said the Deputy Head. "Using school resources for non-school use, including the use of the photocopier, is in breach of your contract. It's fraud. Have you no integrity?"

He'd been told he was signing to confirm he'd returned any school property that he'd been issued. Then Mr Wingett seemed to be reading out some small print with all the urgency of a dodgy loan company during a commercial break. The chances were that even Mrs Spratt couldn't honestly claim to have heard what he'd said.

"Under the terms of the settlement agreement you, Mr Timothy Cocker, henceforth referred to as the ex-employee, are banned from returning at any time to Wildside Academy, henceforth referred to as the Academy, talking to anybody about your time at or experience of the Academy or contacting any employees, ex-employees or future employees of the Academy in any way. Furthermore if at any future date the Academy, its Governing Body, Headteacher or Senior Leadership Team decide that they wish… "

As he was escorted towards reception Tim noticed that the Fairtrade logo was nowhere to be seen. Instead a display in the corridor announced that '*Wildside Academy supports Children With Diarrhoea!* That just about summed the current situation up perfectly!

Still feeling like he was playing a part in somebody else's life Tim reached the end of Cemetery Road. He waited to join the traffic and begin the long journey home one last time. He found himself focusing on small details as if this would help him come to terms with it all. Had he left his chess set in his classroom? What would he tell his wife? Should he wait till after the kids had brought his birthday cake out? Where could he best use his IT skills?

Across the road from him Darren Froggett the lollipop man was arguing with two men in grey suits and blasts of his conversation hit him as he waited. Apparently the Council had decided to replace the Advanced Road Safety Operations Lead Executive with a pelican crossing. As he drove away Tim Cocker reflected philosophically that he was not the only one facing an uncertain future.

CHAPTER 63

"You do not need to keep running once you have caught the bus."

There were many things that people would miss about Tim Cocker thought Harry Greenfield as he glanced over at the empty deckchair in the centre of the PE office. They hadn't yet been able to bring themselves to fold it up and make a little more space although his name had been added to the wall of remembrance. As a mark of respect Marcus Deeside had waited a few days before collecting the money he'd made out of Mr Cocker's sudden departure.

Sports Day loomed on the horizon and as an honorary member of the PE Department as well as a Geography teacher Tim had always played a vital rôle in the success of the day. It was Tim who understood weather forecasts well enough to be able to predict which day in the final week of the summer term would be the wettest. The record was currently set at seven consecutively cancelled Sports Days and they had been hoping to improve that record this year too.

Of course Sports Days were never actually cancelled. They were merely postponed on a daily basis until they were forgotten. The skill of the PE teacher came in thinking up new reasons to prevent them having to haul all their athletics equipment outside where teachers would be on crowd control beneath a crackling sound system. They often relied on the phrase *"the front field is still waterlogged from all the rain at the weekend"* but one unusually dry July they had had to resort to hiding the little line-marking machine that Bob used.

With Sports Day provisionally pencilled in for the final Tuesday, the day Storm Elvira was predicted to hit the North of

England hardest, Harry went back to his television. The Wimbledon repeats had finished but he'd found that the channel was now re-running old episodes of *A Question of Sport*. Harry always knew that he himself could have won Wimbledon if only he hadn't gone into teaching. Maybe he just wasn't competitive enough? Well, he'd be the first to admit that.

And so, the last week of the school year slowly dawned amid reminders that handing out wordsearches was a hanging offence. There was a rumour going around the staff – in truth there were always rumours going around the staff – that Ms Stonehart herself would be conducting the final assemblies of the year. With the exam season finished and the invigilators no doubt already on some distant cruise this was the chance to celebrate everything that had been achieved throughout the year at Wildside Academy. It was usually possible to fit all four assemblies for the different year groups into a single hour and still have time to spare.

The Music Department now consisted of supply teachers so there was no final rendition of *"All things bright and beautiful"*, a tune that was only wiped from people's minds around late-August. Just in time for the start of the new school year. The school prayer was not recited largely because the temporary Acting Head of RE, Mr Livingstone, was an atheist. As they waited Mr Haddenough looked around the hall to see how many of the other Year 8 form tutors had managed to go the distance and survive a full year at Wildside Academy. It looked like he was the only one apart from Mr Ansari but there were still two days until the summer holidays began so that could still change. Even some of the supply teachers in the hall were replacing supply teachers from the previous week. It was getting harder to remember everybody's names with the result that even the teachers just referred to each other as "Sir" or "Miss." It often felt like you were playing a game of 'Guess who?' trying to work out which teacher a pupil was talking about. *Does he teach in a Science lab? Does he have glasses? Has he been here more than a week?*

Mr Haddenough's form, 8Z, seemed to have survived most of the turmoils of their second year at Wildside Academy. They'd only lost one member of the class throughout the year but as Cordelia had transferred to Upper Steem Academy it was never mentioned again. In return Ivor had inherited five more pupils who had moved into the area, making his form the largest one in the year group. As he didn't have thirty-seven seats in his form room it was probably a good thing that three of the boys regularly didn't attend. Two of them suffered from anger issues which seemed to be all the rage at the moment whilst another insisted he needed to be home schooled.

The last of Wildside Academy's values was being considered today and Mr Haddenough found himself considering whether "Excellence" would be spelt right on the certificates that would be handed out. During the working day it was as if sweeping changes had been made to the English language and nobody had thought to tell him. He was surprised to see Mrs Spratt venture into the Main Hall followed by Stan who wheeled in a large box and carefully manoeuvred it onto the stage. Miss Hughes quietened the pupils down as soon as she saw Mr Wingett arriving at the doors to the hall. As he walked down the central aisle alone, up on to the stage and took his place it seemed that the rumour about Ms Stonehart conducting assembly was without any foundation.

"Year 8," began Mr Wingett as he stood at the plinth, "it is a sad time as we prepare to go our separate ways for six weeks. I did have an assembly prepared for you on the nature of suffering but I believe this is traditionally the time to celebrate our successes. Our excellence. And so, for your final assembly, Year 8, I pass you over to your Headteacher. A round of applause for Ms Stonehart!"

More out of a sense of surprise rather than anything else staff and pupils found themselves clapping and those who could turned to look towards the back of the hall. For many of them this would be the first time they'd seen the Headteacher. That went for staff as well as pupils.

But the door remained firmly closed and as the ripple of applause died down a cough echoed from the front of the hall as though to get the attention of its audience. The cough had not come from Mr Wingett who had now sat down and was looking up at the screen above his head. Some of the pupils on the front row shuffled back nervously as Ms Stonehart's face filled the screen.

"Good morning," her voice came through the speakers all around them. She glanced down at her notes before continuing. *"Erm, children. This is an important time for you all as the school year comes to an end. Tempus fugit! Under my leadership you have all gone from strength to…"*

The screen went blank. A moment later the recording was

replaced by a slide reminding everybody that Mr Cocker's Chess Club meet in Room 27 every Thursday after school. Everybody welcome! It was unclear whether this test card was just some sort of scheduled repeat or whether somebody had hijacked Ms Stonehart's seasonal message to her people. Either way she wouldn't get to utter another word in assembly unless she came through in person. Mr Wingett led assembly with Mr Cocker's smiling face beaming over his shoulder the whole time.

For some reason Mr Haddenough found the lines of the Kipling poem running through his mind.

'If you can keep your head when all about you
Are losing theirs and blaming it on you…"

"And I allus tell lads before we go out on t'field," concluded Mr Fitt, "matters not if y'win or lose it's 'ow thee laiks in t'game. And I tek me cap off t'under 13s who've allus put up a reet old fight against all t'posh schools out there every week even if it's chucking it darn. We've never lost a match yet. Not one. There are three places on podium at Olympics. Coming second isn't losing in my book."

At the thought of returning home for six weeks to Yorkshire, God's own country, Jim Fitt's accent was starting to become a little broader again. Even though she was an English teacher Miss Hughes had to watch the pile of sporting certificates disappear to know when he had finished. With the annual demise of the Sports Day the PE Department had become quite inventive with the certificates they awarded, making sure that everybody achieved something. One boy had even got a certificate congratulating him for achieving no laps in the inter-form cycle race. In truth he'd flatly refused to take part.

"Thank you for that," said Miss Hughes as Mr Fitt came back down off the stage. "Now the final awards before you return to lessons. The Form Tutor Awards and the awards for attendance and punctuality."

There really isn't any data to go on when nominating the Form Tutor Award and no matter who you select another thirty pupils will complain that it's not fair. As five of the form tutors had only known their pupils for a matter of days they had had to choose a name at random. Mr Ansari gave his award to the pupil who had annoyed him the least during the two years he'd known them. Mr Haddenough gave his award to a girl called Jennie who'd joined midway through the year. It was like a consolation prize for not having got into Upper Steem Academy.

There were some surprises when the certificates were handed out to reward attendance and punctuality. Three of the pupils with outstanding attendance weren't in to collect their certificates and as Miss Hughes had obviously read the data upside down the award for the best attendance went to Ashley Henry even though he had only been in for two days all year. He could be very proud of his first ever certificate, even though he wasn't in to collect it in person.

"We've been celebrating excellence at Wildside Academy this morning," continued Mr Wingett, "and now we come to the most important award. The award for the most improved attendance."

Mr Haddenough found himself wondering why the most important achievement wasn't for academic accomplishment in a particular subject but merely for the ability to get out of bed and turn up at school in a morning. Or in some cases early-afternoon. There had been awards for doing well in all the different subjects, of course, but those pupils had been given tatty monochrome certificates that looked like they had been churned out of Mr Cocker's old inkjet printer. The award for the most improved attendance somehow warranted a full colour laminated certificate, a small plastic statuette and something that was in a large box at Miss Hughes' feet. It wasn't all about Ofsted but clearly attendance was now an issue at Wildside Academy.

"Now when I was a lad," Mr Wingett was continuing, "I never missed a single day at school, even though I had to walk eight miles each way in the cold without any breakfast. But look at where that got me today. Deputy Head at Wildside Academy, the best school in the North of England!"

Mr Haddenough was sure that last phrase would appear on the school's website soon enough. If it wasn't already there.

"So the award for the most improved attendance in Year 8," announced Miss Hughes when he had finished, "goes to a young man whose attendance this year is 200% better than in Year 7. Well done to Wesley Burke. Is he in today, Mr Ansari?"

Mr Ansari indicated a boy on the second row who was looking around, surprised that somebody had mentioned his name. Miss Hughes didn't think she'd ever seen him before.

"You know what, mate," Mr Ansari whispered to Mr Haddenough as Wesley stumbled up on to the stage. "It's only 200% up on last year because he was only in for about eight days in Year 7."

"I know. Most of mine could only improve if they came in for 110% of the year. Apparently that's possible though you know," added Mr Haddenough thinking about his Bright Sky target.

Teachers had targets but there were no awards for staff. It was probably coincidence but Ms Stonehart had even stopped rewarding staff at the end of each term after Mr O'Brien left. There were now just end of year bonuses for her SLT and anybody she had promoted.

Wesley had managed to find his way onto the stage and was holding his certificate and award while Mr Wingett heaved the mystery prize out of the box. Mr Haddenough happened to notice the puzzled looks on the faces of his form as they compared the scrap of paper that they had been given for all their hard work with the amazing prize Wesley was receiving.

"You've won a ghetto blaster," said Mr Wingett. "A boombox, I think they're called."

"It has twin speakers, a cassette deck and a radio," said Miss Hughes enthusiastically reading the label. "And best of all you can play CDs on it."

Wesley looked at the object he was being given. He had no intention of lugging that thing all the way home with him. He'd only come in for the last week of term because his Mum had said she'd get him the new Zombie Kombat 24/7 game if he did.

"Right," he grunted, making no effort to take the huge box from them. "What's a CD then, man?"

CHAPTER 64

"All questions will eventually be answered."

Ms Stonehart was having a good morning and with just a few hours left until the summer holidays she was looking forward to many more good days over the next six weeks. She looked down at the little cactus on her desk. Tempus fugit! It had been a present from Bob on their first date when he'd taken her to a garden centre. A symbol of his undying love for her. She'd heard that Bob was going back to Cornwall next week but with Deirdre the cleaner of all people! Well, good luck to them. She herself would be spending the whole summer in Australia and getting away from all the responsibilities of being a Headteacher as soon as the school closed. It was something she'd always wanted to do and now was her chance to seize the day. She was going with Phil, a man she'd met on an online dating site shortly after she'd dumped Eddie. Phil was a Business Studies teacher at Wildside Community College so they had a lot in common and it was nice to find somebody she could really trust at last. She knew that he would pay her back his part of the holiday as soon as they returned. He just had a temporary cash-flow problem at the moment, the result of a messy divorce coinciding with his redundancy. Anyway, like Phil had said, it made better financial sense for one person to pay for the holiday in one go so that they got a discount for having paid in full. He'd researched it and had managed to save them quite a bit of money by choosing the option that didn't allow cancellations or amendments to their booking.

She'd just had a meeting with all her Senior Leadership Team to thank them for their efforts throughout the year, assisting her in taking the school from strength to strength. They'd enjoyed a few glasses of champagne while Mr Thicke had had the orange juice all to himself. She'd generously handed out an end-of-year bonus to each of them and she'd listened patiently to their holiday plans although frankly they paled into insignificance beside her own. Mr Wingett was going to stay at home as he felt it was a waste of money going off somewhere, especially when there were DIY jobs to do about his flat. Mr Thicke was going to Scotland with his family as he didn't want to be surrounded by foreigners and not be able to get a meal that wasn't swimming in garlic. Last time he'd gone abroad he'd left his son behind at a service station outside Düsseldorf and had had to go back for him. Ms Payne was jetting off to the Greek islands with a friend tomorrow and would be going off for a girlie break in Barcelona later in the summer with Ms Winter. Mr Humble said he was looking forward to going to Glastonbury with Ms Lovall and would then find a cheap holiday somewhere abroad, maybe Ibiza again. Ms Stonehart approved of their holiday plans as it would mean that somebody would be around when the GCSE results came out.

Putting her empty cup down it crossed her mind that Phil would have to know how to make a proper cup of tea if he was going to move in with her when they got back from Australia. He was so excited and had said he couldn't wait to go Down Under with her. It might even be worth adding Business Studies to the curriculum at Wildside Academy so that there was a job for him here in September.

She'd made so many changes to the business over the last year but it was only as she'd started writing her newsletter to parents that she realised how much she'd achieved. It was amazing really that one person could have so much impact on the educational outcome of the pupils. There was the telescope, the improved website and social media, the new car park, Wildside's new core values, her Words of Wisdom, the school charity, the redesigned Parents' Evenings, her new-improved SLT…the list was endless! The GCSE results really were going to be off the scale this year and Ofsted would not be able to believe what she'd done to the school. She glanced up at the counter on her wall. If she was being honest, and it did happen occasionally, she probably also felt relaxed knowing that there would not now be an inspection until the next academic year at the earliest.

An ominous chime rang out from her computer, interrupting

the silence of her vast office. She'd had Trevor set up her desktop to alert her whenever certain key words came up in any email across the school. It was a system that had been very effective in tracking down dissidents amongst her staff and supplying the evidence for speedy redundancies. This particular chime though heralded something more important than just poor teachers who weren't team players committed to her vision for the business. This particular sound warned that she had received a message directly from Ofsted HQ. Ms Stonehart sank into her chair and took the time to read through the email twice before grabbing the phone and bellowing for Mrs Spratt, Mrs Timson and her two Deputy Heads.

"What do you mean you didn't know they were Ofsted Inspectors?" exclaimed Ms Stonehart.

It had taken them quite a while to go through the office rota to work out who had been in charge of the main reception desk two days earlier. Judy Timson, the Office Manager, had initially narrowed it down to one of the Julies but Ms Stonehart had insisted on further details. Mrs Timson had finally worked it out by cross-referencing the office duty rota with the office cake rota. Now Julie Tomas, having only just completed her first week back after her maternity leave, found herself standing in front of the firing squad in Ms Stonehart's office as Mrs Timson had quietly made her excuses and left. Ms Stonehart had written herself a note to tell Trevor to simplify the system of staff codes before September.

Quite understandably Julie was feeling somewhat disorientated that particular morning. Before she'd even had a chance to come through and tell anybody what had happened she'd found herself being marched through to Ms Stonehart's office without a chance to speak to any of her colleagues.

"Well," said Julie, focusing on the matter in hand, "we had an Ofsted visit on my first day back, last Friday, and then we all got told afterwards that they weren't really Ofsted inspectors." The previous Friday felt like a lifetime ago to her now.

"Those 'inspectors' were members of my SLT," explained Ms Stonehart, gesturing towards her Deputy Heads. "Surely you must have recognised them even after all your time off enjoying yourself!"

Ms Winter had seemed a lot bigger than she remembered her and she hadn't really had much to do with Mr Thicke in the past. She had thought that Mr Wingett was vaguely familiar but he'd looked different somehow. Later she'd realised that she'd never seen him smile before.

"But then at the end of the day we were all told that we shouldn't have let those 'inspectors' in," she continued calmly. "You said if we weren't sure we should have just turned them away."

And that was precisely what Julie had done the following Wednesday when four men had turned up at the front desk, claiming to be Ofsted inspectors once again. It was obviously not genuine. She was pretty certain that one of the men was that Mr Hoskins from Upper Steem Academy. She couldn't help noticing that Ms Stonehart's left eye had twitched when she'd mentioned his name.

"That man is no longer in charge at that place," said Ms Stonehart.

"There was some talk of him becoming an Ofsted inspector though," added Mr Thicke without thinking. Mr Wingett shuffled his chair a little further away from his colleague.

"So the first I know," continued Ms Stonehart, "as Headteacher of Wildside Academy, the first I know that Ofsted inspectors have visited my school is when I receive an email from them two days later to say they've been refused entry by a woman on the reception desk!"

"I was just doing as I'd been told," said Julie reasonably.

"There are protocols to be followed," exclaimed Ms Stonehart. "Why do you think we have so many policies?"

Julie hoped the question was a rhetorical one as she knew her answer probably wasn't the right one under the circumstances.

"The policy concerning procedures during an Ofsted visit is policy number 1. The first thing you should have done if you had any doubts at all about these visitors was to refer the matter to the Head of HR."

"That's what I did," replied Julie. "I asked them to wait in reception while I came through to speak to Mrs Spratt."

"Oh really? And what did she say then?"

"I told her what had happened and she said that she'd heard what I said but she was very busy. She said I just needed to do what I'd been told to do. So I did." It all seemed so unimportant to her now.

For her part Mrs Spratt seemed to be fascinated by the intricacies of the pattern in the carpet.

"I see," said Ms Stonehart as though she was slowly piecing together a particularly difficult jigsaw. "So you heard what she said but you were too busy to do anything about it! And what, may I ask, was keeping you so busy while four Ofsted inspectors were sitting waiting in my school's reception?"

"There were problems in assembly," Mrs Spratt found herself saying. It sounded like her way of completing that jigsaw involved just shaking the box with her eyes closed. She wished now she hadn't had that third glass of champagne. "I'd gone down to the Main Hall with Stan to deliver the prize, that radio thing, and... Well, it was that Mr Cocker's fault. His face popped up on the screen and I had to race off to try and find Trevor or Adil to sort it out."

She suddenly realised from Ms Stonehart's reaction that nobody had told her that her message in the assembly had not been broadcast. It had taken her ages to record it and even in his absence Mr Cocker had got in her way once again.

"You've all got no idea what it's like to be a Headteacher!" bellowed Ms Stonehart furiously.

"And neither have you!" Mrs Spratt shouted back before she'd even realised she'd said it. She'd never had to deal with Ofsted at the dog food factory. In fact more to the point she'd never had to put up with anybody like Janine Stonehart in her entire life before. She'd heard what she said and she'd finally heard enough. Without waiting for permission to leave she turned and headed back to her own office to start packing. The smell of burning bridges lingered in the air. If anybody had chosen Mrs Spratt on Mike Stringer's sweepstake the odds of this being her last day were so high that they could probably have retired on their winnings. Goodbye, Norma Spratt!

"I'll deal with her later," muttered Ms Stonehart turning her attention back to the Julie in front of her. "I can't think of a single good reason why I shouldn't fire you too!"

"I can," said Julie quietly. "I can think of at least two."

Ms Stonehart looked up. What was happening to her staff today?

"You see when Ofsted inspectors turned up here again this week it seemed like some kind of prank. Like an April Fools Day prank except it's July," continued Julie. "And that got me thinking about other April Fools Days. You're wanting me to lose my job and yet I remember so well that April 1st when you got your job here. I'm such a hoarder really. I've still got a copy of all the paperwork from the day you were interviewed if you're interested. I'm sure Mr Chambers would want me to return it if I wasn't employed here…"

Ms Stonehart was beginning to look even paler than usual. Mr Chambers' portrait seemed to be watching the shoot-out very carefully as Julie looked across at Mr Wingett. You didn't often get a day like this.

"It's interesting talking about paperwork," she continued. "I believe Trevor changed everybody's email details while I was off on maternity but he forgot about me. Out of sight, out of mind. Just another Julie! Only last night I was re-reading a very interesting email you sent to all staff on April Fools Day this year, Mr Wingett. Something about the Maths Department? April Fools Day really does live up to its name at Wildside Academy, doesn't it?" She smiled sweetly. "Anyway, what were you saying, Janine?"

A bell tolled in the distance. For nearly a minute nobody spoke. Nothing like this had ever happened before. Even the Deputy Heads were now beginning to find the carpet pattern fascinating.

"I'm sure we can come to some sort of arrangement," the Headteacher of Wildside Academy finally said grudgingly. "Something to tide you over while you look for employment elsewhere."

Julie knew she was pushing it when she asked for a reference but she was enjoying the moment. It was amazing how free it made you feel when your husband had just phoned to say he'd won the Lottery. She couldn't wait to tell her best friend, Verity.

CHAPTER 65

"It doesn't matter how quickly you make umbrellas,
if it isn't raining nobody will buy them."

As always Ms Stonehart had left it up to Mr Wingett to make all the necessary arrangements and then escort the two ex-employees off the premises. She was not a religious woman but the significance of the number displayed on her wall was not lost on her. It was exactly 666 days since the last time Ofsted had come in to inspect Wildside Academy. The final day of term had been going so well until she'd had this revelation about the four inspectors of the apocalypse coming to bring judgement on her world. It suddenly felt quite chilly in her shadowy echoing office.

She'd managed to delete Upper Steem Academy from the list of websites that was labelled, rather ironically, as her favourites and was now scrolling through the emails in her inbox. As far as she knew Ofsted didn't just turn up at a school unannounced, did they? Wouldn't there usually be a sign? A warning phone call, an initial email or even just a postcard? *Wish you weren't here!* Surely Trevor's system would have warned her like it had this morning if they'd sent an email?

And then she found it.

An email had arrived at the start of the week, two days before their intended visit. Monday July 15th at 14:28. It was hidden away, sandwiched between an email about another lost mug and an invitation to the next Local Headteachers' meeting. How had she missed the one email she'd been expecting for over two years? What had she been doing that afternoon that she'd not heard its arrival? She looked in her diary and could hardly believe it. It was that Mr Cocker yet again! When the email had come in she'd been over in Mr Wingett's office instructing him to get Mr Cocker in and sort out his departure. After that it would have been her afternoon tea before Phil had taken her out for a meal and a film. The poor man had been so embarrassed when he'd found he'd left his wallet at home.

When she opened up the email Ofsted had sent her on Monday it confirmed her worst fears. The details of their proposed visit were all there in black-and-white along with requests for various documents she was meant to supply in advance. She wasn't sure what the various acronyms stood for and made a list of what she would need to search up on the internet. SEF? SIP? SEND? FSM? GCSE? She was fairly confident that the 'S' in most of them stood for 'School.' There was a question about bullying. She would be able to tell them that the school had a zero-tolerance policy on bullying and there wasn't a single teacher working in the school who would disagree with her. Looking down the email at the list of inspectors who had visited her school reception area two days earlier she found that one of them had indeed been a Mr Hoskins. The email ended by saying that they would be in touch in due course to make further arrangements. Ms Stonehart felt sick.

Mr Haddenough was also going through his emails now that the day and indeed the school year had come to an end. He always liked to make sure there were no loose ends before he headed off for the summer. His form, 8Z, had all wished him a happy holiday, tumbling out of the room and racing towards the exits as soon as they thought they'd heard the bell. The classroom was unusually silent now with the hum of his laptop the only sound.

Mr Wingett had sent out provisional timetables for next year but this time the attachment was blank. Mr Thicke was concerned about the state of the staffroom, commenting that if anybody had a big dump in there they should clear it up before close of business. Mrs Ramsbottom had let colleagues know that the staffroom photocopier had now been repaired. Four more mugs had disappeared but on the plus side a table tennis bat had been found. There was an email from Ms Lovall asking staff to evaluate the training they'd had this year and list what training they felt should be included next year. He smiled when he remembered what Mr Ansari had said about the INSET they'd done. *It's best to leave fire fighting to the professionals and if you can't print off your training certificate*

Ryan Spivey can do you a very convincing copy for a reasonable price. Ivor wanted to suggest training on 'how to achieve 110% in anything!' but knew the comment would be seen as facetious. The thought did make him click on the link to his Bright Sky targets. He'd not found time to upload any evidence of what he'd been doing since September as he'd been too busy. Luckily Ms Winter had very kindly made sure that his forty-two lesson observations and nineteen work scrutinies had been uploaded. The only feedback that seemed to be missing was from the lesson that had been observed that morning. And the one Mr O'Brien had watched, of course.

He didn't expect any emails thanking him for his continued hard work but he was surprised to find that Ms Stonehart hadn't sent out her usual cheery end-of-term message. Perhaps she was too busy?

Another email from Ofsted arrived, its warning chime sounding like another nail being driven into a coffin lid. It seemed to take forever before the message opened up and Ms Stonehart could read the bad news. Why did it have to be from Hoskins? Who did he think he was?

Having been refused entry to Wildside Academy on Wednesday, July 17ᵗʰ for the purpose of carrying out an inspection under Section 5 of the Education Act 2005, notice is hereby given that a full inspection will occur in September of the forthcoming academic year.

Ms Stonehart found she'd been holding her breath and let it out slowly. Well, that wasn't as bad as she'd anticipated. The autumn term was still a long way off so there was plenty of time to plan everything. Obviously she couldn't cancel her well-deserved trip to Australia and her SLT would not want her to miss out after she'd worked so hard all year. If you want to be the best, delegation's what you need. Fortunately all the members of her SLT would be free at some time over the next six weeks so it shouldn't be too hard to make up a rota for them that was fair. She reached for her phone to call through to Norma before she remembered. Well, she would be easy to replace. She was only Human Resources after all. She put the receiver back down and read the rest of the email.

Furthermore as the inspection team was not supplied with the documentation that was requested on Monday, July 15ᵗʰ, Ms J Stonehard is required as Headteacher of Wildside Academy to make herself available for a series of preliminary meetings with the Lead Inspector prior to the full inspection visit. Since this inspection has had to be re-scheduled for the start of September these meetings will take place at Wildside Academy each Monday over the summer beginning on July 22nd at 8am prompt. As highlighted in the attached schedule these interviews will give you the opportunity as Headteacher to expand on the details contained in your Self Evaluation Form and School Improvement Plan. Since these documents were not supplied following our first request they should be forwarded by close of business today. Failure to do so will lead to further actions as outlined in Section 23 paragraph 19 of the attached document 'Ofsted guidance for Schools and Academies' such as the school being placed in Special Measures. In the initial meeting next week we will be focusing on staffing concerns, pupil progress, exam regulations and the financial management of the school. It is anticipated that each meeting will last a minimum of ninety minutes. Questionnaires have been sent to all staff employed at Wildside Academy during this academic year as well as parents and / or guardians. Failure to comply with this directive, including, but not limited to, the absence of the Headteacher, will result in additional…

Feeling a little dizzy, Ms Stonehart stopped reading for a moment. Perhaps she'd had a little too much champagne earlier as it was odd the thoughts that now went through her head. Her first thought was that she had been right, of course. The 'S' in some of the acronyms did stand for 'School.' Her next thought was that they should perhaps have gone for the option that allowed them to cancel the holiday without any forfeit. If she was having to come in for a meeting every week she was not going to be seeing a lot of kangaroos this summer.

Mr Haddenough switched the lights off and closed his classroom door. The Halloween skeleton he used to teach parts of the body in French swung gently on the wall in the slight breeze. Along the MFL corridor the displays he'd put up still looked good although it was a bit of a mess where Mr Buonanulla had tried to paint over the phrase *Ma patrone est une ordure.* He'd seen both his Head of Department and Madame Loups-Garoux heading off together about half an hour earlier. Neither of them had looked in to wish him a good holiday. Never mind. He was looking forward to six weeks where his every move wouldn't be observed, scrutinized and graded.

The reception area had been empty as he'd clocked out one

last time, loosened his top button and put his lanyard away in his jacket pocket. There were very few cars in the car park and Jim Fitt gave him a cheery wave as he drove past. As always his radio could be heard through the open car window.

"You're listening to Wildside FM and that was Pink Floyd with 'Another Brick in the Wall'. *With the time just coming up to three o'clock Steve Oldham will be up next with the DriveTime Show straight after the news and weather. For those of you breaking up for the holidays today it doesn't look too promising from tomorrow, I'm afraid..."*

This is the way the school year ends then, thought Ivor. Not with a bang but a whimper. Most of the people he would have said goodbye to had long since disappeared, picked off one by one as though by some unreasoning, inhuman alien creature. Sometimes he couldn't believe he'd been a teacher for over thirty years, the last twelve of those at Wildside Academy. It wasn't all about the holidays, whatever people said. He genuinely enjoyed teaching, knowing that the majority of pupils were trying their best and appreciated what he did, even if they'd never ever admit it. He didn't even mind it when Ofsted came in. They were just doing their job and they too seemed to appreciate what he was doing. The only trouble with Ofsted was when SLT became like headless chickens running around with even less idea of what they should be doing than usual. And then there was the real problem hiding behind Ofsted – the self-confident, faceless government ministers like Jeremiah Grimes pulling the strings and letting their algorithms play Russian roulette with young peoples' lives.

As for working at Wildside Academy, if it weren't for the endless lesson observations, criticisms, lack of support, double standards, meetings, data and paperwork then every minute of the working day would be a joy. People would often say to him that they wouldn't want to do his job nowadays. All those unruly kids! To be honest, the kids weren't usually the problem. Kids were kids. *If you are determined to learn, nobody can stop you. If you are not willing to learn, nobody can help you.* You all just did the best you could.

His daydreaming was interrupted by a football bouncing off the roof of his car just as he was about to get in. He threw the ball back to the boy standing by the gate. It was Sam Nixon from his Year 9 class.

"Thanks, sir," the boy called out. He paused for a moment. "Au revoir, Monsieur Haddenough! Merci beaucoup. Bon voyage!"

Ivor Haddenough smiled. He'd taught them something after all!

As he turned into Cemetery Road the sound of Zombie Kombat was already echoing from countless bedroom windows. With no sign of Darren Froggett the traffic was flowing smoothly and Ivor was able to turn left without any real delay. As he headed towards the motorway and the freedom it offered he happened to notice a sign in the window of Sharkey's, the local betting shop. *"When the fun stops, stop!"* How true!

Bob the Senior Ground Maintenance Supervisor looked at his watch. It was five o'clock. Time for him to pack it in for the day and go start packing for his holiday with Deirdre instead. He noticed a light on in Ms Stonehart's office and it sounded like she was not alone in there. Experience had taught him that it was probably best not to disturb her. Stan could always lock up when he finished his shift later.

Ms Stonehart's office was busier than it had been all year. All her Senior Leadership Team were there, along with Mr Devlin, the Head of Maths, who'd only called by looking for Ms Payne. The large mahogany conference desk was hidden beneath countless print-outs of policies, data and information gleaned from the internet. Laptops bathed the room in an unearthly cold glow whilst everybody present scribbled on sheets of paper or tapped on keyboards. As Headteacher of Wildside Academy Ms Stonehart was naturally at the centre of it all, sitting at her desk willing her telephone to ring. For a brief moment she experienced a flashback to her days as a secretary at Derby Road Primary School in Berryfield.

"I was just thinking," said Mr Wingett breaking the silence, "we're presuming all this is actually from Ofsted and not just some wind-up? Somebody who knows about schools and is good with IT?"

A number of possible suspects had already crossed his mind.

Mr Thicke dismissed the idea.

"It'd have to be a pretty good forgery," he said. "I've not found a single discrepancy in the fonts used and the logo's right too."

He peered again at the symbol that seemed to be three blue stickmen of increasing size beside the slogan *"Raising standards.*

Improving lives." It certainly wasn't improving his life at the moment. He should have been halfway up the M6 by now before the holiday traffic really started.

Ms Payne and Mr Devlin were clearly taking it all very seriously as Ms Stonehart heard them discussing something about flight paths. With everybody working together she felt confident that they would manage to compose the necessary Self Evaluation Form and School Improvement Plan and get them scanned in and sent off today. Mr Humble's suggestion that they should adapt something from another school had really helped to speed things up. She'd insisted however that they didn't use the one from that place up the road. On her third try she'd managed to get through to Phil and tell him the bad news about the holiday. She hadn't been impressed with his suggestion that he just went to Australia on his own. Then she'd phoned Ofsted HQ to see whether she could delay the planned meetings until after the summer. She'd got through to a secretary who informed her that she had heard what she said and that somebody would call her back before close of business. That had been over an hour and a half ago.

"Should we send out for takeaway," suggested Ms Winter, "if we're going to be here a while, yeah?"

Ms Stonehart was just about to tell her to shut up when the phone on her desk rang out. This was it! If it was all just some elaborate hoax she would find out. If it was genuine there was a chance she could get the meetings re-arranged if she played her cards right. She could just picture herself in front of the Sydney Opera House enjoying a cocktail with Phil in the afternoon sunshine. This was it. Here we go. I can do this! Deep breath!

She picked up the receiver, the members of her Senior Leadership Team all watching her silently. This was the moment when they would truly appreciate why she was such an outstanding Headteacher. Her leadership and negotiating skills today would take Wildside Academy from strength to strength and beyond.

"Hello, Janine Stonehart speaking. How may I help you, please?"

"Hello, love. Right. I'd like to order two sweet and sour chicken, egg fried rice, prawn crackers…"

ACKNOWLEDGEMENTS.

A lot of *"The Secret Life of Teachers"* was written and drawn during lockdown for the Covid-19 pandemic, meaning that I've really had to rely on my memory and my imagination. Had I set the book during the 2020 academic year I would have ended up with a much different and probably shorter novel. Having said that, I have no doubt that Wildside Academy would, of course, have continued to go from strength to strength in these difficult times. Ms Winter would have had to observe lessons online, regularly checking that Mr Haddenough's top button was done up, and naturally sports day would have been cancelled yet again.

I have worked with so many wonderful people over my years as a teacher that it would be impossible to name them all for fear of missing somebody out. You know who you are, particularly those of you who are still in touch after all this time.

Mr Hoskins, the fictional Head of Upper Steem Academy, is named after my first French teacher who instilled a life-long love of foreign languages in me which ultimately led to me becoming a teacher.

After a year teaching in France it all really began in Yorkshire. Thank you to the teachers I worked with in my first school in Morley before Ofsted came into being. Moving on to Skipton, Ian - as well as teaching me all I needed to know about stick insects - your words *"Nothing that's meant for you passes you by"* have been good advice to us all over the years. Then there were the special days in Bradford and fond memories of all the other Mr A's and the members of the Three O'Clock Club. Those were interesting times.

I'd like to say a special thank you to all my colleagues and friends at my current school which is a world apart from the fictional classrooms of Wildside Academy. You make teaching, support and leadership seem so effortless but so effective. It really is inspiring. It's a shame we've had to spend so much of this year online! And of course, *muchas gracias* to Rhian and Colleen for checking over my Spanish.

The Secret Life of Teachers' isn't just about teachers though. As Mr Haddenough might say, schools are all about pupils, not data, flight paths or algorithms. I hope my novel shows the kind of young people I have worked with over the years in quite different schools : pupils with a sense of humour, determination, resilience and an inspiring way of looking at the world. I'm glad I've had the opportunity to teach for so long. *"Teachers affect eternity ; no one can tell where their influence stops."*

Thank you to former Head Girl Gill Barnard for taking the time to proof-read *"The Secret Life of Teachers."* It really was appreciated and I hope you'll share your novels with the world soon. Any mistakes in my novel are, of course, entirely my fault. To be honest the errors that remain, in particular the inconsistent font size, were deliberately included to annoy Mr Thicke!

As always none of this would have been possible without my amazing wife and family. Whilst Wildside Academy does not actually exist and the events and characters in the novel are purely fictional, Rachel has lived through my whole teaching career with me. Don't worry, there won't be a sequel! I'm so glad you suggested I write a proper book rather than another graphic novel and thank you for inspiring the words on the back cover. Last but not least, of course, a massive thank you to my three fantastic, talented sons, Peter, Ben and Mark. You have always inspired me and will always mean the world to me.

Tempus fugit! Calamus gladio fortior.

August 2020.

ABOUT THE AUTHOR

David Adamson was born and brought up in Yorkshire but now lives in Manchester with his wife, Rachel, and their three sons, Peter, Ben and Mark.

He has taught for over thirty years and is the author and illustrator of the *'Planet of the Grapes'* series of graphic novels.

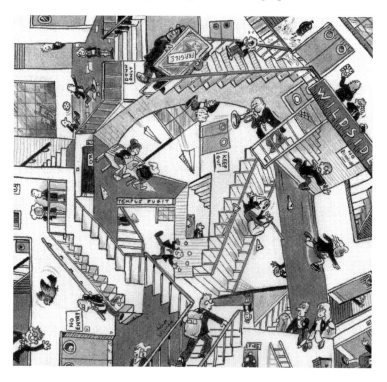

For more details of how Wildside Academy continues to go from strength to strength, please visit the school website :

www.wildsideacademy.wixsite.com/secretlifeofteachers

A final note from the author : Please be aware that as Mr Thicke organises the school website it may not currently be available. Thanks.

Printed in Great Britain
by Amazon

47441631R00255